Magnolia Parks

written by
Jessa Hastings

THE EPHEMERAL HAPPINESS OF THE
HOUSE
OF
HASTINGS

First published in 2021 by
Also Industries and The Ephemeral Happiness
of the House of Hastings

Text © Jessa Hastings, 2021
Cover design © Emily Pappas, 2021

All rights reserved. No part of this publication may
be reproduced, stored or transmitted in any form or
by any means electronic, mechanical or photocopying,
recording or otherwise, without the express permission
of the publisher

ISBN 978-1-7372811-0-8

Typesetting and ebook creation by
Ten Thousand | Editing + Book Design
www.tenthousand.co.uk

Magnolia Parks

For the 2018 version of me who wanted to throw in the towel and become a history professor because creative rejection is hard on the heart.

Also for that version of you who nearly gave up on the thing you were made to do because creating is so costly.

But here we are… Like Glennon says…
We can do hard things.

How many loves do you get in a lifetime?

How many people do you get to call yours? There are
all sorts of loves in this world, not all of them, but
most of them are beautiful. Some are old, some noble,
some brave. Others are dishonourable and weak and
make you so by association. Some are a low whisper
on a sombre night, some are maddening. Some you
can't ignore—they slow-burn inside of you, never quite
going out completely but you're too scared to dare try
to fan that flame. Some loves you pretend you don't
feel, even when you can, even when you know you do,
even if he's the first thing you think of in the morning,
even if he's like a match in the darkened room of your
heart—because loving something how you love him
is a painful love that puts rocks in your pockets and
melancholy in your eyeballs and if time has taught
you anything it's that it doesn't matter.
You'll love him forever anyway.

ONE

Magnolia

"I like this." He tugs on my dress, coming up behind me. Black, Amiri Thrasher jeans (extra torn knees, obviously), black Vans and the black and white raglan tee from Givenchy.

I stare at my reflection in his bedroom mirror. Tilt my head, squint my eyes and pretend like I'm the only girl who's been in here lately. I make sure the necklace with his ring on it is tucked under and away where no one but me and probably he later can see it, then flatten the Peter Pan collar of the red, blue and white floral, satin jacquard dress.

"Miu Miu," I tell him, catching his eye in the mirror.

I love his eyes.

He nods coolly. "Slept with a Miu Miu model last week."

I hate his eyes. I glare over at him for a second, swallow heavy to compose myself before smiling carefree. "I don't care." Our eyes lock and hold and I don't just hate his eyes but all of him for a second—for knowing me how he knows me, for seeing through everything I say, for doing that with anyone but me. He shrugs indifferently.

He, being BJ Ballentine, my first... everything, really. Love, time, heartbreak. He's the boy with the golden hair and the golden eyes even though his hair is brown, and his eyes are green, the most beautiful boy in all of London they say—and probably I agree. On his good days. But why am I explaining him to you? You already know who he is.

"I know you don't care." He runs his tongue over his teeth absentmindedly. He does that when he's annoyed and I can tell he's annoyed, but it's just for a second because then his eyes soften like they always do for me.

"You had a boyfriend at the time, Parks—" He looks for my eyes but I don't let him find them because I like to make him think he has to work for my attention.

"Right," I blink as I tell him again: "I don't care."

"Yeah," he sighs, fake-bored. "Shields up, right?" he says, under his breath. That's a thing that the boys say to each other when they see my heart switch gears.

He gives me another look because he knows that I'm lying, and our hearts have a Mexican stand-off with our eyes.

I miss you, I blink in Morse code.

I still love you, say the turned-down edges of his perfect mouth.

Fairly top heavy, like somehow it always manages to get stung by bees. Once upon a time, he balanced my whole heart atop that lip.

"When, anyway?" I ask as I turn on my heel and face him, grabbing his wrist to cuff the sleeves of his black denim patch scarves trucker jacket, also from Amiri, without his permission. I can feel his eyes on me, watching me, waiting for me to look up and when I do, it hurts in the centre of me like it always does when our eyes catch. A fish back in water. A sore relief.

"What?" Beej asks, brows low, watching me closely.

I tug on the centre of his jacket, trying to work out if it'd look better buttoned or not. I do the buttons up. He shifts his head, still looking for my eyes and when I don't offer them, he lifts my chin up to face him, holding it between his thumb and his index finger.

The physical distance between us is meagre, but somehow still a forest grows between. Pine trees of mistakes so tall we can't see over them and rivers of things we didn't say so wide we can't get around. We're nowhere near where we thought we'd be, we're completely off grid, and I feel lost and alone for a minute, but I'm lost and alone with him. "I was just wondering when, is all." I blink a lot. It helps keep the memories at bay. I undo the buttons. "Because you were with me almost all of last week so I just don't really know when you had the time to fornicate with some very, very white girl whose eyeballs are undoubtedly too far apart."

He smirks down at me, amused. Tall, that BJ Ballentine. Six feet, two inches.

"What?" I shrug innocently. "Ghoulishly white with googly alien eyes is undeniably Fabio Zambernardi's aesthetic."

BJ squashes a smile. "You had a boyfriend, Parks," he tells me again, and I ignore him because that's beside the point.

I jerk his jacket back together, rebuttoning. "But I was with you almost the entire time, so I just don't understand like, literally when—"

"Do you want me to share my calendar with you?"

"Your sex calendar?" I ask sharply, but I wonder if I should say yes either way, because it'd probably be handy to have for organising what nights of the week I'd plan to wash my hair, and also knowing his general whereabouts which I like to know at all times but cannot—under any circumstance—admit to, so I just give him a look.

His eyes pinch. "I don't have a sex calendar."

I give him a look. "Well, you certainly don't have a work calendar—"

"I have a job." He rolls his eyes.

"What, taking your shirt off for your Instagram fan club?"

He scratches the back of his neck as he grins sheepishly. "I'm just trying to pay the bills." He shrugs playfully. "Not all of us are sitting on a cool $800M, Parks."

"Quite right, quite right," I concede. "Say, how is that small island your family owns off the coast of Grenada—"

He licks his bottom lip, grinning. "You had to say small…"

"—Smaller than mine," I cut in and he laughs.

He looks me up and down, his eyes dragging over me like his hands used to—he takes a sharp breath in and breathes loving me out—he looks past me at himself in the mirror. He shoves his hands through his hair. "Where'd we land with the buttons?"

I undo them again and he peers down at me, a grin playing about his lips.

"Always trying to undress me…"

I roll my eyes, but my cheeks go pink. "You wish."

I pluck the sky blue Le Chiquito Noeud nubuck shoulder bag from Jacquemus from the fourth level of my handbag shelf.

"I do wish," he concedes, then peers around my body. "Got any buttons that need undoing?"

I smack him away, laughing. "Fuck off."

"Come on." He hooks his arm around my neck, pulling me to the door. "We're going to be late."

"So, Parks," BJ asks, small smile, eyes pinched, "what's your number one pet peeve this week?"

"This week?" I frown. We're sitting at a table with the Full Box Set, our closest friends but even still, sometimes a thing will happen and then all the world falls to black and all we can see is each other.

"Well," he shrugs. "I know what it is of all time."

I arch my eyebrows. "Do you now?" He nods and I drum my fingers on the table, waiting. "Enlighten me."

We're at Annabel's, and next time you're there I highly recommend getting a bottle of the 1995 Dom Pérignon Rosé.

That's not what BJ's drinking though. He's drinking a Negroni. Always a Negroni, unless the night's heading south and then it's 1942 Don Julio.

"Your number one pet peeve of all time... when other girls pay attention to me. Obviously." He does a little shrug with his mouth, as if to say, "so there."

I scoff and shake my head vehemently. "No. That's... not even remotely close."

Though it definitely is, and is absolutely, one hundred percent correct.

He rolls his eyes, ignoring the lie. "This week then, go on—"

"Girls who announce they're not wearing makeup on Instagram who are obviously not wearing makeup on Instagram—"

"Oh," chimes in my best friend, Paili Blythe. "I hate that!" She tucks a piece of her platinum blonde hair behind her ear and her little button nose pinches in frustration. "What do they want from us, a Purple Heart?"

I give her a "thank you very much" gesture before continuing on.

"I don't really understand why being intentionally unkept is a bragging point."

"Some concealer, perhaps?" Paili offers. "A nice creme blush."

"Oh, what's that, Charlotte? You're not wearing any make up today?" I ask no one. "Yes, I know—it's terribly obvious when you have the gift of sight."

BJ runs his tongue along his back molars, smiling. Sniffs a laugh, shakes his head.

"Not everyone rolls out of bed looking like a cartoon deer, Parks—"

"I—" My face falters. "Is that—is that supposed to be a compliment?"

"Absolutely." He nods.

"Come on now," says Henry Ballentine, my oldest friend in the world. Looks-wise he's much like his older brother with the brown hair and the smile that might make you pregnant, but with blue eyes instead of BJ's green, and occasionally in glasses none of us are entirely sure he needs to be wearing. He pokes his head into the conversation, "We all know Bambi was BJ's sexual awakening."

"Ey, Bambi's a boy," Christian Hemmes announces, his Mancunian accent coming through, as it always does when he's amused. We dated once, Christian and I. Sort of. We wouldn't say that now, but we did, I think. And it was bad. Bad for me, bad for him (especially bad for him), bad for Beej (especially, especially bad for Beej)—bad for everyone, really.

But he is beautiful, Christian. Golden-y hair, hazel eyes, heavy mouth. Angelic almost—in appearance, not action. He's terrifying in action, actually. I try not to think about it, what he and his brother do… They think I don't know. But I know. I know everything about these boys of mine.

Henry and BJ both look confused and perturbed by Christian's revelation.

I give him a glib look and turn back to Beej. "So if I'm a deer, what are you?"

"A wolf," he tells me without missing a beat.

I roll my eyes. "The lone kind?"

He shakes his head, eyes going the kind of soft they shouldn't at a table full of people we know in a room full of people we don't. "The kind who finds a deer in the forest who can't reach the top of her medicine cabinet by herself, or change her engine oil, or—"

"She sounds like a very advanced deer," Henry whispers to his brother.

"Well, she's definitely a complicated deer," BJ tells him and I frown. He grins.

"Without the wolf the deer probably couldn't have done up that dress she's wearing." BJ nods at me. "Wouldn't have fed herself since 2004—so the wolf sticks around out of the goodness of his heart."

"I think wolves eat deer," Henry interjects unceremoniously.

BJ rolls his eyes, but I'm worried Henry is right.

Perry Lorcan—slicked back brown hair, big brown eyes, bigger smile, dug-out cheekbones and completely gorgeous, completely fabulous, shakes his head from the other side of the table. "Henry's confused. Bambi was my sexual awakening. BJ's was Ariel—" He gestures to his chest. "The shell bra. He's a sucker for boobs."

7

I don't mean to, but I glance down at my chest and when I look back up, BJ's watching me. He throws me a subtle wink and smirks.

I do my best not to combust into flames on the spot.

"So," Beej leans in towards me, brushing off a rogue eyelash that isn't on my face... just any old reason to touch me, really. "We both know what your real one is"—I try not to smile at him—"but what's your fake all-time pet peeve then?"

I try not to smile at him. "You know this one too."

"Too?" He beams and I roll my eyes. He pauses for a second to think. "Roses and ranunculus in the same bouquet?"

I nod once. "Fucking disgusting. Completely distasteful."

He laughs from the back of his throat and I love it when he laughs at the things I say, I want to make him laugh forever but I can't because he broke forever and still I fight the urge to kiss him anyway. Jonah Hemmes, Christian's older brother, stretches his arms up from the other side of the table—always in all black. Black denim jacket, black T-shirt, black jeans, black Cons but he's very shiny on the inside though—precarious nature of his job aside. His hair could be blonde, but I think it's brown, and his eyes could be green, but I think they're maybe a brown or a hazel? All his angles are sharp: sharp jaw, sharp nose, sharp tongue. Except not with me, because I'm his favourite.

Jo cocks his head at me. "She talking about Monty Python again?"

BJ shakes his head at his best friend as I put my nose in the air, indignant about it all.

"It's a scar on the face of British cinema and I won't hear another word about it."

"I know what we're watching tonight, then." Beej winks.

"Yeah." I give him a look. "Me too. We left Jack Bauer in a very precarious position last night."

Jonah swats his hand as he reaches over and picks up my drink. "That poor bastard's always in precarious positions…"

He samples the cocktail, then pulls a face of disgust. Too sweet.

Henry elbows his brother. "Last night?" he probes in a quiet voice—they don't think I can hear them. "How many nights this week, then?"

"Every?" BJ's eyes pinch. "What's it to you?"

Henry cocks an eyebrow. "Taking that break-up of hers well…"

BJ's jaw sets, defensive. "She is."

Henry gives him a look. "Because you're staying over every night this week?"

BJ's defiant. "I stayed over every night the week before when they weren't broken up, so—"

"Not every night," I butt in. "Just three out of seven."

They both look over at me, a bit surprised, as though they forgot they were having the conversation right in front of me.

"Four," BJ whispers so only I can hear him and our faces are so close I'm dizzy and my breath catches on a shard of my broken heart.

Four? No wonder Brooks Calloway dumped me.

I don't know why that pierces me, but it does. Like an arrow.

The four nights thing?

He's the only man I've ever grieved the loss of, the only love I've ever loved.

Before I even know I'm doing it, I push back from the table, feeling light-headed—spinny and panicked—but I'm not having a panic attack, because I don't have those, those are for people who aren't in control of their lives and I have a handle on everything, absolutely everything, especially my heart. It just comes and goes in waves, the grief of losing him. Rears its head at funny times, in peculiar places.

Like three years after the fact, at The Dorchester with him sitting right there next to me in the Amiri jacket I picked out for him an hour ago, all unbuttoned like my brain goes whenever he's around me.

Did you think I was talking about my boyfriend from a week ago?

How silly of you. So optimistic of my ability to let go of the sinking ship my heart is chained to.

"Is that Magnolia Parks?"

"Where's her boyfriend?"

"Is she here with BJ Ballentine?"

"Are they together again?"

"They're never not together."

"Doesn't she have a boyfriend?"

"I like her dress."

"I hate her dress."

"Are they fucking again?"

These are some of the things I hear as I weave my way to the loo, trying not to faint before I get there.

The four nights thing—that's not why Brooks Calloway and I broke up, by the way. Brooks doesn't know about that. Or he does, probably, because everyone seems to know more about me than I think they do. Brooks doesn't care, he's never cared. In its crudest form and most secret, unspoken terms, we had a mutually advantageous relationship, Calloway and I.

I look between him and Paili, confused. "Going back to the table?"

He purses his lips together. "No." He shakes his head at me like I'm silly. "Nah. Let's go back in the bathroom." He starts pushing me backwards.

"What are you—" Paili starts. "Oh." She stops. She sees something I don't. "Yeah. Bathroom."

BJ nods at me. "Have… you… seen… the new… Dyson air blades they have in these bathrooms?" BJ whistles. Paili nods along enthusiastically. "Wow."

"Yes," I nod at him, like he's a crazy person. "I have. Just now, in fact." I give him a look. "You also have the same ones in your house."

"Yeah," he nods. "Bit weird, don't you think? Should I get them taken out?"

"Well, I mean, actually, yes, if you don't mind because they're quite loud, and Jonah has such a small bladder— he's up four times a night and I can hear it through the walls. Also, I personally prefer those disposable non-paper, cloth-y linen, towel things but could we not just talk about this back at the table, because while we're on the topic there are some other things in your bathroom I'd quite like to change—"

Just then, I see my ex-boyfriend of one week holding hands with some girl I've never seen before a few tables from ours.

"What the fuck?" I say much louder than I mean to.

I'm actually making my way over to him before I realise I'm making my way over to him. Like a little masochistic moth to an idiot flame. Brooks Calloway looks up at me with his big, stupid, dopey brown eyes all round and surprised.

"What are you doing here?" I ask, hands on my hips.

"Um." He looks between me and the girl he's with. "Having dinner?"

I give the girl he's with a cursory glance. "Hello, I'm so sorry, I'm Magnolia—" And then I look at Brooks. "And what the fuck is this?" I ask, hands on my hips. "You're here with another girl?"

It hasn't even been printed in the society pages that we've broken up and he's out dating other women?

"I am," he nods, sitting tall.

"What the fuck!" I all but stomp my foot in protest. "That's so rude."

He looks past me to BJ, who's standing close behind me. He gives BJ a considered look and me a long one. "Is it?" He squints. "Hello BJ."

BJ nods once, tight smile. Never been a fan, really. "Calloway."

"Um," I say, pulling my head back in disbelief. "Sorry, but wait, people still think we're together. You're here with another girl."

"Right. But you're here with another man?"

"I'm here with several men," I clarify.

"Much better." He nods but I don't think he's being sincere.

"I'm here with my friends."

"You're here with Ballentine," he tells me with a look that makes me wonder whether he was less pleased with our arrangement than I previously thought. He clears his throat. "Anyway. This is Hailey—"

"He gets manicures, you know," I warn her. Hailey glances at him, unsure.

"Man-manicures," Calloway clarifies.

"They're the same thing—" I start.

"They're not!" he interrupts. "Not the same thing!"

I shake my head. "It's a buff, a shape—"

"And a clear polish at the end," Brooks says, with an innocent shrug. "Why do you need any polish at the end?" I squint at him. "Brittle nails."

"Ooh," I fake-coo. "Sexy."

He rolls his eyes at me. "Hailey and I have been seeing each other for the last three to four months."

I stare at him for a few seconds. "We only dated five."

Calloway nods cheerily.

"Come on, man," BJ says and scowls.

And up Calloway jumps, almost like he's been waiting for this. "So which are you tonight, her guard dog or her boyfriend?"

BJ shifts in front of me a little, gives him a tight smile. "I'm whatever the fuck she needs me to be."

"Oh," Brooks nods coolly. "So you're her bitch,"

BJ's head pulls back, surprised. "Do you want to go outside?"

Beej steps towards him, and a barrel of nerves rolls over Brooks like a wave. You don't want to be on the wrong side of a fight with BJ in general, let alone if the topic pertains at all to me. He can't see straight when it comes to me, Jonah says. I put my hand on BJ's chest, trying gently to push him away but he yells over my head, "Try it—" BJ tells him. "You piece of shit."

"Woah." I shake my head at them both, reading the room, watching the phones come out.

And, honestly, I don't quite know what Calloway's plan is here—he's mad dogging him or something.

"Come and say that to my face!" he calls to Beej and something about his fight stance reminds me of the Cowardly Lion in The Wizard of Oz.

He's a bit poncy, old Brooks, and while he's not

literally rolling his fists in the air saying "put 'em up," he might as well be. Meanwhile, Baxter James Ballentine could be anything from a rugby player to an Avenger—why Brooks is trying to pick a fight with him is beyond me and I feel uneasy about it either way. I'm uneasy too about BJ punching someone for me. Again. Uneasy about the headlines in the morning. Again. Uneasy about what they'll say, about us, about me. They're not very nice about me sometimes.

"I did say it to your fucking face, you knob," BJ yells and there are camera phones flashing and the wait staff loom nearby, nervous.

"Funny you mention it, do you know who loved my knob?" Calloway starts, looking smug and my jaw drops.

My eyes pinch as I point a finger at him. "Don't you dare say it—"

BJ gets a look in his eyes—and it's a bad look. I know it's a bad look because suddenly the other boys are around us.

I can already see the headlines: "Ballentine cuffed at The Dorchester", "The boys go starkers for Parks!", "Magnolia Parks loves a knob" (—that'll be *The Sun*). Brooks is never in the papers without me, maybe that's why he's doing this? He cares about things like the papers. Beej gives Brooks a long look, daring him to finish the sentence.

It hangs there. And I have hope for a sliver of a second that Calloway has the good sense to retract it all—

"She did." Brooks points at me.

"That's factually inaccurate!" I announce loudly to the entire room, because that feels like the most important part to clarify. "Not true! That's—it's—well, I'm sorry to say, it's actually somewhat underwhelming, to be honest with you." I give the new girl an apologetic look.

"I've seen it," she tells me.

"Of course you have." I nod at her once. "My condolences."

"Hey." Brooks frowns.

I ignore him and turn to look at BJ. His jaw's tight, fists clenched, ready to throw down for my honour any day of the week.

"Let's go," I tell him, but he doesn't move.

Beej glares past me at Calloway and I take his face in my hand, turning it towards me, ignoring the flashes of cameras swirling around us and for a second I don't care if the *Daily Mail* runs a piece on us because it's all bullshit anyway. Everything is. They all go to black. All I can see is him.

I look for his eyes.

I find them and they soften as soon as I do.

"Take me home, Beej," I tell him with eyes he can't ignore. "Jack has a bomb to diffuse."

He takes my hand in his, kisses the back of it. "Fuck David Palmer. Bauer for president."

TWO

BJ

My dad's going to flip a switch. A man's reputation is everything, he says. He can say that because he's got a good one. I don't know what my reputation is these days but I'm pretty sure it wouldn't be something my dad's going to be yelling about from the rafters.

"Another fight, BJ?" he'd say.

I'd say nothing as I'd roll my eyes.

"How many fights do you need to get into before you understand that it's too late. You lost Magnolia a long time ago." That's what he'll say to me tomorrow morning.

Probably in a voice mail because I won't go home tonight.

I don't know how he knows I lost Magnolia, not that she lost me—but he's right. He doesn't know he's right; he's just assumed he's right, which actually is annoying as fuck because he is right. Used to it though. Used to his rightness and also, the long voicemails filled with unsolicited wisdom that's wasted on me but he shares anyway. I think he might wish I was different. Better, or some shit. Parks says that isn't true, that my parents love me stupid—they do—but doesn't mean my dad doesn't wish I were a better man.

I mean, fuck—even I wish I was a better man.

That voicemail he'll leave me, that's just what he says to me after every fight I have over her. They're all over her though. That's the point—not just because I love her and she's her but because she's my family. They're all my family. Boarding school does that to you—makes you make your own family—and whether I love her or not, she's mine.

And honestly, you know what? Of all the shit reasons I've had fights about over the years, Parks' knobby ex announcing publicly at The Dorchester that she loved his dick seemed like as good a reason as any.

Technically didn't even fight him.

LMC and *Loose Lips* won't care; they'll run it like I did anyway.

Parks said she'd call Richard Dennen in the morning, curb anything *Tatler* might run.

The car pulls up at her place in Holland Park.

"A modest little detached ten-bedroom house on Holland Park," I heard her explaining it to someone the other week. "It does have an indoor pool, but not an outdoor one, which is a shame but we make do," she'd solemnly told the shop assistant who didn't ask a thing about her home. We walk through those heavy black front doors I've kissed her up against a million times and I can't help it—what this house does to me—I've loved her in every corner of it. Undressed her in every room. The house turns me to fucking mush. Nostalgia on steroids with a shit-ton of oxytocin whenever I stand in this foyer—a lifetime worth of memories watching her walk down this curving marble staircase, heart in my throat, her in my hands…

Loving someone like I love her fucks you up a bit. Fucking up how I fucked up also fucks you up a bit.

She closes the front door extra quiet and extra slow, her finger pressed to her mouth, shushing me silently.

"Why are you shushing me?" I whisper to her, my mouth closer to her ear than it needs to be but exactly where I want it.

"Because if we wake Marsaili she'll yell at me for bringing you home—"

"Ah." I nod like it's not a punch in the gut that the most important adult in Parks' life thinks I'm trash. Terrifying little thing, Marsaili MacCailin. Her childhood nanny, carer, guardian—you name it, she was it for Parks. Been around since day dot, could have literally yanked her out of her mother's womb, for all I know. She's in every family photo, the parent her parents weren't. Red hair, about 5'1", pretty face but it's always scowling—at me, anyway. Mars used to be my biggest fan, but now she probably lights a fucking smudge stick every time I walk out of a room.

"And also because if my mother sees you she'll probably try to mount you or something, I don't know." Magnolia rolls her eyes, and I smirk. Mostly because she's joking, and a bit because she's not.

Not a regular mother, that Arrie Parks. The bag designer.

Super fun, pretty loose, always found it endearing every time she caught me with my hand up her daughter's skirt, not a pain in the arse when she'd find us with contraband as teenagers (and would occasionally join us). Her number one attribute as far as I'm concerned is that she's still my biggest fan despite my transgressions.

"Where's your dad?" I glance around. I like the feeling of being alone with her in this house.

Feels like we're kids again, sneaking back in after sneaking out.

"Atlanta." She shrugs. "Back in the morning."

Her dad—I mean, you know who her dad is. Harley Parks? The producer? Thirteen Grammys in the last twenty years, and like thirty-five nominations. The man's a fucking legend. Kind of terrifying.

Do you know what it's like to date the daughter of a big, burly black guy who has 50 Cent on speed dial? High stress, man—that's what it's like.

I spent her seventeenth birthday party sweating fucking bullets because I'm pretty sure her dad told Kendrick Lamar and Travis Scott to stare me down and keep me in line. Parks was trying to feel me up every chance she got because she's a handsy little thing when she has a drop in her and I was having to swat her away, so she was shitty at me and they thought it was funny—it was a clusterfuck of a night.

I'm glad her dad's not here, to be honest—if Parks and I were doing it I'd do her on his bed as a fuck you, but we aren't, so I'll just fall asleep in her bed like I do most nights anyway.

Still a bit of a fuck you, I suppose.

When we get to her room I take my shirt off, head straight to the bathroom. She's got a weird thing about showers and bedsheets. Can't get into a bed without a shower.

Do you know how shit a rule that is when you're drunk? Fucking unbearable. Probably had a million fights about it, and never won one of them.

She walks into the bathroom while I'm showering. Grabs her toothbrush, and spins on her bare little foot, watching me. Just my top half, the bottom half is behind this shit tiled wall that you can't see through that I wish wasn't there every day and I know what you're thinking—what the fuck? It's weird. I know we're weird.

But I'm in love with her. And this is the only way she lets me have her, so fuck it, I'll go down with the ship.

"You wanna join me?" I ask her, just to get a rise.

"BJ," she growls but it's hollow. Her eyes flick up in fake annoyance, but her cheeks go red. Turns around, looks at herself in the mirror, fusses with her face that needs no fussing.

"Do I get to watch you shower at least?"

She frowns. "You most certainly do not."

Tilt my head at her. "Bit hypocritical."

She's a sucker for a head tilt. She swallows heavy and I hate this. Hate whatever we are. Hate that I can't just rush her and kiss her and take her in the shower. Hate this box she's put me in, hate the walls she's built around her. Hate these bones of a relationship, but it's all we have left. And it's the best part of my day.

"Pass me a towel," I tell her, as I get out of the shower.

Her hands fly to cover her eyes but she's trying to fight a grin. "Oh my god."

"I know, right." I sigh, proudly just to rile her up.

"BJ!" she cries, cheeks the colour they'd used to go before we were about to… you know.

She blindly swats at me, both passing me a towel and also trying to hit me.

"Watch those hands, Parks."

Eyes still closed, she shoves me out of the bathroom, her hands slipping down my body. We both know it's on purpose, but she'd swear to her death it's an accident. And in another lifetime, I'd drop the towel, grab her by the waist, kiss her stupid and carry her backwards to her bed but in this lifetime she slams the door in my face.

I pull on some sweatpants Parks bought me this week out of the drawer she'd tell you isn't "my drawer" but it's my fucking drawer and we both know it and I climb onto her bed. Sit on her side of it so she'll pretend to be pissed when she gets out of the shower and then she'll shove me over to my side and she'll have to touch me again, because I'm like a junkie with her hands on my body.

She walks out ten minutes later in a light pink silk chemise from La Perla. I know it's from there because I bought it for her. It's not really sexy. No lace or anything. She'd crucify me if I bought her sexy lingerie. I did for Valentine's Day this year, actually. Worth a shot because Valentine's Day is my birthday too. Told Parks they were for me as much as they were her, and that she should just do me this solid favour. She threw them at my head. Wore them the next day, mind you. Not that she told me she was wearing them, but she wore a see-through top to brunch on the coldest February 15th London's seen in a decade.

It happens how I thought it would.

She gets this cross look on her face... walks on over, shoves me as hard as she can muster which is barely at all and I laugh and she shoves harder still, and I pull her down on top of me and for a few seconds she lies there, pretending to push me to my side of the bed, but really we're just trying to hold each other in the ways we have left, and it lasts three, four, five, six—six seconds before her eyes go big with remembering the way I hurt her two and a bit years ago and she rolls off of me, bottom lip heavy in a way that's not fair when you can't kiss it better.

"You good?" I look over at her.

She looks back at me and the Rolodex in my mind tries to find a way to make her feel better, but it doesn't exist. I need a fucking time machine.

Her eyes flicker over me—presses her finger onto the tattoo on my thumb. A little string bow forget-me-knot. Got her a necklace from Tiffany's for our one-month anniversary—which isn't a fucking thing by the way, but I guess it is when you're fifteen and you land the girl of your dreams. Anyway, she loved it. Lost it after a couple of years and they'd stopped selling them. First tattoo I got for her.

They're all for her though—with the exception of...

"This is new." She touches a little tattoo I got a couple of days ago on my chest. A whale. Because of Jonah? He thought it was clever. I don't care—it's barely bigger than a two-pence coin.

I grimace. "Lost a bet to Jo."

She glares over at me a bit, makes a "humph" sound.

"What?"

"Nothing." She sticks her nose in the air. "I just think you're a bit reckless with your body is all." She shrugs like she doesn't care but I can tell she does.

"You didn't think the other twenty-two were reckless."

"That's because they're about m—" She catches herself before she says it, flashes me a tight, controlled smile.

It's all deep, mythological relationship lore, symbols and shit that she knows and I know and no one else does, and I love having her marks on me. She used to leave them in other ways but not anymore. She presses her lips together, gathers herself, clears her throat.

"That's because the other twenty-two are pertaining to someone who cares about your body."

I roll my eyes. Not just at her but at me and us and whatever the fuck we're doing with our lives. "That why I've had blue balls the last three years, then?"

"BJ—" She looks over at me, incredulous. "You literally have more sex than any person I know. If you still have blue balls, you need to see a doctor."

And then I start laughing and she starts laughing, even though it's not that funny because she hates it, so I hate it, but she dates and I fuck and this is what we do, so we laugh.

Her bedroom door swings open and her sister fills the frame. Barely.

"Well, well. If it isn't London's most dysfunctional couple." Bridget Parks grins at us, folding her arms over her chest. She's two years younger than Parks, brown eyes, curly hair, prettier than she thinks she is, but doesn't care either way. Bridge is my youngest sister's best friend.

"Fridget." Parks nods at her, sitting up straighter. "How was yet another riveting evening hitting the books?"

"I love how you make education sound like a bad thing," Bridge sneers back and Magnolia squints over at her.

"I'm educated," Parks tells her, nose in the air.

"You've got a Bachelor of Arts," Bridge scoffs, "which we all know is just higher-education speak for 'not knowing what you're doing with your life' and you paid Imperial College a considerable amount of money to confirm that for you on a piece of paper."

"Yeah but"—I give her a squint—"she did get into Imperial College—"

Her sister rolls her eyes. "As if Dad didn't pay her way in…"

"Colleges need new wings." Parks shrugs, unbothered by the accusation. "It's the circle of life."

Bridge gives her a look. "Is it?"

I snort.

"Tell me, Bridget, what's it like to have nothing in your life but university and essays and assignments?" Parks turns to me. "Isn't that sad? Don't you think that's sad?"

I blow air out of my mouth. "Don't bring me into this."

"Well," starts Bridge. "I see you two are in this"—she points to Magnolia's bed—"again? Do we need to have the talk?"

"You're about as qualified as a potato to give that talk, Fridge—"

"I have sex," Bridge growls.

"With who?"

"People."

"People?" Magnolia blinks a lot, wide and antagonistically. "Plural? Really?" She clocks me. "Are you buying this?"

"What are you talking about, plural?" Bridget shoots back. "The only person you've ever had sex with is him."

Parks' cheeks go hot. "Penetratively speaking, perhaps, but—"

"Oh, fuck," I groan.

This is what they're like. They've been like this since they were kids.

And there's no one on the planet Parks loves more than her sister except probably me.

"Beej." Bridge nods at me. "No shirt, once again." She winks badly. "Thanks for that."

"Was that a wink?" asks Magnolia, knowing full well it was. "Or is there something wrong with your contacts?"

"Oy, Beej." Bridget ignores her sister. "Would you do us all a favour and give this girl an orgasm so she's less of a bitch?"

"Believe me, Bridge," I say with a grin, "I am trying."

Magnolia hits me with a long, gangly arm, and I can tell it hurt her more than me. Bridget rolls her eyes at us, leaves, closing the door. I look at Parks and she looks at me and the same thing that happens every night happens again. We stare at each other. My eyes nearly as round as hers, both of us frozen in what we used to be as everything we've done in this room floats off the walls and dances around us like ghosts from another time.

Have you ever had someone stare you dead in the eyes and wearing all the ways you hurt them? It's fucking intense. But you know what, she hurt me too.

She claps her hands twice. The lights go off and she stares at me through the darkness a few seconds longer, and I love her in the dark. I mean, fuck it—I down and out love her in all spectrums of light, even the absence of it.

She lies down, burrows under the covers, then pokes her head out the top of them. Both of us staring at the ceiling. Her breathing's quiet. She's got a few different kinds of quiets, Parks does. A thinking quiet, a tired quiet, a safe quiet.

This one's weighted, a bit angry. But she's always a bit angry at me, I think.

Which is okay, actually. I get it. I hate myself for what I did 100 percent of the time, none of this "comes and goes in waves" shit, it's constant. I just try my best to drown it out.

She drowns it out better than anything else. Even her quiet breathing.

Then I ask her our question.

"How's the weather over there, Parks?"

She looks over at me, and I see her mouth twitch with a smile.

"Warm enough," and she wriggles closer to me. "How's the weather over there, Beej?"

I turn on my side to face her. "Clear skies."

THREE

Magnolia

I wake up before BJ does most mornings, I have since we were little.

That's how long I've known him. Since we were tiny kids. Henry and I were in the same reception class at Dwerryhouse Prep and were in all the same classes until we left to start at Varley in year seven.

I don't remember a lot about BJ before high school, other than he was just there.

Once when we were little, I would have been seven, maybe—our families were in Capri sharing a super-yacht. We'd docked, and the parents were at this little beachside bar and we were playing on the shore and I fell off a jetty. I was all cut up from the oysters. Lots of blood. That's one of my only real vivid memories of Beej before we got to high school—him diving in, pulling me up to the surface. His hair was blonder then. "I've got you," he told me as he dragged me out of the water. He carried me back to the shore. I had to get like, twenty-two stitches.

He came with me to the hospital. I didn't know why. He told me a hundred years later he already loved me by then, but I didn't really pay much attention to him in those days because BJ was just Henry's older brother and I was besotted with Christian. Probably a bit of a sore spot for all of us now, actually.

Anyway, Henry, Paili, Christian and I were all in the same class, it was kind of the four of us. We never hung out with their brothers; the age difference felt too big to cross. BJ and I did kiss once when I was thirteen. Spin the bottle. It was a little party at the Hemmes' house and the kiss was good but still, he just felt like my best friend's big brother.

However, the further I got into secondary school, the more difficult it became not to acknowledge Baxter-James Ballentine. He was a fifteen-year-old hot shot, not top of his academic classes but a pretty renowned First Fifteen Rugby player (good enough to be scouted for both the Harlequins and Ulster after he graduated, but he tore his hamstring beyond repair in pre-season training). He swam for the district, played hockey, he was centre midfielder too but that's not why people knew who he was. People knew who he was because he had this shaggy mop of light brown hair that oozed teenage sex appeal, and this crooked smile that would have had the teachers throwing their knickers at him if they wouldn't have lost their jobs for doing it.

You know how when you're in high school, the hottest things in the world are sexy bed hair, shoulders and skating?

He hit the trifecta.

Plus, he had these bedroom eyes that look at you like he's undressing you on the spot and I know that sounds so inappropriate, but that's just because he's never done it to you, because if he had, you'd know and you'd live your life waiting for him to look at you like that again.

You couldn't not know who BJ Ballentine was at Varley.

You couldn't not know who he was in London.

It was the first week back from school after summer holidays—the Ballentines took all of us to the Canary Islands for a few weeks, because Lily always said that after three kids, it's a slip and slide, and what's an extra six? I was fourteen, and that was the summer I stopped liking Christian and started liking BJ, and I'd wondered whether maybe he liked me back, but by then he was BJ Ballentine, and I was probably dreaming.

I was standing by my locker with Paili and he walked straight up to me, hand against the locker, cornering me, like the quintessential bad boy in every teenage movie. Except he wasn't a bad boy. He maybe liked to think he was, but he wasn't. He's never once forgotten his mum's birthday, and he'd always bring her flowers every weekend he was home from school. His all-time favourite movie is *Mary Poppins*, who was also his first crush. I was his second.

His shoulders, even back then, were so big and broad, just the sight of him whispered of badassery, except it was a ruse. When his grandfather died, he started taking his grandmother out on weekly dates. He still does, actually.

Besides Henry, there are three sisters, all are younger but one, and Beej was dreadfully overprotective of them, neither Allison nor Madeline had a boyfriend the entire time they were at school because no one wanted to be offside with the Ballentine boys.

He shoved a hand through his hair, glanced down at me—this strange, newfound confidence. Like he'd woken up that day and realised he was the hottest boy in the world.

"Hey Parks," he said and gave me the cool boy nod.

"Hi," I said back, locking eyes with him because that's what the girl magazines told you to do.

"I want to take you on a date," he told me.

"Oh." That's all I said. I blinked a few times. "Why?"

He laughed once, all cool and calm and I think if we all could have peeked behind heaven's curtains at that moment we'd have seen those old Fates knotting our threads together, me and Beej, in this pure, sunny, inexorable, undoable way. I said knotted, not tied. Because I don't know whether we'll ever come undone. Not easily, anyway.

"Can I?" he asked again. "This weekend?"

I pursed my lips together. "No."

Paili looked at me like I was insane, and his face fell.

I shook my head. "It's actually my grandparents' anniversary party at the Four Seasons. I can't miss it. My nanny said she'll take my phone away if I don't go—"

"Oh shit." He laughed. "I'm meant to be going to that too. With my parents."

"Oh." I went pink.

"So you'll be my date then?"

I nodded a tiny bit, but it felt pertinent to clarify, "It's going to be pretty boring?"

He gave me a smile with twinkly eyes that meant trouble. "I'll make it pretty fun."

He did, by the way. Make it fun. He makes everything fun.

We went to the party; our families were overjoyed that we were there together. A dream come true, the marriage of our perfect families. Written in the stars, fated, imagine the wedding, and all that jazz! It was a strange amount of pressure to apply to the first date of young teenagers who aren't Saudi royals. I definitely heard my mother toss around the word betrothed several times, but I didn't even mind because I was all in the second he looked up at me as I walked down my marble staircase.

He swallowed heavy. His eyes fell down my body the same way they do now but it's worse now because he's seen me naked.

"Woah," he said. And then he just smiled shyly, dropped his eyes to the ground.

At the table that night in Trinity Square, while my Uncle Tim was making a drunken speech about my grandparents ("To Linus and Annora, my friends an flarents in paws, an inspiration to live by") I thought BJ was being cute, fiddling with my hand, but midway through realised he was slowly piling my lap with bread, and I couldn't stop laughing, and he felt like the best person. Like I found a secret that was all mine. I remember they played Billie Holiday's "I'll Be Seeing You" and my grandfather standing up and inviting my grandmother to dance, and after a minute, BJ offered me his hand, and I stood up, a million pieces of bread tumbling off me, and he started laughing, and took my hand, and pulled me into him—I love it when he pulls me in to him—dancing in the way that all boys from money know how to dance because they grow up going to galas and royal weddings, and that night he waltzed my heart right out of its chest.

Usually when I wake early I tell him I do it to meditate on the beautiful parts of life but really, I just watch him. He is a beautiful part of life, I suppose. Painful things can still be beautiful things, in case you didn't know.

The way he's asleep this morning, head tossed back, neck stretched out and exposed, his jawbone jutted out—I swallow away all the things I'd do to him if we were doing things but that's not what we're like anymore. His eyelids flutter awake, staring at me for a few seconds. "What are you thinking about?"

"Billie."

He rubs his eye all tired and gives me a small smile. "I love her."

It hangs there. What we're really talking about. "Me too."

Beej pulls on the navy tapered, grosgrain-trimmed, striped, cotton-jersey sweatpants from Thom Browne—different sweatpants than the ones he slept in but don't read into that—it's not like he has a million clothes here, just a drawer. Or two. Or three. They're not even really his drawers, they're my drawers in which—for convenience sake—I permit him to keep a few personal belongings within them. Sweatpants, T-shirts, undergarments and the like, also Ombre Leather by Tom Ford, which I definitely never spray on my pillow if he doesn't stay over, and also I think it's worth noting I store my label maker in those drawers too, so actually, they're barely his at all, and anyway he throws on a T-shirt and I put on a nightgown and we trot downstairs to breakfast.

My family look up from the dining room table.

"BJ." My father looks up from his açai bowl, nodding at him once.

"BJ," my mother says and smiles, like it's not the seventh day in a row she's seen him at breakfast.

"BJ," Marsaili says in a very different tone. Not overly big on second chances, our Mars.

I sit down, huffy. "Do you all not see me?"

My sister sneers. "Quite the contrary—we see too much of you. What are you wearing? Is that underwear?"

"No, Bridget. That would be terribly inappropriate."

Bridget gestures to me. "And that is…."

"It's pretty easy on the eyes, to be honest, Bridge—" Beej offers, and I feel chuffed with myself, but Mars looks cross.

My father glances over at BJ, pretending to look annoyed by the comment.

This used to be scary to BJ when we were kids but now he's the cockiest son-a-of-bitch in every room, so he just grins at him. My father likes him. He acts like he doesn't sometimes, I think in a way where he thinks, as a father, he's supposed to act like he doesn't like the man his daughter's sleeping with—but we're not sleeping together. Even though we're technically sleeping together. And he's barely a father, even though he's my father.

"Harley." I smile over at him curtly. "How was your trip?"

"Magnolia," he says, and sighs. "I have asked you repeatedly to call me 'Dad.'"

"And I have asked you repeatedly to act like one, and yet here we are." I give him a dazzling smile at the same time that BJ kicks me under the table, making a "shut up" face.

"Magnolia." Marsaili gives me a look.

My father shifts, annoyed. "It was good."

"Who were you working with?"

Father reaches for half a passionfruit. "Chance."

"Chance Who?" asks Bridget, completely hopeless.

"Chance the Postman." I roll my eyes. "The rapper, you twat."

"Language." Mars rolls her eyes.

Marsaili is the only responsible adult I know.

She's a small, little Scottish woman who once beat Jonah in an arm wrestle.

She's fiercely protective and aggressively maternal which has proven useful over the years as we've otherwise—as a family—lacked a hands-on parenting approach across the entire board. Mothering and fathering. Bunch of F's, if I were to grade them, which I oft try to do.

My mother could zip off for a girls' weekend that would last a week with Fergie (the former Royal, not the Black Eyed Pea). As for my father, he probably missed several milestone moments throughout my life because he was with the Black Eyed Peas.

Bushka shuffles in and slops a plate of borscht down in front of me.

"Do you mind?" I look at her like she's mad. "This is a £2000 feather-trimmed, satin dressing gown."

My Russian immigrant grandmother. About 50,000 years old, running on diet of Beluga and pickled vegetables. My mother brought her over here for a visit when she married my father and she refused to leave—I don't know why.

My Uncle Alexey is substantially more attentive to her than my mother has ever been. He and his family have a room waiting for her at his place in Ostozhenka. It's nice... Part of the Noble Row complex, views of the Kremlin and Christ the Saviour Cathedral but she keeps on staying here with us. She won't be put into a home (or rehab) and Marsaili has to schlep her around to a bunch of old people's activities every day because she has to be out of the house during work hours, otherwise she tries to get in on my father's writing sessions; She swears up and down that she had a hand in writing that big One Direction song.

"Is good for you." She gestures to the plate as she sits down next to me.

"It's disgusting for me and an absolute hazard."

She scowls at me. "You embarrass to be Russia?"

"I'm not embarrassed to be from Russia." I give her a placating pat on the hand. "I'm not from Russia. You're from Russia. I'm from Kensington."

I look over at my mother for help, but she's distracted—ogling BJ. Can't blame her. That silly mouth of his showing off extra this morning all puffy like it's been kissed all night even though it hasn't, that's just how his mouth is, and I bite down hard on a strawberry.

He catches me, swallows a smile. "You right there, Parks?"

I ignore him.

"This is heritage." Bushka pulls the plate dangerously closer to me.

"Cold beetroot and beef broth is our heritage?" Bridget chimes in.

My father doesn't look up from his phone but pulls a face.

Bushka nods with conviction. "Plus special ingredient." She winks.

"It's vodka," announces Marsaili. "In case there's any mystery about it, let's go ahead and clear that right up."

"Oh cool." Beej takes the plate, sniffing it. "Like a Russian Bloody Mary?"

He slurps some back, then gives Bushka an encouraging grin and a thumbs up. When she looks away, appeased, he gags silently. ("The beef," he whispers hoarsely.)

"So." Marsaili clears her throat. "You two were in the papers this morning."

"Ooh," I sing. "Do I look pretty?"

Bridget rolls her eyes. "Because that's what counts—"

"Very trim, darling." My mother nods. "Décolletage looks phenomenal. Only wear shoulderless clothes this week."

I snap my fingers to communicate to her: noted.

"Too skinny. Eat Borscht," Bushka demands.

"On-again-off-again couple Magnolia Parks and BJ Ballentine caused quite a scene last night at The Dorchester as the pair ran into one of Parks' many ex-lovers—unnamed—"

"How many is many?" my father asks without looking up from his phone.

"Several," Bridget tells him unhelpfully.

"Does it actually say 'unnamed'?" I ask, snatching it over, positively gleeful. "Brooks would just die over that."

Mars ignores me and keeps going. "Jealous Ballentine appeared ready for fisticuffs, but the situation was diffused before it went any further."

Beej shrugs. "Not bad."

"Fisticuffs," I muse.

"And then there are several photos where it looks like the two of you are together—"

"They are," Bridget interjects.

I roll my eyes and BJ pegs a bagel at her.

"Trauma bond!" Bridget announces as though she suffers from some sort of Tourette's syndrome.

"I beg your pardon?" asks my father.

"That's one we haven't explored in the interminable search for a reason as to why these two are the way they are," she prattles on and I roll my eyes at her. "Trauma bonds!"

My father pipes up. "Right, what do these two have to be traumatised about?"

Beej and I stare over at each other, just for a second and then it's gone.

Bridget's terribly vocal about how unhealthy she thinks this all is. Bridget thinks she knows everything because Bridget's in her third year of studying Psychology at Cambridge. Jokes on her though—all I've got is a stupid BA and even I know that we are, at best, maladjusted.

"You two," my mother starts, "Friday is the launch of my new fragrance at Harrods. You'll be there, yes?"

"And by 'you two' you mean one"—I point to myself, then point to BJ—"two? Not the absolute obvious and forever number two in the room."

Bridget ignores me.

"I'm calling you a Two, Fridge. Like a poo."

Bridge glances up, bored. "If you have to explain it, Magnolia, it's not a good joke."

"We'll be there," Beej tells my mum.

"And I'll have security keep her out." I gesture to my sister, who pelts an apple at me.

"I'll bruise from that!" I pout.

"That's because you're malnourished," she tells me.

Bushka pushes the plate in front of me. "Borscht."

FOUR

BJ

I walk into Hide over in Piccadilly and the boys erupt in a cheer.

It's a bit past breakfast time, don't know what day it is.

Paps outside. Love it when they get the four of us together.

The Billionaire Boys—that's what they call us. Joke's on them though, because none of us are billionaires. Maybe if we combined trusts.

"Ey!" my brother cheers.

"The man, the myth—" Christian starts.

Jonah smacks me on the back as I sit down next to him. "I can't believe she let you out of the house, mate." I roll my eyes. "Do you have an ankle bracelet on?" He checks.

I flag down the waitress. She's cute. Short hair, button nose.

"Excuse me, hey." I smile at her. "Can we get some drinks for the table?"

"Coffees?"

I grin at her silliness, shake my head.

"No, sweetheart," grins Jo. "The hard stuff."

I point at the Hemmes boys: "Two Bloody Marys." I point to Hen: "A screwdriver." Point to myself: "Greyhound."

"You got it." She smiles at me in a way that tells me I could have her on her back later if I wanted to.

Jonah catches it, gives me a slight wink. "So," Jo says, looks around the table. "I just want to be clear—Ol' BJB hasn't slept in his bed at our place for over two weeks."

I shake my head. "That's not true."

"Without Parks," he adds.

That might be true. Won't say that out loud.

My brother combs his hands through his hair. "Interesting, interesting—because Allie said Bridget said you nearly kissed the other night." Roll my eyes. Parks and me, we always nearly kiss.

"And," Henry continues, "Mum was saying to me just this morning that you and Magnolia slept at their place two nights the week before last."

I breathe out my nose. Are these clowns keeping a fucking logbook or something?

"Mum also noted that Magnolia didn't sleep in Magnolia's Room, she slept in yours."

"Okay." I wave a dismissive hand. "So the takeaway here is that you, Mum, Al, Bridget and Jo all have too much time on your hands."

Christian's quiet, I notice. He's just watching me, not a lot of expression. That's not crazy weird for him either, he's pretty stoic. Extra stoic when it comes to Parks though.

The waitress brings over our drinks, slips me her number and I pocket it out of habit.

"You gonna call her?" Christian asks.

I scratch my nose. "Nah." I look back at her. Pretty hot. "Maybe."

I make a point of not looking at him, I don't want to see his face—tell me that I'm doing something wrong.

I don't know what's with him. He's not some fucking moral compass—not with what their family does. And I mean, they're all protective of Parks. They'd have ripped that shite Calloway a new one if I barked once, but Christian's different to Henry and Jonah. He's just protective of Parks because of their—whatever, I guess.

We came to blows about it once. About three years ago. Me and the lads were supposed to nip off to Prague for a boys' weekend but Christian pulled out last minute, said he had a work event or some shit—they run clubs, the Hemmes brothers—anyway, our flights were cancelled so we just went out that night anyway.

It wasn't long after me and Park had ended. Fresh. Like we're talking, under three months.

Got to The Box over in Soho—me, Hen and Jo, and I swear to God, the second we walked in, my heart fell fifty floors.

She was in the darkest corner of the club, but I could spot her anywhere, my girl, being kissed and felt up by some fuckwit. I was incensed. Couldn't believe it.

Barreled over, pulled the guy off her—it was a reflex. Tossed him to the side. I didn't realise it was Christian straight away. And everything about this part of it lags in my brain—I remember Parks looking sad—maybe a bit ashamed? And I was looking at her like she betrayed me, and even though she hadn't, she had. I remember the feeling my heart had—like, fuck. This is what you did to her but a hundred times worse.

And then my brain went into overdrive. Christian lied about the trip so he could be with... Parks? He lied to me? To be with her? My her? My brain instant-replayed their kiss in my mind—that wasn't their first fucking kiss.

My insides went from ragged to hulk.

I turned towards Christian, who had barely gotten up off the floor, and charged at him. Grabbed him by the collar of his T-shirt, dragged him through the crowd, knocking people and glass over. There was smashing, screaming—I didn't care, I couldn't stop. Slammed him up against the wall, looked him in the eye—I wanted him to be drunk or high or some shit, but he was dead sober, so I cracked him in the jaw.

The sound was loud but not loud enough to drown out the screaming of Parks.

I looked back at her—Jonah was holding her back.

"Beej—" Christian started, but I couldn't—so I hit him again.

He wasn't fighting back, which was weird, because Christian's the best fighter out of all of us, but he did nothing. Just looked up at Jonah, waiting for him to intervene, but Jonah just shook his head, shoved Parks towards my brother.

I threw him into the wall again.

"Stop!" Christian yelled, shoving me back and away as he squared up, but he didn't want to fight me.

"Excuse me?" Jonah said, getting in close to his baby brother's face.

Christian's eyes went all tired and hurt. "You going to let him beat me up, Jo?"

"No." Jonah gave him a long look. "I'm going to help him."

Me and Jo, right? Thick as thieves. Brothers.

My mum was a bit nervous about me and Hen hanging out with the Hemmes because even though it's not really spoken about, people know what their family does, you know? I mean, you have a tea with their mum for thirty seconds and Rebecca Barnes will blow all your worries away. It's why she's good at what she does.

Jonah and I were always close through primary, played the same sports and shit, but in year eight, we came home after Saturday sports. Found his sister drowned in the pool.

We were twelve. She was four. Dove in, fished her out. I tried to resuscitate her. Jonah called for help. She was blue. Gone. Gone well before we got there.

The boys stayed at our house for a month. Bridge was right about trauma bonds.

So, Parks, right—standing in The Box, screaming at me and Jonah to let Christian go, to leave him alone—made it worse if I'm honest, hearing her care about anyone but me.

"Hemmes," said the bellowing voice of a club bouncer from behind us all. He shook his head. "Outside."

Jonah pulled Christian up off the wall, tossing him in the direction of the door, shoving him as we walked, hard enough that he tumbled out onto the street.

And then I don't know what happened, I was just kicking one of my best friends in the stomach.

"Is she your work thing?" I yelled at him and Parks was sobbing in the background, I couldn't even focus on her to hear.

Jonah sort of just stood back, watching. Letting us work it out.

"Beej," Christian croaked, wiping blood from his face. "You don't—"

"What? Understand?" I growled. "It's Parks. She's mine." I picked him up off the ground and shoved him again. "She'll always be mine."

"No!" she spat at me, shouldering her way out of Henry's arms and grabbing mine, spinning me to face her and she looked me dead in the eye. "Fuck you."

I looked over her head to Henry. "Take her home." I couldn't even look her in the eyes, mine were a mess, all teary and shit, and she's there screaming, "You can't make me leave, come on Christian. Let's go—"

She looked afraid. That makes me feel sick now when I think back to that night, that we scared her.

"He's not going with you, Parks," Jonah told her.

"Yes, he is." She sniffed, reaching for Christian, but Jonah shoved him away from her.

"Take her home now," I yelled at Henry again, giving him warning eyes.

"Just go, Magnolia," Christian told her. The way he looked at her still pisses me off now. "I'll call you in the morning."

Jonah made a growl at the back of his throat, but Christian shot him a look and something about it made Jonah back off. "I'll call you in the morning," Christian repeated.

Henry grabbed Parks' arm, pulling her back towards a car.

"I hate you," she choked out to me, barely meeting my eyes.

I don't think she'd ever hated me before, even when I did what I did. My jaw clenched, and then I punched Christian in the stomach. Beat him up 'til he was vomiting in an alley behind the club he was kissing my girl in, left him there. Makes my ribs feel like they're twisting inside my chest remembering that shit. Christian's beat up-face, my fucked-up fists, all the questions I needed to know the answers to so I could figure out how to breathe again. Did they have sex? Had he seen her naked? Where had he touched her?

I still don't know, actually.

"So, Beej." Jonah bumps me in the chest. "Be honest. Are you shagging Parks?"

I swat my hand through the air. "No, man."

"Jo," Christian says and snorts, "the second Magnolia Parks lets him back in her bed, this one'll throw a fucking parade."

I toss him a bored smile. "I've been in her bed since I was fifteen."

"Yeah," my brother tosses me a look. "But he'd throw a parade if she let him back in her though—"

"Watch it." I point at him. But also, it's probably true. Jonah chuckles. Christian doesn't. Tries to smile. Doesn't land.

"What's on the agenda for the rest of the day, lads?" Jonah glances around.

"Uni," sighs Henry.

"I'm having dinner with Baby Haites tonight." Christian yawns.

"Eyy." I grin over at him. Happy genuinely, both for him and for myself. "I like her."

He glances over, gives me a sort of amused, sort of unimpressed look. "Yeah, she likes you too, actually."

Henry looks between us. "Oh, fuck me, boys—let's not do that one again."

Jonah leans back in his chair, yawning. "What about you, big man?"

I lift my T-shirt up, showing my stomach, smacking it a couple of times,

"Gains?" Jonah asks. "What are you pumping these days?"

"Besides Miu Miu models," Christian offers.

My brother leans in, curious. "Oy, how did you manage that?" I roll my eyes at them all collectively. "I'm asking seriously," he presses.

"Oh, fuck off." I throw back my drink.

"In the loo?" Jonah whispers.

I snort a laugh. "My car."

FIVE

Magnolia

My mother's fragrance launch tonight—Velvet Seduction. Gross, I know. A little too much information offered there regarding the sex life of my parents which I was quite certain they'd retired from immediately after the conception of Bridget but anywho. I'm glad she's doing a fragrance though. For one, they're a cash cow, and two, I think fragrances are important.

They leave a mark on your mind in a way other things can't.

Old books. My sister.

Milky sweet tea. Marsaili.

Hoyo de Monterrey. My father.

Menthol cigarettes. Bushka.

Chanel No. 5 and Rosehip oil. My mother.

Cardamom and leather. A one Baxter-James Balentine.

Musk and orange blossom? The worst day of my life.

The launch is at Lecture Room & Library and I arrive by myself which I hate and love to do. Hate it because socially it leaves you wide open to conversational misfires but love it because I know for certain that everyone is staring at just me. Which they are. I'm wearing the moss green, layered tulle, beaded, plunge-neck gown from Marchessa and I dare you not to stare at me.

The neckline is too plunging to wear the necklace I always wear in secret, so I had to take it off and my heart feels like it's sitting on uneven ground without it.

I grab a glass of champagne from a server and throw it back quickly—it's the only way to survive these things. I start scouring the room for people I like, of whom there are perhaps six on the planet at any given time, depending on how BJ is behaving.

I was supposed to arrive with Paili and Perry, the two P's, but London traffic worked against us.

I duck away from a boy I dated a while ago, Breaker was his name. New money from dairy farming over in the U.S. We dated for a loose three months, tops. He was an absolute infidel, and he was undoubtedly using me to get into high society, but I didn't care because BJ got to sleep in my bed as much as I wanted, and that's really the only qualifier I look for in a relationship these days.

I'm wandering around, looking for a familiar face when I walk right into Hamish Ballentine. "Magnolia," he says, leaning down to give me a kiss. "You look beautiful, darling." I squeeze his hand because I love him more than my own father. "Your travel piece was lovely, sweetheart," he tells me. "On the little spa in the Dolomites? We're definitely going to go."

"Oh!" I clap my hands gleefully. "Lil will love it. Let me know when—I'll call ahead and make sure they treat you extra special."

He gives me a grateful little wink.

"And where's my son?" He glances around. Much to his parents' disbelief, BJ and I in fact do not spend all our time together. We each have our own. Well, I have a job. He has a... thing. He's attractive, he's signed to a big agency, has sponsorships, posts shit all day.

He doesn't like to call himself a model and I'm reluctant to call him an influencer, because that's incredibly embarrassing and dare I say, lacks any kind of professional longevity—but he's not...not an influencer?

He had a shoot today—a proper one—not some thirst trap photos on a train track, shirtless with a generic dog. I think he was shooting with Fear of God.

Me, you ask? Oh, I put in a hard two at the office and then headed to George Northwood to get my hair done.

"He's meeting me here," I tell his dad.

"Still not together?"

"Still not together, Hamish." I nod playfully.

"Yes, sure, sure." He rolls his eyes, not buying it. "Still in love though?"

I pick up the skirt of my dress and glare over at him playfully.

"Nice try," I call back as I march away and over to the safety of August Waterhouse.

One of London's rising music stars. He produced five of the UK's #1s last year.

He's a tad older than me, Gus. Thirty, maybe? A long-term, worthy, faraway crush of Perry's and a very sweet, somewhat sage man. He works with my father.

"Gus," I smile. "How wonderful to see you. I didn't know you were coming?"

"Your dad dragged me along." He gestures to my father, who's in the corner of the room with Marsaili, looking as grumpy to be here as each other.

I snort a laugh. "He could at least pretend to be supportive. Mum pretended to like that garbage song he did for Dua Lipa last year."

"Oy." Gus gives me a look. "I wrote on that—"

I make an uncomfortable sound.

Gus makes a tsk-tsk sound under his breath. "I should have known you'd be here, Parks—Tommy might have actually left the house for a brief twenty seconds."

Flattered as I am that I might have propelled Tom England out of his home momentarily, I still find myself frowning a little. I don't mean it. It's just all so sad…

Tom is Gus's best friend. His brother died rather suddenly a few months ago from a brain aneurysm.

"Anyway," Gus shrugs to himself. "Heard your break up was splashed about in the papers?"

I wave my hand through the air. "Always,"

He chuckles. "Taking it like a champ, I see."

"It's very easy to take break ups like a champ if you strictly date twats."

He laughs. "I'll remember that."

"Gussy," my father jeers, clapping him on the back. "Glad to see you could make it. Magnolia—" He leans in to kiss my cheek. I allow it.

"Harley." I nod at him, with a terse smile.

He rolls his eyes at Gus as they exchange a look that implies I'm a somewhat taxing person occasionally before Gus spots an up-and-coming rapper he'd liked to work with and excuses himself.

"Darling, listen—" My father folds his arms over his chest because we don't know how to talk to each other. "I have a writing retreat I'm supposed to go to. Rural America—"

"Sounds murdery." I nod along.

"I'm not all too keen on it, if I'm honest with you, darling. I'm trying to rally them over here instead, but they want a quiet, off the radar place to be. Any ideas?"

Firstly, though it pains me to admit it, I'm chuffed that he's asking for my professional opinion on something.

Seeking your father's approval is such a terrible cliché, I know—but it's so seldom given that when it is, it's a real thrill.

"Hmm," I ponder out loud. "Heckerfield Place, in Hampshire?"

He shakes his head. "If I've heard of it, it's too known."

I purse my lips. "Do you know what, actually? Just a few weeks ago a little estate opened its doors up in Toms Holidays—" He looks confused. "By The Towans?" I offer.

"Oh." He nods, intrigued.

"It's called Farnham House. I haven't been yet, but I need to. Beautiful, they pulled one of the sous chefs from Le Gavroche up there. Amazing spa. On the water, super gorgeous. But no one really knows about it yet, it's so new—"

He leans in again, kissing me on the cheek again but I am less annoying about it this time. "Sounds perfect, darling. Thank you."

He walks away.

"Who's the artist?" I call after him.

"Hm?" He looks back.

"The artist. That you're working with."

"Oh." He nods. "Um. What's his name? Your man—" I eye him, confused.

"You know." He gestures to his face nondescriptly. "With the—and the—"

"Post Malone?" I offer.

"That's him," he says before he jiffs off.

Perry and Paili finally arrive. Slim-fit, satin-trimmed, cotton-velvet tuxedo jacket in burnt orange and the Eggsy's black wool and mohair-blend tuxedo trousers, both from the Kingsman's label; royal blue mini, velvet-trimmed, shirred, tiered, taffeta gown from Molly Goddard respectively.

"Was that Gus Waterhouse?" Perry asks, looking after him. "I love him. Does he love me? Do I look good? Should I talk to him?"

I count the answers off my fingers. "Yes, it was. Yes, I know. I don't think he does—yet! Uh—yes, you do look good. And definitely talk to him." I pluck the champagne from his hand and toss it back.

Paili looks up at me, brightly. "You look perfect. What is that dress, holy shit!"

I'm sure it's some sort of best friend's bias but my head floats up to the clouds nevertheless.

"And where's the woman of the hour?" Paili asks. "Should we make our presence known?"

I wave my hand dismissively. "Last I saw of her, she and the Viscountess of Hinchingbrooke were trying to take a selfie with a peacock. Lot of feathers—not expert bird wranglers, either of them."

"What does a peacock have to do with velvet seduction anyway?" Perry asks very validly.

I purse my lips. "I've never wanted to know an answer to a question less."

"So." Paili glances around. "Where's your boy?"

"I don't know." I sigh. "Said we'd meet here"—I pause—"and also, actually, what boy?"

They both roll their eyes.

"You've been spending a lot of time together." Paili smiles, eyebrows up.

"No more than usual," I say, nose in the air.

That much is true. With the exception of the initial few months following our break-up, the Christian debacle and the aftermath of the beating Christian senseless debacle—we've never really... not...spent all our time together.

"Yes," she concedes. "But now you don't have a fake boyfriend to throw in his face whenever you remember that you love him."

I scowl at her on both accounts of what she said. Fake boyfriend? Love him? Absurd. Sort of.

"Speaking of Boy Wonder." Perry nods at the door. And in he walks.

Claret slim-fit, velvet tuxedo jacket in wine, the black, virgin wool, tuxedo trouser and the white bib-front, double-cuff, cotton-poplin, tuxedo shirt, all from Giorgio Armani except for his little Tom Ford bowtie.

Henry, Christian and Jonah follow after him and then a calculated millisecond later follows the velvet gown by Alaïa, also in wine. I can't tell which bothers me more—that BJ brought her to my mother's launch or that I'm worried that they coordinated. Taura Sax. She is regrettably, very beautiful. In a different way to me though, and that's maybe the worst part.

For all my brown skin, dark hair and light eyes, Taura Sax is sort of olive, bronde hair, freckles and hazel eyes. I think her mother is from Singapore. And we literally look nothing alike.

And sure, perhaps at this point it's safe to say that BJ's type is simply just definable as a sexually willing female, but Taura Sax is the only repeat on his roster that he says doesn't exist.

Taura Sax is also who he cheated on me with, by the way. That's what I've concluded. The second worst night of my life floats to the surface of my consciousness— orange blossoms. There was something else... what was it? Think, Magnolia, think. I stomp out those thoughts like a fire in my mind.

I can't think of it. Not now. My chest goes tight as my heart bucks at the feelings I'm feeling but I can't feel in front of him because he can't know he still does this to me. I can feel my mouth is agape, so I snap it shut quick smart.

I don't want people to know that this has caught me off guard, that this—him, bringing her here, wasn't pre-planned, pre-checked with me, isn't exactly what I was expecting from him, never in a million years did I maybe think that he'd be different for once, just once in his stupid lifetime, maybe he'd try to not swerve us off a cliff.

But they can see it on my face too, I know they can. Perry's grimacing, Paili's got the sad eyes she always has when she looks at me and BJ. She swallows, looking apprehensive. She touches my arm. "Are you okay?"

"What?" I blink a lot. "Me? No. Yeah! I'm fine—it's just—rude, is all. To bring her here. Don't you think? The girl he fucked me over with?"

"We don't know that," Paili offers, gently.

Perry gives her a look. "Yes." He pauses. "We do."

It's not really known, by the way. That that's why we broke up. It's known among our friends now, it's trickled out over time to the P's and the boys and my sister, but no one else knows.

I don't know why.

I think I was afraid of what it would say about me, that he threw away what we had for one shitty night with Taura Sax. I stare over at BJ darkly and our eyes catch, because they always do if we're in the same room.

His face sparks up, a half-smile appears, and he walks over. "Hi." He leans in to kiss my cheek and I subtly pull away from him and our eyes catch again and he looks confused and hurt and annoyed, all at once.

Perry makes an uncomfortable noise in the back of his throat and points to something on the other side of the room. "Fancy a peacock selfie?" He pulls Pails away.

BJ watches them go before glancing back at me, jaw tight with apprehension. "Problem?"

"What'd you get up to this afternoon?" I ask brightly, but it's a trap. He knows it's a trap. "Did you do anything after your shoot?"

"Uh," he breathes out a small laugh. "Not much, just hung out—"

"With?"

He licks his bottom lip, bracing himself. He says nothing.

"With Taura Sax," I say for him.

He smells like freshly applied Tom Ford. That's a bad sign. He smells like a shower, like he's scrubbed his body clean but not with his Malin & Gotez Rum body wash that he usually uses, something else—and you're there thinking, sure well, he's just showered before an event but no. These events are a dime a dozen for us, and he doesn't shower any other time of day except the morning unless he's getting into my bed or he has to, but he's showered now. At 5 p.m. on a Friday evening. I know what that means.

He gives me a look. "Yes, with Taura."

I raise my eyebrows. "And you thought it was appropriate to bring Taura Sax here to my mother's launch, given all our history?"

He sighs, tired. We've walked down this road before, a thousand times, we know it well. It's dark and shadowy and one of us always emerges with an arm gnawed off or a broken bone or heart. "Parks." He shoves his hand through his hair. "We've talked about this before. She's not—that's not who I—"

"So you haven't slept with her?"

His jaw juts. "I have."

"When?"

His eyes go heavy. "Parks."

"Today?"

His eyes drop from mine. And I stare at him, feeling more betrayed than I want to, more betrayed than I should. He's crushed. He's crushed he's crushed me. This is an old dance we do. A ritual, almost. Breaking our hearts open on the altar of each other.

"Parks," he starts.

I shake my head dismissively. "No, I know, I get it, I had a boyfriend"—I pause, glare over at him—"wait, no, I didn't."

He looks sorry. "Parks—"

"But I will." I cut him off.

His jaw sets. Worried and annoyed. "Magnolia—"

"—Magnolia?" I interrupt him. He barely ever calls me that. "I'm the one in trouble?"

He reaches for me, holding my arms, trying to keep me close. "Parks, you're being ridiculous."

I smack him away and glare at him. "Don't touch me with those hands."

I realise that the world has fallen to black but in the bad way. The room is watching us. Drinks stop clinking, waiters stop serving, breaths are being held—Perry's about to pass out from the drama of it all over in the corner. This fade-to-black thing BJ and I have, I know it sounds romantic—written in the stars, two people who can just home in on each other so much that no one else around them seems to exist, but that skill when fighting in public is front page press for people like us.

I'm embarrassed for a second, all those eyes. I wonder: what did they hear?

I turn on my heel, away from him and as I do the room jerks back into motion.

I walk up to the bar, grab another champagne and throw it back, then pick up another to sip.

"Good chat?" asks Henry.

I down my sipping champagne in one go.

"Fantastic."

00:39

Parks

How's the weather, Parks?

Stormy very vrty stromy

Are you drinking

Ye

S

Where are you?

I'm find

Fine

I didn't ask if you're fine, I
asked where you are

Pick up

Answer your phone

I'm home xxxxxxxxxx

The xxxxxxx was an
accidenn still stormy fuck
you

SIX

Magnolia

I blink awake the next morning, a little worse for wear—
and roll over towards my bedside table praying to the
Lord on high that drunk me (understatement) had the
good sense to leave sober me (overstatement) a glass of
water.

She did, bless her.

I don't remember how I got home, actually. I want it
to have been BJ, but it wasn't because he's not here in my
bed. I haven't woken up without him being next to me
for a while now. We're having sleep overs too often if I'm
waking up feeling strange that he's not here.

But I've never really liked it when he's not here—
we were together too long, loved each other in such an
intertwined way that his absence makes me feel uneasy.
And he can't be alone, so I know if he's not with me then
he's with someone else and that's too heavy a thought
for the morning time.

I can't help but wonder if he went home with Taura?
Probably he did. That's what we do. Spend all our time
together, get too close, get too scared. He'll fuck around,
I'll get a boyfriend again soon. He'll hate him, probably
so will I, and BJ and I will be back to normal.

Normal is relative, I know. Normal for two broken
hearts who can't fit their pieces with anyone but each other.

My bedroom door swings open and Marsaili marches in, carrying a tray table full of breakfast and a pot of tea. She clatters it down on my bedside table extremely loudly and extremely on purpose on account of my hangover. I glare over at her and she gives me an amused smile.

"One's head must hurt this morning," she tells me.

I sweep my hair over my shoulders and pour my own tea like a normal person; I like it better when Louisa brings me breakfast. She actually serves it.

"Yes, well—" I give her a delicate look. "We can't all stand sullenly in the corner of our employer's fragrance launch, can we?"

She rolls her eyes, and then gives me a look. "Velvet Seduction?"

I put up my hand to silence her. "Please stop."

Marsaili does an involuntary shiver. And then my bedroom door swings open again. In walks BJ with a Chanel gift bag.

Black and white, zodiac map shirt from Valentino, the black and very torn wash-blowout, slim-leg jeans from Purple Brand and the black and marshmallow earth Old Skool Vans.

"Listen, Parks. Are we—" BJ starts then stops when he sees Marsaili. Gives her a big grin. "Mars."

"BJ." She rolls her eyes. "You didn't stay over?"

He grins at her brilliantly. "Thought I'd give you a night off; we don't want those frown lines setting in…"

I give him an exasperated look. She rolls her eyes again so far back I'm just positive she must have gotten an ocular headache, and then she saunters away.

"I think she's warming to me," he says, watching after her.

("She's not," Mars calls back without turning around.)

"So." He gives me a look. "Last night was fun…"

"Last night and in the day time?" I ask, eyebrows up. "Busy boy."

"That's not what I meant." Beej sighs, shoving his hands through his hair.

It's strange, actually. He has so much sex, so much— and he'll bring it up whenever he pleases if it'll get a rise out of me, but he doesn't like it when I talk about it.

"I hate fighting with you, Parks," he tells me.

"Then don't do it." I shrug, wondering when he'll just hand me that bloody gift bag.

"Can't help it," he tells me and my eyes snag on his mouth.

Beej clears his throat, and I flick my eyes back up to his eyes, my cheeks flushing ever so slightly.

"You're just a massive pain in the arse," he tells me, his cheeks a bit pink too.

I wonder whether we're going to kiss. I always wonder whether we're going to kiss. We never do. Nor should we. Our eyes hold like our hands won't.

I love you, he blinks.

Prove it, I sigh.

I feel glad that I'm wearing the Noelle Martine lace-trimmed, satin pyjamas from Morgan Lane + LoveShackFancy co-lab because it's very short and it shows my midriff which is terribly toned right now and I hope he thinks about me without my clothes and I think he must because he presses his hand into his mouth and swallows.

"Alright, Parks." He gives me a measured look. "Scale of one to ten, how mad are we talking?"

I eye him. "Ten! Very ten! Now give me the Chanel bag."

He chuckles as he tosses it down on the bed.

"Which one is it!" I grab for it, excited.

He smiles, eyes watching me in a way that one could argue might be too familiar and too comfortable for exes, but I don't want to argue that. "The one you wanted."

"Pink lambskin, gold-tone metal with the jewels?"

He nods as he sits down on my bed, laying back on it.

I clasp my bag to my chest and lie down next to him. "Thank you."

Beej nods again, his eyes tracing the cornice on my ceiling like he always does when his mind and his mouth can't quite connect.

"I'm sorry," he says eventually, glancing at me. "—About Taura. I know she makes you sad."

I pull back, swallow a bit nervous. I don't know why. "You never say sorry to me for that kind of thing."

He looks a bit raw; his eyes go back up to the ceiling. "Yeah but—I don't like making you sad."

I copy him, staring up. "I don't like making you sad either." I wish we could stop. I don't know why we can't seem to.

I look over at him. "Take me shopping?"

He smiles and nods. "I get to watch you shower though."

"Deal." I nod.

He sits up, cannot believe his luck. "Really?"

"Nope!" I sing as I skip away.

He calls after me, "I'm taking this bag back."

SEVEN

Magnolia

You're wondering—I know you are, everyone does—why we aren't together?

Infidelity aside, you think he's perfect. That we're perfect, and that nothing in this world past, present or future could be big enough or bad enough to justify us not being together. I get it, I've been there. I've thought that too.

There were these couple of months after everything that had happened with Christian where Beej and I began to drift back towards what we used to be. It wasn't intentional or conscious. It was just easier to be with him than not to be, and maybe that's not a good thing—I don't know anymore. I can't objectively tell with us. With anything to do with him, my heart's logic is as blurry as the lines we pretend we don't cross. I was still broken, and I was still sad, and I still didn't trust him how I used to trust him, but I think at one point, I loved him more than he hurt me, and it sort of began to feel stupid to me to love someone how I loved him and to throw it all away because he had sex with someone else one time.

I'm not belittling that, by the way. Or making excuses. It makes me feel sick to say it even now. It's not that it didn't matter. I think it's just that how much I love him mattered more.

But Marsaili wouldn't have a bar of it. I'd never seen her before with anyone the way she became with him. When he started showing up again around the house, she'd practically lurk in the corners with daggers for eyes, waiting for moments to make snide comments, to undercut him, pour a salt ring around him, toss him under a bus. He'd leave and she'd make me an extra sweet tea in the kitchen and tell me that what he did couldn't be undone, and he couldn't be trusted, and if he did it once, he'd do it again, and that actually, if he loved me how he said he did, he wouldn't have done it anyway. And I'd cry, every time, and I'd tell her I think it was an accident, and she'd tell me people don't accidentally have sex with people, that it doesn't just happen, you have to want it to happen. Which was always hard to wrap my head around.

It was easier for me to default back to the idea that it accidentally happened, that he slipped over accidentally into having sex, that there was no thought to it, that it happened the way you fall, a trip and then you're falling, falling without your permission, it's not conscious, and then you hit the ground.

That's how I needed it to be for us to get back together, but Marsaili helped me see that's not how infidelity happens.

It happens because people are careless and callous and casual with hearts and emotions, and those people are dangerous to be involved with and so even if you love them, you shouldn't love them because nothing is worth feeling how he made me feel, and there was no guaranteeing that what happened before wouldn't happen again because the word of a cheater, she said, is void.

So BJ and I didn't happen again either. It's what put us on a funny path, I think. Those few months where we were obviously headed towards being together again before I 180°-ed the fuck out of there, started dating other boys to cover my heart's tracks.

I think it killed him for a minute. Maybe even literally once.

We sort of were like we are now, I suppose. I had just begun dating someone—Reid Fairbairn, an Australian boy whose dad is in mining. He was new on the scene, pretty hot like most Australian boys are. It didn't last long—I think we were together two months or thereabouts. I didn't need it to last, he'd served his purpose. It stung BJ at first but all it took was a hot minute and a long weekend in Amsterdam and he was back to normal.

We'd all spent the previous night out with my friends at EGG, and Reid told a joke that was actually pretty funny, and I really laughed, and it was one of those rare occasions where I actually had fun with the person I was technically dating at the time.

Anyway, the next night, I don't know where Reid was, but I went to dinner with Henry and Christian at Gauthier Soho, and Jonah came to meet us after for a drink.

"Not this again," he said, as he waved his thumb between Christian and me, who were sitting next to one another.

"She has a boyfriend." Christian rolled his eyes, giving me a tired look.

Jonah tossed me an unimpressed look. "She's got a beard."

"She does not!" I huffed. Henry threw me a look that told me they all knew anyway, and I reached across his plate to "sample" his dessert for the fifth time.

"Where's Beej?" Henry asked Jonah.

Jonah shook his head. "I haven't seen him since last night."

They all glance at me nervously.

"Guys!" I rolled my eyes. "I know he's fucking all of London! No need to tiptoe around me. Besides," I plopped my shield up in front of me, "I have a boyfriend."

"Are you okay?" Henry asked, cautiously.

"As okay as I'd be to hear that you were fucking all of London." I blinked with faux indifference.

"Well," he sighed, contently. "I am."

"Then great." I grinned at him, lying through my teeth. "That's great, because I am great. With all of it. Because it's great. Good for him. I'm happy for him, even."

"Right," Jonah said, smirking. I gave him a megawatt smile to shut him up, and he shook his head, suppressing a smile as he poured me some wine.

The magical ingredient in our social circle that enables us to still function after everything we've been through and done to one another: denial. (And alcohol.)

And then my phone started to ring. "Speak of the devil." Christian nodded toward my phone.

"Hey." I tried not to grin too big as I answered.

"Parks?" he called into the phone, and his voice sounded weird.

"Beej?" I pressed the phone into my ear and covered the other with my hand.

"Parks?" he yelled, then took a big, long sniff.

"Beej, where are you?" I asked quickly, and I felt the atmosphere amongst the boys shift. "You sound strange?"

"I think I'm—" I heard him taking deep breaths. "My heart's going funny," he said, but I could hear someone in the background. I don't know which of us he was talking to. A girl.

"Give me the phone," the girl said urgently.

I asked him again, clearly: "Where are you?"

"Give it to me!" she said. There was a scuffle at the other end.

"No!" he growled at her, didn't sound like himself, and that's when my heart sank, because I knew. I knew what'd happened. I could tell, even though it didn't make sense. But I'd seen it enough in our circles, knew the signs. The way it can change you. I didn't know he'd been using. There was more scuffling, more arguing for the phone. BJ was slurring. The girl was panicked.

"Beej?" Me, all urgent and nervous. All the boys' eyes were on me, brows furrowed.

"BJ?" I called loudly.

"Hello?" the girl said, breathless into the phone.

"Where are you?" I demanded.

"Magnolia, it's—" she started, but I jumped in.

"I don't care who you are." I was doing my best to keep my voice steady. I stood up. The boys mirrored me. "Just tell me where are you?"

Jonah snatched the phone from my hand. "Where the fuck are you?" he barked, heading for the restaurant door before he had an answer. "You don't let him take another thing, okay?" Jonah commanded in his voice that frightened me. "I'm coming." He threw a wad of cash at the maître d and walked up to his car that was parked right out front.

He opened the passenger door to his Escalade and shoved me in, closing the door behind me. "What the fuck is going on?" I asked, my voice so much smaller than I wanted it to be. Jonah threw Henry and Christian in the back seat a dark look.

"Fuck." Christian shook his head, nervous. They were all so nervous. I'd never seen any of them nervous before and it was the most unsettling thing.

"Has this happened before?" I asked Jonah specifically. He stared straight ahead. "Once."

"When?" I looked back at Henry, who gave me a long look, his eyes brimming with nervousness. Obviously whenever it happened it was sworn amongst the four of them that I was never to know.

"When?" I asked, my tone sharp as I turned to Christian. He pressed his lips together, not wanting to betray his friend.

"In Amsterdam," he said eventually.

"What the fuck, man!" Jonah glared in the rear view.

I still haven't quite shaken the feeling from that day. It's made me not trust blue skies, because the sky was so blue that morning, and as Jonah swerved through traffic down Piccadilly Circus I remember thinking that how the sky had looked that morning was a lie, like it had lulled me into a false sense of safety. It made me feel like that day was going to be a good day, but it was unfolding in front of me to be the worst.

I felt like I was driving to my doom. I felt like I was on my way to finding the love of my life dead. I remember gripping the chair of Jo's car so tightly my nails tore the leather. I remember Henry reaching around to me from the backseat behind and holding my arm, steadying me. I remember at a stoplight Jonah turning to me and wiping tears from my face I didn't know I was crying.

And I remember, viscerally, the feeling that my chest had been sawed wide open and the nerve endings of my heart were exposed.

The car jerked to a stop and Jonah barreled out, jogging up the stairs into the lobby of the Courthouse Hotel, us following after him. He smacked his hand down on the counter of the receptionist to get their attention. "Ballentine," he barked. "The room number for Ballentine."

"Sir—" The woman looked up, flustered. "We can't just give—"

"He's overdosed," he told her without flinching.

She blinked rapidly a few times, then nodded quickly, typing something. "305," she barely uttered before Jonah spun on his heel, running for the stairs not the elevator.

"Do we need to call an ambulance?" I asked no one in particular as we ran after him. Christian, who deeply distrusts all law enforcement like every member of the Hemmes family, shook his head. I flicked my eyes to Henry, who nodded subtly as he whipped out his phone.

Jonah tore down the hallway, hurling himself at door 305. On the second hurl, the door gave way and Jonah tumbled in and on to the floor. I pushed past him, ignoring the girl in black lacy lingerie, hovering over him looking distraught, and ran to the bed where Beej was flopped up against the headboard, looking pale, beads of sweat on his brow and bare chest.

I scrambled up onto his body. "Beej?"

"Magnolia?" he slurred, looking up at me, his pupils completely dilated and unable to focus on me. He smiled faintly at me.

"What have you done?" I whispered to him, stroking his cheek.

"I—" BJ said.

I could hear Henry on the phone in the background. "What did you take?" I was urgent in tone, but I pushed my hand through his hair like a compulsion. He just blinked at me. "What'd he take?" I blinked tearily at the girl, finally acknowledging her. Once our eyes locked I realised we were sort of friends. Lila Blane. A party girl from Cheltenham.

She looked at me, guilty, panicked and confused. "I—I don't know." Her hands were on her face. "I think just cocaine?"

"He's burning up!" I called out to no one in particular, my hand on his forehead.

"But he's been racking up since last night," she said, panicked.

"And drinking?" Jonah held up one of the dozen bottles of champagne that was littering the floor of the hotel room. The girl nodded. Christian shoved me off of Beej and pulled him up off the bed, calling for his brother—Jonah ran over, helping drag Beej into the bathroom, me trailing uselessly behind. They pulled him into the shower and made the water tepid—his eyes jerked open landing on Christian and me.

"Are you together?" Beej roared, angrily and barely coherent.

"No." I shook my head, heartbroken.

"Then why is he here!" BJ yelled.

I glanced between the Hemmes boys, hurt and unsure. Jonah shook his head at me. "He's just paranoid. Makes him more aggressive."

I clambered into the shower next to Beej, whose eyelids were heavy, his head kept rolling back.

"Beej!" I smacked him in the face. "BJ!"

"Parks," he whispered, voice shaky. "I love you,"

I didn't realise I was crying but I was. I nodded. "I know. I love you too." He started shaking and I looked over at Jonah, jaw agape, completely panic-struck.

"Tremors," Jonah told me.

"Is he dying?" I swallowed, nervous, not taking my eyes off of him.

"No." Jonah shook his head quickly, pressing his hand into his mouth, nervously. "Henry?" he called. Henry jogged to the bathroom door, phone pressed against his ear.

"ETA?" Jonah asked without looking back.

"Any second."

Beej started shaking more.

"Take her out of the room," Jonah commanded, nodding in my direction as he turned off the shower, and I was moved out of the way just in time for BJ to vomit and then start convulsing.

Christian ran and grabbed a pillow, putting it under his head, and Henry was trying his best to block out the world for me as he pressed me into his chest and covered my eyes.

And then the paramedics arrived, yelling for us to move, wheeling in a stretcher. It's funny how your brain copes with trauma. Everything fell silent at that point. Silent and slow. Billie Holiday playing in the background of my mind as they lifted his limp body onto the stretcher. I remember Lila Blane hugging her knees on the bed, crying, pointing as she tried to relay what happened to one of the paramedics. I remember seeing from afar Jonah step out of the shower, covered in vomit and water, both hands in his hair, looking down at BJ, frozen in some kind of sorrow. I remember Christian on his knees in the shower, heaving like he was about to be sick himself. I remember wondering if this was it, if that was the last time ever I'd see him. Him with the starry eyes and the hair I loved to knot my hands up in. The most beautiful boy in every room, the great love of my life—how many loves do you get in a lifetime? I remember wondering that. How many people will look at me like he does, not just like I'm the sun but like I'm the whole god damn universe. I remember hating him for doing this to us. I remember hating him for dying before we had a chance to be okay again, because I always thought we would be. I thought we'd be fine, I thought one day we'd sort our shit out and I'd forgive him for everything he's done, and we'd grow old together and we'd finally get that house in Tobermory but then he was dying of a coke overdose because I looked happy the night before with another man I don't give a fucking shit about. I remember resentment pounding through my body and then I remember it, like a physical punch in the gut, how much I loved him. Really loved him. To the bone, loved him. Cut me and I'd bleed him. How much I needed him, still needed him, would forever, always, never couldn't even if I tried, needed him. And I remember being deeply afraid of what my life would be like without him in it.

From there, he was taken in the ambulance to the hospital. After about two hours, a doctor came and told us that he'd stabilised but was hypoglycaemic. Christian flopped his head on his brother's shoulder, sighing relieved. One single tear slipped from Jonah's eye, which he wiped away before anyone could see, but I saw it. Our eyes caught and we traded a heavy glance because even though the whole world would feel it if BJ wasn't in it anymore, me and Jonah would feel it the most. The Hemmes boys sat in the waiting room for BJ's parents, and Henry took my hand, leading me to the recovery room. "Come on." He tried to smile, but he couldn't really. We got to the door of the room, and I stopped, looking up at Henry.

"Jonah said that happened once before?"

Hen shook his head. "Not that."

"What then?" I folded my arms over my chest, trying to feel in control of something, because it became raucously apparent then that I was in control of absolutely nought when it came to loving BJ.

"He just took a lot once."

"When?"

"A few months ago."

"How long has he been using?" I looked up at him with dark eyes.

Hen's brows furrowed and he sighed. "We all use it sometimes."

"I don't." He gave me a look. "How long?" I repeated, rubbing my eye as a ruse to cover up the fact that I was crying.

Hen scratched his throat, pursing his lips. "Since Amsterdam."

I nodded once. "Regularly?"

He tilted his head, thinking. "Recreationally."

"That"—I pointed to the room—"wasn't recreational."

"No," he conceded quietly. "It wasn't."

We opened the door, and BJ was asleep on the bed. There was a seat in the corner that Henry collapsed on, exhausted. Beej was still a bit pale, his big puffy pillow lips parted in the centre, his chest rising and falling in a rhythm that was the soundtrack of my youth and I'd never been more grateful to hear it. I walked over to him, cautious, like he might break if I moved too quickly, and reached up to touch his hair. "Family only," a young, pretty, brunette nurse appearing at the doorway told me.

I looked over at her, feeling a bit like someone slapped me.

"I know who he is," she told me. "You're not his family."

Henry stood, frowning. "If you know who he is, you know who she is. She is his family." The nurse looked between us, then nodded once, and left. I climbed into BJ's bed, snuggling up next to him like no time or boyfriends or overdoses were between us.

You think big things like that change a person on the spot, but the changes that happened were invisible. He felt the same to me, to hug and to hold. His whole body was a familiar mountain I'd climbed and conquered so many times in our lives that until that night had felt vast, but it suddenly felt so fleeting. My eyes kept catching on his wrists with the IV needles in his veins. I remember shifting into his neck, breathing him in—deliberately ignoring the hickeys all over it made by people who weren't me. His nose was raw from how much blow he'd done, and my chest panged because I didn't understand how I could know him how I knew him and not know he was doing this.

About ten hours later, he came to. His mum and dad were sitting next to his bed which I was still lying on. I hadn't moved once. I felt him shift under me, his butterfly eyelashes twitching before they opened. I pulled back, looking up at him. Drearily, he blinked at me a few times. "Parks." He slowly smiled. My heart surged at him waking. His voice, I remember it sounding like Christmas morning and my birthday and Valentine's Day and home and I loved him.

"Is he going to be okay?" I asked his doctor.

He nodded. "He's going to be fine—"

Relief flooded me as quickly as I found myself smacking him in the face. The whole room gasped, then froze. Both his parents, Henry, Jonah and a doctor. Beej looked wide-eyed, confused, still a bit dazed.

"If you ever," I started, my voice shaking. "Do that to me, ever again—" I shook my head. "I will never forgive you."

"Okay." He blinked, kind of teary.

"Promise me."

"I promise." He barely nodded.

Then I climbed out of his bed and walked out of his room.

No one knows that, by the way. We never talked about it, we didn't tell anyone, not even Paili or Perry. The only person who knows is my sister and that's because I came home from the hospital that day crying, and she wouldn't leave me alone—I'd been missing for going on two days. I didn't even notice. I didn't realise hours were passing, let alone days. I was at the precipice of losing the love of my life and time had suspended. Allie would have told her anyway.

Reid didn't notice—or if he did, he didn't say anything. He knew, I think—they all did. What they were to me. Or perhaps more aptly, they knew who they weren't to me.

I didn't talk to BJ for a week. He texted me constantly, called, IM-ed, DM-ed—everything. But I couldn't.

I was undone. Ruptured from the inside and bleeding out.

That's what him nearly dying did to me.

So, I ignored him for as long as I could.

It was Saturday a week and a half later, and our friends were going to see a rerun of *It* at Leicester Square—not exactly like us but with Beej secretly on substance lock down, it was slim pickings for social activities. I walked into the foyer—and all the boys' eyes fell on me, like I had a bomb strapped to my chest. I remember BJ looking over at me, eyes big and round, him swallowing nervously as I walked to him. And then it happened, not even consciously—I took his face in my hands and pressed my lips against his. He tasted like popcorn. He's never been able to wait for the movie to start to eat his snacks.

That kiss, it wasn't sexy or full of lust, but it was laced with a desperate, thirsty, nameless love that we had and have still now and we can't quite shake. I pulled back a little, our faces hovering only a few inches apart. We blinked at each other, our faces still like our hearts weren't—all of our friends, utterly baffled. Then I stepped around him, linked my arm with Henry's and marched into the cinema.

None of us ever talked about that kiss. Paili and Perry never asked. And thank goodness because how could I ever have explained it? I'd already banished that night into the same corner of my heart where our other terrible night lives.

There are three memories that live there, all ones I never look at. All ones that shape me still all the same. All of them involving BJ.

He's a time bomb for me, do you see now? That he'll hurt me. He'll always hurt me. I'll never be safe with him, even if I'm always safe next to him.

So, it doesn't matter if I love him—which I don't— but if I did, it doesn't matter, even now. Because loving him is the same thing as tossing the keys to my heart to a valet without a driver's license. He'll drive me off a cliff.

EIGHT

BJ

Park Lane parties are legendary. There are some we bring the girls to, some we don't. Tonight's is a don't.

Me and Jo's place is sick. Park Lane, four-bedroom bachelor pad. Parks likes it but I feel weird bringing her here sometimes. Probably because of nights like this. Christian was hellbent on getting completely obliterated tonight—seems girl-related—didn't want to ask.

Jonah's obliging him by having it here because Henry refused to have it at their place because my brother doesn't want to upset their little next door neighbour, Blythe. Fair enough, neither would I. Blythe was a World War II nurse and her stories are ace. She's a down and out legend and her eyes still sparkle, so no parties over on Ennismore for a while.

I stayed upstairs for a while, chatting to this girl from France. Don't know how she wound up here—but I also don't particularly care. That's shit of me, I know, but girls are kind of the same—at least the hook up ones. Look them in the eyes, listen to them, touch their face, they're yours.

"Do you like stars?" I ask every girl who's in my living room who I'd prefer to be in my bedroom. They all say yes because I don't think anyone's ever said no to me besides Parks.

France says yes.

I appreciate it when women aren't emotional about sex and treat it more as transactional, not pretending it's something it's not. Like, we met in a club. You were grinding on a bar stool. You already kissed my friend. This isn't the fairytale. I'm not who you bring home to your mother, I'm the wildest story you tell your friends about when you're trading dirty secrets.

She's in all black, France. Magnolia never wears black.

I bring her downstairs to my room and it's all a ruse, to make the exchange less calculated. She'll look through the telescope, I'll duck behind her, head close to hers, point to a star neither of us can see because you can barely see the stars through the London smog, and this is a bad night.

"Waouh," she says, accent thicker than I realised. Looking at me, not at the telescope. I sit on my bed, watching her. Waiting. Her eyes drop from mine, down my body, back up again.

"I can use your bathroom?" she asks, and I nod. I point to it. She's pretty hot, this one. Porcelain skin, dark, choppy chin-length hair, brown eyes. She doesn't look like Parks. No one does. That's the interminable problem of my existence post Magnolia Parks. She's the only one. Only one whose shit I'll put up with, the only one who fucks me over and around and I'll stick around for, the only person who's ever had my heart in a headlock.

Lean back on my bed. Wonder what Parks is doing tonight? Maybe she and the P's—Paili and Perry—are out. Don't like it when she's out without me, but I guess I'm about to sleep with someone who isn't her, so, not a lot of ground to complain.

France appears at the doorway. Leans against it. "Do you have a girlfriend?" Her accent's cute enough. Most girls I hook up with know who I am. They know not to ask. Guess they don't get *Tatler* in France?

I squint over at her. "No."

She gives me a doubtful look. "I do not care if you do—"

I give her a tight smile. "I don't."

"This is your Foreo then?" She palms Parks' little pink face scrubber thing, rolling it in her hands.

I make a mental note to buy Parks a new one. I watch Parks' pink thing, not the girl. "No."

France tilts her head. "So who's is?" I glance up at her. Not a huge fan of pre-intercourse chit chat, especially when the conversation is about Magnolia.

"My best friend's." I stand up, taking the Foreo from her, putting it in a drawer.

France gestures to the sink. "Est-ce que c'est sa jolie brosse à dents rose aussi?"

I nod. "It is."

She reaches for it. "Can I use, actually? Ma bouche sent dégueulasse—" She picks it up, and I push her hand back down.

"No."

France blinks, a bit surprised, a bit annoyed. "Non?"

I shake my head. "She has a thing about other people and touching and germs."

And girls I have sex with.

The girl rolls her eyes. "Elle a l'air géniale—"

"She is." I nod once.

"Désolé, dois-je y aller?" She lets out a cool laugh. "Would you rather be here with her?"

I give her a long look, measure her up. "Yeah, actually. But she doesn't want me like this so—"

"Pourquoi pas?"

"Because." I shove my hands through my hair, give her the grin. "I'm a massive fuck-up."

She snorts a laugh. "Lucky me."

"You have no idea." I grab her by the waist.

And then, you know. It is what it is, and I'll spare you all the gory details. Suffice to say, there's nudity, touching and orgasms are had. And I don't think of the girl I'm inside of one time. Deeply fucked, I know. I have this one memory of Parks that my mind can't ever shake and it's where it always goes. Me and her on Lake Como in the back of a 1971 Riva Aquamara. Broad daylight. So unlike her to be carefree and not worry that people might have seen us or recognised us. She was in this lilac string bikini—I have a thing for her in lilac—the sun was in her eyes, made them this ice kind of green. I think about that every time I have sex with someone else. I don't know why. Kills me a bit.

Afterwards, France grabs her handbag, pulls out a little baggy. She pours out some cocaine on my bare chest, uses her credit card to cut a line, then snorts it. She rubs her nose, then looks up at me. "You want?"

I shake my head. "Best friend?" she asks.

I chuckle. "She'd fucking kill me."

10:09

Lil Ballentine

Hello Sweetpea. Can you have my son call me please?

He's not picking up.

81

I'm not with him :)

Oh!

Silly me.

I'm kidding. He's right here.

Don't read into it.

I'm day drinking again.

Lily, it's fine.

He's not my boyfriend.

But he could be 🩶🩶🩶🩶

No, he couldn't 🩶

💔

.

Love you my darling

NINE

Magnolia

"What'd you do last night?" my sister asked as she perused the menu of Belvedere. It's not my favourite, but it's just across the road from our house.

"Me and the P's had some drinks. Privee. 109. Callooh Callay—" I swat my hands. She knows what I mean.

"Did you just have an aneurysm?" she asks, deadpan and I roll my eyes.

We're quite different, Bridget and I. There were two ways you could go really, having parents like ours. I went one way; she went the other. I am very much so in an obvious way the daughter of a wildly successful music producer and an ex-supermodel turned high-end accessories designer.

Bridget is, in a very obvious way... weird.

Like now for instance, she tried to leave the house in just a pair of vintage 501s and a plain white brandless T-shirt. I practically had to tackle her into wearing my red, black & white jacquard wool cardigan from Gucci, and stuff her unpedicured little feet into the fringe-studded sandals I bought her from Marni last week because they look like something someone who drinks almond milk and eats a lot of buckwheat would wear. She doesn't like things, she doesn't care about people's opinions of her, she doesn't care about boys. I know she's not a lesbian because I ask her every few days in case she is, I want her to feel like she can come out to me—she doesn't like parties, she doesn't care about the society pages, she doesn't care that she's never mentioned in the Social Set. She's just weird. She's very smart though. And a good listener. She's aggressively observant, lacks a good bedside manner and oftentimes is annoying as shit. But then somehow she's lovely and safe, and seems older than me. Even though she's younger than me.

"So just you and the P's, then?" she follows up. "No Beej?"

I shake my head. "They had a party."

Her face falters. "And you weren't invited?" I shake my head again, nose in the air. "And you're okay with that?"

"Mm hm." I fold my hands neatly on top of my menu, nose extra in the air now.

My sister leans in, curious. "Did he invite you and you didn't go or he didn't invite you?"

I fiddle mindlessly with the Mini Flower By The Yard bracelet from Alison Lou that Beej got me last week. "The last one."

Bridget is horrified. "Why wouldn't he invite you?" I give her a look. We both know why.

"Girls don't touch him when I'm in the room." I shrug to suppress an involuntary shudder.

"Because you're touching him?"

I give her a different kind of look. "Bridget."

"You two," she groans. "You'll be the death of me, one day."

"Here's hoping!" I sing.

Those Park Lane parties—I don't know. I'm always scared about what happens at them when I'm not there.

When I'm there, BJ and I last a solid thirty minutes with the crowd before retreating to his room to watch a Nat Geo documentary. When I'm not there, I don't know who he's retreating with. And I have a sinking suspicion that what happened with Taura Sax that fateful night, happened at a party like the ones they throw there.

"Hey, isn't that Daisy Haites—" Bridge nods her chin towards the door.

Daisy Haites. Haites, as in, Julian. Yes, that Julian. The gang lord who somehow still manages to appear in *GQ* and gets write-ups in *VICE*. Jonah's other closest friend, I'd say. Daisy's his sister. She's a few years younger than me, completely beautiful, sort of terrifying: dark brown hair, bright hazel eyes and skin a little more tan than your standard issue white girl.

She's sharp and fast and could be carrying a gun, so I'm always very friendly.

"Yeah." I watch her and then who should walk in behind her but Christian Hemmes. "Oh my god"—I smack Bridget in the arm with excitement. "Are they together? They look together. He told me they weren't."

Autumn colours and black floral-print dress from Saint Laurent over the top of the embroidered logo, cotton tee from Fendi with the pocket-detail combat boots from Prada that I'm dying over but aesthetically is a bit of a hard swerve for me.

Daisy didn't go to our school—she went Elizabeth-Day Morrow, I think? A day school here in London. She's a bit younger than us, but there's always been a bit of an overlap. Same house parties, same clubs, same boys—apparently?

If this is actually a thing—Christian hasn't told me yet.

"Christian!" I yell, waving them over. He looks up—he's happy to see me, and I wonder for a second whether he came here for that reason? But surely not. He gives me a cool guy chin nod and they walk over. Daisy Haites doesn't look too excited to see me and if I didn't know better, I'd think she whispered something smarmy to him on the way over.

"Parks." He leans down and gives me a kiss on the cheek. "Bridge." He ruffles her hair. Bridget knew about Christian and me when there was a Christian and I. She, Henry and Paili, they were the only ones and even still it was enough for all hell to break loose.

"Daisy—" I stand up and give her a hug and she doesn't hug me back, she sort of just stands there, stiff like a board.

"Hi." She gives me a tight smile. That's all. Just hi.

"Sit, sit," I tell them both, gesturing to the two spare seats.

She looks from me to Bridget. "Oh, we don't want to intrude."

"Oh, no, not at all." I swat my hand. "Bridget's a terrible conversationalist. Please—I beg of you."

Bridget rolls her eyes and Christian sniffs a laugh, sitting down.

Daisy reluctantly follows suit.

"Do you know my sister?" I gesture to her.

"We've met a few times—" Daisy nods. "Hey."

Bridget says hey back and then it's this terrible, clunky silence and Christian and I stare at each other from across the table, and it feels loaded. Why does it feel loaded?

"How's school?" I ask her warmly.

Daisy Haites shrugs. "Fine."

I persevere. "Are you enjoying it?"

She shrugs again, mostly with her mouth this time. "Sure."

I'll win her over yet. "What's your favourite class?"

"Mortuary procedures."

I swallow. "Cool."

I try to smile. Christian looks amused. Bridget is fascinated. "Is that... what... you want to do?" I ask, cautiously.

She looks at me like I'm an idiot. "No."

"How's your brother?" I ask.

She gives me a dirty look. "Fine."

"And your parents?" I ask mindlessly.

"Dead."

...As I imagine I too will be after this conversation. I'm sweating. I'm literally sweating. I press my mouth together. "Cool," I say and nod, nervously.

Bridget makes a weird peep. Christian's eyes go wide with delight. I'm flailing. "Okay, okay," I raise a hand in mock protest. "Slow down. No need to waterboard us with information."

Christian chuckles but Daisy is stone cold. Bridget's mouth rounds out into an O. She absolutely cannot believe her eyes. Frankly, neither can I. I'm a sheer wonder and an utter delight wrapped in Gucci and sprinkled with cheer and goodwill, and I'm being motherfucking stonewalled.

I let out a small laugh. "So glad you guys sat down,"

"I didn't want to—" she starts, jumping up. "He made us."

I look at Christian. "Made you?"

"Bye," Daisy says, walking away.

I frown after her and look up at Christian. "What's her problem?"

He shrugs. "No idea." Then jogs after her.

Bridget looks over at me. "She knows about you."

15:17

Christian H

That was weird...

Was it?

Seriously??

She's just not that friendly.

There are prison guards in Guantanamo Bay more personable than her.

Hah

Are you actually dating?

Nah

But do you like her?

Not like that.

I'm glad.

She's kind of mean...

💙

TEN

Magnolia

Full Box Set dinner at Seven Park Place. It's a favourite of mine, gaudy wallpaper aside. Tonight, I'm in the Gucci Intarsia wool sweater, red tweed buttoned mini skirt from Miu Miu, and Marmont fringed, logo-embellished, leather platform pumps from Gucci..

I do my makeup in a way I know BJ likes, which is barely any (that he knows of). Flushed cheeks and stained lips. He doesn't realise it, but he likes it because it looks like I've just had sex.

We're at a round table, the same one we're always at, Beej on my right. Black shredded Amiri Shotgun jeans, grey Zenga Fear of God tee, the black wool Teddy Varsity bomber from Saint Laurent and black Con hi-tops. His arms slung around my chair. Not around me, around my chair. It's not touching. We're touching around touching. That's how we touch most of the time, especially in public. It's hard going from what we were: teenage love unbridled and set on fire, to what we are now: fucked if I know.

I have missed him though. I'm glad his arm is on my chair. I'm angled in towards him. If I were to lean back—which I won't, but if I were—I'd be leaning back into him.

The dinner's going fine, everything's coming up roses. And then a song starts to play.

You know when you hear something and you recognise it, but you can't place it, you look off to the side, far away, peering back into your past lives to find the memory? Christian and I both do this at the exact same time, and it is not lost on BJ. Nothing about me and Christian ever is.

It was an accident. Us, happening. I never meant for it to happen.

I was a wreck when Beej and I ended. Not one of those wrecks you slow down to peer at, just... pure carnage, keep driving, cover-the-eyes-of-the-children kind of wreck.

It wasn't just what happened, it was an absence of him and the way my life had grown around him, like ribs around a heart.

My whole world felt off-kilter, and me and BJ breaking up caused the sort of breakdown you'd expect in a friendship group like ours. He got the boys; I got the P's. But it was hard because those boys were mine as much as his, I'd loved them as long as he had. Longer, in some ways actually.

I hadn't just lost BJ when I couldn't be around him, I lost all of them.

Anyway, about ten weeks or so after Beej and I had broken up, I was having breakfast one morning by myself at Papillion, Christian saw me through the window, sat down with me, ordered breakfast, and then we accidentally spent the day together.

By the time he dropped me home that night, the strangest thing had happened: I realised I hadn't felt sad all day.

It was unbelievable, really. Since BJ and I had broken up, I'd been shattered, all day, every day. Then one day accidentally spent with Christian Hemmes, and I felt a little bit like a human again. Like someone had taken me off the conveyor belt of my breakup.

So I texted him the next day, and we hung out again. And again, and again.

I don't know at which point we morphed from friends into more than that; one day we got caught in the rain on Regent Street and we ran into a phone booth, and I was freezing and my hair was wet and ruined and sticking to my face, and he was laughing at me as he peeled it back, and it was like his hand on my cheek was the jumpstart one of us had been waiting for, because his hand slipped behind my neck and pulled me in towards him—our eyes caught before our lips touched—a tacit "are we doing this?"—then he kissed me.

I felt guilty when he did, but it was good. It was a good kiss. The kind you feel through your whole body. I liked it and I liked him, and I knew probably I shouldn't like him, and I knew that me liking him would have killed Beej, and that made me like him more.

Christian was pretty torn up about it all, that was fairly obvious from the get-go.

The more time we spent together, the bigger an elephant it became. Me, him, and BJ; the ghost that followed us around everywhere.

Sometimes he'd try to justify it—all the ways we weren't doing the wrong thing; I liked Christian first. BJ poached me out from under his nose. BJ cheated on me. Christian and I were friends before me and BJ were friends—but sometimes the justifications weren't enough and he'd call it off. He'd bubble up with guilt, couldn't believe he'd been hooking up with me—of all people. If BJ knew, he'd kill him. Christian would tell me he was sorry and it had to stop and we couldn't see each other anymore. And actually, it happened so many times when we were together, practically weekly he'd end it; and I wouldn't fight it, I'd just put on an episode of *Outlander*, and he'd be back before it was over.

It was maybe only a month into us that BJ and the boys found out, that horrible night where Jonah and BJ beat the living shit out of him, Henry dragging me out of the club, finding out on the way home the real reason BJ and I broke up.

Henry helped us sneak around after that. It was stressful and heightened and Christian is so handsome and so strong and so stoic, it was curious to me, and I loved not being alone. I loved spending all my time with someone, filling my rib space with someone else.

We ended a few months later anyway.

It was fun and tender and I liked him, I maybe even loved him, but I was completely still in love with BJ.

Christian knew it and I knew it, and he's no one's place holder, he told me and then he ended it.

I place the song around the same time Christian doesn't at all disguise the small smile that appears on his mouth and I catch it unfortunately right when BJ spots us and his eyes go dark.

"What are you two smiling at?" He looks from me to Christian.

The table shifts uncomfortably. I shrug it off. "Nothing."

"Nothing, man." Christian swats his hand. BJ doesn't say anything. His brows are low, his eyes go from me to Christian.

"Nothing?" he repeats. The P's exchange nervous glances.

"Yeah." I shrug airily, smiling up at him like I'm breezy, not at all like I'm a tiny bit afraid. He stares at me for a long few seconds then moves his arm from around my chair.

BJ looks at Christian, eyes full of resentment. "That wasn't a fucking nothing smile, mate—"

"Beej—" I touch his arm.

BJ stares down at me and his eyes won't budge. "What the fuck was that smile?"

He gets extra in his head about Christian and me when he's not sober and he is not sober.

"When we were together, we went up to Gwynedd. It was raining like crazy. We got bogged in the mud. Only thing around for miles was a chippy, we went inside. They were playing this song—that's all." That's what Christian said but there were two problems.

They were the bare bones facts, zero flesh, and we all know the flesh is the tastiest part.

That night we slept in the back of his G Wagon, and to this day it remains one of the sexiest nights of my life, and we didn't even have sex. We never had sex, actually. It's a bit telling, I suppose. We almost did, lots of times. But that night, I don't know whether it was us slow dancing in the chip shop or us freezing in the back of his car, our breath fogging up the windows of the car we were stuck in 'til morning when roadside assistance arrived. Needless to say, he was very resourceful.

The other problem with what Christian just said is he didn't take his eyes off me once as he said it. Also not lost on BJ. He glares over at his best friend's brother. They're not best friends themselves tonight, I can tell you that much.

"BJ—" I hold his arm, shake it so he looks at me. "It was so long ago—"

"Yeah, and you're over everything I did ages ago too, hey?"

I frown, shaking my head. "That's not the same thing."

He pushes back from the table, looking from me to Christian. "You can both get fucked." He looks back at me. "I'm going to." Then he saunters to the bar.

My hands are on my cheeks from both stress and embarrassment. Paili reaches out, touches my hand. "Are you okay?" she whispers but I don't answer.

I'm counting the shots he's taking back-to-back. One, two, three, four.

Four. Shit. I know what happens next.

It takes him all of twenty seconds to pick a girl. Super long (probably hair extensions), platinum blonde hair, ultra-straightened. Deep red lipstick. Dark eyes. Tight dress. He leans in, boozy and dreamy, and I can see in her eyes: she's in. Of course she is. How could she not be? They have another shot, this time together.

I look over at Christian, distressed.

"What are you doing later?" I ask him, mostly joking.

He looks at me a fraction longer than he should. "Fuck you," he says, angry. I wasn't expecting angry. I pull my head back, surprised. "Like, genuinely, fuck you."

Then he grabs his drink, sinks it, stands, pulls out his phone and walks out. Jonah sighs, shoves his hand through his hair.

Henry looks over at me. "Nice one."

I frown, confused. Perry dabs himself with a napkin. "Fuck me, the *Daily Mail*'s going to have a field day with this one." Paili elbows him.

I look back at Beej at the bar—his whole routine, it's always the same. He points to their eyes. "Are they real?" he'll say. Even if they're the plainest pair of brown eyes

94

you could ever imagine, he looks into them in a way that makes you think he means it. Then he shakes his head, incredulous. How could eyes be that beautiful?

Did you have braces? He'll nod at her mouth. But he does this so they'll look at his mouth, because once you look at BJ's mouth, you're a goner.

He'll bite down on his bottom lip and grin at you, and by then, you're done for. You're having sex with him in the back of a car or in a toilet cubicle. You won't make it home. You can't wait that long. You don't have the will power. No one has the will power.

He's up to the point in his routine with the lip bite, and my chest feels like someone's sucked all the air out of me and it could cave in on itself. This isn't new. He fucks around. That's what he does. It's why we're not together, he's done this before, he's done this a million times—in front of me—and it never feels good, and I usually feel like I'm dying some, but tonight feels different.

Tonight, him doing that, being like this, feels frightening. Like he's far away? Like he's adrift? Or maybe I am? And it doesn't matter normally, we're anchored in the same port. I don't know what port it is, but we always find each other there, but I miss him, and my eyes feel wet and before I even really know what I'm doing, I'm walking over to him, and then I'm standing there.

He glances at me, eyes bleary, now quite drunk. "Parks."

"What are you doing?"

"You know what I'm doing," he slurs.

"Beej—" I shake my head. "Stop."

"It's fine, Parks." He shrugs. "Me and…" He trails. Touches the girl's arm. "And…"

"Ivy," she offers.

"Ivy." He nods too heavy. "Are just going to have a couple more drinks and piss off."

I shake my head. "You don't need a couple more drinks."

"And you know what I need?" He glares at me a bit.

I push some hair from his face, and I'm see-through. "Yes," I tell him softly.

His face changes a bit.

"Now," I stand up straighter, straightening the collar of his shirt. "Do you want to go home with her"—I ignore her—"or me?" His eyes flicker from me to her to me, then he nods his chin wordlessly in my direction. "Come on," I pull him up, and he's a bit woozy. I look over at our table, signal that we're going to leave, and pull him outside, into the town car.

"Home please, Simon," I tell my driver.

"Yes, Miss." He nods.

BJ's slumped against the seat, staring out the window. I'm sitting in the middle to be closer to him, not because he needs me, just because I want to. He looks over at me, tired eyes all raw with things he'd never say out loud if he were sober.

"He still looks at you like he wants you."

I shake my head. "No, he doesn't." Though I don't know, if I were to be entirely honest, that that's entirely true. BJ doesn't buy it either.

"I don't want him," I clarify.

Beej looks back out the window for a minute or two, thinking drunken thoughts. "It killed me when you were with him," he tells the window.

I wriggle closer to him, rest my head on his shoulder. "I'm sorry." He takes my hand in his, then lifts it to his mouth, kissing it mindlessly, then keeps it there.

I hope he keeps it there forever.

Paili

Is everything okay?

We're good.

I think.

I think we're okay?

It sort of seemed like you & beej were... together last night?

It sort of felt like it?

!!!!!!!!!! 😱😱😱😱😱😱 😱💀💀💀💀💀

💀💀💀💀💀

Stop..

Holy shit. Do you think?

Is this happening?

Hahaha

I don't know. Maybe.

Maybe not? I don't know?

13:02

Jonah

Man. What the fuck happened last night?

Nothing.

I went home with Parks.

After she cock blocked you.

Definitely cock blocked me.

Bro it was heavy couple vibes???

Hah.

I guess.

We'll see.

You know her. Spooks easy.

Why don't you try talking to her?

And not shagging a random
this week?

K thanks mum xx

ELEVEN

BJ

I don't really know what happened the other night with me and Parks, but it felt like something. I've hooked up with too many girls in front of her over the years, she's never intervened... Even if I've wanted her to, hoped she would.

We're both stubborn and shit.

I don't remember a ton from last night. I do remember holding her hand in the back of the car, though. Bit weird for us, to be honest... Maybe I'll grab her hand to lead her through a crowd. Hold it a few seconds longer than I need to, but we're more for the touching around touching. Buttons that need done up, cufflinks, zips she can't reach even if she can, necklaces to place around her—that's how we make do these days.

But this was different. It was overt. She undressed me in her bathroom. Took off my jacket, lifted my shirt up off over my head. She swallowed nervously, put her hands on my chest and watched me for a few seconds. I should have kissed her. I don't know why I didn't. I didn't want her to pull away, I didn't want to make her angry. We fell asleep that night and I was holding her. I sleep in her bed all the time, but I never hold her in bed. And I kissed her on the cheek when I left in the morning to head for a shoot, and it felt like something.

All of it, felt like something.

So, when I called her today and asked her to come out with me and the boys, it threw me that she said no.

"Oh."

"I'm just—I'm quite tired," she said. She was lying. We slept like fucking babies. Plus, she's a shit liar and clear as glass. She's scared or some shit.

"Cool." I shrugged, even though she couldn't see me.

"I'll see you later?" she said, her voice sounding nervous.

"Yeah, maybe."

"Okay," she said.

"Yep," I said but what I really meant is I love you and you're killing me. Then I hung up.

Tonight, I head out with the sole intention of getting fucked up. It's my MO, we all know that by now. The boys are already at Raffles when I get there. I guess it's on my face, whatever the fuck's going on with Parks, because Jo takes one look at me and says, "Uh oh."

"On the pull, mate?" Henry eyes me and I ignore him.

And then the drinks are flowing.

You know how there are a key few moments in your life that stand out, like, your first kiss, and the first time you realise your parents are just people too and hearing Coldplay's "The Scientist" for the first time and falling over and really fucking up your knee, like your first hospital visit, all that shit—meeting Parks is one of them for me.

She was four, probably? She came over for a playdate with Henry and I was kicking about with a ball in the yard. I don't know how she wound up outside, but she did, and she was watching me. She was tiny. Long little brown legs, scraggly almost. Her hair was lighter back then. Little kid hair.

"You're a bit good," she told me from a few metres away.

"Thanks." I grinned up at her, pleased with the attention. I did a few kicks that I thought were cool to show her just how good I was.

"I would probably be better if I wanted to be," she said.

And listen, I have sisters. No way was I going to tell this girl she couldn't be better than me, even then at all of six years old, I knew it was true. She was. In every way, at everything...

"You probably would," I agreed, picking up the ball and walking over to her. "I'm BJ."

"I'm Magnolia Katherine Juliet Parks." She paused. "Henry's my friend."

"Henry's my brother," I told her.

She looked at me, really looked at me. "I like your face."

Parks doesn't remember saying that. But I remember her saying it. It set me on a course for life.

I was high as a fucking kite for the rest of that day. Probably been chasing that feeling ever since. And sometimes I wish I could go back in time and tell little me to fucking run—that this girl is going to ruin you, she'll be all you think of, all the time, she's going to bake biscuits, grind up your heart and use it for sprinkles, she'll hurt you and you'll hurt her, and you'll never, fucking ever, get past her. But I can't.

And even if I could, what parts would I change? The parts where I had her? Never.

But this old fucking dance we do. I hurt her, she hurts me, I sleep with a girl, she dates someone else— it's well-rehearsed now. It's my move. Imagine if I was above it... Imagine if I hadn't already picked out which one of these girls flocking our table is the one I'm going to take home.

Imagine if I just called Parks—said, I'm in love with you, let's just... figure it out. I wish I was that guy. I'm not. I'm the guy in Raffles with a table littered with bottles and surrounded by girls I've never seen before. Mostly out-of-towners, I reckon—one of them, she's been eyeing me since the second I sat down. Pale skin, brown hair, big blue eyes. She edges closer and closer to me over the course of the hour and I'm drinking more and more because that's the sort of night this is. Once she's next to me I work out she's from Surrey. She speaks closer than necessary, but she's just making her intentions known. Nice-looking girl, actually. Quite posh.

So, I'm dead surprised when Surrey stands up and pretty much gives me a lap dance in the middle of everything.

Not the first time this has happened, I'm hardly a monk. Just wasn't expecting it from someone who smells so much like sherbet.

Jo gives me a wry look from his seat. Arse in my face, grinding, kissing my neck, kissing me, my eyes are closed, don't really care that I'm in a club and people can see me, people have seen me before—and then someone's hitting me.

Jonah. Jonah's whacking me in the arm. I open my eyes and see past Surrey a blur of pink and realise that Parks decided to come after all.

Her mouth's open. She's gone pale.

"Fuck," I say and shove the girl off me and that's Magnolia's hint to move.

She turns on her heel, hurrying through the crowd but I grab her arm, pulling her back to me.

I shake my head. "Parks—"

She shoves me off, eyes ragged. "Don't touch me."

"You said you weren't coming—"

"Oh! Of course!" she calls loudly. "My mistake! Please do go on—"

"Parks." I sigh, reaching for her.

She gets close to my face, looks me square in the eye, thumps me in the chest. "You disgust me."

TWELVE

Magnolia

It was late on a Saturday night, about three years ago. He'd been at a party. I was sick, I think. That's why we weren't together. He and Jo had already planned it, he said he'd skip it, but I didn't really mind. I was so tired and I didn't want him to catch it.

He walked into my bedroom, closed the door, pacing back and forth. We'd been together more than five years by then, I'd never seen him this way. He looked high almost, but not in a fun way. Manic. "Parks," he started. His breathing was funny. I could hear it. "Parks." He was walking around in circles.

"What are you doing?" I frowned.

He shook his head. "I've done something."

"What do you mean?" I got up and walked over to him. "Are you alright?"

"That's not what I mean—" He shoved his hand through his hair. "I did something wrong."

"Okay?" I said. My voice was small, so much smaller than I knew it could ever be and there was a pit that began to grow in my stomach, like a sink hole opening up in the centre of me.

I could feel it coming before he said.

"I slept with someone."

I think my blood turned cold. My eyes didn't meet

his. His hand was over his mouth. He looked like he was going to be sick.

"What?" I asked, blinking lots. He said nothing. "What do you mean?" I pressed. He looked at me, silent still, his eyes begging me not to make him say it again. "When?" I asked quietly.

"Just now." He reached for me.

"Just now!?" I swatted his hands away as I stumbled backwards away from him.

"It was an accident." His breathing was shallow as he reached for me.

"How was it an accident?" I yelled as I searched his face, looking for something familiar to grasp onto.

"It just happened—"

I shoved him away.

"How?" I shrieked; my hands flew to cover my mouth. I didn't recognise the sounds coming from my throat. They felt foreign. "Who were you with?"

"We were just at home, there was a party and then I was drinking and—"

"Shut up." I shook my head, urgent.

"We never meant to—"

"Stop it!" I hurled a Lalique vase at him filled with hydrangeas he'd brought over for me yesterday. He dodged it.

It smashed on the floor.

"Parks—just let me explain." He reached for me again, his eyes were wet.

I jerked away from him. "Don't touch me. You're disgusting."

His heart broke on his face and I ran into my bathroom, closing the door and locking it behind me. I stayed in there crying for four hours, and he sat outside my door, crying the whole time. He cried so much he worked himself into a sort of panic attack. His breathing went gaspy, like it was stuck in his throat and couldn't get to his chest. Like he was suffocating. I opened the door, rushing to him, sat in his lap, took his face in my hands and breathed with him silently. In and out, in and out. I did what he did to me all those times I had panic attacks that I don't like to think about. And his breathing eventually fell in pace with mine, his eyes didn't look away from mine. So blue from the redness of crying.

What a mind fuck it is to comfort the person who just blew your whole heart open with a rifle. Carnage everywhere, men down, blood spilled.

But the truth is, when you love someone how we were in love, it didn't matter what he'd do to me—he could have hit me with a bus, kind of he did—I innately still would have done everything I could to make him not feel what he was feeling.

For so many years, his pain was my pain. But that pain, the one he was crying about then, was mine. He was crying my tears, feeling what he had done to me, broken by his own actions. He cried into my neck and said sorry so many times, the word lost meaning... the word stopped sounding like a word.

He held me tight, tighter than I think he ever has, he told me it was a mistake and that it'd never happen again and it was just one time and then he tried to kiss me. I pulled back and looked at him, my face, very serious.

"We are—" I grabbed his face so he was looking me in the eye. "Listen to me—listen. We're done." I ran straight to Marsaili's room, and she locked the door behind me. She held me as I cried until I fell into a sleep that would last thirty-six hours.

You know the rest…

My devastation over what had happened and what he did was eclipsed by how much I missed him and wanted to be around him because he's the kind of person you be around at all costs and believe you me—it was all cost. I learnt to look him in the eye again, I learnt not to cry every time I left him again, I learnt how to breathe through him flirting with other people, I realised we could still talk to each other without using words, and somehow, in the bloodshed of it all, I found my friend.

It's because I'm weak, I think. It was easier to be his friend than not to be. Too much of my life, maybe even too much of who I am entirely can be traced back to him or us.

Everything wonderful, everything magical, everything painful, everything beautiful and spectacular and wretched and defining that has happened to me happened with him.

And I hate him for that.

THIRTEEN

Magnolia

I only said no because I wanted to think. I needed to... I didn't want to be in a club and have to be around all these other girls who want BJ while I was trying to work out how I could be with him again, if I could be with him again, because the other night felt rather consequential to me.

It was the closest we'd come to being together since we were together, and it was the happiest I'd been in years, and when I realised that, then I felt afraid. Afraid that he'd do it again, afraid that he'd fuck up—and so when he called about going to Raffles tonight, I said no, because I didn't know how to be around him after the other night, with the holding hands and the cuddling me to sleep, and the brushing the hair from his face— and I didn't know how to figure out what any of that meant moving forward in front of him.

But then as I sat in my bedroom missing him, wishing I was with him, feeling frustrated that he wasn't there with me, I decided that the responsible thing to do—the grown-up thing—would be to go and find him and tell him all of it. That I like holding his hands, I want to keep holding his hands. That I like him cuddling me to sleep, that it was the best sleep I've had in three years that wasn't medicated. That sweeping his hair from his face, was the closest I've felt to someone since we ended.

So, I put on my candy pink, square-neck knitted, mini dress from Balmain and the over-the-knee, suede stiletto boots from Casadei and took a car to Raffles, and then I get here and the first thing I see is that awful girl, grinding on top of him.

Him reclined back in the chair, loving every second, eyes closed, lost to it... Holding her by the waist, gripping her stupid thighs. Is this what he's like when I'm not around? Is this what he was like the night he broke us?

He sees me and he rushes to me, and I'm blind. I can't see anything, I think I'm having an anxiety attack, the edges of my vision are fading. The music goes softer but it can't be going softer, we're in a club. Maybe the pounding in my ears is getting louder? Am I going to be sick? Are my eyes wet?

Then the world goes to black. We lock eyes. And this sheet of impenetrable glass slides up from the ground between us. We can't touch and we can't talk and there's nothing to say anyway besides him screaming through the glass that he misses me and me screaming back that I miss him too and him screaming that he's sorry and me screaming that it's not enough. Our faces are frozen in what feels like hopeless love but couldn't be, because I don't love him anymore. I cannot.

The moment passes. The glass slides down.

"You disgust me," I spit at him and rush towards the bar, hoping it offers me some sense of safety and it does more than leaving. If I leave, he'll just follow me home. If I stay here, at least there are bodies between us.

There are always bodies between us.

He stares at me from the other side of the room, but I won't meet his eyes. They look droopy sad. He's completely shitfaced. He watches me, picks up a bottle of Patron, bites out the cork, spits it on the floor then drinks straight from the bottle—holds his arms open wide like, "what are you going to do", and then falls back on the sofa behind him and the girl keeps dancing on him, her hands slipping into his short-sleeved, yellow and brown, floral print Marni shirt. There are too many buttons undone. I want to go over and fix it. I don't want anyone seeing that much of him but me.

I breathe out through my mouth, tiny small breaths, they're too shallow to be helpful but the feeling of the air passing over my lips distracts me enough to keep bad breathing at bay.

And then I feel someone saddle up beside me. "Magnolia Parks." It's a voice I vaguely recognise but can't completely place blindly on the spot. I look over and I'm delighted to see *Tatler's* most eligible bachelor since Harry was nabbed from the list—practically 7ft a million inches, glacier blue eyes, dirty blonde hair swept to the side, muscles and shoulders for days and a smile that's only rivalled by my ex-boyfriend's.

"Tom England." I grin up at him, surprised.

Besides being a full-time, professional dreamboat, Tom is also a pilot. I mean—of course he is. He doesn't have to be, by the way. He's worth about a bajillion dollars. He just likes flying. He likes having a thing he has to show up for. That's what Gus told me anyway.

"What are you doing here?" I glance around, a bit in awe.

"I'm sticking closer to home for a little while." He gives me a strained smile. The upper crust of British society is built upon such smiles.

"How are you?" He gestures to me warmly.

"Good," I nod. "Yeah, I'm good—"

He pauses, "Really? I saw—" Then glances past me and nods his chin in BJ's direction.

"Oh." I sniff a laugh. "Then no."

I should be embarrassed. It's embarrassing Tom England saw that, but I'm not. He smiles. "Can I buy you a drink?"

I nod once. "Do you know what, Tom England? You can buy me several."

He smacks the bar twice to get the bartender's attention. "You're on."

Tom England didn't go to Varley. I think he went to the Hargrave-Westman. He's a bit older than me too. Twenty-nine, maybe? Could be thirty.

We all had crushes on him growing up, even the boys, I think. He's so dashing and so dreamy and he's like London Society's very own prince-elect. He's charming, and clever and you kind of lose time with him a bit? There's nothing boyish about him, which is so lovely. So far from what I'm used to with my little brigade of lost boys who make terrible, slutty, stupid, regrettable decisions, all the time. Apparently. Tom just makes good ones, I'll bet.

He's not in the media much. Tends to be more private, tends to steer clear of the parties that might get him photographed and for some reason it makes him a bit sexier.

We're at a table now, Tom and I. BJ's gone. God knows where. To a loo stall, probably. But I can still see Henry and Jonah, they're watching me closely. I can feel their eyes on me.

More so than normal—

Normal is: BJ's not around, they're just keeping an eye on it all.

Abnormal is: this. It's like they're one step away from night vision goggles and a remote control drone. I stare at my old friends, try to tell them with my eyeballs to fuck off and leave me alone, but they don't speak the same silent language BJ and I do.

Tom watches me for a few seconds, eyes pinching at the edges. "Are you feeling any better?" he asks as he swills his Scotch around his glass.

"Ah," I say, thinking out loud. "It's going to take a few days for me to oust that one from my memory."

He sniffs a laugh. "He's always been a bit of an idiot, Ballentine"—he pauses—"love him, good kid." I can barely contain my glee that Tom just referred to BJ as a kid. Beej has always said—in his words not mine—that Tom England is "the shit." Beej would just die that Tom England referred to him as a kid. "But he's just…. sort of… stupid. Especially with you." He sounds annoyed about that part.

"With me?" I smile, feeling awfully high and mighty.

"Yep." He nods. The eight-year-old who followed him around at a party at Windsor Castle can hardly keep it together. I give him a small, grateful smile.

"Hey." He nods at the door. "Do you want to get out of here? Grab a drink somewhere else?" I nod quickly, confused. I try to look confident and self-assured, but I think I just look dazed. Is Tom England asking me on a date? He picks up my coat, opens it for me to slip into— so dreamy—and then grabs me by the waist, spinning me around to face him.

"Wait—I just need to do one thing." Then he knocks my chin up with his hand and kisses me softly. I don't even kiss him back, I'm just starstruck. He leans in closely and whispers, "The boys will tell him I did that."

Then he takes my hand and leads me away. I look over at Jonah and Henry through the crowd, and as predicted, both their eyes are wide, Henry can't believe it. I hold my hand up to wave bye.

They both wave back with a sort of paralysed uncertainty and then Tom pulls me out up onto the street.

I look up at him, awaiting further instructions.

"Any suggestions?" He smiles down at me merrily, his hands in his jacket pockets. I shake my head. I like him telling me what to do. He smiles and nods. "There's a place about a ten-minute walk from here—"

And then he does that incredibly sexy, incredibly grown-up guy thing where he puts his hand on the small of my back but definitely not my arse to guide me someplace. It's just for a few seconds but I'm positively living for it, because Paili cut out a picture of Tom from *Tatler* and we had it in a hot-boy collage on our dormitory wall when we were at school, and now here I am on my way to have a drink with him after watching the love of my life get a lap dance from this Plug-Ugly girl whom I can only assume is from Surrey with the aggressive eyebrows she was sporting.

"Wait." I pause, confused. "Did you say walk?"

"Do you ever get bored of it?" he asks me, sitting back in his chair at Barts, combing his hand through his hair.

"Of what?" I frown.

"This… shit?" He shrugs. "Society. Money?"

I shake my head playfully. "I find material possessions incredibly fulfilling."

"Good to know." He smirks over at me.

"Love fades, things are forever." I merrily pat my £3000 Devotion knitted shoulder bag from Dolce &

Gabbana. He starts laughing. "I don't like the eyes," I concede. "*The Sun, LMC, Loose Lips,* the *Daily Mail*—" I point to someone in the corner. "He's been trailing me for a few weeks trying to get a bad photo."

"Impossible. Couldn't take one of you if his life depended on it." He smiles, then considers all this. "Honestly, I don't get a lot of this." He nods his head towards the idiot in the corner with the telephoto lens.

"They sort of just disappear into the crowd after a while," I shrug.

He taps me on the arm. "How are you feeling?"

"Actually, I'm having a really nice time."

He pulls back in faux-offence. "Actually?"

"Well, considering how my night began with BJ being straddled by the next member of Little Mix... my expectations for the evening were somewhat tempered. But this has been fun."

"So I've redeemed it then?"

"Redeemed it?" I let out a shy laugh. "I'm sitting in a bar with Tom England and just before, he kissed me in a club to make my—I don't know, whatever the fuck he is—jealous."

His eyes pinch in amusement. "Why do you keep saying my full name?"

I purse my lips. "When we were kids, we all had crushes on you. You and Sam. I was a Tom England girl through and through but Paili flip flopped between you and your brother—" I smile at the memory. "You felt so much bigger than us then."

He gives me a look. "I'm still so much bigger than you." And I don't know why that was a sexy thing to say, but it was.

"There was this one summer," I say and start to blush at the memory, "where we were all on the Amalfi Coast at the same time as you and your brother and the girls. And me and Paili took the little Aquariva out to Tordigliano Beach, and—" I start laughing. My cheeks on fire.

"Oh god—"

"You and Erin were on the beach"—I pause to choose my words delicately—"skinny-dipping."

He eyes me, amused. "That's a polite way of putting it."

"And I guess you didn't hear the boat or see the boat, or you just didn't care, I don't know, and we were so embarrassed that we saw you but also—" I look away to the side with over-exaggerated wide eyes and a pursed mouth.

He starts chuckling. "Fuck! That's embarrassing."

"No!" I shake my head. "It was very—"

"Illegal? Smutty? Something my mother would cry over?"

"Yes, all of the above, but still not the word I'm looking for."

He smirks.

"Inspiring!" I land on, and he laughs loudly, banging his fist once on the table.

"And what exactly did it inspire?"

"Oh." I bat my eyes at him. "Wouldn't you like to know."

"Yes, I would. Very much." He smirks. Then his face changes a bit. "You seem in a better mood now."

He bites into a padrón pepper.

"I am," I nod.

"So then." He wipes his hands. "Tell me—what's it like being in love with someone who hurts you all the time?"

I'm completely thrown for a moment. I blink a lot of times. I let out a bewildered laugh. "Horrible."

He nods, coolly. "Thought about as much."

"You'd hurt him too though," he tells me.

I frown at him. "How do you know?"

"Face like yours?" He nods at it. "Fuck, it's hurting me now. I'm just sitting here, across from you, without a history, not in love with you, and you look sad that I said that, and I want to slit my wrists." He sniffs a laugh and looks a bit sad himself.

I think for a few moments. "I don't trust him."

He nods. "Seems fair."

"I had a boyfriend before," I start. "He was sort of a prop for me to hide behind? Like a barrier, that BJ couldn't cross because someone else was there." I don't know why I'm telling him all this. I've never said that out loud before. "And then, we broke up. Because he was shit. And actually, I was shit." He gives me a sad smile, like he gets it. "But now, I'm in the middle of no-man's land, under attack, without a foxhole."

He gives me a long look. I mean, long. Ten seconds at least and I can see the cogs ticking in his mind. "I could be your foxhole," he says eventually. I sit back, a little surprised, and give him a funny look. He shrugs. "I could."

I give him a look. "You could have any girl you wanted in London."

"Yeah," he considers. "But actually, I've always had a bit of a thing for you." I die. He continues. "And I can't date anyone right now. After Sam—" He shakes his head. "I've a lot of shit I've got to deal with and… happening at the minute."

"Oh." I'm sad for him. He looks sad.

"I'd be a garbage boyfriend," he tells me, quite seriously but then his eyes go bright. "But I'd make a knockout foxhole."

I rest my chin on my hand, frowning curiously. "Are you being serious?"

He nods.

"So—what?" I fiddle with my Sydney Evan diamond hoop earring mindlessly. "We'd just pretend like we're together? That we like each other?"

"Yeah, like your last boyfriend except I'm in on it," he quips, grinning at me.

I give him a suspicious look, as though the thought isn't the biggest thrill.

"Are you trying to have sex with me?" I ask, half joking.

"Oh," he says. "I'm definitely trying to have sex with you. Whether we do or not"—he shrugs—"up to you."

I give him a look. "I'm not really a random sex... kind of girl."

He shrugs. "I figured as much. Worth a try." He folds his arms across his big, burly chest. "So, what do you say? Are you down for a sexless foxhole?"

"Are you?" I laugh, bemused. He nods, effortlessly. "You'll come to places with me?" I ask. He nods. "Hold my hand? Take me shopping?"

"Yes and yes."

I bat my eyes at him. "You'll kiss me?"

He snorts. "Yeah, I've been trying to all night."

"Oh," I lean across the table. "I'll make it easy for you then."

He smiles a little as he leans in, brushes his mouth against mine and kisses me softly. There's the distant flash of a camera phone from somewhere in the restaurant. He smiles, our mouths still pressed against one another.

I pull back a little. "I think this is going to work out just fine."

Henry

You good?

Grand!

Hah

You get home okay?

…You know I did.

Haha

Why don't you just ask me
what you're really asking,
Nosy Parker.

Did you go home with him?

Who's asking?

Me.

Your oldest friend in the
world.

Just you?

Yep.

No.

And if Beej asks…?

I definitely shagged Tom England.

Twice.

On it.

FOURTEEN

BJ

I wake up and there's this girl next to me with the most insane eyebrows I've ever fucking seen asleep in my bed. Are they painted on? Are they tattooed? What the fuck? How drunk was I? I never let girls stay the night. She's still sleeping, so I MI5 roll out of bed, scared to wake her and have a sober conversation about whatever the fuck we did last night and creep out of my own bedroom, venturing upstairs.

The sun looks pretty high. Midday, I'm guessing.

"Eyy," sings Jonah as I walk over to the fridge, cracking open a bottle of water.

"Didn't we have quite the night?" says my brother, sitting up from the couch. "How are you feeling, big man?"

I glare over at him, the smarmy git. Do a big yawn and stretch. "Rusty." I rub my head. "What happened?" And then Jonah and Henry both go kind of still, catch each other's eyes.

"You, uh—" Jonah clears his throat. "What do you remember from last night?"

I rub my temples with the heel of my hands. "Got there, got shit-faced—I think the chick downstairs gave me like... a lap dance? And then—" Jonah's nodding. So far, correct—Jo looks weird though. And then I remember. My face freezes. "Fuck. Shit!" I look between them both. "Parks."

Henry pulls an uncomfortable face, then nods. My hands are on my cheeks, I feel like I might throw up. I can see her face in my mind's eye. How much I hurt her. How could I have hurt her like that all over again? I groan, laying my face down on the bench.

"Um," Jonah clears his throat again. "That's not all." I roll my face over the cool marble, peering up at him, hopeless.

"You or me?" Henry says, walking over.

Jonah shake his head. "All you, my man..."

Henry takes a breath and thinks for a second. "Beej," he starts. "Do you remember Tom England?"

"Yeah!" I perk up. Bit of a legend. Probably one of the coolest lads on the planet. "What about him?" I panic. "Oh, fuck—I didn't punch him or some shit, did I?"

("Not yet," Jonah sighs under his breath.)

"Well," Henry says, scratching his chin, "Magnolia left Raffles last night with him."

"What?" I shrug my lips, confused. "Like he gave her a ride?"

("Of a lifetime, maybe?" Henry whispers to Jo.)

Jonah's mouth is pressed together tight. "Mm," Jonah hums, high-pitched. "I don't think so. They, um, they left... together."

"No, but like—he just dropped her home." I shrug. "He has a girlfriend."

"Erin?" Henry frowns, shakes his head. "Beej, they broke up like a year ago."

"Wait—" I blink. "So you're saying that he and Parks left... together. Together, together?" Doesn't compute. Tom England. We're mates.

Henry gives me a look, shakes his head. "He kissed her, Beej."

I look over at Jonah. "What?"

Jonah's cringing and nodding.

"What kind of kiss?" I ask, panicked.

"Oh, the worst kind, for sure"—Hen grimaces —"affectionate."

"Fuck!" I yell. Jonah nods, getting it. "You're telling me that last night, after I fucked up massively—that the girl of my dreams went home with the man she has out-loud fantasized about being with since she was nine?" I stare at them, incredulous.

"I mean, he is well, fit." Jonah nods. "He was on her list, right? Like her, get out of jail free list?" I stare at him blankly. "Sorry." He scratches the back of his neck. "Don't know why I—never mind. He's a bastard—"

"Fuck!" I yell again. "Shit! Fuck. Fuck!"

Henry squints at me. "Are you having a seizure?"

"Why didn't you stop her?" I ask him, my eyes desperate.

"Right, yeah." He nods. "Hey, Magnolia, I know that you and Beej shared a really tender moment the other night and then you've just watched him be vigorously dry-humped by a random girl but do me a grand favour and don't go home with the hottest man in England."

"Henry!" I roar. My hands are fists in my hair. I'm sweating.

"Beej"—Jonah touches my arm—"it's gonna be fine."

"I don't know." Henry shrugs. "He's right. Parks and England? Kind of makes sense."

"Fuck," I bellow again.

And then Surrey appears. "Er—" She stands nervously to the side.

I look at her, my eyes wide. "Shit!"

"Are you o—"

I shake my head at her. Don't have real words left in my vocabulary. No, though, is the answer. Henry lets out an appeasing, apologetic laugh. "Hello. I'm Henry—this is my brother. He's just found out that last night the girl of his dreams went home with the man of her dreams and he's just taking a minute to process—"

I kick the fridge. Say "motherfucker." Kick it again.

"Um." She blinks, looking at me, concerned probably mostly for herself. "Oh. Can I—should I… do anything?"

Henry nods. "Leave, probably? Yeah—"

"But I'm—" Surrey starts.

"Listen," Henry gives her a sorry smile, "does he have your number?" He pauses. "Doesn't matter—he's not going to call—he's one swear word away from usurping Samuel L. Jackson—"

I yell fuck again. Jonah's laughing a bit, trying not to, I think. I'm not trying to be funny. I feel like my mind is melting. This is my nightmare. Parks and Tom England? My actual nightmare. Because it works. It makes sense. They make sense. More than we make sense. He's never fucked her over, he's never hurt her. He's a clean slate.

And he's older than me, he's a god damn pilot, he looks like fucking Thor—I press my hands into my mouth.

Surrey's gone now. Henry wanders over. "What are you going to do?" He asks this casually, like the sky isn't falling.

"She came to the club." I look up at them. "She told me she wasn't going to come and then she came."

"And then you came," Henry says, and eyeballs me playfully. "But differently."

I give him a look.

"I wonder if England came?" Henry ponders, just to shit me.

I peg my water bottle at him. "Fuck you! This isn't funny!"

Jonah gives Henry a look. "It's kind of funny." Henry shrugs.

"Hen—" Jonah nods in my direction, like I can't see them.

"What?" Henry shrugs. "Like, it's ironic. Because BJ went home with the Anti-Parks, and Parks went home with the BJ deluxe." I rub my hands over my face, stressed. Henry gets his thinking face on again. "Hey, what if she said no because she was just thinking things over for a minute and decided to come because she wanted to like, get back together or some shit and you, because you're an arsehole—"

"Henry—" Jonah says, eyeballing him.

"Because you're an arsehole," Henry says louder. He likes Parks more than me most days. His oldest friend… Never really forgave me for cheating on her. "You dropped trou at the first sight of trouble."

Jonah gestures to me, staring off into space. "How is that helping?"

Henry shrugs, equally optimistic and ambivalent.

"Listen," Jonah looks at me, "Parks isn't like that. She wouldn't sleep with him just because she saw you…" He leaves it open-ended. Looks uncomfortable. "You know," I stare at him, waiting for more. "Just go and talk to her."

FIFTEEN

BJ

I drive myself over. I like driving. Don't get to drive a lot of places because cars in London are annoying as shit. But I have a little Chiron Sport "110 ANS Bugatti" and it's nice to take her out for a spin when I can.

The drive feels three times longer than it actually is and I'm sweating fucking bullets the entire way as I wonder whether Jo's on the money—I think he is. Parks doesn't sleep around. She's not like that. I wonder for a few seconds what it would feel like to walk into her room and see another man in her bed. I hate the thought. Push it away.

I let myself in to the Holland Park house. I have a key. I don't tell anyone I'm here. I don't have time for her Bushka's wandering hands today, I just need to see her.

Bust into her room, she's lying in her bed, still under the covers—alone, thank fuck—staring straight at the ceiling. She looks up at me. Hair in ridiculously sexy disarray, mouth all blushy the way it goes in the morning, no make-up. Fuck. That face. I'd do anything for that face.

She frowns when she sees me.

"How's the weather over there, Parks?"

She looks me in the eye, blinks a few times, then stares back up at the ceiling. Fucking icy. Shit. This is bad.

That's our question. She never doesn't answer.

I walk over to her bed, sit on the edge. "Oy."

"Oh!" She sits up a bit. "How nice of that girl to remove her tongue from your mouth long enough for you to come and say good morning to me."

"Parks—"

She looks over at me and I can tell she's been crying a bit. They're glassy, those eyes of hers. Extra jewel-like or some fucking shit that I'm sure I've fallen for a million times and I'll fall again because look at her. It's not fair that they do that, it's crippling. What to say? What can I say?

"Are you okay?" I ask a bit tentatively. She looks over at me. No, is the obvious answer.

"Yes," she says, nose in the air. She glances away from me. "Fine."

"You don't look fine."

"Why would I not be fine? Because I saw you practically fornicating in public with a rancid girl wearing a skirt from Prada's 2017 fall collection which, if you recall, looked like its mood board was based solely upon Mackelmore's 'Thrift Shop'—" I try not to smile at her because I know she's being dead serious. "I'm used to that by now," she says and shrugs, demurely.

I sigh. "You came to the club?" She glances away again. "For me?" I ask.

She gives me a long look. Inside of it she's crying and screaming and hitting me. But she says nothing, does nothing, doesn't even flinch and then she says, "I went on a date with Tom England."

"I heard." I nod, coolly. "How was it?"

"We're going out again tonight."

Fuck. "What are you doing?" I frown.

"I'm going on a date with Tom England."

"No, you know what I mean—what are you doing?" She looks away. "Why did you come to Raffles last night?" I press. Her eyes look sad and I'm worried Henry's right.

"It doesn't matter." She shrugs. "I'm with Tom now."

"You're not with Tom." I roll my eyes. She's ridiculous. "You went out once. Don't send out your save the date just yet."

She gets out of bed—she's barely wearing anything. Tiny baby yellow pyjamas set—starts doing fake tasks around her room. Doesn't like being called out and I love doing it. I sit down on her bed and she comes over and pushes me off it so she can make it. Properly make it. Want to know how many times Magnolia Parks has made her own bed since she left boarding school? A grand total of zero. She might pull up the duvet once in a while herself—refer to it as a hard day's work or some shit, but here she is making this bed with the precision of an ophthalmologist and the determination of an Olympian just so she has a reason to touch me as she yanks me off it.

I stand there watching her, arms folded across my chest, trying my best not to watch her arse as she bends over in these lacy little undies I know are from La Perla because I bought them for her. I feel relieved that she's in them. If she hated me for real she wouldn't have put them on. It's how I know we're not done.

She never gave my ring back.

We've had each other's family signet rings since we were rug rats. I gave her mine the day I graduated Varley, something to remember me by I think I said, or some shit like that. It's funny to think back now, I was definitely just marking my territory. But she wore it everywhere.

Never took it off. That same Christmas she gave me her family's ring.

I remember opening it, glancing up at her—she could have given me a Chocolate Orange and I'd have thought it was the greatest present in the world, but her ring, that she had to ask her Dad for—it was so weighty.

"You asking me to marry you, Parks?" I squinted down at her playfully.

"Not yet." She smiled.

"One day?" I asked, brows up.

"Girls don't ask." She frowned, offended.

"But I could?" Me.

"You could." She nodded, resolute.

"I will." I nodded coolly.

She never gave it back, not even after I cheated on her. Took it off her finger. Now she wears it on an extra-long chain around her neck that no one can see, but I know it's there. See it sometimes before she darts into the shower. Magnolia throws on another a ridiculous-looking fluffy robe.

"We are, by the way"—she calls over her shoulder—"together."

"Bullshit."

She tosses me her phone and on the screen is a *Loose Lips* blast.

HOT NEW COUPLE ALERT.

A new couple about town! It's being reported that billionaire dream boat Thomas England has been snatched up by the ineffable and ridiculously beautiful Magnolia Parks.

Watch this space!

"So?" I shrug, but my chest is getting tight. "Everyone runs shit on us all the time. Doesn't make it true."

"Yes," she walks over, talking her phone from my hand. Her hand hovers above mine, grazing it. "Except this time it's not shit."

I stare across at her. "What the fuck are you doing?"

"I'm quite sure I don't know what you mean," she says with her nose in the air so she definitely does know exactly what the fuck I mean.

"I fucked up! It just happened! It was stupid! But—"

"Do you know what it's like to lose you how I lost you?" she interrupts quietly. She looks at me and then her eyes fall away. "Those first few weeks after what happened and we were over, every time I closed my eyes I saw you with another girl. Every girl. Every girl in the world except for my sister and Paili, every girl we passed on the street, every bartender who looked at you longer than she needed, every waitress who held your eyes when you gave her your card, the girl who works in Saint Laurent, the old girls from Varley, girls from shoots you did—it was a supercut of you and them in every way and position my mind could come up with, trying to imagine what the fuck they did for you that I couldn't do. Because I would have done anything for you—"

Her eyes are too heavy for me to hold on to anymore. I feel sick.

"And I thought you knew that. And I think you did? Didn't you? Surely you did." She's looking for an answer I can't give. "All this time I thought it was me, something wrong with me, some deficiency in me, something I couldn't give you, but now, having seen you, seen what you're like when I'm not there—it's not." Her voice goes soft. "It's not me, it's you. You're just...a slut."

She delivers this with straight-faced perfect execution.

I glare over at her. "Take it back."

"Why?" She shrugs insolently. "What are you going to do? Fuck someone else? Fuck me over? Make me look like a fucking, goddamn fool?" She swallows, composes herself. "You've already done that."

"Parks." I grab her by the wrists.

"Let me go." She pulls away, fighting me.

"No."

"Let me go!"

"I can't." My chest feels like it's heaving.

She shoves me away and I look at her with ragged eyes.

"I reckon it's time you left, Beej," says a quiet voice from the door. Bridget's there in the doorframe, watching on, brows low.

I let out an incredulous laugh and walk out the door of the girl I love, brushing past her sister and walking as quick as I can down the stairs.

"It's getting a bit old, don't you think?" Bridge calls after me. I stop halfway down and look back.

"Your sister's serial dating?" I scoff. "Yeah."

She nods. "Also, you fucking anything you can just to hurt her... bit tired at this point"

I shake my head. "I'd never do anything to hurt her."

"Don't bullshit me." She's annoyed. "No one needs as much sex as you have, and even if they do, which they don't, by the way, because if they needed it, they'd be an addict. Are you an addict?" She gives me a long look that makes me feel uneasy about myself. "But let's say, for shits and giggles, you did need it—you don't need to tell her every time you have it. You tell her to hurt her." She folds her arms over her chest. "You have sex with other people and tell her because when you do, it makes her sad and her being sad about that validates your feelings for her. She still cares. She wouldn't be sad otherwise. She's sad that I'm sleeping with other people, it must be because she still has feelings for me. You do it to feel close to her."

I scowl up at her, equal parts annoyed and confronted. "I don't need a psychology lecture, Bridge."

"No, Beej." She gives me a pointed look. "You need a therapist."

SIXTEEN

Magnolia

I'm lying in bed a few days later, reeling a bit from the events of the last few days. The other night I left the house thinking I was going to maybe, possibly, potentially, hypothetically, start things up with BJ again, and yet somehow arrived home several hours later with a new fake boyfriend. The fake new boyfriend doesn't stop the burning hole in my chest from seeing BJ like that with someone. I've seen him kiss other girls before, touch other girls before—but that one felt different. That one was almost exactly how I imagined whatever happened three years ago happened, and now I've seen it, with my own eyes. His eyes closed, head back, hand on her waist, his neck all stretched out and exposed—that's the part that gets me. I don't know why.

Fake-dating Tom England doesn't make that stop playing on a loop in my mind and eating me alive, but fake-dating Tom England will level the playing field.

I don't sleep around. I don't judge girls who do, it's just—it's still something to me. I've only ever been with BJ. Not even with Christian. I've done other things; I've dated lots of boys since BJ. But I just never felt like that was the right thing for me. I never wanted to do it with anyone else. I haven't figured out how to get past that feeling yet either. Feeling like it's just something for me and him.

I wander downstairs for breakfast only to discover an extra body at the table. Our little neighbour, Sullivan Van Schoor—cute as a button, about fourteen years old. Blonde hair, olive skin, blue eyes. Originally from South Africa but has been here since she was three. Her dad is a tough as nails merchant banker who has a very intense gaze as South African men oft do. He's a very hands-on father and she's an absolute handful—so good for him and godspeed.

"Well," Mars says, giving me a look. "Look who finally decided to grace us with her presence." I give her an unenthused smile and go and sit next to my sister. Wasn't expecting company but mercifully, I tend to look fantastic. I wake quite well. I believe it's a combination of the amount of alcohol I consume preserving me, as well as living a fairly stress-free life that requires little to no manual labour. I'm wearing the Mimi Martine floral print, satin-jacquard pajama set from Morgan Lane which make me look extra brown, so extra pretty. I bat my eyes at Louisa, one of our house staff, as she pours me my tea.

"Sully." I'm sure to flash her an extra dazzling smile on account of her mother telling me that Sullivan follows me on Instagram and thinks I'm 'like totally beyond'. "What are you doing here?"

"Sullivan's parents are in South Africa at the last minute," Marsaili tells me. "Family emergency."

She smiles over at me pleasantly. "My dad's... sister's... sons... might have gotten the same girl pregnant."

"Ooh." I lean in, intrigued. "Keep me updated on that one! Sounds like a page turner."

"She's staying with us a few days," Marsaili tells me, passing my dad the marmalade even though he hasn't asked for it.

"No BJ this morning?" my mother asks, cheerily. I shake my head, demurely. "Oh." She looks disappointed. "Where is he?"

Sullivan looks over, waiting for my answer. She was probably hoping to spot him here this morning—and honestly, so was I—but here we are, old girl...

"How should I know?" I reach for a strawberry.

My sister gives me a peevish smile. "Because you have him on LoJack."

"I do not." I scowl. But wouldn't it be great if I did?

"Are you fighting, darling?" my mother asks, tilting her head.

I breathe out, annoyed. "If you must know, yes."

"Oh." Mars sighs with faux-empathy. "What a shame."

My father shoots her an amused look. Marsaili used to love BJ. So much. She used to chase him out of my bedroom with a wooden spoon when we were home from school for the weekends, but she loved him. She loved how he loved me. She trusted him; she wouldn't let me go places unless BJ was going to be there. The disparity of it all now is a bit shattering.

Her fuse for him is tiny. It used to eat away at him, he spent forever trying to win her back, bought her flowers every day for months. One time he handed her a bunch of roses and she put them straight into the Insinkerator. I think he stopped trying after that.

I never told her he cheated on me. I suspect she knows anyway.

"Magnolia"—she starts, "I have a friend's son who's coming to town. I thought it would be nice if you'd show him around?"

I look over at her, confused. "Are you being funny?"

She frowns. "No."

"Oh." I frown. "Then—no." I flash her a smile.

My father looks up.

"Please?" she pouts. "After all I do for you?"

I give her a confused look. "Yeah but—you're employed to do it?"

My mother stifles a laugh.

"Magnolia"—my father starts—"it would be nice—"

"Oh, Harley." I call him that just to annoy him. "I wish I could. But I don't really think my boyfriend would find it appropriate."

"Boyfriend?" Mars repeats, frowning. ("Don't say BJ, don't say BJ." Under her breath.)

"Not him." I flick my eyes impatiently. "A different boyfriend."

"How many do you have?" my sister asks, and I shoot her a look.

"Boyfriend who?" Bushka asks, frowning from the other end of the table. She yells it so loudly and with such reckless abandon for societal norms, I can't help but smile.

"Tom England," I yell back. It's unnecessary to yell but it is worth announcing. My father looks up from his phone, intrigued.

Bridge looks at me with pinched eyes. "You're dating Tom England?"

I glare over at her. "What do mean 'you're' like that? Yes me—of course me. Who else is he going to date?"

"I don't know." My sister shrugs uselessly. "Like, Kate Middleton."

I stare at her blankly for a second. "Um, I think she's taken, Fridge—"

"Tom England?" my father interjects. "As in, Gus's mate?" I nod. "Dead brother?"

I give him a look. "Billionaire, philanthropist, pilot, dreamboat but sure okay, go with 'dead brother' as your mental tag."

"Gus hasn't said anything?"

I flash him a terse smile. "He doesn't know."

"Who's Tom England?" Sullivan frowns.

"He was to my generation what BJ is to yours," I tell her sagely.

"And you're with them both?" Her frown deepens.

"Yes! I mean—fuck—"

"Magnolia," Marsaili sighs. "Don't say fuck."

I look her in the eyes defiantly. "*Ебать.*"

"Don't say it in Russian either." She rolls her eyes. "So, sorry—just to clarify—the same Tom England you followed around like a lovesick school-girl for an entire weekend at Ascot?"

"The very one." I flash her a look like the cat who got the very fancy cream. Mars sits back in her seat as though she doesn't quite know what to do with the information.

"Blimey," she says and sighs. "BJ must be on the brink." My father smirks, pleased.

"Hmm?" I feign confusion. "Who's that now?"

Marsaili rolls her eyes.

"BJ Ballentine?" Bridge starts. "About yay high?" She waves her hand in the air. "Good hair. Great mouth? Love of your life?"

"Doesn't ring a bell," I chime.

"You may or may not have lost your virginity to him in the back of Dad's Maserati?"

Our father looks over at me, head pulled back, eyes wide. "What's that now?"

"She's kidding!" I glare at my sister. Throw a grape at her when no one's looking. "Of course she's kidding!"

I shake my head quickly. "Harley, I would never. Ever. Never."

He gives me a long-suffering look before turning to Bridge. "Which one?" I subtly pinch my sister under the table to silence her, but it doesn't work.

"The white one with the black roof."

"Not my MC20!" he cries, pained. Sullivan Van Schoor is watching on, eyes sparkling with the delight of it all.

"I wouldn't! I didn't! She's kidding!" I glare at her, pinching her harder. "She's joking! She's just—not very funny—we all know that—rubbish comedic timing." I elbow her.

"I'm kidding," she begrudgingly says.

Marsaili watches us with pinched, suspicious eyes.

The consensus, by the way, is I did not lose my virginity in the back of my father's Maserati. There was arguably a hint of penetration but BJ was so distracted by the fact that Marsaili could walk out and see us that he kept ruining it so we waited and that's a different story for a different day.

"Tom England. Wow." My mother sits back, lost to the thought. "His mother's a bit boring though, isn't she?"

"Charlotte England?" I blink "I mean—no? I think she's just a regular... mother? Goes to lunches, runs charity events, gardens a bit, has a couple of small dogs she focuses too much on..."

My mother eyes me suspiciously. "Sounds boring."

"As opposed to, say, calling your eldest daughter at three in the morning because you're locked in a horse stable with the Marchioness of Milford Haven."

My mother points at herself. "Not boring."

Bushka yells from the other end again, "Is Tom England Tom England like I am Bushka Russia?"

"No." Bridget smiles at her gently. "That's his surname."

"He is very British though," I offer.

"He's almost like a prince," my mother inserts.

"Like the purple rain?" Bushka clarifies. We're all silent.

"Yes." I nod. It's just easier sometimes. "Anyway." I look at Marsaili. "I have a boyfriend now and it's new. I wouldn't want to rock the boat—"

"Of course." Mars rolls her eyes. "Who would want to upset The Artist Formally Known As Prince?"

"Sugar, Miss?" Louisa offers me for my tea.

"No, I'm fine." I smile up at her.

"She needs two," Marsaili tells her, and I scowl at her.

"Do not," I say, pouting. "It's not a two-sugar cube kind of day."

"You're fighting with BJ," Marsaili reminds me, but all the sugar cubes in the world can't fix us, I'm afraid.

I nod. "But I have Tom England now, and I believe all the sugar in the world resides in his—"

"—Don't say lips, don't say lips," my sister chants under her breath.

I give her a look. "—Little finger. He is an excellent kisser though."

My father groans.

"Why are you and BJ Ballentine fighting?" Sullivan asks quite suddenly. My whole family sort of freezes; perhaps because we're British and we only ever talk around our feelings? Perhaps because it's a rude question?

"Err." I blink. I guess the fight made its way to the papers. "Why?"

"I know you fight a lot," she tells me.

"Well." I tilt my head considering it. "No, I wouldn't say a lot—"

"You're always photographed growling at each other in public."

"Right, well, yes," I nod, "he can be irritating."

"I have your relationship timeline here on my phone." She flashes it to me. "*Loose Lips* did an article on it."

"Oh dear god," Mars says under her breath. "Can I get a copy of that?" my father asks.

I reach for it and Bridge and I peer down at it. Photos of me and BJ taken both from our Instagrams and from moments we didn't know we were being watched, a few paparazzi photos—a lot of dates. Some of them are actually completely bang on. They're wrong about our break-up date, wrong about why. They think it's me. I would have never unless he forced my hand.

It's not all true. It's not all not true either.

"Lots of fights," Sullivan reiterates.

"Yes." I glance up at her, distracted. "Lots."

She sighs, frustrated. A Queen's College girl. Confidence levels are sky high.

"So," she presses, "is there a reason?" My face falters a bit. "It's just, *Loose Lips* is running a contest—whoever submits the juiciest piece of gossip wins a Chanel 19 Flapbag in the multicoloured houndstooth. I already have it in black so Daddy won't buy it for me—but I need it." She gives me puppy dog eyes.

I sigh. Anything for Chanel, right? It's practically charity to throw her a bone here. I can't imagine how I'd feel were someone to ruthlessly cut me off from Chanel products.

Plus, I'm still level 5 cross at BJ for what happened the other day, and there are only 5 levels.

"He cheated on me," I announce. I probably shouldn't have said it, I think as soon as I do.

Sully's jaw drops.

"A long time ago," I clarify to my plate of eggs. I can't really meet anyone's eyes. "But that's what we're fighting about."

"When?" my mother blinks, looking a bit sad.

I give her a look. "When we broke up."

She frowns. "Which was when?"

Marsaili rolls her eyes at her, annoyed that my mother doesn't know the answer herself. "When she was nineteen."

Sullivan is typing speedily on her phone when she glances up. She's beaming and says, "Well, I'm definitely winning the bag now."

10:34

Marsaili

Tom England.

I can scarcely believe it.

I know!

Fun right?

Very.

Just... Curious is all. You've not mentioned you were spending time with Tom England.

So what?

So, nothing.

Just, the last time Tom England passed you a napkin you practically wrote a soliloquy about it.

I'm very private these days.

Two days ago, despite my insistence to the contrary, you shared a very graphic story about you and the ex toyfriend on a boat in Lake Como.

I did that for you!

Because you don't have so much going on.

Like, when was the last time you had sex?

When was the last time you had sex?

Marsaili, that's so terribly rude.

How vulgar.

And don't call him toyfriend.

SEVENTEEN

BJ

"You want some?" the girl I'm with asks me. Blonde hair, brown eyes, big mouth—too big probably. From Bath.

"Hm?" I look at her, not paying that much attention. We're at Jo's club, Hampton Haus. All the staff dress like they're from the Hamptons and every waitress is fit as anything. It's one of about ten venues the Hemmes brothers own, which I'm grateful for so I don't have to lie to Parks about what they do. I can just divert the question.

"I'm going to run to the loo for a cheeky bump." She grins over at me. "Do you want some?"

I shake my head. "I don't use that shit." Bath looks surprised. Maybe it is surprising. I like it—like it too much, if anything. Bath looks at me funny, her eyes a bit too round and a bit too eager, like party girls' eyes often are.

"You just sort of strike me as someone who... would. You know?"

I shrug. She's not wrong. "Used to."

"But not anymore?" I shake my head, a bit bored of all the questions. What is she, Piers fucking Morgan? "Why?"

Fuck me, I roll my eyes a bit. "Promised someone." That's all I offer her.

"Who—?" she snorts. "Your mum?"

And then I'm annoyed. "Nah, just the girl I love."

This throws her how I want it to. "The girl you love?" she repeats.

"Yep," I nod, back to being bored. "Go do your line. I'll be here when you get back."

I pull out my phone, check my messages to see if Parks texted me. Hasn't. Check my phone to make sure I have service. I do. Fuck.

So, I check Instagram in case she decided to DM me, reply to a story or some shit—relationships are so fucked these days with all the mediums there are to talk to each other on. Not that we're dating. We're not dating. She's dating someone else. "Dating."

I'm about forty seconds into dissecting the validity of Parks and Tom England when I realise my Instagram comments are blowing up and my DM's are through the roof…

I mean, I always get a lot of both, but this is apeshit.

I open my most recent photo and there are hundreds of people commenting 🐀🐀🐀🐀🐀 and a bunch of shit like I can't believe you, you don't deserve her, a couple of fuck u die, losers. I'm confused so I do what you're never supposed to do: I Google myself.

And then I see it.

A close personal source confirms, the REAL reason behind the most confusing and drawn-out public break-up in the history of time—BJ Ballentine cheated on Magnolia Parks.

Fuck. I think I'm going to throw up. Feel light-headed. I can't see properly for a second.

"Are you okay?" asks a bartender. I nod. I'm not. Could faint.

"What's going on?" Jonah's there suddenly, brows low. "Did you take something?" Shake my head. Barely. Flash him my phone. "Fuck." He blinks, his eyes are wide. "Does it say with who?"

I shake my head. Another wave of nausea hits me like a dump truck.

Jonah leans across the bar, grabs a bottle of tequila and passes it to me. I take a few swigs. Big ones. I feel weird, like I'm walking underwater in a dream. Which, funnily enough, is how I felt the night I cheated on her as it was happening… a slow-motion walk towards something I didn't want to do but had to do, and it was like my head was out of the water and the rest of me was under it and I was walking against the current to do it. Every touch, every grab, every kiss, every motion, the current of the entire universe was telling me not to do it and I fucking did it anyway, and now not just she knows it but everyone knows, that not only did I lose the girl we all know I love, I lost her and it's all my fault.

I head out back to Jo's office. Open the door. A girl rolls off of Christian on the couch. Takes a second for my eyes to adjust.

Daisy Haites. Guess that date he took her on a while back went well—

She's very hot. Very dangerous. Not a girl I'd fuck around with. Her brother is more dangerous than the Hemmes boys.

Her mouth looks pink and a bit smudged. "Is he okay?" Daisy asks, looking at me, head to the side.

I sit down. Take another swig. She walks over, squints at me. Med student, second year. What's my pulse going to tell her that I don't already know? My heart lives outside of my chest over in Holland Park and it just wandered into the arms of England's most eligible bachelor.

"It's out." Jonah eyes Christian.

"What is?" Christian asks, ominously. I guess I have a few skeletons at this point. Could be any one of them.

Jo nods in my direction like I can't see him. "Him. Cheating."

"You cheated on Magnolia?" Daisy blinks, eyes wide as she takes my pulse. "150 BPM," ahe tells Jonah, then adds, "Does he get panic attacks?" Jonah doesn't answer.

"Shit!" Christian sighs, coming to sit down next to me. "Who leaked it?" he asks Jonah, who shakes his head.

"Right, well." Christian looks from me to Jonah. "Who knows?"

"Just us all," Jo shrugs. "Our group."

"None of us would," Christian says, listing off his fingers. "Hen wouldn't. Perry wouldn't. Pails definitely wouldn't."

"Why?" Jonah asks, maybe too quickly.

"Because she's shit-scared of being on Magnolia's bad side."

"Bridget wouldn't have said anything," I tell them.

"Does Taura know?" Jonah asks. I shake my head.

Daisy's watching me, looking between my pupils. Stands up, hands on her hips. Turns to Christian. "It was probably her."

"What?" I blink.

"It was probably her," she says like she didn't just send a missile straight into the middle of my whole life. "Have you pissed her off lately?"

"Has he pissed her off lately?" Jonah scoffs merrily— catches himself. "Not the time, sorry."

I grimace. "Yeah, maybe… but she wouldn't."

"She would—" Christian nods, thinking it through. I scowl at him when he says that. Don't mean to; it's just the way he says it, like he'd know, like he knows her like I know her. All that shit between them and how angry it makes me courses through me and then it falls on me like a piano: you broke her first.

"Fuck off." Jonah rolls his eyes. "She would not."

I rub my face as I think about her eyes that night she saw me. Heavy-rimmed, glassy, a kind of hurt that's too deep for me to be able to reach.

"She might have?" I look up at Jonah, a little terrified.

Jo grabs the tequila and takes a long sip. "Well. Shit."

EIGHTEEN

Magnolia

I take one of the town cars into the city to meet Tom.

He's standing outside Cartier on New Bond Street. Neutral-coloured, horizontal-striped T-shirt from Jil Sanders, the navy, garment-dyed cotton trousers from Brunello Cucinelli with the Chuck Taylor All Star HiTops in Farro. Even when he looks casual enough to practically be a window-washer, he's a bit of a dream come true. He opens my car door smiling down at me as he helps me out. I look adorable: Oversized wool-blend cardigan from Jil Sander with the gingham-print dress from Miu Miu (both in navy), black patent Mary Janes from Proenza Schouler with white almost-knee-high socks from Fendi.

We stand there on the street for a brief few seconds, staring at each other and then we each let out a weird, small laugh. He looks a bit nervous. Tom England looks nervous.

He tilts his head, trying to figure it out. "Should we kiss?" I've never had a fake boyfriend before who knew he was fake at the commencement of our relationship, so I don't know.

"Probably." I nod, unsure. "Sure? Yes. Sure." It's quick and strange and awkward and funny and he gives me a long look and then we both start laughing again. His laugh is sort of brilliant. Deep from the back of his throat, making all the heaviness he's carrying in his brow lift a little.

The laughing makes it easier, like it breaks the tension, rubbing out the knots of strangeness between us. He places his hand on the small of my back again, leading me down the street.

"So we're shopping today?" I look up at him. He really is so tall. Six feet four inches, maybe?

He nods. "I kind of need a whole new wardrobe."

"Where's your old wardrobe?"

"At Sam's."

So I just nod. "Okay," I cling to his arm because I don't know what else to do. "A whole new wardrobe, then."

"Up for the task?"

"Born for the task," I nod, resolutely.

We head on into Burberry because someone with Tom's build and colouring belongs almost exclusively in neutrals and navy blues. I sift through the racks, pulling pieces for him—the slim-fit, logo-embroidered, cashmere sweater, the checked, merino wool sweater, the slim-fit, cotton-twill chinos—I try not to pick anything I'd pick for BJ, try my best not to dog-ear in my mind the things I'll probably come back and buy him myself next week when I hate him a little less.

They don't look the same, anyway. Plus, Tom and BJ's styles are completely different.

Tom's style is… Burberry when Christopher Bailey was on board. BJ's style is Burberry in the Riccardo Tisci era, do you know what I mean? Of course you do.

I notice two girls—maybe seventeen-ish years old—who've been sort of just around us since I pulled up have followed us into the store and they're nervously edging closer and closer to me.

("You ask." "No, you." "No!" "Okay, fine.")

"Excuse me?" one of them squeaks. I look over at them, smiling as warmly as I can muster. Tom looks on, curious.

"Can we get a photo with you?" the other one asks.

"Yeah, sure," I nod. "Of course." I don't know why. I never really understand why people want photos with me, nevertheless, I go stand with them. They hand the phone to Tom—hilarious—and he takes a few photos. They're about to walk away when the first girl turns around.

"Where's BJ?"

Tom glances over at me amused and I take a breath, breathe it out of my nose louder than I should—terribly unrefined of me—and I give them an offhanded smile.

"I'm not sure, but this is my boyfriend. Tom." I gesture to him.

"Oh. Hi." She laughs nervously, then scurries away.

("They broke up?" "I told you! I knew it!" "He's single!" "She's never single!")

I glance over at Tom apprehensively, flick my eyes, trying to play it off. He folds his arms over his chest, amused. "That happen a lot?"

"Oh," I ho and hum for a moment. "What's a lot?"

He shrugs with his mouth. "Once a day?"

I squint up at him. "Will my answer impact the state of our"—I glance around, then whisper—"fake relationship?"

He ducks a little (a lot) and whispers back, "No."

I pull back and smile up at him. "Then yes." He laughs and pushes some hair behind my ears, looking at me in a way that if I didn't know it was fake, might have made my heart go funny but my heart is just fine, thanks. Maybe just a murmur.

We go to the fitting rooms and I wait outside while he tries on the clothes for me.

He comes out in the slim-fit, cotton chinos in navy and the camel long-sleeve, icon stripe-detail merino wool polo shirt. So sexy. "I'm in, by the way," he tells me as I tug the shirt around on his body, tucking it in, untucking it, tucking it back in.

"In what?" I look up at him.

He brushes some hair behind my ear again. "This. Us."

"Fake us?" I smirk.

He squashes a smile. "Come hell or high-water."

I spin him around to inspect the back of his pants. "I'm glad to hear because I'd imagine both are on the way."

"Do you now?" he says, standing over me, looking down.

My breath feels a bit caught in my chest. "I do." I breathe out, grab the Vintage Check panel cotton hoodie and shove it in his hands, closing the door quickly because my cheeks are going pink. That hoodie was maybe too like something BJ would wear? Anyway.

"Why's that?" Tom says from the other side of the door.

"Because BJ is insane when it comes to me."

"Oh." He chuckles. "Great."

He opens the door and shows me the hoodie. It doesn't suit Tom, but it's perfect for BJ. I shake my head and he takes it off. On the spot. In front of me. Just whips it off of himself—and, oh my dear lord.

He's a masterpiece. An absolute, fucking masterpiece. He could be a centrefold. I swallow heavy, looking away from him.

He looks over at me, perplexed. "What's the matter?"

"Nothing." I blink, suddenly riveted by the latte-coloured carpet in the change room.

"Am I going to get a black eye from this?" he asks with a laugh.

I glance up with a grimace. "Probably."

He walks over to me, ducks down so we're level, brushes his lips against mine.

"Worth it."

NINETEEN

BJ

I pretend like it's an accident as me and Jo cruise into Bellamy's for a casual lunch. Pretend like I don't know it's where she always is at lunchtime on a Tuesday.

"Eyy," Jonah calls when he spots them. Parks and Paili. He glances at me quickly, looking amused. "What are the chances?"

Parks look up at me, glaring. But I reckon I can see it in her eyes, she's relieved to see me. Not glad, but relieved. I know she feels like that because I feel the same.

Jonah sits down at the table next to theirs, grinning stupidly. Magnolia rolls her eyes at both of us. Paili smiles uncomfortably in that overly-dutiful friend way.

"Did you tell them we were coming here?" Parks asks, as she fidgets with the collar of her blue shirt.

"No," Paili frowns, nodding her head in my direction. "He stalks you."

"No, he doesn't," Jonah shakes his head and I'm grateful he's defending me. "He just put a tracking chip in that bracelet he got you."

I wave my middle finger at him half-heartedly and he shrugs, eyes on the menu, not on me. I stare over at her for a second, then frown.

"Are you wearing pants?"

She frowns at me. "They're the Fumato pants. Max Mara."

"But they're pants," I tell her.

"Fuck." Jo shakes his head. "You've broken her. Where's the reset button?"

I give him a look. I wish I knew, brother.

Watch Parks closely, who's deliberately not watching me. I bang my balled-up fist into my mouth a few times as I glare over at her.

"Wanted to talk to you," I say eventually.

She looks up from the menu she's fake-reading. Her eyes are wide, brows are tall. She's waiting.

I stare at her a few seconds longer. "Did you tell the rags I cheated on you?"

Jonah makes a weird noise in the back of his throat, Paili shifts uncomfortably, avoiding all eyes.

"Did I?" Parks repeats. "No, I did not." Big pause. "However, do I know of a certain fifteen-year-old who was in dire need of a specific Chanel bag to which she was otherwise tragically and barbarically declined who might have leveraged the information to acquire said bag?" She shrugs innocently. "Perhaps."

I push my hand through my hair—I can't believe it. Holy shit. How angry is she? I try not to feel betrayed. I did cheat on her. It's her prerogative, I guess. I didn't make her keep it a secret all these years, but she did. I thought she did it for me—maybe she did it for her? I rub the back of my neck, look up at the waiter, order an extra strong Negroni—glare back over at the twat I'm in love with. "You sullied my name for a Chanel bag?"

"Oh, Beej—" She lets out a carefree laugh full of cares. "Your name has been sullied now for a very long time, and that had nothing to do with me." I try not to look like that hurt me. I stare over at her, jaw set. "There's a photograph of you feeling up a Kardashian." She eyes me pointedly. "And it's neither of the good ones."

She's being a little shit and I don't want to smile, but I do a bit. Shake my head to disguise it.

"Come on, Parks," I groan. "Hen's not talking to me. Mum's not talking to me."

"Well." Parks gives me a curt smile. "That makes three of us!" I give Parks a look. "Bridget got to Al, so she's not talking to me either." Allison—my youngest sister by four years—and for some reason, her not speaking to me appeases Parks a bit. She peers at me out of the corner of her eye. "And Madeline?"

Second youngest by three. I tilt my head, uneasy. "Never liked you that much." And with that I've lost her again. It's nose in the air, menu up extra high, body angled away from me.

"Magnolia," I groan. "It's been four days, can't we j—" The menu smacks down loud onto the table.

"Magnolia?" Her eyebrows shoot up.

("Uh oh," Jonah whispers under his breath.)

I never call her that. Don't know why? I just never have unless I'm shitty at her.

I dig my heels in. "It is your name."

"Oh—" She folds her arms over her chest and I'm already rolling my eyes at her. "Well, Baxter-James David Hamish Ballentine—"

("Fuck me," I groan under my breath. Catch Jo's eye, he's trying to hold it together.)

"Excuse me for not being able to instantly process the hideous image forced upon my retinas the other night," she says. "Sorry for being a little bit perturbed at the sight of you in the sexual throes—"

"—You're ridiculous," I interrupt. "You're a ridiculous pers—"

She talks over me. "In the erotic embrace—"

"Oh my god," I breathe in through my nose, steel myself. Paili's hands are covering her mouth. Can't tell whether she's amused or horrified. Can't tell if I am either.

"—the venereal clutches of the twerking slut."

"—Why do you care, Parks?" Jonah asks, nodding his chin at her as he leans forward.

"I beg your pardon?" She blinks at him.

"Why... do you... care?" My best friend shrugs, eyebrows up. "If you're just friends with Beej, if there are no feelings"—he gestures to her—"which is your official party line, you shouldn't care." She stares at Jonah—glares, actually. Wouldn't want to be Jonah right now. Invisible daggers are being tossed, wrapped in grenades at him, by her eyeballs. It lasts about five seconds. This weird stalemate between them. She won't admit anything, he won't admit anything on my behalf. All one of them can do is retreat, and knowing him, it won't be Jonah.

And then she squares her shoulders. "Fine." She shrugs. "I don't care."

"Because you're just friends, right?" Jonah clarifies.

Her eyes pinch. "Right."

"So what would you have to be upset about?"

She smiles tightly at him. "Exactly."

"Just friends," he tells her.

"Just friends." She nods back. Doesn't look at me when she says that though and I'm glad because I can see it in how she's blinking that all this shit is hurting her, and I can't really look at her when she's being hurt.

I glance over at Parks—don't know whether I'm relieved or nervous. "So, we're... fine?"

"We… are tremendous." She nods, but her eyes still look mad.

I rub my tongue over my teeth. "Great."

"Great." She gives me a tight smile.

"Great." Jonah grins, looking between us, then claps his hands loudly. "So, Full Box Set dinner this weekend? I'll book Le Gavroche."

"Perfect," Paili smiles, eager to get the ball rolling away from whatever the fuck is going on.

"Can't wait," Park smiles but not with her eyes. "I'll bring Tom."

I breathe out, exasperated. "Of course you will."

She glowers at me. "Problem?"

"None at all, Friend." I give her a look. "And because I'm not a child, I'll be bringing no one," I tell Jonah.

Parks looks over at me. "Yet isn't it astounding that you not bringing someone to dinner somehow still doesn't preclude someone coming… with you… later." She gives me an overly-twee smile and Jonah snorts into his glass.

She's really mad. I bite down on my bottom lip, not wanting to give her the satisfaction of a laugh. I look up at her, shaking my head. She flips her hair over her shoulder, holding my eyes, not smiling, but softening all the same. And then I see that long chain around her neck, the one she wouldn't want me to see but wants me to see and all the clouds fuck off from around my head.

She sees me see it and she adjusts her dress quickly. Can't help but smile. She looks out the window, but I can spot her quarter smiles a mile off.

TWENTY

Magnolia

I plan it so we arrive fifteen minutes after the start of our reservation because I want the whole room to see us when we walk in, and boy, do they. Tom's in a plain white T-shirt from Sandro Paris, the reversible, check bomber jacket from Burberry, the Gucci tapered, cotton-poplin trousers in indigo and the cornstalk and true white Old Skool Vans; Me—the gathered, floral-print, silk-satin jacquard mini dress by Magda Butrym, the fire-engine red, double-breasted cashmere and wool blend coat from Saint Laurent and the 105mm, bow-tie pumps from Aquazzura to match. Every single eye is on us—except BJ's—as Tom and I walk into Le Gavroche hand in hand.

BJ's not looking is intentional. Its intention is to infuriate me. It's working.

"England." Henry stands up to shake his hand.

Jonah follows. Christian just nods at Tom. BJ stands and hugs him. "My man," he says, smacking him on the arm. "Good to see you." He glances at me and nods. "Parks." He looks so good. I don't know why he looks so good. All he's in is the black MX1 skinny-fit, distressed, leather-panelled, stretch-denim jeans from Amiri, black logo-print, loopback, cotton-jersey sweatshirt from Givenchy, and black Vans.

Bit of a nothing outfit, really. But still, my heart still goes funny.

Tom pulls my seat out for me, slides me in. Paili mouths at me, oh my god.

And I look at her like, I know.

I point to the P's. "Do you know Perry and Paili?"

Tom shakes his head, then shakes their hands. "Heard a lot about you both though." He sits down, leans back into his chair—the most confident man in the room, and he's at a table full of men who could respectively be megalomaniacs, narcissists and down and out sex legend—so it's really quite saying something.

He flips open the wine list, points to the 2005 Latour. "That's the one I was telling you about."

I lift my hair over my shoulders. "Oh, get it." Tom orders it and he's a jovial delight with the maître'd, which is usually BJ's forte and he looks pissed. He's avoiding my eyes.

"So," Perry leans in. "You have to tell us—how did this happen?"

Tom stretches his arm around me and gives me a fond look and a small, covert wink. "Well, I was actually on the shittest date of my life the other night. Called it early, went to meet up with Gus at Raffles, and when I walked in, I saw her at the bar. Looked a bit glassy eyed—" He touches my face gently. He's a very good foxhole. Meanwhile, BJ is not loving this story. He's sullen and annoyed and muttering things under his breath to Jonah who's occasionally elbowing him as subtly as possible. Tom pretends he doesn't notice (or genuinely doesn't notice because he's a grown-up).

"We had a couple of drinks and I got a bit braver so I kissed her. To be honest, I've always fancied her

a bit, but she's always been otherwise... preoccupied."
His eyes dart over towards BJ just to annoy him. "It just
happened that everything aligned that night." He gives
Perry a pleasant smile. BJ's building towards something,
I can see it in his eyes.

And then: "But you're thirty and she's twenty-two,"
BJ pipes up. "So what, when you were twenty-three and
she was fifteen, you were keen on her?"

"Shut up," Henry whispers, looking embarrassed.

"No," BJ shrugs innocently. "I'm just saying—it's a
bit weird."

"You first felt her up when she was fourteen, man,"
Jonah announces.

My hands fly to my cheeks. "Jonah!"

"What?" He frowns at me. "I'm helping."

I scowl at him. "Are you?"

Christian chuckles, amused. Tom gives Beej a long,
sobering look, then says, "Since she was of age." He
pauses, to give BJ another look. "I have always fancied
her."

"But you had a girlfriend then," BJ tells him, in case
he forgot. "So, once again, bit inappropriate..."

"Sure, yeah I guess. But sorry"—Tom pauses—"didn't
you cheat on her?"

Jonah makes a sound in the back of his throat and
Christian's now full-blown laughing.

BJ looks over at me, eyes all guilty, sorry, sad. His
mouth goes tight, he nods once.

"So!" Jonah says loudly, commandeering the conversation, steering it into safer waters. "How's being a pilot
these days?"

Tom pushes his hand through his hair. "Yeah, good.
Fun. It's always fun. It's never not fun to fly a plane, you

know?" Then he glances at me. "Speaking of, I actually got put on a run to the Americas next in a few days. Do you want to come?"

I smile over at him, and my eyes catch BJ's, who's watching me altogether too closely, and his face looks a tiny bit afraid and I want to reach out and touch his face but I can't, so I touch Tom's arm instead.

"I wish I could—I have a work thing I can't miss."

Tom nods understandingly and BJ licks away a smile.

"So," Tom glances between us all, "you're all friends from high school?"

I nod.

He points to me and Paili, "Dorm mates?"

"Yeah," Paili nods, gesturing between us. "But we've been friends since year one."

Tom shakes his head, a little fascinated. "I kind of wish I went to boarding school. Mum would never send us away."

"Oh, muffin—" I rub his arm with a sarcastic affection. "How terrible that your mother loved you so much she wanted to keep you around."

He rolls his eyes playfully.

"It just always looked like fun," he says.

"It was," BJ says, looking just at me.

My cheeks go hot.

"There was a bizarre amount of independence given to us at such a young age," Perry tells him.

"That developed into a co-dependency." Paili laughs.

Jonah shrugs. "You're in each other's pockets all the time."

"You kind of have to be though. Because you're so disjointed from your family that you make your own hotchpotch one," I tell him.

"Parks' parents forgot her sixteenth birthday," Christian says, nodding his chin at me

Tom looks horrified. "No?"

They did. It was sad and I was heartbroken, because even Marsaili forgot, which was so unlike her. Bridge remembered though, of course, and by the time we got to school, BJ and Paili had executed a redemption plan: Jonah procured the Hemmes family jet (their parents always asked the fewest questions), they all piled into the stretch my parents sent us to school in and off we flew to Paris.

I can't even imagine how ridiculous we would have looked, the seven of us with our school bags in our uniforms, in the foyer at Le Bristol.

Beej squared up his shoulders and walked straight up to the concierge. "Booking for Ballentine. Three rooms."

The woman's gaze flickered from BJ to us all behind him.

"Is—erm, you 'ave an adult?" she asked, French accent.

"No." BJ smiled at her, shrugging his shoulders.

"Erm." She glanced around.

BJ slid his Coutts World Silk card across to her.

"Is this yours?" She picked it up, inspecting it.

"Are you saying I don't look like the kind of person who would have a Coutts card?" he asked, giving her a playful smile.

She looked at him a little like a beetle—which never happens, because he was heaven back then, so she probably didn't like men. "No, I think you look like a child," she said.

"Here, take mine then." I offered her my AMEX Centurion card, but BJ swatted it away.

"I can pay in cash, if you'd prefer?" he tells her.

The woman looked at us skeptically for a few seconds, then blinked, and began typing into the computer.

"Ballentine." She pronounced it Bally-Teen. "Erm, you have requested—"She clicked her tongue in thought. "Two Junior suites and le Saint-Honoré Suite—oui?"

"Oui." He nodded.

She ran his card through, then looked up and smiled at us as warmly as she could muster.

"Bienvenue à Paris."

They all piled onto our bed that night. I cried a bit, happy and sad tears. "Parents are shit, Parks—"Christian shook his head, passing me a glass of champagne.

"Forgetting their first-born's sixteenth birthday, shit?" I asked, eyebrows raised.

"All of our parents have sent each of us away to boarding school," Paili reminds me. "They're all shit."

"Our parents don't talk anymore," Jonah offered, looking at Christian a bit uncomfortably. "They haven't—not since—" His voice trailed.

Not since their sister drowned five years ago. Beej and Jonah held eyes, faces sombre. She'd been under the water in their family pool for more than fifteen minutes when they found her. They dove in and pulled her up. Jonah was too distraught, BJ tried to revive her, but she was gone.

Beej and Jonah were already best friends before that happened, but after it they were brothers.

"They can't talk," Christian downed a full glass of champagne before he continued. "If they do, they just blame each other."

"Mum's okay, she's pretty normal still—like," Jonah shrugged, "insane—she bought an octopus last week—but okay enough—she leaves the house still. But Dad—"

Christian pursed his lips. "He just sits and looks at photos of Rem in his office."

"My parents still think I'm straight," Perry offered. "I can't tell them." He told us before we could say anything—"My uncle's gay. My dad won't speak to him."

"You're their son," Paili reminded him gently.

"I don't want him to look at me how he looks at my uncle."

BJ smacked him on the arm apologetically.

My eyes fell next on Henry, but he flicked his gaze to Beej.

"Erm." He sniffed a laugh. "I don't know—our parents are pretty great—"

"Well." Christian rolled his eyes. "Fuck you, then—"

Hen and Beej laughed.

"My mum is pretty slutty these days," Paili announced, despondent. "But only with younger men."

"How young?" Christian asked.

"Like, university. First year." She sighed.

"Your mum's pretty hot." Jonah shrugged. "Reckon I could have a crack?"

Paili smacked him in the head with a pillow before shrugging. "And I haven't seen my dad in forever. He's moved to Berlin with his new family."

I remember looking around at the group of people assembled in front of me, piled on my bed in a hotel room I ran away to in Paris with my boyfriend, and thinking—maybe they're what family actually is. Maybe they're who have been my family all along. Maybe it was these people who had raised me this whole time.

It was Christian Hemmes in a stairwell when I was thirteen who told me what sex actually was. Not just rolling around under sheets and kissing.

It was Jonah that same year who first gave me alcohol, and then took care of me all night as I threw it up.

It would be Perry who, when he eventually did come out to his parents, taught me about taking pride in who I am, no matter what.

It would be from Henry that I'd learn about steadfastness and what it's like to have a brother. Paili would teach me how to be selfless (a work in progress) and how to show up for the people you love.

And it would be BJ who would make me fearless and safe and hopeful all at once, and it would eventually be BJ who would strip me of those things one day also when he'd come home smelling like musk and orange blossom.

Tom gives me a sad look back in Le Gavroche. "I can't believe they forgot your birthday." It's sweet how foreign an idea that seems to him.

BJ looks over at me, eyes too soft for this table. "We sorted her out."

Tom gives him a small smile that maybe has seeds of genuine gratefulness.

"I like your friends," Tom tells on the way home later that night. "It's kind of special what you have."

I nod, feeling proud of them.

"Even BJ?" I ask.

"Even BJ." He nods. "Does the younger Hemmes have a thing for you? He was looking at you a lot—"

I swat my hands because I can't right now. "He's just a starer."

Tom snorts a small laugh. He looks over at me. "So how's the foxhole working out for you?"

"You did very well."

"Yeah?" He grins.

I kiss him on the cheek as we pull up. "Yeah."

00:14

Parks

Hi

Hey

How's the weather, Beej?

Better now.

Goodnight BJ.

Goodnight Parks x

TWENTY-ONE

BJ

I'm waiting for her outside her work, leaning back on the hood of my car.

Tom's somewhere overseas. Got Henry to check with Parks that he was actually gone, and he is. Thank fuck. I miss her. I need a minute with her.

She walks out, chatting to some girl from the office and for the full two seconds before she sees me, I take her in. Bright green little sundress with puffy sleeves, matching strappy high heels that make her legs go for miles and miles. Her friend sees me before she does and elbows her. Parks looks up. Our eyes catch and maybe the whole world falls into step with her blinking—I don't know.

"Hey." I nod my chin at her.

"Hey." She walks over to me, closer than she needs to. "What are you doing here?" she asks, like until a fortnight ago I didn't pick her up every day she was in the office.

"Thought you might be lonely." She gives me a look and it makes me snort a laugh. "Want a ride?"

She purses her mouth. "I think my car's here already—"

"So send it home," I say and shrug. She thinks for a minute, and I love how her mouth goes when she does. Then she nods and I open the car door for her.

We drive right into London rush hour and I've never been so happy to see a thousand gridlocked cars. She's mine for at least an hour. She takes off her shoes. She wouldn't do that around Tom, I know that much. She only comes undone around me.

"Still angry at me?" I ask, looking over at her.

"No," she says, staring straight ahead. And I wonder if she's telling the truth. Less angry, more sad? Way worse.

"Need a hard reset?" I ask, watching her closely.

She faces me. "Probably, actually."

"Go on then." I nod at her. "How many seconds for?"

"Fifteen."

"Fuck me—" I snort. "You've never gone higher than twelve." A smile twitches across her face. "Fifteen it is," I concede.

We're in standstill traffic. I turn up the song. "Say You Will." Kygo. She shifts her whole body to face me, tucks her feet under herself.

I mirror her. "Ready?"

She nods. "Go."

We've done this since we were in school. After every fight, stare at each other in the eyes for ten seconds or something—I don't know why. I think she saw it on *Oprah*. It works though.

Especially with her—I find it pretty hard to stay shitty at her for very long anyway, but she can hold a grudge like you wouldn't believe, but when we do this, I watch it all melt off her.

And here I have her in my car, stuck in endless traffic, and I get to just stare at her, unapologetically, for fifteen seconds. My thought process is almost the same every time.

One... two... Holy fuck, she's beautiful. That's my first thought every time we do this. She's so fucking beautiful. I can't believe she loves me.

Her eye-lids flutter, she always blinks extra when we do this.

Three... four... I don't know that she does anymore. Does she still love me? I don't know. I used to think she did. Sometimes I still do. But maybe it doesn't matter because maybe you can't go back after you fuck up how I did?

Tilts her head to the side, she only does that when she wants something from me.

Five...Six... I don't know how I could do it to her. I don't. I don't know what was the matter with me or even how it happened. It just happened. And once it was happening, it felt worse to stop it. But I didn't want to hurt her. It wasn't about her.

She rests her elbow, chin in her hand, on the middle console. Her eyes don't shift from mine and my heart drops forty feet.

Seven...eight... Will we ever get past this? Could we work again? It'd be different. I'm different now. I think it'd work. I think we could make it work.

I can see the undoing inside of her starting to happen as her face starts to relax.

Nine...ten... Look at her mouth. Fuck. I love her mouth. It's sort of crazy to me that I've lived without that mouth on mine now for three years.

She can see me watching her mouth and it starts twitching with a smile.

Eleven...twelve... I remember the first time I made her smile. It felt like such a worthwhile pursuit when I was a kid. Still feels like a worthwhile pursuit now.

Even though her smile hasn't fully cracked the surface, it's too late. Her eyes give her away, always have. One look and they'll tell me anything I need to know.

Thirteen…fourteen… She's never needed fifteen seconds of this before, this is new territory. God, I want to kiss her.

And I think she wants to kiss me too. Her eyes flicker from my eyes to my mouth—against the rules, you're not supposed to break eye contact, but I don't want to say it because I want her to kiss me—our heads are so close, centimetres, maybe, barely between us—I can smell her perfume. She smells exactly how she has since forever, she's worn the same perfume since she was fourteen. Gypsy Water. I hope she never changes it. Whenever she gets out of the shower and she puts it on, sometimes I hug her and she fights me because she's strange about it now, like we can sleep in the same bed, she can touch my face when she thinks I'm sleeping, but if I want to hug her when the sun's up and the lights are on, all hell breaks loose, but sometimes I do it anyway, and then the smell gets on me, and I can smell her on me all day how I used to before I fucked it all up.

Fifteen. She had me at one.

She gives me a small smile, and then looks back out the window.

"How's the weather, Parks?" I ask, staring straight ahead.

It's a toasty 21°. Barely a cloud in the sky.

She peeks over at me out of the corner of her eye. "It's quite lovely right now—but I heard it might rain later."

"Oh?" I frown over at her.

She nods, eyes on the road. "Ghastly weather to drive in. You might have to stay."

I lick away a smile. "Safety first."

TWENTY-TWO

Magnolia

BJ stays almost the entire time Tom's in America. Nothing happens—but I guess nothing ever happens. We just stayed at my house, watched National Geographic documentaries. Sometimes in my bed. Sometimes in the home theatre.

Actually, the home theatre poses a few complexities, the largest of all being that I have to come up with new and creative ways every time we go in there about why Beej and I can only sit on the snuggle seat, even though there are several other options. These excuses range from "I think there's a bee on that seat" to "No you mustn't, that was just reupholstered."

I don't need an excuse for him to sit next to me—he'd sit wherever I tell him, I know that. The excuse is for me.

National Geographic is the height of romance for Beej and me—ancient of days relationship lore for us, from the first night we slept together. In the actual way that people sleep together.

It was all incredibly planned, our first time. Which is funny now when I think of it, because now I'm older, spontaneous sex seems much more exciting—not that I've had an awful lot of it over the last three years—but that night, the way he planned it—it all felt so romantic and so serious at the time. I guess it was.

After the Maserati debacle and a disastrous first New Year's Eve in Mykonos (don't ask), everything needed to be perfect, he said. He was adamant about it, the romance of it all, the lead up, everything was going to be perfect. I didn't really mind much how it happened because I just wanted him. I'd never wanted anyone before, really. I'd never really had the want before. But when you get it, you get it, and how couldn't I have gotten it with BJ Ballentine? It was like someone switched a light on in a basement full of hungry bears, that's how I was every time BJ walked into the room. Like someone lit a match in my belly, there was a growing heat always under my skin. I would have sooner, if he let us.

We were just babies, really. Doing grown-up things with hearts the size of Texas and a lust as deep as the Mariana Trench. We were too young, I think. When I think about it now. Bridget says we were, that I transferred my paternal dependency onto him and latched. Hardly my fault though, is it? I didn't send myself to boarding school at the ripe old age of eleven. I didn't ask to have checked-out, ridiculous parents who preferred yachting with Jay Z over weekends at home with me and my sister. What was I supposed to do? Not become disproportionately attached to the world's most perfect boy?

Anyway.

He booked us the Knightsbridge Suite at the Mandarin Oriental.

There were so many times where we almost—almost, nearly but never quite. So many times where it could have just happened organically, but it was so plotted out... so discussed. Paili and I went shopping for it.

It was the first time for both me and BJ, which is strange, don't you think? It was such a big deal to him then but now he sleeps with everyone.

We arranged to meet at the hotel at eight. I skip dinner (thanks Cosmo Girl!)—and I remember walking into the lobby, wearing the sexiest, most uncomfortable underwear imaginable under my white Calvin Klein mini dress, carrying my overnight bag, and he was sitting there on a couch in the lobby, reading *To Kill a Mockingbird* for the billionth time.

Hair pushed back, lips pursed, thumb loosely between his top and bottom teeth, thinking. Focusing. Then he spotted me. First a smile broke out on his face, then I saw him swallow nervously. He reached for my hand, then pulled me into him.

"Hi," he said, into my hair.

"Hi," I said, barely meeting his eyes before I broke out into a blush. My discomfort put him at ease for some reason—a purpose to be braver, and his mouth twitched into a smile as he took my hand, leading me to our room.

He stole a few bottles of Moët from his parents' cellar at home. It's not my favourite flavour profile as far as champagne goes, but it will forever be the specialist drink in the world to me because we had it that night. We got tipsy pretty quickly, I think because we were so nervous.

We got into robes and stood far away from each other for a long time, pretending to be casual about what was happening, which neither of us had acknowledged since we got there.

"I brought Uno," I told him, as I rummaged through my Marc Jacobs duffle bag.

He looked at me for a few seconds and then a smile burst onto his face. "Yeah?" He put his hand out to take the cards from me. "Best of three?" he asked, and as I nodded, our hands touched and there was a spark like when you jump-start a car. Our hands touching jump-started us, and then it was like something came over him, maybe finally the champagne kicked in, and he yanked me in towards him, as confident as ever, one hand on my face, the other on the small of my back, walked me backwards towards the bed, like he was already a professional and lay me down.

I'd never before had lust be met with having. I remember how heavy he was on top of me. I equated that feeling with safety for the longest time. Him lying on me like the best quilt until he lay like that on someone else and changed everything.

He says I talked the whole time. Nervous chatter about breadsticks being a seriously underrated food and how much I fancy the colour lilac, because it brings out my eyes. He still teases me about it. Because apparently I didn't just nervous-talk at the start, I nervous-talked the entire time, even when I came. He says that in lieu of one of those pornstar climaxing moan-gasps, there was the briefest second of silence—a few staggered breaths on my behalf where I steadied myself, one nervous swallow, and then with flushed cheeks and the fullest heart in the world, I said, "It's Brussels Sprout, not Brussel Sprouts, did you know? It's not a plural noun. It's a pronoun. Singular. Until there are multiple. Can you believe it?"

And he held me tight against him, laughing softly as his body trembled inside mine involuntarily.

I remember at one point him peeling his face away from mine, everything sweaty and sticky and breathy, bodies locked and intertwined.

"Wait—are the bees really dying, then?" he said, looking intrigued.

"Yeah, like, really, really alarmingly fast." I nodded, earnestly.

And he pressed his sweaty forehead against mine and laughed in a way where I felt it through my whole body.

Afterwards, we spent the night tangled, googling bees and watching documentaries about them and I think that after, in bed with the bees and him, is one of my favourite memories.

That's where we're constantly trying to revert to, I think. To a place from before we began killing each other for our hearts to stay alive.

And it's mid one of these reveries that Tom England waltzes into my bedroom to find my ex-boyfriend in my bed, shirtless, wearing nothing but the black and camel webbing-trimmed, tapered, silk-velvet and printed satin sweatpants from Gucci and a pair of Anonymous ISM socks.

Tom hovers in the doorway for a few seconds, reading the room, then he takes a few more steps in. It's odd, actually. It all just hangs there, suspended in time. And I don't know what any of it means. What the seconds mean, what they're counting down towards. I can feel the room shift instantly to tense, but I can't quite put my finger on why.

It feels like we're doing something wrong. Maybe BJ thinks we are. But I feel that off Tom too. I'm frozen still, staring at him and out of my peripheral, I can see BJ, mouth gaping, like he's been caught with his hands down his pants or something. He looks terribly unintelligent.

I'm out of my bed like a light, so is Beej.

"Tom!" I throw myself towards him. He catches me somewhat hesitantly.

BJ hustles, shoving his Dezi Bear slippers from Ralph Lauren into his weekend bag—he grabs a Celiné hoodie that he doesn't even put on.

"See ya, Parks." He does his best not to be grinning ear to ear. He walks by Tom, clasps his hands together as though they're full of his shit, and does this weird "thank you" bow. "Later, man," Beej says on his way out the door.

Tom doesn't say a thing, just watches him. He waits a few seconds, just watching me. They feel longer than normal person seconds, and it doesn't feel dissimilar to being sent to the principal's office when you're a kid.

He closes the door. Takes a few breaths, looks at me out of the side of his eyes. "Did you sleep with him?"

"No, well, yes," I concede. "But no."

He isn't overly enthused by my sudden penchant for semantics. His jaw tightens. "Did you have sex with him?"

"No!" I shake my head quickly.

He gives me a look. He doesn't believe me. Why would he? BJ was half-dressed. I'm in pyjamas. Which is about to be my next point:

"Do you think I'd wear these if I were attempting to seduce someone?"

I gesture to my printed Gisele pyjamas, the white ones with the little printed pink hearts from Eberjey.

"No." He fights a hint of a smile. "But I can't imagine you'd have to try that hard to seduce anyone—you could wear a shower curtain and he'd still want to sleep with you."

Is he jealous? He looks jealous. The bridge of Tom England's nose gets rosy when he's jealous, I think. It's quite cute. I purse my lips. "I didn't."

His eyes pinch and he shrugs like he doesn't care. "Listen, it's fine if you did, because this is—you know, we're—"

I don't like to see him flailing. It makes my chest feel tight. "We didn't"—I shake my head as I touch his arm, trying to placate him. "I promise."

He nods once. "Why was he in your bed then?"

I frown at the question. "He's always in my bed,"

"What?" He blinks a few times.

"He sleeps in my bed all the time." I shrug. "But it's just sleeping!"

He blinks more. "He sleeps in your bed all the time but you're not sleeping…together?"

"Right." I nod.

"You sleep in your bed with your ex-boyfriend all the time but you're not sleeping together?" he clarifies.

"Correct." I nod again.

"That is fucked up."

I pull back, affronted. "I beg your pardon?"

He laughs. "That's so… fucking fucked."

"No, it isn't." My cheeks have gone hot, but I'm glad he's laughing. Tom England being sad isn't something I want happening on my watch.

He gives me a look that's equal parts amused and confused. "That's weird," he tells me, shaking his head. "You're weird. That's a weird thing to do—"

"Oh, alright, okay"—I roll my eyes—"like you're so perfect, you're like that, you have that—you're just so— with your…" Fuck. "Your hair's parted weird."

He shoves his hand through it, smile cocked. Very cocky. Very sexy. Tom falls backwards onto my bed, staring up at the ceiling. I lay down, facing him. He looks over at me and goes back to serious.

"I don't want to look stupid," he tells me. "Don't make me look stupid, yeah?"

"We're in a fake relationship to bury my feelings for my ex-boyfriend. We're being stupid."

His cheeks do that thing again. The jealous thing. "Just make sure no one sees you being stupid with him," he tells me. He rolls in towards me, kisses me on the cheek, ruffles my hair, and leaves.

Ruffles my hair!

Like I'm a fucking Labradoodle!

I watch after him—incensed and yet, mildly aroused.

I'm going to suggest that to my mother for the name of her next fragrance.

15:32

BJ

See you tonight?

Yep xx

Are you good?

Yep!

Is the weather not good?

Clear skies, Parks

You promise?

I'll see you and Tom in a bit xx

TWENTY-THREE

BJ

The RHS Chelsea Flower Show Gala is probably the wankiest floricultural event on the planet. The royal family comes to it, celebrities come to it, people like us come to it, it's about £800 a ticket—not a lot in the scheme of things but stings a little because I've paid 800 quid to watch the love of my life flit around this fucking garden with some other fucking man. Taura asked me to go with her but I said no. I'm already in the doghouse with Parks, that'd probably be pushing the boat out a bit far. Plus, it's her favourite social event of the season so I don't want to ruin it for her.

Me going with Tausie shouldn't ruin it for her, because she's not who I cheated on Parks with, even though Magnolia doesn't believe that. Nothing's going on with me and Sax anyway. Hasn't been for a few months now.

She's definitely shagging Jonah, and also, I thought I saw a weird little spark between her and Hen the other day? I don't know.

I arrive late. Parks arrives later. Tom on her arm, who's looking more and more comfortable holding her by the second and I wonder—panic for a second—maybe they've had sex.

Magnolia not having had sex with anyone else is both a relief to me and my own personal nightmare. A relief because something about it makes her still mine. More mine than anyone else's, anyway. And a nightmare because she looks how she looks. In a gown or pyjamas, doesn't matter. She looks the same to me. Eyes that I see every time I close mine.

She's in this dress that looks like it's a watercolour painting, green and pink and fucking lilac—she did that on purpose, and she looks fucking perfect, and I get this weird feeling like maybe she's going to fuck my heart up in that dress tonight or something.

She catches my eye from across the room, holding like our hands can't.

Hello, she mouths.

I give her a small smile and she looks away, her cheeks pinking up a bit. Placates me for a second, that I can still do that to her. Make her body do what I want it to with a look. I stay where I am because I know she'll come to me. Magnets. That's what the boys say about us. Sometimes we're the same pole, sometimes we're opposites, but we move each other. Pushing away, pulling closer. You should have heard Jonah the day he thought of that metaphor, like he'd won a fucking Pulitzer.

She wanders over, makes it look like it's Tom's doing but it's not. No one can work a room like Magnolia Parks. Which is funny and annoying, because I don't think she even knows she does it. I didn't care when we were together that all eyes were always on her because her eyes were always on me. Since we broke up though, it eats me alive watching her in a room, because she doesn't see it. She gets fidgety about me and old ladies and waitresses and random girls at bars, but I'm not oblivious to it, I know it's happening. Parks, on the other hand, doesn't have a fucking clue.

I remember sitting across from her a few months back, we were at this little cafe in this little town somewhere far away on one of those drives we take, and everyone was watching her. All of them, and she was perusing the menu, completely unaware. Didn't even notice 'til she caught the look on my face—somewhere in the vicinity of amused terror (not that I found almost the entire population of Rye all that threatening).

"What?" she blinked.

I threw her a small smile. "They're all watching you."

"Yes, well." She sat up a little taller. "I am wearing a vintage Chanel, fur-trimmed, houndstooth coat from 1977."

"Yeah," I snorted into my beer. "That's what they're staring at."

"Beej," She smiles up at me, tilts her head to the side, bats her eyes a lot.

"Parks," I kiss her cheek as close as I can to her mouth without crossing the line and she rolls her eyes in fake and silent protest.

"Ballentine"—Tom grabs me by the shoulders, grinning. "You look great, man."

He grips my chin in his hand, grinning playfully but it's a power move and it throws me for fucking six because if anyone else did that to me, I'd fight them on the spot, but Tom England? I don't know. I don't know how this stupid, fucking guy who looks like a pirate and a Greek god can make me feel like a million bucks and a five-year-old twat all at once. Dickhead.

"That is a sick suit," he tells me and I can tell he means it. Just to add insult to injury.

Parks looks at me for a second. "Tom Ford. Slim-fit, satin-trimmed, stretch-wool tuxedo jacket."

Tom glances at her, then to me, then back to her. "You buy it for him?"

She plucks a glass of champagne from the tray of a nearby waiter and takes a bored sip. "No."

I do my best to keep my amusement in check.

"It's her thing," I shrug. "Always has been."

Tom looks at her, confused. "You just…. know… what people are wearing?"

She nods once. "Yes."

"What am I wearing?" he asks.

She looks at him for a few seconds. "Fawn slim-fit, grosgrain-trimmed, cotton-velvet tuxedo jacket, with the…" She squints. Spins him on the spot. "—Pleated, cotton-twill chinos from Prada." Points to his shoes. "John Lobb, Prestige Becketts Leather Oxford Shoes."

Tom sniffs a laugh and points to a lady who walks by us who's in a long, black dress covered in glitter with weird shoulders. "Her?"

"Alex Perry, the Houston glittered, velvet gown."

"Her?" He points to a girl in a black dress that's got no sleeves or straps. Gold spots.

"Strapless, ruched polka-dot, sequined, tulle midi dress. Marchessa Notte." She barely looks at that one. "I've got it."

Tom points to a lady on the far side of the room in a weird kimono that's covered in woodland creatures or some shit.

She squints at it. "Lanvin, asymmetric, frayed, printed silk midi dress."

Tom lets out an amused snort. "It's like she's some sort of clothes… Rainman?"

"Speaking of—" She looks between us. "How do we feel about Taura Sax in the floral appliqué midi gown from Marchessa Notte at the Chelsea gala? Bit on the nose, no?"

I look over at her dress. It's nice enough, I suppose. Taura sees the three of us staring at her, waves uncomfortably and I feel a pang of guilt. I give her a nod. She's always tried to be friendly to Parks, but Parks can't see past the part where she's seen me naked. Fair play, I suppose.

"I like it," I shrug.

Parks rolls her eyes. "You would."

"I mean seriously, what's next?" She looks from me to Tom. "Plaid and tartan at Christmas time?"

I give Parks a look. "You wore plaid Christmas Day last year.. wore tartan Christmas Eve…. you called it inspired."

She looks up at me, jaw dropped a bit, eyes pinched. "What are you, some kind of festive season fashion savant? Fuck off."

She grabs Tom's hand, pulling him away.

"Later, man." He tosses me an amused smile and something in it slices me to the bone. Like he gets that she's being annoying as shit. Like he gets her.

She's angry I defended Taura.

Probably shouldn't have done it, probably it wasn't worth it.

I'll pay for it later with Parks, but me and Taurs are friends now. Couldn't leave her in the lurch. Henry spots me, danders over with Taura.

"Were you talking about me?" she asks.

"Oh—what?" I play dumb. "No, Parks was just saying she liked your dress."

"Yeah, right," Hen snorts.

Taura smacks him in the arm. "Are you okay?" she asks me, nodding in Parks' direction.

"Yeah," I scoff. "Why wouldn't I be?"

"Because Parks is probably getting wheelbarrowed later by the sexiest billionaire in the world?"

"Henry!" Taura blinks. I give my brother a look. More hurt than I wish I was, angrier too. I breathe out, annoyed. Walk over to the bar.

If anyone else talked about Parks like that I'd fucking wipe the floor with then, but Henry does it 'cause he loves her and they're like brother and sister. Plus, he likes shitting me, and nothing shits me more than it being shoved down my throat that actually, Parks isn't mine now.

Henry's always been angry at me for it, for what I did. It comes out in weird ways every now and then. Passive-aggressive comments, aggressive-aggressive comments, planting visuals of my worst nightmare in my mind at a garden party, you know—shit like that. I order a whiskey from the bar, down it on the spot, and then order a Negroni. Jonah saddles up next to me.

"Oy." He gives me a cautious look. "You good?" I take another drink. "He's just playing, man—" Jo shakes his head. "Parks couldn't be wheelbarrowed, she's about as limber as a tooth-pick." I give him a look, because I can't tonight. He frowns. "What's up with you?"

I stare over at her on the other side of the room. "Do you think I'm losing her?" Jonah stares at me for a couple of seconds, like he's never even entertained the possibility. And then maybe, the worst thing happens. I think I see it on his face. He wonders if I am too.

Because she's there, with Tom, with his parents—Andrew and Charlotte England, nice people, good people, rich people, people who have a son who hasn't fucked her around for the last three years. And Parks is the kind of girl parents dream about their sons ending up with—she's honey on toast personified, and they're eating her up.

And I'm watching her with him, her hands on his chest, laughing as she tells them something, all eyes on her and that's fine because there's something magnanimous about her that makes you lean in closer, but they're his parents.

Why is she with his parents? She never meets the parents. And every boy she's dated 'til now, if she touched them, she'd touch them watching me; if she hugged them, she'd hug them holding my eyes. But now she's touching his chest, and she's looking up at him, and they're laughing, and I think they're a real couple because she doesn't clock me once.

Then Tom tilts her face up with one finger—he's so fucking cool, I hate him—and he kisses her. I haven't seen them kiss before. It's strange, the feeling it gives me. Nothing at first. Just... nothing...and then it was like someone lobbed my fucking arm off with a machete. Nothing, and then everything. Everything bleeding out everywhere, dying right here on a bed of peonies with the love of my life on the other side of the room with a man who isn't me, who's actually fucking probably finally worthy of her and the bleeding out starts to feel too real. That thing in your brain that sounds an alarm: we're not okay? It's going off. I'm not okay. I feel like I've fallen into a hole. No edge to grab, no end in sight, arse in your stomach, stomach in your throat, heart in the hand of a girl who's holding someone else's—just a kind of forever falling, this fucking suspending always falling, which is sort of what it feels like to be in love with her at this point anyway.

I grab Jo, urgently.

"Do you have any coke?" I say under my breath.

Jonah frowns. "What?"

I don't flinch. "Do you have any?"

"Beej—"He follows my gaze, sees the problem. Looks nervous. "This isn't a good idea—bit reactionary—"

I nod once. "Yep."

"You promised her," he reminds me.

"Yeah." I shrug. "I've broken promises to her before, so—"

"Yeah, but this is the one she'll care about." He shakes his head.

"Jo, look at her—" I stare over at her. Her head's leaning on his arm, they're posing for a photo. "She's happy." And my heart is breaking right there on my face.

Jonah starts guiding me away, "Just, let's get out of here—"

I stand in my tracks. "Do you have any or don't you?"

"Yeah." He gives me a reluctant look. "I do." I nod towards the bathroom. I lead the way, my best friend follows, dragging his feet. I go into a stall. He follows me in. Hands me the baggy with a big sigh and heavy eyes, but it's heavy eyes all round tonight so fuck it. I've not had it in nearly two years, not since I promised her I wouldn't.

I just have one line, it's all I need to take the edge off. Jonah watches me as I do it, eyes me down. He's not on board. Seems hypocritical as shit, what with his gang lordship and all but I guess he's not the one who overdosed...

He plucks my drink from my hand. "You're done with alcohol tonight."

I shrug. "Don't need it."

I shove my hands through my hair, feeling better already and head back out to the party. I spot Vanna Ripley on the other side of the room. Hair pulled back, low-cut dress, eyes like a cat. I like Vanna Ripley. She's insanely hot. A fucking terrible actress, definitely knows it too. Makes her an overachiever in the bedroom though. And she likes me more than I deserve to be liked. I think we're kind of friends now.

I think I'm going to fuck her anyway.

01:05

BJ

I didn't get to say goodbye before I left tonight.

Goodbye

?

Are you okay?

You looked kind of wasted as I was on my way out.

Yea in goodl

Really?

Yrp

Yep

Okay.

Hey parsk hos your boyfirne

What are you doing?

Notging

I'm find

Will you answer your phone?

Im with somweobe

I'm with someone too.

Thatsd not what I menat

I know what you meant.

Whaas did I mean. Then?

Stop it.

Afe you angehy at. E?

Arenyou angry art me

Yes.

But call me when you get
home anyway.

Im not gfoing homw tonight

Perfect.

14.06

Parks

Fuck.

Fuck fuck

I'm sorry

I was shitfaced

Clearly..

I'm sorry.

Who did you go home with?

Do you actually want to know?

Yes

Vanna

Ripley?

Yeah.

Right.

Great.

Parks?

What?

Sorry.

It was just drinks, right?

You last night? It was just alcohol.

A few too many Negronis…

Okay

Feel better 🩶

TWENTY-FOUR

Magnolia

Tom doesn't pick me up for dinner with his family tonight; he said he couldn't make it from his place to mine and there in time and for a second, that prickles as strange, but then I remember firstly, he's not my real boyfriend and secondly, there's every chance in the world I'm being overly sensitive purely on account that BJ slept with a minor celebrity one night last week and I feel a bit sick about it.

That Vanna Ripley isn't as pretty as me but she's a cracking actress and a scoundrel in the bedroom, according to Christian who told me far more than was required or requested.

Anyway, I take a town car to the Mandarin Oriental, which makes me feel a bit like I'm cheating on BJ because this is our hotel, and I think he'd die a bit if he knew I was here with Tom, because I'd die if he took someone else here too. It wasn't my suggestion though. Heston Blumenthal is a friend of Charlotte's and her favourite chef in the world, so hopefully I just don't get photographed here and Beej is none the wiser.

Also, I remind myself, *BJ actually cheated on you.*

While you were home sick with a flu, the love of your life had penetrative intercourse, at a party, at his old house, in a waterless bathtub, with someone else who smelt like musk and orange blossom and... tuberose (I think?) and so, if you feel like going to Dinner by Heston at the hotel where you lost your virginity to him nearly seven years ago, you should be allowed to, because he gave up Mandarin rights when he gave up you.

That's the pep talk I give myself as I walk over to an already-seated table of Englands.

I wear something safe and sure to be parent-friendly—the Miu Miu scalloped-collar, cropped blouse, the logo-plaque, flared skirt from Prada with the v-neck cashmere cardigan from Versace. Adorable, but conservative.

I don't know why I'm nervous. Or why I care about impressing them. And it's not as though I haven't met them before—of course I have, a hundred times since I was a child, but now that I'm not a child, and Tom England is my fake boyfriend with real parents whom, apparently, I am hellbent on delighting with my diamond eyes and meekness.

I actually hadn't even thought about Clara England being there—how terrible of me, of course she'd be. Just because her husband died doesn't mean she's not an England anymore, it's just that I forgot sort of that she was. She's twenty-six, I think. Imagine being twenty-six and a widow.

They got married very young, she and Sam. Straight out of school. Quite strange for people of our station; there was a lot of speculation that she was pregnant. I don't think she was though. They didn't have any kids.

Tom stands as I approach the table.

Tan, suede bomber jacket from Gucci, paired with the Steady Eddie II slim-fit, tapered, organic, stretch-denim jeans from Nudie, paired with the black leather Converse Chuck Taylor All Star 70s. He looks handsome, and I wonder when that'll wear off—that schoolgirl heart-puddle feeling I get whenever he looks me in the eye. It happened when I was seven and he was fifteen and he handed me a napkin at Windsor Castle for a party, and it happened just now when he did nothing but blink at me.

He steps out from his chair, walks over to me and takes my face in one of his hands and kisses me a bit deeper than I wish he did in front of his parents because I want them to like me and take me seriously, even though technically I'm not taking their son seriously, but impressions are everything! He takes my hand, leading me over to the table.

Polite, British cheek kisses from both his parents, but a warm hug from Clara that I don't feel I deserve. "It's so lovely you could join us." She smiles at me.

"We're just delighted about you and Tom, Magnolia," Charlotte tells me.

"Yes," Andrew nods. "It's wonderful. We haven't seen him this happy in a while."

"Though—can I ask—" Clara cuts in, looking at Tom for a couple of seconds before looking at me—"and I'm so sorry if this is inappropriate"—she glances quickly at Tom—"I thought you were still dating BJ Ballentine."

"Ah." I shake my head once, let out an uncomfortable laugh. "No—it's not an uncommon mistake though, we're still quite close."

Tom puts his arm around me, and for a second it feels like a shield, like he's protecting me from the curious eyes of his family, and their eyes are curious—most people are when it comes to BJ and me, with our love that's like a sideshow—but then I catch Tom's face, jaw set, brows low, not tender nor protective, and I wonder if perhaps I'm shielding him from something I don't know about.

"And tell me," Clara asks with a smile, but she's smiling at Tom, not at me, even though the questions for me. "How did you and Tom meet?"

Tom gives her a look. "We've known each other for years."

Clara concedes with a head tilt and rescinds her question. "Sure, no, I just didn't realise you'd been spending any time together."

Andrew nods. "Nor did we actually, but a welcome discovery nonetheless."

I give him a grateful smile, prattle on about that night, leave out the part about BJ and the lap dance, interchange club for a restaurant, make it a bit more parentally appealing.

Tom hasn't taken his arm from around me. Nor has he looked at me once. "And you're the leisure editor for *Tatler*?" Andrew nods, answering his own question.

"I am."

"How did you get that job?"

"Well, I'm very experienced in leisure and also"—I give him a playful smile—"a dash of flagrant nepotism."

He chuckles heartily. "Are you going to say Albert Read is your godfather?"

"Just my mother's good friend." I smile at him like he's silly. "Elton John's my godfather."

That gets my fake-boyfriend's attention. Finally. "Shut up—really?"

"Thomas." His mother blinks.

"Elton John?" His jaw drops.

"Mmhm." I nod.

"The Elton John," Clara clarifies.

"No, the other one." I roll my eyes sarcastically. "Yes, him."

Tom scoffs a laugh. "How. Why?"

"Well, it was 1997 and my father was working with George Martin at the time, kind of his protégé. And he was mixing for the re-release of 'Candle in the Wind', and my mother became pregnant with me, and Elton was around a lot, and it just happened."

"Is he a very hands-on godfather?" Clara asks, leaning across the table, riveted.

"Yes, quite! Yeah." I nod. "He's come to all my birthday parties. He's outrageously flirtatious with the Ballentine boys—"

"—Can't really blame him," Clara interjects. "What's the best present he's ever given you?" she asks, chin in hand.

"For my eighteenth birthday, he bought me a 12th century chateau in Aquitaine. Actually"—I reconsider—"for my twenty-first, he bought me a ten-carat diamond necklace I quite like."

"Ooh. I'd love to see it some time," Charlotte says, smiling at me.

Before our food comes and I excuse myself to the ladies' room, Clara comes along. I don't know why girls go to the loo together, I'd rather go alone. Do you not think it's harder to pee if someone's listening?

When I come out of the cubicle, I think she's waiting for me at the sink, primping herself in the mirror. I wash my hands, dry them slowly. Uncomfortably.

It's not like I'm going to powder my nose—I follow a fifteen-step skincare routine, my face is practically pore-less. Still, I play along with the charade. Dab on some lip colour as though my lips aren't this colour by themselves anyway.

Clara looks at me in the mirror for a few seconds, heavy in thought.

"—I'm sorry if that was overstepping before," she says.

"About BJ?" I clarify. She nods and I shrug.

"It's fine." The truth is, it is. I'm always happy to have an excuse to talk about him.

"You were together for how long?"

I don't mean to do it, but I sigh. "We started dating when I was fourteen." A sad smile whispers across her face. "I'm twenty-two now," I tell her before she asks.

"That's a long time."

"But we're obviously not still together."

"Right." She nods once. "When did you break up?"

"Three years ago,"

She keeps nodding. "How come?"

I purse my lips, curiously. "You don't read the papers?" She shakes her head. That makes me like her more. The click of my Hourglass Confession, Ultra Slim, High Intensity lipstick lid echoes through the bathroom. "He cheated on me."

"Oh, shit." She sighs. "Sorry—" She shakes her head, looking away.

She looks upset.

Are her eyes welling up?

"Are you okay?" I ask, watching her cautiously.

She sniffs a laugh. "I don't mean to be nosey—you two have just always kind of reminded me of me and Sam."

Something about that endears her to me. "Really?"

She nods. "Just so young when you fell in love, all tangled up in each other." It's all over her face how much she misses him, and then she looks me in the eye, quite serious. "There are worse things you know, than cheating—"

I hold her gaze. "Like dying?"

She nods again. "Like dying."

She presses her hands into her temple. "Listen to me, shelling out unsolicited relationship advice to Sam's brother's poor cornered girlfriend in a bathroom." She shakes her head at herself. "I've lost the plot."

"No." I shake my head but it's just me trying to shake the thought of BJ dying from my mind again.

I don't know what I'd do. I don't know what the world would be like without him in it.

My heart breaks for this girl; if Sam England was her BJ, and now he's gone in a way where there's no far away hope that maybe you'll be okay again and you'll work it out one day when he stops fucking everything and you can stomach the idea of trusting him again, then she must be a shell of a person and the bones of her heart must be entirely broken.

We join them back at the table, and once seated, Tom kisses me again, and once again, it's more than necessary.

And it's only when he pulls away and I see Clara watching his mouth on mine, and inside her eyes, I watch a peculiar jealousy bloom that I don't think even she understands because I can assure you, I do not. I glance from Tom to Clara, and there's something. Some sort of weightiness. And maybe if I had eyes that could see invisible things I'd find a heavy chain from him to her that binds them—but my eyes can't see that.

They can see, however, Tom's eyes—who find mine finally. And he looks, well, he doesn't look like a deer in headlights as much as a lamb caught in the thickets. And I don't know what it is but I know I'm not an idiot, and I know that I just caught something between them. I try to catch his eyes, give him a chance to talk my mind down. I don't know why it's up, if I'm honest, but I feel funny suddenly. On edge? Kind of exposed.

And then our food arrives.

After the bill is paid, the senior Englands are standing, ready to leave.

"Shall I run you back to Holland Park?" Tom asks me. I nod, smiling at him, relieved to have a minute alone.

"Oh," sighs Clara. "I was hoping I could grab a lift?"

"Oh," Tom says. And then there's a strange pause. I look at him, waiting for more words to come. His eyes hold mine, and then it occurs to me: he's waiting for me to excuse him from driving me home. I don't offer him one. "I could drop you both home," he says. "Holland Park's not too far and then I can just run you to Rosie's." She nods, smiling a small smile, placated.

My eyes pinch. "No, actually. I'm fine. I have a car here. I forgot."

"You do?" Tom asks, maybe a bit too eagerly.

"You couldn't pick me up either, remember?"

His eyes drop from mine, guiltily.

I look at his parents. "Thank you for dinner, it was lovely."

I turn to Clara and give her a subtle look. "Worse things." Her face falls. Tom leans in to kiss me but I dodge it, offering him my cheek instead.

"I'll call you," he tells me.

I look back at him over my shoulder. "Mmhm."

Why that made me sad, I don't know. It did though— teary even, in the car on the way home.

I head straight to my room, avoiding all my family but especially my sister and especially Marsaili, because I don't much feel like explaining my feelings which I can't even really explain to myself. I shower, then pull out a jumper from BJ's drawer—the Ralph Lauren teddy bear print hoodie. It's baggy on him, swimming on me. It smells like him and it feels like him, and I just want to feel close to him because I don't understand what happened before, and I hate not understanding things, but I can almost always understand BJ.

And then my phone rings. It's Tom. I don't answer it. It rings again.

23:53

Tom England

Pick up.

No.

I'm outside.

I look out my window, and he's on the street. By his car, looking up at me, his phone to his ear, waving his hand, beckoning me down.

I mouth go away, but he just waves more and keeps phoning me.

I roll my eyes, make my way downstairs.

Gucci socks, slides and the sweater, that's all I'm in—I've never looked so unkept in my whole life. I close the front door ultra-quietly because I'm convinced my sister is listening close by and I suspect she already suspects Tom and I are a variant of pretending but I don't want her to know for sure.

He tugs on the sleeve of the Mastermind sweater and his eyes fall down me. "This yours?"

I give him a pinched look. "No."

He sniffs a laugh. "He upstairs, then?"

"No." I frown indignantly. "Am I not allowed to wear it?"

Now he frowns. "Course you are, it's just—"

"Don't make me look stupid," I interject. "That's what you said to me last week—don't make you look stupid—and then you took me to dinner with you family whilst leaving out a piece of incredibly crucial information."

"What's that?" He sounds defiant, but he swallows, nervous.

"You need a foxhole too." He avoids my eyes. "She's your brother's wife—"

"It's complicated—"

"—Yeah, no shit," I cut in. "I'm not playing mind games with a grieving widow."

His jaw goes tight and he shakes his head. "You're not—we're not."

"Then what are we doing?" I look up at him, eyes wide and impatient. He takes a shallow breath that makes his barrel chest heave a bit. Blows that breath out of his mouth like there's a candle I can't see. He looks white as a ghost.

"I'm in love with her."

"Tom!" I yell a bit and I'm sure the whites around my eyes are showing. "Does she know?"

His face pulls in a weird way. "We kissed."

My face goes slack. "Tom!"

I can't believe it. I'm staring at him like he's told me he's got a slave labour camp in his basement. I'm blinking a lot.

"Not tonight," he clarifies with a frown, and I must admit—I'm a bit relieved. Why am I relieved? "It was a week before we"—he trails—"you know. Happened, I guess?" He shakes his head. "I needed to shake it off."

God, I could use a martini. I blow air out of my mouth and look at him with pinched eyes. "Was it just a kiss?"

Something in his face shifts. It's the first time I've ever seen him look a bit afraid. "I need it to be."

I nod once, processing. I cross my arms over my chest and sit on the front step. "How did it happen?"

He sighs. "It's complicated."

I glare over at him. "So uncomplicate it for me."

His eyes plead. "I can't. Do you trust me?"

"No," I shrug. "Not particularly." This is a lie. I know it as soon as I say it. Tom England is trustworthy, and I do trust him. Quite a lot, actually. But I want to hurt him for some reason.

And I do, I can see it breeze over his face.

"Okay." He says this, nodding a few times, not holding my eyes anymore. I press my hands into my eyes and sigh. "Do you want to stop"—he pauses—"this?"

I keep my hands on my face as I answer. "No."

"No?" He sounds surprised.

I peer at him. "No."

"Why 'no'?" The real answer is because I didn't like how his face went just before. I don't like seeing Tom look a bit scared—it makes the little guards in my heart stand to attention.

But instead I say, "Because I still need a foxhole."

"Right." He nods once. "But—we're okay?" He looks for my eyes as he asks this, with earnest concern. I roll my eyes.

"I guess," I say, glancing away being extra petulant, just because I like to have men at my service.

He sits down on the step next to me. "I'll buy you a pair of shoes tomorrow?"

I eye him. "You'll buy me three."

Tom cocks a smile. "Okay."

"Okay." I nod, looking out onto the street.

He follows my gaze, stays there for a minute.

It's nice, the air between us. And I feel safe next to him here, which strikes me as peculiar because I've really only felt safe around one person before. And as I begin to peel back the layers of that, and what that might mean, Tom leans back against the step and looks up. Under the inky black of tonight's sky, his pushed-back blonde hair looks much darker than it really is but somehow his eyes look lighter. Bluer and clearer. Maybe a bit like a weight's lifted.

He looks over at me for a few seconds.

"Were you jealous?" he asks. "When you found out I kissed her?"

I feel embarrassed that he could tell and I'm grateful it's dark out so the colour in my cheeks can't be seen.

"Yes," I tell the stars. "But you mustn't read into that—I'm quite possessive and renowned for being a terrible sharer."

He sniffs a laugh. "Good to know."

TWENTY-FIVE

BJ

Parks took Vanna better than I thought she would.

Don't know whether that's a good sign or a bad one, but I was happy that she asked me to come up with her to suss out a new hotel for the leisure edit.

Somewhere new I've never heard of—Farnham House? Off St Ives Bay, I think. She just turned up on my doorstep. It's why I don't have girls stay over after. She has a key, but she never uses it. I think she's scared to in case something's happening on the other side of the door that she doesn't want to see. Fair enough. Probably safer for her to knock anyway.

I pulled open the door and I know that face like the back of my hand; she's nervous about something. I don't know what, don't know why. But I was glad that she came to me.

"Oy," I grinned down at her as I stepped out of the doorway to let her in.

"Are you free?" she asked. "For the next few days?"

The answer: No, actually. I had a shoot that afternoon and was supposed to take an American model out on a date tomorrow, but that face in front of me and I'm as free as a fucking bird. I nodded. "I can be."

"Do you feel like taking me to Cornwall?" she offered. "For work."

I tilted my head, curious. "You don't want Tom to take you?"

"No." She shook her head a tiny bit. "I don't." Our eyes caught and I felt like she was reaching out for me, like she thought I was far away, but I wasn't. That pulled at a weird thread in my head actually, because her being like that, her feeling a distance between us that wasn't coming from me, meant it was coming from her.

"Me drive or you drive?"

"I took the Mullsane," she told me, "but you drive it. I like it better when you drive."

I pulled her inside my apartment.

"Give me five, I'll pack a bag."

She lets me drive and I love driving down the M3 with her. I've driven her down this motorway a billion times and it always feels like we're driving back to what we used to be.

Her family has a place up in Dartmouth that's a thing for us. We go there sometimes. Not often. Sometimes though.

These roads remind me of her, of that night, of everything that happened. I sigh louder than I mean to, trying to breathe out the memory. She looks over at me and I know she knows. She picks up my phone from my lap and changes the song to "I'll Be Seeing You" and looks out the window. She knows. She always knows me, and I always know her, and it's probably unhealthy and it's probably fucked up because it's not just that I can't move past her, it's that even if I could figure out how to do it—I wouldn't anyway.

Because her eyes right now, all raw and weighed down the same way mine are, they anchor us to the seabed of whatever the fuck we are and were and will be. And I wonder what love is like for other people… Is love for everyone wordless exchanges and a million memories that fuck you up to the bone?

She perks up a bit by the time we're driving through Plymouth. From there it's about an hour and a half's drive to Toms Holidays and I'm just happy to have the time with her.

No one else, no prying eyes, no weird eavesdropping, no boyfriends—just me and her and grazing hands and wandering eyes recalibrating us back into the good old days.

"I'm an ideas gal," she tells me.

I give her a look. "Are you though?"

She frowns, indignant. "Obviously."

"Alright then, hit us with your best shot—"

She turns in towards me, her brown legs tucked up under her, clears her throat. Dramatic pause. "Titanic: The Waterpark"

I shake my head. "Absolutely never."

"What?" She frowns, miffed as anything. "Why?"

I peer over at her out of the corner of my eye, and shrug as though I'm making a light suggestion. "It's maybe a bit insensitive?"

"To whom?" She blinks. "James Cameron? Don't worry about that, he's a friend—"

"No—"

"Okay, fine," she concedes. "We were seated next to one another at a state banquet 'til he asked to move, but I don't think that was about me I think it was because he was right under an air duct. Imagine seating James

Cameron under a fucking air duct. Someone lost their job that night!"

I'm doing my best to rein it in, not to laugh. She doesn't like it when I laugh at her. It's a skill that's taken years to hone and has probably shaved days off the span of my life. I leave it a few seconds before I carefully ask, "Did you tell him about your water park idea?"

She's frowning again. "Yes?"

My mouth twitches. "He moved because of you."

Parks pauses, thinking on this. "Do you think he's going to steal my idea?"

"I really don't." I shake my head.

Her eyes go to slits. "Are you sure?" I nod once. "Why?"

I let out a laugh that sounds like a sigh and it doesn't match up with how happy I am to just be shooting the shit with her. "Because it'd be like someone making an Apollo 11-themed space ride. Or an Amelia Earhart aviation ride."

She stares at me for a long few seconds and I think she finally gets it. "Shit! Beej, that's brilliant! Inspired! A disaster theme park! We'll be rich!"

I'm laughing now. "We are rich."

"….er," she offers.

We pull into the grounds of Farnham House.

The building looks a bit like a French chateau. Old stones, maybe sandstone? Slate roof, massive windows.

"It's nice." I look over at her as I toss the valet the keys with a wink. Then I nod at a car. Looks familiar. "That looks like your dad's car."

She looks over at the black Quattroporte GTS GranSport.

"HP1977?" She looks at me, confused. "That is his car."

I frown a bit.

"Do you know what? A couple of months back he asked for a hotel recommendation that was quiet for an upcoming work trip. I think it was with Post Malone."

"Your dad's inside with Post Malone?" I blink, then I nod towards the door. "Let's go find them."

I want to pause here for a second and say this: Parks and I had very different childhood experiences.

My mum is the best mum: five kids, not Catholic.

Five kids because she loves kids—the fucking weirdo. She cried when she sent us to boarding school, but it was just really what families like ours do. And Dad, we have a bit more of a complicated relationship because I think he thinks I'm disappointing—wasting my life away, and probably he's right—I don't know—but I've never thought he didn't love me. Parks though, her and Bridget's childhood was completely dotted by these weird occurrences where they were made to feel like they were the impositions.

Like her parents had them because they felt like they were meant to have them, not because they wanted them. And I don't think that they don't love them. They do. I've seen her mum fight for her once—just once—but it was once that mattered. And her dad—when Parks and I first started sleeping together, my dad was furious, drove to her house, stormed in, I hid under her bed, Marsaili covered for us, lied—said I'd gone to Jonah's—Parks' dad didn't say anything to her, but he did pull me aside later that night. "I'd kill you if I had to," he told me.

But they're hands off. She could have been dealing cocaine for all they knew. Both of them were off with the fairies. Did a lot of shit like forgot birthdays, would go away for Christmas without the girls, would piss off for a few weeks at a time, wouldn't answer their phones—all that shit-parent shit. You could ask Parks and she'd tell you for sure that the only reason she's a vaguely functional person (and depending on the day I think we can all agree that there are varying degrees to her functionality) is because of Marsaili.

So, we walk into the lobby and over to the front desk—Parks does the talking, and I fight the urge to shove the check-in chav who's behind the desk because he's looking at her like I'm not fucking standing right here, but she doesn't notice. She never notices. I hover behind her closer than I would if we were in London. She doesn't move away from me—she never does when people can't see us.

It's why we love quiet English towns. No one gives a shit about who we are, and I can touch her on the waist without a photo ending up in *The Sun*, and I can rest my chin on top of her head while the fuckwit behind the check-in desk avoids my eyes for flirting with my girl.

"We have a suite with two double beds, or one with a king. Which is your preference?"

I pinch my eyes at Check-In. "What do you think, mate?"

His mouth pulls tight and he starts typing.

They're still sorting out the rooms, says they'll be probably another hour—pretty sure it's some sort of power move Check-In's pulling, trying to delay us from having all the sex we won't be having anyway.

We go to the bar while we wait.

I've got both my hands on her shoulders and I'm walking her through the door frame, and she's laughing and smiling and then she stops dead in her tracks.

I follow her gaze over to the far back corner of the bar.

Her dad…and Marsaili?

She frowns. "That's strange."

And it doesn't compute to her, because it wouldn't, because Parks isn't like that, she's not wired to think about the underbellies of emotion and because she's put Marsaili up on a pedestal all her life as the only adult who hasn't disappointed her, and I get this feeling like I need to get her the fuck out of here, like I need to keep her from seeing what she's about to see—

"Come on—" I grab her hand, pulling her backwards. "We should check on the room."

"No." She snatches her hand back. "What are they doing here?"

And as soon as she asks that, she gets her answer as they lean across the table and kiss in that fucking gross tender way old people kiss.

Her jaw hits the floor.

"Parks"—I grab her wrist—"come on."

She turns to look at me, and her eyes are wide with surprise and something else—something I can't pick. A bit like hurt but worse.

I squeeze her hand. "I think we should just go."

"Absolutely not." She shakes her head, spins on her heel and marches right on over.

"Well!" Parks claps her hands together. "What do we have here?"

"Shit," says her dad, standing reluctantly.

"Magnolia!" Marsaili jumps up, the colour draining from her face.

Parks looks between the two of them for a few seconds. "I mean—wow."

"Darling—" Harley starts.

She holds up a hand to silence him. "I mean, really—wow."

"Magnolia," Marsaili starts, glancing from her to me, like I might toss her a line. "I can explain—"

"Can you?" Magnolia blinks, pleasantly. "By all means, have at it."

Harley shakes his head, stepping forward. "Darling, listen—"

She looks at him, gesturing. "You, doing this—fine. Whatever. You've been fucking girls from rap videos for years." He pulls his head back, indignant. He's a big enough guy her dad, six feet, two inches, probably. Maybe a half an inch or so shorter than me. But rock solid. Gladiator status. I've seen him train with Dwayne Johnson and keep up. She—Parks, is like five feet, eight inches, Bambi legs, big mouth and fighting eyes and she is incapable of backing down from a conflict with this man.

I've always wondered if I'd have to fight him one day. I wonder if today will be the day.

"Excuse me?" he growls at her.

"Do you think I didn't know what you were doing with that girl you were with at Britannia Row when I walked into the sound booth? I was thirteen." She shakes her head. "I expect this shit from you, Harley, but you?" She eyes Marsaili. And I low-key love that my Parks has turned into a little dragon. "On your high horse, looking down at the rest of us—spouting all self-righteous about him"—she thumbs in my direction—"and his misgivings, and how unforgivable his behaviour is, and all the while you're screwing my married father?"

Marsaili's face falls. I press my lips together.

"Magnolia—" Harley steps between them. "That's enough."

"How long for?" Parks asks, ignoring him.

Her dad glares at her a bit and I clench my fists.

"Six years," Marsaili says, quickly.

At that, even my jaw goes lax.

"Six years," Magnolia repeats slowly.

Something about the air between them shifts.... Shifts from shock and maybe a bit of betrayal to—I don't know... I'm watching Parks' eyes and I know all their colours and tells and my best bet here is... they're sporting some kind of grief?

Parks looks too pained for the feeling to just be anger.

Mars and Parks stare at each other and there's this exchange happening between their eyes, Mars' are pleading and Parks' are just gutted, and they don't look away, they're locked on. And I wish I could tune into whatever they're saying because I feel like it's maybe about me?

Magnolia points a weak finger at the woman who's loved her all her life, says nothing for a heavy few seconds.

"Don't you ever speak to me again," she tells her.

And then she grabs my hand and pulls me back to the car.

TWENTY-SIX

BJ

We get in the car and go. Just drive for a while in silence. Her chest is heaving. I'm watching her close for tears. They'll come, now or later, I can't tell yet with my focus split between her and the road, but she will cry, and I'll make it better.

"Where do you want me to take you, Parks?" She looks over at me, a little dazed. Shrugs. "We're not far from St Ives?" She nods. Looks back out the window.

Carbis Bay and Spa Hotel is where we land. I get us the best room I can last minute, then lead her up to it. How many times since we've broken up have I thought about taking Parks hand in mine and leading her up into a hotel room? I don't know. A million over easy.

But her face is crushed. All of her is, sort of. I think she just watched her hero fall into a fiery inferno.

For as long as I've known her, Parks has had Mars on a pedestal. Never used to bother me because when we were younger she loved me like I was hers too, but after what happened—which is strange now, to think in context of all this—maybe it was too close to home? Like a mirror being held up or something.

Seven years.

The affair must have started when Parks was fifteen or sixteen and it's a weird thought to land because Marsaili was the best. On weekends home from school when we'd come home drunk from parties she'd pick us up and bring us in McDonald's and she and my mum had a deal they thought we didn't know about, but it was a no questions asked policy if it meant we came home safe. It meant we always called one of them. Almost always anyway.

She used to chase me out of Parks' bed with a wooden spoon—give gnarly smacks, those things—there's a lot of shit Parks and I did looking back now that we're adults, that we can't believe we got away with when we were kids. Magnolia's parents didn't really give a shit. Her mum took her to the doctor to put her on birth control about a month after we got together. I don't know it for sure, but I don't think Parks was a planned pregnancy. That's what I've picked up on over the years. Trickled out over time and bad conversations that shouldn't have happened in front of us but did anyway because they were sort of emotionally negligent like that.

I wonder if her mum knows. I wonder what'll happen to Bushka.

I sit Magnolia down on the bed, pull over a chair to sit across from her.

"What do you need, Parks? Whatever the fuck you need." Then she reaches out and touches my hands. She looks strange in her face—a bit conflicted? Sad.

"I'm so sorry," she tells me and her voice cracks a bit.

My heart falls off a ledge and I don't know for what. "Why?"

"Nothing." And then she shakes her head. "Beej?" I look over at her. "You know that night you overdosed? You didn't do that on purpose, did you?"

"What?" I pull back. "No. Why would you—? No."

214

She nods. Looks very breakable. "Was it about me?"

I sigh as I stare up at the ceiling. Big breaths. "Parks, there's not much about me that isn't about you." I look over at her for a second, then eyes back on the roof. "But I wasn't trying to kill myself, if that's what you're asking."

"Okay." She nods.

Then she presses her hands into her eyes, shakes her head again and stands up.

"I need a shower."

She gets up and starts walking there, then pauses without looking back.

"Are you coming?"

I stand up wordlessly, follow her in. Don't read into it. She's done this forever. She doesn't like being in bathrooms by herself. Doesn't like to be alone with her thoughts. Her brain gets loud in the shower. I sit on the edge of the bathtub, stare at my hands—do my best not to peek out of the corner of my eyes and watch her get undressed.

But I do peek and she's watching me watch her. Our eyes catch, and she looks at me, maybe even like she wants me, then she swallows heavy and slips into the shower.

My knuckles are white as they grip my knees to steady myself—rein in how much I love her and all the things I wish I could do about it.

The shower runs and I wait a minute. "You're taking this pretty badly," I tell her.

"And how should I be taking it, then?" she calls back.

I stand up and move closer to the shower. "I don't know."

"Right." She sounds justified.

"What are you avoiding thinking about in there?"

"Hmm?" she mumbles, but I can tell she heard me.

It's steamy now in the bathroom. The windows are foggy. I lean with my back up against them.

"What's wrong, Parks?" I fold my arms over my chest. She's standing under the water; it's running over her how I wish my hands were. She sighs. "She told me something once."

"And what happened?"

She looks over at me, eyes all round and teary. "I listened."

TWENTY-SEVEN

Magnolia

"Where's Beej?" Bridget asks, leaning against my door frame before she walks in, sitting on my bed and it takes all my self-control not to scream with delight that she's wearing one of the outfits I laid out for her. Striped, mohair cardigan with the stripe-detail track pants (both from Marni), paired with the logo-printed flipflops from Isabela Marant. Every night I lay out outfit options for her for the next day—bit of a thankless job but some-one has to do it otherwise I'd have a sister who wears Birkenstocks that aren't the Proenza Schouler special editions.

"Where's Beej?" she asks as I toss another bikini into my Chelsea Garden Globe Trotter suitcase.

"Angler." I glance up at her. "It's his parents' anniver-sary dinner."

"You didn't go?" She frowns.

I give her a look. "It's a bit on the nose at the minute, don't you think? Besides," I shrug, "Lil would have just spent the entire night fretting. I'd have ruined it for them."

Lily Ballentine has just officially been elevated to #1 adult in my life as of the last day.

I wrote that on a card, as well as "Sorry, Hamish. You're #2," and sent it with BJ to the dinner I should be at with them all—the dinner he tried to make me go to, the dinner he also tried to stay home from—because "Whatever the fuck you need, Parks." That's what he said to me. That's what he always says to me.

"I think it's a good idea," she tells me.

I glance over my shoulder. "What?"

"This"—she nods at the bag I'm packing—"you, going away." I turn back around. "Where are you going?"

"Monemvasia."

"With?" she asks, open-ended.

I look back at her and I don't feel like answering because she knows who with, so I pinch my eyes instead. "Did you know?"

She takes a measured breath. "I'd suspected—"

"And you didn't tell me!" I blink, horrified.

"No, I know." She sighs. "I just had this strange feeling you wouldn't take it particularly well."

I give her a look as I fold the same cropped, rose-print blouse from Miu Miu that I folded just a moment ago because I'm not really pay attention. "Do you think Mum knows?"

"I think Mum's been dating a hot French guy for the last year in anticipation of what I assume is a pending divorce."

"What the fuck!" I growl. "Since when did we all become so casual about infidelity?"

Her face softens. "We're not, Magnolia—it's just—it's different. I don't think they ever really loved each other."

"Then why did they marry?" I ask, eyebrows up. Her mouth purses a little and she carefully points at me. I roll my eyes because that can't be true. Elton would have told me.

There's a knock on my door, and I don't turn to see who it is because I can tell by the way the knock sounds.

Two light taps in quick succession only using the knuckle of her index finger, and she never waits for permission to enter.

"Can I have a word with you for a minute, Magnolia?" Marsaili asks.

I look over at her and look at her blankly. "No."

She's wearing the tie-neck, polka-dot, silk-crepe midi dress from Valentino and she never used to wear Valentino dresses before; she didn't care about Valentino dresses before, so why does she now?

"Magnolia, look—"

"I told you never to speak to me again," I cut in.

Her face flickers a bit amused and I hate her for it. "Did you think I was going to listen to that ridiculous demand?" I roll my eyes at her insolence.

No wonder she's gotten so big for her boots lately, what with her doing my father and all.

"Listen, Magnolia," she starts again, walking towards me. The clip-clop of her sensible black Gilda 60, suede pumps from Gianvito Rossi makes me extra angry. "This is seeming less and less about your father and I, and, somehow—increasingly about you."

"Somehow?" I repeat, blinking a lot. "Somehow?"

She takes a steadying breath, bracing herself I think, which is wise of her because I feel like the water just drew back from the shore of my reason, the way it does right because a tsunami hits.

"You knew"—I point at her—"when I was twenty, that BJ and I were going to be together again, you knew that's what I wanted, more than anything, and you—knowing that, told me that he was a cheater and he was bad and he couldn't be trusted again and—"

She shakes her head, rejecting it. "Don't you hold me

responsible for decisions you made on your own after getting some advice—"

"On my own?" I blink. "Advice?" I let out a small breath in disbelief. "Hypocritical, bullshit, manipulative advice from the person I trusted most in the world, who told me that the boy I love would only ever hurt me, that that's all he was capable of because he cheated on me one time and all the while, you're having an affair with my father—"

"Magnolia—"

"He nearly died," I say quietly and I don't mean to say it, it slips out because I think it's her fault. Even though she doesn't know what happened, it's her fault. She and her shitty advice that made me feel like I could never be with him and I shouldn't want to be with him either and so I started dating Reid all of a sudden, completely all of a sudden—and BJ was so blindsided and so fucked up over it he—well, you know what happened... she doesn't, but you do.

Marsaili's face falters. "What?"

"I hate you," I whisper.

"Magnolia—"

"Get out."

I point to the doorway that Tom's standing in. He knocks, apprehensively, watching me carefully. Marsaili is tearful as she bustles away. Tom steps to the side, letting Marsali pass, then flicks his eyes over at me.

"I just heard the news."

"The news?" Bridget repeats. "It's out, then?"

Tom walks towards me. "Are you okay?"

His face is super serious, and I wish Bridget wasn't here, because it's probably a dead giveaway that he's not hugging me or kissing me but is instead being super British with his arms folded over his chest.

"I guess," I shrug.

"When did you find out?"

"Yesterday," I tell him.

"You didn't call," he tells me and I wonder if he sounds a bit surprised.

I glance over tentatively at Bridget, hoping she'll leave but she doesn't.

I purse my lips. "I was with BJ."

He nods once. "Of course you were."

That strikes me as a weird response considering where we last left things, him being in love with his dead brother's wife and what-not.

He nods at the half-filled suitcase on my bed. "Going somewhere?"

"Um." I nod. "I'm thinking I might get out of here for a while. Wait for the press to die down a bit? Blow over—"

He nods. "Am I invited this time?"

I'm thrown for a second. "Of course?"

Tom glances at Bridge, then back at me. "Is BJ coming?"

Bridget looks from Tom to me, like she's watching a tennis match.

"I mean—" I tuck some hair behind my ears. "It was his idea."

Tom's face goes funny, somewhere between amused and annoyed.

"Of course it was."

I toss the colour-block, stretch-lurex bikini by Oséree into my case, as I eye him. "You don't have to come if you don't want to."

His face flickers again. "Would you rather I didn't?"

"No," I say quicker than I plan.

"…No, you don't want me to come?" he clarifies.

"No." I shake my head. "I do."

Bridget looks between the two of us, head tilted to the side, kind of fascinated. "Wow."

I glance at her, roll my eyes.

"I'll bring Gus." Tom tells me. "We'll take our plane. I'll fly us."

And just as I'm about to meditate on the wonders of having a fake boyfriend who's a pilot, something happens and it happens quite quickly—there's some sort of loud sound—a crashing of sorts—I hear Harley Parks growl my name like he's never growled it before and then my father tears into my room, pushes past Tom—his eyes are wild, he's got one phone to his ear, another in his hand that he's pointing at me, menacingly—

"Did you leak it?" he roars, standing over me. "Was it you?" I blink up at him, my face unflinching, but a little bit scared on the inside because I've never seen him like this. "Was it fucking you?" he yells louder. I don't like how he says the word "fucking". It's horribly angry.

"I don't know what you're talking about," I tell him calmly.

His nostrils flare and he shakes his head. "Yes, you fucking do."

I straighten out the skirt of my crystal-embellished, polka-dot, silk-jacquard mini dress from Miu Miu and I give my father a tight smile. "I'm quite sure I don't know what you mean."

"It's all over the news," he growls.

"Your infidelity, you mean?" I clarify, sweetly. He doesn't respond but his teeth are clenched. "Oh dear." I shrug delicately.

My father edges closer towards me, jaw tight, fist clenched. "I swear to god, Magnolia, if you leaked it, I'll—"

"You'll what?" says Tom, stepping between us and shoving my father back a bit. My father is quite a large man to be honest, but Tom is bigger. His eyes are fierce, his jaw is set, and his face isn't one to be trifled with. "Finish the sentence," Tom dares him, glaring down at him.

I don't know what the end of that sentence would have been. My father's never threatened me before, he's never been angry like this before, he's never looked before like he wanted to hit me, much less kill me, not even the time I accidentally leaked a Kendrick Lamar song in the background of an Instagram video.

"You do realise whose house you're standing in?" my father asks, squaring up.

"I do, yeah—"Tom nods, coolly. "I think I could probably wipe the floor clean with you any place though."

"Okay, champ"—Harley snarls, and he gets a mean smile—"want to give it a go?"

"Not particularly." Tom shakes his head and starts rolling up his sleeves. "But I will."

"Okay." Harley grins, and maybe it's a little sinister and maybe I feel more nervous than you want to feel of your own father. "—I wouldn't mind making an England bleed," my father says before he shoves Tom backwards and into me. It's a bit of a domino effect: Tom falls on to me, I fall onto my bedside table, my lamp falls onto the floor.

My father looks like he's seen a ghost. Tom looks like he might murder someone. And my hand is bleeding, but only a bit. It's not deep.

"Magnolia," my father says, his voice sounding quite different all of a sudden. "Darling, I'm—"

Tom shoves Harley away, aggressively. "Take one more step, I dare you," he says, then pulls me up off the ground.

"What's going on in here?" Marsaili runs in.

Bridget's gotten me a cloth for my hand.

Tom cocks his head towards my suitcase. "This ready to go?"

I nod, a bit dazed.

My sister hands me my passport from my fallen nightstand, then kisses my cheek. Tom grabs my suitcase, lifts it off my bed like it's a paper plate even though it weighs well over five stone, takes my good hand in his other and leads me towards the door.

We're in his car. Dark grey, SVAutobiography Range Rover. He's gripping the wheel pretty tight with one hand; with the other hand, he's gnawing down mindlessly on his index finger. Tom looks over at me. "He been like that before?"

"No." I shake my head. "Never." He keeps driving. "Where are we going?"

He watches the road for a few seconds. His face looks strained. If he were a MacBook he'd have the swirling rainbow of death on his face.

"Where's BJ?" He glances over at me.

"His parents' anniversary."

"Where?" he over-annunciates.

I frown a little, confused. "Angler."

He nods once. "We're going to Angler."

20:32

Tom England

We're on our way to you
now.

224

What?

Why?

Everything okay?

Big fight with Harley

Bad

Oh shit. Okay.

Is she okay?

Angler, yeah?

Yeah. South Place Hotel.

TWENTY-EIGHT

BJ

I'm waiting outside before they pull up. Feel a bit sick about all of it—whatever it is…. That she had a fight, and I wasn't there. I should have been. Glad that Tom was there though—sort of. But even that makes me feel off. Why was he there when I wasn't? I only dropped her there a few hours ago, and he went over already?

His car pulls up. It's not a Bentley.

Not a Rolls, not a Lambo, not a Porsche. It's a Range Rover and it annoys me that he's this unpretentious. It's a grey SVAutobiography, which is a £140,000 car that pretty much looks the same as a £35,000 car. Such a fucking flex to buy a regular-looking car that's four times the price of the normal kind.

Parks opens the passenger door, jumps out and straight into my arms. I hold her against me, her face in my chest, my hands in her hair, press my mouth down into the top of her head. Tom England stands there by his car, frowning as he watches us. And I feel a pang of bad for him—wish I could tell him he's not doing anything wrong, that it's not his fault, we're just like this.

I don't know why he brought her to me.

And then I notice the blood. "What the fuck happened?" I grab her hand.

She shakes her head. "Nothing—it's just a cut."

"What happened?" I ask louder and clearer as I look from her to Tom. "Your dad did this?" I inspect her hand; it probably doesn't need more than a few butterfly strips, then I don't let go of it.

"It was an accident," she tells me, eyes all heavy and shit. She'd lie to me if it meant I wouldn't do something stupid, so I look over at Tom, eyebrows up, asking without asking. He nods and walks towards us and honestly? Fuck him. For being this cool, and this smooth, and for bringing his girlfriend to her ex-boyfriend in the middle of a low-grade crisis and not acting like an insecure arsehole even when Parks' face is buried in my chest like it is right now.

"So what happened, man?" I ask, shaking my head.

"Her dad came in yelling—" He gives me a look. "Really yelling—"

I frown. "Why?"

Tom shrugs with a bit of a grimace. "It's on the news."

I pull back and glance down at her in my arms. "Was it you?" She doesn't say anything but gives me the Bambi eyes…. So, it was her. Hah. Hell hath no fury like a Magnolia Parks scorned. I nudge her in the chin. "My girl."

Tom shifts on his feet. "You alright?" I nod at him.

He shrugs, dismissive. "Fine, yeah—just a bit of shoving."

I nod and look back down at Parks. "What'd he say to you?"

Tom shakes his head a little. "Threatened her a bit."

"No!" I scowl, looking from Tom to Parks. "Harley did?" Tom nods. "What the fuck?" I scowl. "Fuck, I'm glad we're leaving—"

She pulls back and looks up at me. "About that"—she gives me a quick smile—"Tom's going to come."

"Oh," I say and then tack on a smile at the end, and I swear I see his mouth twitch, amused. "Great. That's—yeah. Cool."

"We can take my plane—" he offers.

I shrug. "I have a plane, she has a plane. We all have planes—"

"Yes." Parks gives me a look. "However, he's the only one who's licensed to fly us there himself."

"Right, then." I nod casually, cursing the fucking day I didn't go to pilot school myself.

I could be a pilot if I wanted to be.

Tom backs away towards his car.

"We'll fly out tomorrow afternoon," he tells us, that smarmy git. "Farnborough." He points to me and says something I hate more than anything anyone's said to me before: "You look after her."

TWENTY-NINE

Magnolia

It's just under a four-hour flight from London to Monemvasia, this little island town on the east coast of the Peloponnese region of Greece. It's only linked to the main island by a little causeway so there's obviously not an airport there, and it's usually a six-hour drive from Athens but in a dreadfully convenient turn of events, Tom is an England and a pilot, so I don't know why I didn't start dating him sooner. Oh wait, yes I do. Two letters, phenomenal mouth, stayed in his bed last night, cried in the crook of his neck all morning—

I could tell Tom dropping me to him threw Beej a bit. It threw me a bit too actually, if I'm honest. Tom was so calm, so quick to my defence, so brave against my father, and so casual about dropping me to BJ when he thought it'd be better for me—

I mean—who does that?

I'd have to be high as a fucking kite to drive him to Clara for any reason and he's just my foxhole. And that's it, I suppose. We're just each other's hideout 'til the storm rolls over and it's safe to come out. Probably my time with Tom is drawing to a close, I think—but even thinking that makes my skin prickle a tad. I don't love the thought of not being in each other's lives anymore. I guess we've become a bit close through all the pretending.

I think for me, it's passing—the BJ storm. If it even ever was a storm. It was maybe more like, a drunk person who stumbled onto a news set who then proceeded to give a convincing, yet factually inaccurate, weather forecast for a completely terrible monsoon of death and so you hid, and you hid and hid and hid, waiting for the storm to pass but there was no storm.

Maybe there was no storm with BJ.

Maybe all the ways he's hurt me 'til now are because I hurt him, and maybe now it'll be different because I can trust him?

We're all standing in the lobby of Kinsterna. It's one of my favourite hotels, actually. It's a restored Byzantine mansion that cascades down a hill towards the sea. I've been here before with my sister. It's why BJ picked it, because he wanted to come with me last time, but I think he'd slept with Taura or something, so I brought Bridget instead. It's a fun little crew. Me, Beej, Tom, Paili, Henry, Gus, Perry and Christian. No Jonah on account of a work thing—hopefully of the legal variety, but one can't be too sure.

"We're after eight rooms," Beej tells the woman at the front desk, shoving his hands into the pockets of his Bassike Karamatsu tie-dye track pants.

"Actually, just seven, mate," Tom calls to him.

"Oh," BJ says, and turns to face us, then looks at me. "Are you sharing with Pails?"

"Um." I glance at Tom, then shake my head.

"Oh." BJ blinks. "You're going to share a room? You two?" I press my lips tight together. Christian's watching on, probably a bit too amused.

"Okay," he says and nods. He nods a lot. "Of course you are, you're boyfriend and"—BJ's eyes snag on mine—"girlfriend." He keeps nodding. "Two doubles?"

Tom looks a bit pleased. "One king's fine."

BJ's jaw goes tight. "One king's fine." Nods. "Yep. Of course, it is. Big beds—very much—space with the—"

"Oh, fuck." Henry pushes him out of the way, and takes over talking to the lady. "Seven rooms, please. And maybe put some Xanax in his?"

Tom goes off to organise our luggage and BJ hovers close by, watching me carefully.

"Have you slept with him?" he asks, eyes pinched. I frown, shaking my head. "Do you mean asleep or sex?" he clarifies, which probably no one else on the planet would need clarification over, but we would.

I offer him a weak shrug. "Neither."

He nods, thinking it through. "But it's going to be you and him. In a bed. In a room. Alone. Together."

"BJ," I interrupt.

He ignores me. "And I'll be in a... different room. In a bed, as well. But you'll be in... his bed?"

His eyes hold mine, and they look wired and stressed. I nod once, carefully. "I guess so?"

"Okay." He nods. "Yep, that's—" He nods again. "Okay."

I purse my mouth. "Okay."

"Room's ready," Tom calls to me.

I look over at him and nod. "Coming." I look back at BJ and his whole heart is raw all over his face, and I want to make him feel better, fix it, blow it all away—but I don't know how. I could just tell him, I guess, that it was all a ruse, but today when BJ and I arrived at Farnborough Airport and Tom waltzed over, hand on my face and kissed the shit out of me, I began to wonder... How much of the ruse was left?

I walk away, a few metres before I stop and turn around. Beej is watching me, his eyes rounder and heavier than he'd want anyone but me to see them. Tom's watching me too, but I don't mind so much.

"Do you want to do something tomorrow?" I call over to BJ.

Beej blinks a few times. "What?" I walk back over to him. A foot between us, maybe.

"Do you want to do something tomorrow? With me." Pause. "Just me."

BJ looks past me to Tom, then back to me. "What about England?"

I shake my head. "Don't you worry about England."

"Okay." He nods once. Smiling a bit. "What are we going to do?"

"Oh, piss off." I roll my eyes, a teensy bit outraged that I just practically asked him out on a date and he had the audacity to assume I'd also arrange it. "Do I have to do everything? Plan it yourself." He laughs as I walk away.

Tom's waiting for me.

"You good?" he asks with a warm smile. I nod. "He good?"

My mouth twitches as I look up at him. "He's probably been better."

Tom sniffs a laugh. "The poor bastard."

"I'm going to spend the day with him tomorrow—is that okay?" And I wonder if I see it there for a second, it's tiny, almost imperceptible—but maybe a tumbleweed of jealousy breezes over his face. There one second, gone the next.

Then Tom shrugs indifferently. "Course it's okay. You don't have to check." I nod, flash him a smile that feels both disingenuous and forced. "I know what I am to you," he adds as an after-thought.

I pause and look over at him. "And what I am to you."

He nods once. "Right."

I nod back. "Right."

"We're wrapping up, aren't we?" Tom asks after watching me for a few seconds.

"Maybe." It's non-committal because for some reason I don't feel fully ready to commit to that. Probably I'm just afraid of being alone again. "I don't know."

Tom's face is hard to pick, the emotion on him is a bit unreadable and I find this frustrating about him. I never cared for reading the emotions of the men I was seeing before except for BJ and Christian and I knew how to read them because I'd known them forever, but Tom who I desperately want to read, who I would die to understand and to hear his mind and his secret thoughts about me, Tom, to me, is speaking like he's from County Kerry with Spanish subtitles.

I think he's annoyed. That's my best guess judging from the way his eyebrows are right now.

"What don't you know about it? You're going to get back together with him."

"I am?" I blink.

The frown depends. "Aren't you?"

"I—" I just shrug.

"That's what you want," he tells me.

I nod. "I suppose."

He nods again. "Right."

I nod back. "Right."

Although I'm not really sure all is.

THIRTY

BJ

She asked me out on a date. I think. Right? In front of
Tom. For real, I thought I was going to chunder when
England said one room, one bed, but then she asked me
on a date?

Spent the afternoon planning it with Henry, who was
pretty long suffering about it all.

"—Ready for this saga to end," was his reasoning for
his level of personal investment but actually I reckon
he just loves us. Loves me, loves her—loved us together
like the rest of my family. I'm less fucked up when
I'm with her. More grounded. Weird, I know because
she is the least grounded person in the entire fucking
Commonwealth, but she just does something to me—I
don't know what.

We head downstairs to the restaurant, the fine dining
one—rather go out for a bite, if I'm honest but Parks
loves a hotel restaurant, and she's a very domineering
holiday presence.

Self-appointed Activity Captain, self-appointed
Cuisine Captain (her words, not mine) and just in general, High Lord Empress of Holidays (my words, not
hers).

She's already down there with Tom when Hen and I
arrive. Circular table. I sit on her other side, do my best

not to stare at her stomach in that Dolce & Gabbana bra top she's wearing that I bought for just my eyes to see. The rest of the party dribbles in, Lorcs being the last one seated because he's forever fucking late to everything but especially late to things he wants to make an entrance for—like Gus Waterhouse, for one. Who's sick, by the way. We listen to his stories all night. They're funny and ridiculous and he loves what he does, and Parks' dad is insane in all of them, and I still want to kill him for what happened the other day, but the stories about him are funny as shit.

"Can't believe it about your dad, Parks." Gus says eventually.

"Really?" She blinks. "You can't believe it?" She gives him a look. "That one time you and I got lunch and he stayed in the studio for a 'meeting' and when we came back there was a very terrible actress leaving the building with lipstick all smudged?"

"No," he shakes his head. "That I can believe but I can't believe he was overt enough to get caught, in public, with your nanny—"

I sway my head, weighing up what he said. "Caught? Tipped off by vengeful daughter? Hard to tell."

She gives me a look.

Tom looks at Parks. "Why do you have a nanny?"

She glances at him, confused. "Hm?"

He shrugs. "You're just... you're twenty-three."

Fair play, Tom. Absolutely valid question. Wondered it a million times over the years myself. Why the fuck did Parks need a nanny when we were at boarding school majority of the time? Why did Parks need a nanny when she'd finished secondary and Bridget was away at boarding school? Why did Parks need a nanny when the nanny never cooked or cleaned or performed any household task...that we knew of. In retrospect, it could be concluded that actually a fair few tasks were... performed but their household value might be up for debate at this point.

"I mean—I'm twenty-two," she corrects him, and I feel relieved for a second because he can't like her that much if he doesn't even know how old she is. "But yes, it's a solid question, Tommy. Why do I have a nanny?"

"Well—I mean, I think we know the answer to that now." Henry pulls a face. "And it's convoluted, at best."

"Oh, come off it." Perry rolls his eyes. "She looks like Kate Winslet. It's hardly shocking—I mean, the woman can't dress for shit, but she was locked away in Jonah's spank bank for years."

Parks' jaw hits the floor, and Jonah would be so glad he's not here because what Lorcs just said is completely true, and Jo'd die over it now.

Paili folds her arms over her chest and leans in. "Do you remember about a year ago, we were at an event— something for your mum, and we nicked off to the bathroom, and Marsaili walked out of the disabled room all flushed—"

"Oh my god!" Parks recoils.

She continues, "And you said, 'She looks like she just had an orgasm,' and your mum was flitting around asking where your dad was. I bet they were shagging in the loo."

I choke back a laugh.

Henry tosses me a look. "Like you're one to talk, man—you've had so many orgasms in disabled toilets."

"Oy," I jeer. "Not just disabled toilets—all toilets, I don't discriminate." Tom chuckles and I try to catch

Parks' eye, make sure that one didn't sting her too much but she won't let me find it.

Perry holds up his wine glass. "Never have I ever had an orgasm in public." And then every boy at the table drinks. Me, Tom, Henry, Christian, Lorcs and Gus.

Christian laughs and nods his chin at me. "You better drink that whole glass, mate."

I ignore him, try to win Parks back.

"And you," Christian says, eyeing Parks down from the other side of the table, "you should have had a sip."

She blinks, pulls back her head in surprise. "I beg your pardon?"

The back of my neck goes hot. Tom stiffens up too.

"We all know you had an orgasm once in public," he tells the table, and I frown at him.

Do we all know?

"You all know?" she repeats, looking at him eyes wide.

Christian nods. "Yep."

"Shut up," Paili whispers to him, softly.

"Well, I didn't." Her nose is in the air, so she did.

He shrugs, indifferent. "—Except that you did."

"I'd never—" Her cheeks are flushing. "That's so improper."

"Yeah," he scoffs. "You were real focused on societal proprieties at the time." He gives her a look and I can tell he's a bit drunk. He likes to antagonise her a bit when he's drunk. Never really goes well for him.

He doesn't look away from her.

"The speakeasy in Paris. You and him"—Christian nods his chin at me, and I could fucking deck him for it. "Back corner. His hand. Under a table."

Fuck. He's not wrong, that did happen. Pretty unlike her to even let me, too. It was a very good night.

I feel Parks tense up next to me—hope it's just me that notices it because it's me and her and we notice shit like that with each other.

"Christian," Paili tries to diffuse the mounting tension, and rolls her eyes dismissively. "How would you even know?"

And then he says this looking square into Magnolia's eyes: "Because I know what she looks like when she's having an orgasm."

Henry gapes at him. "What the fuck, man?"

I shake my head, mouth tight. "Hate that—"

Tom's staring down at the table. "Can't say I'm a fan either—"

Paili can't believe it, Perry's eyes are about to fall out of his head, Gus is watching on in curious fascination. I should hit Christian for it, probably. I know I should. If it were anyone else I would. But I feel shitty at her too. Not her fault, I know. But then again, she's the one who went and had an orgasm with my best mate, so.

Magnolia's frozen, staring at the table, and it's this fucking weird tension between me never wanting her to feel how Christian's made her feel just now, all exposed and embarrassed and shit, but also, I never want to remember what happened with her and him and when they make me, the house rules seem to fly out the fucking window, and it probably makes me a piece of shit, but I don't feel like defending her in the moment.

I push back from the table. "I'm going to grab a drink—"

Tom eyes down Christian. "Yeah, I'll come with you."

England and I get to the bar. I blow air out of my mouth. Order two shots of Casamigos Repasado, slide one over to him. Throw it back silently.

Tom stares at me for a few seconds. "What the fuck was that?"

I glance back over my shoulder, and don't meet Magnolia's eyes as they watch both me and England, nervous. "They dated."

Tom pulls back in surprise. "Right. When?"

I tilt my head, thinking. "Not long after we broke up."

"Wow." He blinks a lot.

"Yeah." I stare over at Christian, grinding my jaw. "Wow."

A few minutes pass before Parks walks over to us gingerly.

Tom gives her a weak smile. "You okay?"

And fuck him for being a better guy than me, asking her that. I should have asked her that, but I'm still fucking pissed at her for all of it. And anyway, he doesn't love her like I do.

She nods and it's unconvincing at best.

"Want me to hit him?" I offer, wanting to be as good a guy as Tom.

She sniffs a laugh. "Yes." But then frowns at me. "No. That was a joke—please don't."

I give her a look. "He'd deserve it."

She shrugs. "He's just drunk. You know how he gets."

"What?" scoffs Tom. "Bitter and belligerent?"

"Arseholey," Magnolia offers.

Parks looks knackered and I nod my chin at her. "You should go to bed. Big day tomorrow…"

"Yeah?" She smiles up at me.

I nod once. I glance at Tom, trying not to cringe. "Thanks for letting me borrow your girlfriend for the day."

He sniffs a laugh and he swallows. "Course, man— just make sure you bring her back in one piece."

Then he hooks his arm around her neck how I do and pulls her away to their room. She looks back at me. I give her a small wink.

She looks a different kind of tired now, but she smiles at me anyway.

23:54

Christian

Why did you say that?

Because it's true, Magnolia.

Which part?

All of it.

You did and I do.

Are you trying to hurt me?

Nope.

Are you trying to hurt him?

Which him, Parks?

Wow.

Are you and Daisy having a row?

Fuck you

Oh that's so funny—

I was under the impression
you already had.

THIRTY-ONE

Magnolia

I'm laying out by the pool—Tom's gone for a run. BJ's not awake yet. Gus is by me, but his headphones are in and he's not paying attention to me, which means my new Sole embroidered, seersucker, triangle, halter-neck bikini top from Marysia that I've paired with her Broadway reversible, scalloped bikini briefs is being completely wasted on the inattentive gay man next to me.

A shadow falls over me, and with one eye open I peer up.

Christian Hemmes is staring down at me in the black and white Palm Angels, logo-print, short-sleeve bowling shirt, all undone with the logo-print, drawstring swim shorts from Balmain. Face as serious as ever. Brows kind of knitted into a frown. Jaw set—but his jaw is always set.

"What's your face so serious all the time for?" I asked him once when we were together, and he held my chin between his fingers, and for a second his whole face lightened up.

"It's a serious business, loving you."

But that wasn't why—I knew that even then. It's whatever he does. All the things those boys keep from me, all the whispers about the Hemmes they think I don't know about, all the whispers that are true, those are why he's serious.

Christian kicks me gently with his big toe, nodding at the bed next to me.

"Can I sit here?"

"Oh, of course." I wave my hand dismissively. "However, you must be careful as I have been known to orgasm spontaneously in public—oh wait, no—you know what that looks like. You'll be fine."

His head rolls back to the sky and sighs. "Don't be a bitch."

I look over at him, eyebrows arched. "I beg your pardon?"

He turns to me. "I'm sorry."

I give him a sharp look, folding my arms over my chest. "I should think so." He groans, leaning back onto the sun bed. I watch him for a few seconds, then shake my head. "Why would you do that?"

He shoves his hands through his hair as he grinds his jaw. "I don't know."

Yes, he does, and so do I. These little flare-ups of his aren't anything new. He never really forgave me. He might have been the one who ended it, but it was my fault and he's held it against me ever since.

"It's fun"—he shrugs—"to fuck with you."

"Oh." I nod, wide-eyed. "Excellent."

He gives me a look. "You know what I mean."

I glare over at him. "No, Christian—I actually don't. I don't like fucking with people."

"Really?" He blinks. I tilt my head and he stares at me, a bit incredulous. "You don't like fucking with people?" His brows are up, eyes dark, and I can tell before he starts he's about to come in swinging all over again. "You've dated, like, five guys in the past two and a half years, present company excluded, and you weren't fucking around with them?" I open my mouth to say something, but he cuts me off. "You were fucking around with me."

"No, I wasn't—"

"Then what were you doing?" he asks, sitting up, swinging his legs to face me.

My eyes pinch. "You know what I was doing."

"No." He shakes his head. "I know what I was doing." He gives me a look that makes me want to cry. "You... I don't have a fucking clue."

I glance away, tired. I can't win this fight. "Are you done?"

"Nope." He shakes his head defiantly. "What about Tom?"

I roll my eyes, crossing my arms. "What about Tom?"

"Are you with him or aren't you?"

I let out a mirthless laugh, shaking my head. I should just lie. I don't know what the answer is anymore though. "How is that any of your business?"

Christian's head pulls back. "How's that any of my business?" His brows shoot up. "Really?"

My eyes are slits by now. "Yes, really."

His jaw juts out. "You're a piece of work, Parks. You know that?"

"What is the matter with you?" I stare at him. "I haven't done anything."

He snorts this hollow laugh and looks away from me and it makes me feel a weird kind of guilty and exposed, but I think that's his fault, not mine.

He stands, shaking his head. "It's funny—I think the only person you think you're not really fucking over is Beej, but you are. You're fucking him over, he's fucking you over. He's also just fucking. Everyone, all the t—"

"—You should walk away, man," Gus says, standing up.

"Should I?" Christian smirks.

"Yeah." Gus nods again. "You run your mouth about her like a real big man when your brother's not here to keep you in line."

Christian sniffs a dry laugh, looking away because what Gus said stings with the truth.

"Go on." Gus nods his chin in the opposite direction of us. "Fuck off and cool down."

Christian doesn't meet my eyes as he walks away. I turn and look at Gus towering over me.

He sits back down, watching me closely for a few seconds. "You okay?"

"Oh, yeah." I sniff and shake my head because I'm not really, even though my mouth will say otherwise. "He's been angry at me for about two years now, so—that's nothing new."

He nods a few times, looking out over the pool.

It's so dramatic here, olive groves that spill down onto a beach that runs right into the Aegean. It's a much nicer kind of dramatic than my love life, which is also dramatic and also is probably all overgrown with things I should have done differently, with seas of fears and regrets so deep it'd rival the Challenger.

"So," Gus says, "how many men here are infatuated with you?" He looks over. "By my count it's three."

I squash a smile. "Is this your way of telling me you're not infatuated by me, Gus?"

He runs his tongue over his teeth, amused. "Me and the other gay one are immune and so is the brother. Ballentine Brother, not Gang Lord Brother. Gang Lord Brother—"

"—I don't think they love that term," I interrupt.

He shrugs, indifferent. "Probably shouldn't have become gang lords then." Pause. "He has feelings for you, yes?"

"I don't know." I shrug, demurely.

He eyes me. "Yes, you do."

I scratch my chin as my eyes pinch at him before answering carefully. "I've wondered."

Gus considers this. "Does he know?"

I purse my lips. "Does who?"

He gives me a look. "Either of the ones you like back."

I take a measured breath, then breath it out. "Tom asked about it… I palmed it off. And I suspect that BJ has to ignore it at all costs in order for our group to function… somewhat."

"And you?" He nods his head at me. "How do you feel about him?"

"About Christian?" I pause. The question sits heavy in my chest for a moment, the truth fizzing up in me like a shaken can of Fanta. "I loved him once." I've never told anyone that besides Christian, actually. I don't know why I'm here telling August Waterhouse. I shrug. "I just never loved him as much as BJ."

"Have you ever loved anything as much as BJ?"

I shift uncomfortably, carefully avoiding his eyes by taking in the wondrous sights around me. How blue the Aegean is today!

"I know about Tom, by the way," Gus tells me as he watches me. "What you're doing—"

I look over, frowning. "We said we wouldn't tell anyone!"

He sniffs a laugh. "He didn't tell me."

Oh shit.

I think Gus sees that sentiment on my face. He swats his hand to dismiss it.

"—Please. Tom kisses Clossy—which I assume you know about, yes?" He doesn't wait for my answer. "And then a week later, out of the blue, he's dating London's It Girl, who just happens to be a recently single chronic dater who's never severed ties with her ex? Are we supposed to think that's a coincidence?"

I frown over at him. "How do you know about Clara and Tom?"

He shrugs. "Walked in on them."

Something about that makes me feel funny.

Something about someone seeing Tom touch Clara makes it more real than before when it was a thing that happened once in a theoretical way that Tom'd told me about and I'd never tell anyone else. Someone catching them animates it to life in a way that I very much dislike. I want it abstract, 2D, on paper. Like Picasso's Dora. True but estranged, real but not really.

Tom touching someone else—it shouldn't make me feel funny, I know that. My mouth shouldn't feel dry, my hands shouldn't feel clammy and my heart rate should be regular.

This is the gig. We're doing this because we each respectively like touching other people and we shouldn't, so here we are, this is why we are what we are but what I am right now in this moment, is jealous.

My breathing feels heavier than I want it to. I hope Gus doesn't notice.

"The plan is excellent," he tells me, nodding. I'm chuffed and relieved to have pulled the wool over his eyes. "There's only one major flaw." He looks at me.

"Oh?"

"He's falling for you and you're falling for him."

Fuck. Am I? Are we? I don't know. But I certainly don't want him to know I don't know so I make a pfffft sound.

Gus ignores me. "You're falling for him, he's definitely into you, and simultaneously you're still in love with BJ, and Tommy's still in love with Closs. So this is shaping up to be..." He claps his hands together once. "Horrible! Really, really bad. An iconoclastic disaster— titanic, even."

I glare over at him. "You are... a huge know-it-all."

"I know." He shrugs as he puts his sunglasses on. "Awful, isn't it?"

"You're wrong, by the way," I tell him.

"Am I?" he says, unbothered to even glance at me. "Because I feel like I'm not."

"Well, you are."

He gives me a big smile with his eyebrows up. "We shall see when you return from your date with your ex-boyfriend to your romantic suite at the romantic hotel you share with your current boyfriend, who is allegedly fake, but decreasingly so by the second I dare say—"

I roll my eyes.

"—who says he is fine that you're going out for the day with your ex-boyfriend, but he is currently running a half-marathon 'just for fun.'"

I shrug dismissively. "So he likes to run—"

"Tom hates to run." He doesn't look up from his book, Adam Kay's *This is Going to Hurt*.

I breathe out loudly. "That doesn't mean it's because of me."

"Oh, sod off." Gus rolls his eyes. "All these boys are loopy because of you."

I frown. "That's not a compliment."

He raises his eyebrows and glances up at me. "I didn't mean it as one."

THIRTY-TWO

BJ

I'm jittery as shit, which is insane; I've spent more time with Parks than literally any other person on the planet. We grew up together. She's seen me naked; I've seen her naked. She's seen me fall, break my bones, she's seen me cry, vomit on myself, overdose—she's seen me at my worst, and I've taken her on a million dates over the course of our lives, and still, this one has me sweating fucking bullets.

Because I think it's a big deal. I don't know—we haven't talked about it yet. But it feels like a shift. Like an "East Wind", to quote my other favourite girl.

Like maybe—I don't know—maybe we're happening... again? It felt weird trying to plan this for her—we're in fucking Greece—we flew here on her pilot boyfriend's private jet. When we were babies I took her to Spain for our first proper date on our private plane. A couple of weeks ago I took her shopping on Avenue Montaigne because I felt like it. She thinks Evian tastes like piss but is "okay enough to wash your face with in a pinch." Elton John practically gave her the Hope fucking Diamond for her birthday last year—

Luxe doesn't cut it. Luxe is the usual to her.

And whatever this is—whatever's about to happen— it's a finite window, I know that.

Like the universe just gave me the time machine I've been praying for all this time and they're giving me another shot. And it's a trick shot.

I've got to ricochet the disaster of what we've become off of the glimmering light of what we were and land it in what we could be again. Both eyes closed, one hand behind my back.

This is my Hail Mary, and this has to work.

I'm waiting for her in the lobby. She's running late. Always. So, I pull out my book, read a couple of pages when a pair of long legs appear in front of me.

She plucks the book from my hand and flips it over. *The Little Prince.* "You're reading this again?"

Her hair's out, skin's extra brown, eyes extra bright. She's in a top she'd only ever wear on holidays with a lilac bikini under it. I nod, trying not to smile up at her like a schoolboy because I fucking love her in lilac. "I read it every year."

"I know," she says, flicking her eyes, annoyed. "What's it telling you this time?"

"That I've been tamed."

"By whom?" She blinks and I know she knows.

I look over at her, my eyes steadier than my heart feels. "By you." Her cheeks go pink and I sniff, amused and pleased. I stand up. "Let's go."

And then... I stop in my tracks.

"Are you wearing denim?" Can't believe it.

Known her almost twenty years, never seen her in a pair of jeans in her life. A material for "the working man," she says.

"Denim shorts, no less. With holes in them." She grins, proud. "Do you like them?"

I feel self-conscious for a second, feel my cheeks go pink.

"I like you in everything," I tell her and she looks chuffed, so I feel chuffed. I walk ahead of her a few steps and then turn back. "Also like you in nothing—"

She swallows heavy, follows after me and catches up after a small jog.

Like the feeling of her running after me.

Levels the unlevel playing field for a second and a half.

She follows me out front and we get into the back of a car that's waiting for us. She slides into the middle seat; I climb in next to her. She's nervous. I can feel it on her, an electric field of anxious energy.

She's staring straight ahead, mouth twitching at nothing. Or everything, maybe? I like her feeling like this, like that I can make her feel like this.

"You good?" I ask, looking at her. She looks over at me, nods. "You nervous?" She pauses, swallows. Nods again and I toss her a tiny smile. "Same."

That makes her happy. She tugs on the collar of my black shirt. Red and pink flowers and palm leaves on it. Bought it the other week while thinking about her taking it off of me.

"Gucci?" she asks, but she already knows. I nod, trying to be cool. "Black and green, dream print poplin." She rubs the material between her fingers. "Viscose and silk-blend."

I wouldn't know. She could be speaking Russian. I've got no idea what the fuck she's saying, but what I do know is that her index finger and thumb slips under my shirt and stays there. Hand on my chest.

I swallow heavy, staring at her. Her eyes don't move, they stay on mine. Her hand doesn't move either, and I should kiss her. I know I should kiss her. How many times am I not going to kiss her, you're wondering—it's a fair question and the answer is hard to pin down.

I think about kissing Magnolia Parks more than I think about anything else, literally in the world. It's my go-to thought when my mind has a minute to spare.

Actual kisses that happened, hypothetical kisses that could have happened, kisses that should have happened, kisses that are completely fabricated and they just drift into my mind while I'm waiting for a coffee and I've thought about kissing her so many times since the last time I kissed her—that right here, right now, when I probably actually could—I can't.

Because there's too much riding on it. I can't rush it. I can't lose control. I can't think with my dick. Today I have to temper how much I love her. Turn down the pot to a healthy simmer.

She can touch my chest, she does it when she drinks too much anyway. Half the time when we fall asleep in the same bed I'll wake up in the night with her snug up against me, we've never talked about it. I don't even know if she knows she does it, and I don't want to tell her if she doesn't know because I don't want it to stop.

I've taught myself to live within the walls of our weird touching—it's dysfunctional as shit—I know, but if being with her was heroin, what we have now is methadone. The shit isn't the same, but it keeps the monsters at bay.

If I kiss her I'm a goner. I'm a goner anyway.

The car stops and we get out at a dock, a Rivamare waiting at the bottom of it. Not the exact same boat as the one from before, newer, fancier, but it does the trick, I can see it in her eyes.

Self-serving, maybe I'll admit. Just my favourite day of my life is all.

I'm not going to shag her on the boat—promise. Wouldn't be mad if she remembered that time on the boat and tried to shag me....

But actually, I just want to be alone with her someplace. I don't care where. We'll get on the boat. I've got supplies for the day. There's a few beaches Henry and I found. All of it's peripheral to just me and her.

I step onto the boat first, take her hand, pull her with me. Our eyes catch. That glass wall she always puts up between us doesn't appear. She doesn't let go of my hand.

I swallow heavy, clear my throat and pull my hand from hers. She's not cut that I do either—her eyes go soft—I think she thinks it's funny.

I walk to the wheel of the boat.

"Do you think I'm going to cook you and eat you?" she calls after me.

I look back, shake my head, smirking. "Nah, just fuck me up."

She tucks some hair behind her ears and comes and stands by me. Undoes her shorts, slips them off, kicks them away. Doesn't look away from me once as she does it.

I lick my bottom lip—give her a look and peel away in the water.

We stop for a while offshore of a little beach— Drymiskos or something, I think? White sand, water the colour of her eyes, no one around for miles. She's picking at some cheese because she always has the appetite of a bird except for when she's drunk and then she has the appetite of a kraken.

She looks over me. "So this is your big date? A boat, charcuterie and champagne?" She shrugs. "Kind of basic…"

I shake my head. "A boat, charcuterie, champagne and your favourite thing in the world…"

She raises her eyebrows waiting for the reveal, "Oh yeah?"

I point to myself. She rolls her eyes. "Am I not?" I ask, chin jutted out. She holds my eyes, downs her champagne. Holds it out for me to pour another. "I am," I tell her.

She rolls her eyes again but wriggles in closer to me.

"So this is a date?" I ask, tilting my head at her.

"Is it not?"

I shrug, shyer than I want to be. "We just didn't talk about it."

"I mean"—she wobbles her head, considering it all—"it's not much of a date."

"Oy—" I toss a fig at her and she laughs.

She's happy. I can tell. She eats the fig I threw at her, wipes her mouth with her hand.

"How's Tom feeling about us on a maybe-date?" I ask, genuinely curious.

She breathes in and out, purses her mouth. "He's quite a bit older than us—"

"—Not me," I butt in to clarify.

"He's thirty-one."

"I'm twenty-five," I remind her. "Not that much older."

She rolls her eyes but doesn't fight me on it. "Actually, I think at this point, he really just would quite like for me to figure… us out."

And I can't help but roll my eyes because fuck him. Truly. I mean that sincerely. Fuck him for being a stand-up legend of a man, who's selfless and thoughtful and considerate and fuck him for making me look like a jack-off on my own date with the girl we're maybe both dating but who I love more.

"You used to like him," she reminds me gently.

I snort, amused. "I still like him—the smarmy prick." I shake my head, thinking. "It was so much better when you just dated the duds."

She nods. "Tom's not a dud."

And that stings me a little but it's my legs that her legs are casually tossed over so, sorry England.

So our day goes like this. In and out of the water, drinking good wine, eating good cheese. If I close my eyes, we could be together, what we were before, somewhere far away, still out loud in love and each other's. She and I, we edge closer and closer together, reasons to touch fall to the wayside and touching for touching's sake becomes the name of the game. I hold her by her waist, I brush her hair behind her ears, I rest my chin on her head. Hands touching, sitting so close she's nearly on top of me. We're going to be together again, I'm sure of the trajectory now. She loves me, she wants to be with me, I can tell she does. I'm watching her climb over the walls she built around herself, tear down the old blockades, looking for a safe place to rest, and her head is in my lap as she looks up and then she asks me the worst thing.

"Beej?"

"Mm," I say, looking down at her.

"Why did you do it?" I blink a few times. I know what she's asking. I don't know how to answer it. "Cheat on you, you mean?" I clarify for no reason.

Hurts me to say it. Hurts her to hear it. I should have seen this coming. Fuck—why did I arrange for a date with so much talking time, of course she'd bring this up.

Is she going to ask who again? I hate it when she asks me who. Her relationship with Taura is already in tatters, I guess it doesn't matter—it doesn't matter how many times I say it wasn't her, she doesn't buy it, and it doesn't matter, because it's done.

Parks holds my eyes. "Because you loved me—I know you did—"

I nod. I did, she's right. Haven't stopped.

"And the more I think of it, the more sure I become that you wouldn't have done it without a reason—"

"Parks—" I shake my head. I feel sick.

"I know you wouldn't have," she presses.

I feel dizzy.

"So what was the reason?" Her eyes look desperate.

"I was drunk," I tell her.

She shakes her head, unsatisfied. "That's not a reason."

I shrug, hopeless. "It is."

She shakes her head, adamant. She's sitting up now, facing me. "No—you'd been drunk before at parties without me—you never would have even looked at another girl. There had to be something else."

I lift my shoulder up, apologetically. "There's not…"

She shakes her head. "No, but you're lying to me."

"I'm not."

I am.

"You are—"

"I'm not—" I dig in, because I can't.

I wish I could, but I can't.

"Beej—" She looks for my eyes. "I need to understand why you did what you did so I can process it properly, and move past it, so it doesn't kill me forever, so I don't have to hold it against you forever—and I know you would never just hurt me to hurt me, so tell me—please." Her voice sounds small and I think she's killing me. "Why?"

I lick my top lip, and my eyes can't meet hers anymore because I know what I'm about to do. I know how it's going to hurt her, sink her like an eight ball.

I say it anyway: "Because I wanted to."

That hits her how I knew it would.

Like an arrow in the middle of her, watch how it changes her right there, on the spot. Like I just dropped a stone in the middle of a lake and now I have to watch it ripple out from her.

Her stomach sucks in from the blow, shoulders hunch. Her eyes drop mine; her face falls and she turns away from me. Walls up, armour on, swords out.

"Take me back," she tells the water. "Now."

"Parks—" I reach for her but she shrugs me off so violently it knocks me for six.

"Now," she demands loud and clear.

And with that, the finite window closes.

The time machine the universe gave me catches on fire, collapses in on itself.

The trick shot fails. The disaster of what we've become blitzes right past what we were, circles the drain of what we could be a couple of times before it teeters off to the side and lands smack bang right where we don't want to be.

I fucked my Hail Mary.

And this has not worked at all.

THIRTY-THREE

Magnolia

I'm mortified. Completely, completely, totally, utterly mortified. The edges of my vision went black as soon as he said it: because he wanted to.

My chest went tight. My breathing fell out of pace. I think I had a panic attack. I think he tried to help me... I pushed him away, I think? I think I scratched him when I fought him not to touch me.

I don't really remember. It all feels like a weird bad dream now. I remember I sat at the other end of the boat, as far away from him as I could 'til we were back to shore.

I sat in the front passenger seat of the car on the ride home. It pulled up to the hotel and I remember that BJ called my name as I threw the car door open and ran from him as fast as I could.

My eyes felt like they were bleeding, my heart felt like it was going to bottom out.

And it's with those eyes and this air of absolute brokenness that I burst into the room.

Tom's on the balcony. Red wine—he likes red, I like white. BJ just will drink whatever I like to drink but Tom just gets one of each.

He takes one look at me and in two steps crosses the distance. His brows are furrowed, his eyes are bright with a concern that's too much kindness for me right now. It's like, the eye contact version of a kind stranger with an excellent fringe asking if you're okay in the middle of the Cartier store a fortnight after your boyfriend cheats on you and you start crying uncontrollably and hysterically and so you can't even answer Emma Thompson, so she just hugs you and pets your hair—that's kind of how Tom looks at me now.

That but more. He's worried about me, I can tell. He's sad for me, he wants to hurt BJ. He doesn't understand what's happened. He needs to make me better.

And in retrospect, when I'll look back at this moment some time from now, this is when I'll mark it—write it down, dog-ear the moment in my mind that this—right here, is when the molecular structure of who Tom England is to me will begin to change.

Not soon at dinner when he'll nearly fight BJ, not when he steps in front of me, shielding me from the boy who broke and breaks and keeps breaking my unlearnable, untrainable heart, not later tonight when I'll pull him back into our hotel room with rushy hands and a mind eager to forget and have sex with him, but here, now, with his eyes on me like that, spotting the cracks in my finish before I do, preempting them with his hands on my face, trying to hold me together but he can't.

"Hey, hey, hey," he says, trying to stop me from crying. "What happened?" I give no answer, just tears. "Magnolia?" he asks but I don't answer again so he holds me. While I cry over another man. Not man—boy. BJ's no man. He really is just a boy.

Tom pulls away, looking for my eyes. He uses both his thumbs to windscreen-wiper my tears away. He grimaces. "Date didn't go as planned?" I muster a shake of the head and he just nods as he folds me into himself—puts himself on me like a cloak, holding me against himself until the trembling in my chest stops.

There are things I should say.

I owe him more information, but I don't want to give it to him for fear of what it says about me—how expendable I am to even the person who I thought loved me more than everyone else.

Because he wanted to.

Tom shakes his head. "I told you he was a fucking idiot." I nod. "He made you this sad?" he says. It's not really a question, more just an utterance. An acceptance of truth that he doesn't really understand and frankly, neither do I.

"I'll put him in the ground if you want me to."

"I want you to," I tell him, deadpan.

He chuckles and then I sniff a laugh and the way he looks at me, the smile he gives—and maybe for him, if I were able to pick it, able to read his mind in all the ways that I can't—I'd imagine that this is when I begin to be something else to him—at least in a way he's conscious of it.

The smile goes across his whole face and crinkles up, but it's why he gives me the smile he does that gets me, it's how happy he is to have made me okay for a second. I can see in him this expanding need to make things better for me, to pluck me out of all the bad in my life. I saw a fleck of it in him that day with my father but here it is now, flowering into some kind of fullness, growing past a preference into a necessity. If he's to be fully okay, now I am too.

It's a peculiar and wordless shift that happens between us, which is undefinable and unchartered to me.

Do I have feelings for this man? Or has he just been elevated to #1 safest place? Can those two things be mutually exclusive? I don't know. I don't know whether I do; I don't know if they can. I do know though, that I feel safer in his arms than I do out of them.

And I know that he smells like a Sunday morning. Slow, easy, uncomplicated. Like fresh coffee. New towels and a light-flooded room. Oak moss, patchouli, bergamot, lavender. And if Tom smells like a Sunday morning, then BJ smells like a Saturday night spent in the emergency room—don't think of BJ—and I just would love not to be in the emergency room anymore.

He nods his head towards the door. "I'll buy you a drink?"

I give him a small smile. "Buy me several."

We head down to the bar, have a few drinks. Not too many, just enough to take the edge off and at this point I have a lot of edges.

There's an ease between me and Tom that I've grown fond of.

There's an ease between me and BJ too—don't think about BJ—but it's different now because the ease is all tainted with infidelities and broken trust and hearts and years of resentment and a willow tree we don't speak about.

"So," Tom says, nods his chin at me, "did you kiss him?"

I frown at him, shaking my head. "No."

He sniffs a laugh, incredulous. "No?"

My mouth twitches into an almost-smile. "We can't... kiss," I tell him.

Tom squints at me, intrigued and maybe a bit miffed. But we can't. Me and Beej, we're all bridled passion and conscious choices, trying to preserve the tiny bit of us we still have left. We're wild horses running down a cliff face. There's no cantering, no gentle trot into love. We are The Man from Snowy River galloping down that cliff face, tumbling towards the inevitable. We can't go slow. The weight of us is too heavy. Gravity calls us, conspires against us…

"Bit of a Pringles situation?" he asks. I look over at him quizzically. "Once you pop, you can't stop?" Tom offers and I laugh.

And once again, he's pleased that I do.

We stay there for an hour or so, and as we're walking out of the bar, BJ rounds the corner.

Henry and Christian with him. Hen looks tense.

BJ's drunk, I can tell it by his face before I can smell it on his breath—which I can.

He sneers as he shakes his head at me. "Classic."

I look away from him, ignoring him.

"We go sideways for a second and a half and you fuck off running to someone else—"

"Easy," Christian whispers softly to his friend, but Beej just glares at him.

"She's not though, is she, England?" BJ glances at Tom, who just shakes his head.

"You seem like you've had a bit, man—why don't you just go for a walk," Tom tells him.

BJ shakes his head, nostrils flaring a bit as he frowns. "Don't want to go for a walk—I want to talk about how easy Parks isn't—"

He hasn't even said anything yet and I already feel like I've been slapped.

"She doesn't put out—" BJ starts.

"—Stop," Tom tells him.

Beej ignores him. "She's a fucking handful. She's a brat—"

"Stop," Tom says again, squaring his shoulders up.

"She doesn't know what the fuck she wants—" Beej keeps going.

"I told you to stop." Tom shakes his head, jaw tight and I get a nervous feeling in my stomach.

"She's childish, selfish—"

And then Tom shoves him. It's a big shove. Beej stumbles a bit, but he's happy he has a reason to let his hands do the talking so he lunges at Tom, but Christian's pulling BJ back and Henry gets up in his face. "What the fuck are you doing, man?"

BJ shakes his head and breaks free, rushing up to me, pointing a finger. "What the fuck are you doing, Parks?"

Our faces are close. Not 10 cm between us I don't think. He's still wearing the shirt he was wearing when I slipped my hand beneath it in the car at the start of the day before he fucked it up again. Because he wanted to?

I shrug my shoulders lightly, keeping our faces close. "Oh, I'm just doing what I want," I tell him with a little nod. The tone in which I say this surprises me. It's so capricious, it's cutting. I lock eyes with the boy I love and hate. "I want to be here. I want to be on a date with Tom, this is what I want—"

BJ's jaw goes tight and his eyes look wounded as he shakes his head. "You're full of shit," he spits and then I push his face away from mine with my hand.

"Get the fuck out of my face."

He grabs my wrists and holds them tight and I don't want him to let them go because I'm scared of what happens when he does. "Oh, is that what you want now?" he yells, and we're devolving.

Everyone around us can see it. The wheels are falling off. We've gone like this before once or twice, when we're at our worst. When I found out about Taura. When he found out about Christian. When all that's left of loving each other is hating each other.

Tom pulls me behind him, snatching me from BJ, which only makes BJ buck harder as the boys drag him backwards and away from me.

The faces of the boys and Tom, all of them, each somewhere between a quiet shock and muted horror, watching on as we pull at the seams of ourselves.

"What the fuck do you want from me, Parks? Do you even know?" BJ yells at me again.

I shake my head; I can't see properly. "I don't want anything to do with you," I call to him. It's a lie.

"Back at you," he slurs.

"Perfect." A lie.

He points a finger at me, and his eyes look squinty and wet. "I'm fucking over your shit." A lie. His, this time.

My eyebrows shoot up as I nod. "Then why can't you just leave me the fuck alone?" That's not what I want. Another lie. All these lies we can't stop exorcist-spraying all over each other.

His eyebrows shoot up. "You want that?"

"Yes," I yell and it feels like a thunder-clap. Echoes through the ancient mountains around us and the Greek philosophers who waxed lyrical about true love and soulmates roll in their graves as I try for the billionth time to sever myself from mine.

Tom places himself very firmly between BJ and I, shielding me completely.

No one's ever shielded me from BJ before. I suppose no one's ever had to.

Tom looks sad, actually. Not at me, for me. For BJ. He shakes his head. "Bro, can you just fuck off?"

THIRTY-FOUR

BJ

I'm back in my room. I don't remember how I got here. Shoved by my brother, maybe? Dragged by Christian? One of the two.

I'm standing in the bathroom. The reflection I find is weird. Me but not me.

Me but fucked.

I hate fighting with her. We do it too well, better than anyone I've ever seen. We weren't like that when we were together, barely ever fought when we were together.

Marsaili used to say something about how love can go sour like milk and then it turns to hate. Maybe we left our love out.

My eyes feel damp. My hand's trembling—I raise my fist to my mouth, press it into my mouth hard enough I split the inside of my lip on my front teeth. One. Just one. That's all I'll give myself.

It comes out mangled and choked. Quick.

Feels stuck in my chest. I press my palms into my eye sockets, breathe big and deep 'til my chest slows down.

It does a bit but not enough—not enough for my shoulders to not still be dragging behind my breathing.

I reach into my toiletry bag, pull out a different kind of bag. Cut a line with my Centurion card because the titanium crushes it better. Roll a €100 and snort it.

Pinch my nose after, rub it twice and sniff. I do another for good measure. Splash some water on my face, wipe under my nose just to be safe. And then I go find the boys.

They're sitting at the bar and I fall into the seat next to them. Henry and Christian—they're their own version of me and Jonah and I gotta say, I don't love being here without him.

Kind of in the lurch, no one has got my back the way Jo does. He'd have decked England on the step tonight. Maybe not. Fuck.

Maybe I was out of line?

Christian puts his hand in the air, makes eye contact with the bartender. She's pretty. Olive skin. Hazel eyes I can see from here. Big eyebrows but in that hot girl way—he points down at me, signalling for her to bring me a drink.

Henry looks over at me, grimacing. "You doing okay?"

I snort a laugh. "Yeah, why wouldn't I be?"

Both their faces falter. They exchange looks. "I don't know"—Henry shrugs, playing dumb—"I mean, you just had the gnarliest fight of your life with the girl you've loved since you were six—but sure, yeah. Be fine."

"We fight all the time."

Christian blinks. "Like that?"

I scoff a laugh. "You're being dramatic—"

Henry looks at me funny. "Beej, she fucking palmed you in the face. I mean, it was sublime—embarrassing for you, but like—truly spectacular for the rest of us."

I scoff again.

The hot Greek bartender brings over a round of drinks for the three of us and when she hands me the glass our hands brush. I look up at her and she gives me an inch of a smile.

Walks away.

I watch her go—blow air out of my mouth as I watch her arse in that flouncy black skirt she's in.

Parks would know the brand, the make, the fucking SKU—don't think of her—actually, she probably wouldn't because Magnolia only knows about brands that are stocked in Harrods. Nothing Showpo or polyester in her vocabulary.

Still—a lot to work with with a skirt like that…

I throw back my drink in one gulp. Pinch Henry's.

Christian's eyes pinch as they watch me. "What's up with you?"

"Nothing." I give him a dismissive look.

He watches me a few seconds longer, then leans in close to me and grabs my chin with his hand. I smack it off but Christian wins every fight he wants to, so he knocks me back and grabs me again, tilting my eyes up into the light. He breathes out of his nose, sounds annoyed. Shakes his head, still holding my chin. "Oy, fuck it—" Shoves my head away. "I'm out, boys—"

"What?" Henry blinks. "Why?"

Christian gnaws down on his bottom lip—points to me, the fucking snitch. "He's on some shit."

Henry huffs a laugh. Just one. "No, he's not." He clocks me. Blinks. "Are you?" Blinks again. "Are you?"

I make a weird sound. It's dismissive and incriminating all at once.

Christian pushes back from the table, stands, raises his hands, washing himself clean from it.

"Are we just going to pretend that you walking away has fuck all to do with Magnolia?" I yell after him.

He doesn't turn around or back, but raises his hand in the air, flips me off, keeps walking.

Henry eyes me. "I forgot that you talk shit when you're on coke."

"Do not."

He nods his chin after Christian. "What's that then?"

I give him a look. "Did I lie?"

And I've got him there—I know I do. He knows I do too. Hangs his head, breathes it out. I try not to put him in the middle of whatever shit Christian and I have. He hates all this, and I get it because I hate that shit too. Hate that it happened, hate that he went there, hate that I fought him in an alley for her and no one that night left a winner. I hate all of it.

"What are you doing, Beej?" Henry asks, voice softer.

I shrug. I don't care right now. "She'll kill you."

I try to put a lid on how ragged I feel inside my chest when I answer him. "She already is."

Henry stands—he looks angry. Or sad, maybe? Stares at me for a few seconds and feel like I'm failing him as his big brother. I don't feel like his big brother very often. He's more responsible. He doesn't fuck around so much. He's at uni. He never feels like my little brother, just feels like Brother. But right now, the way he's looking at me, I can feel it that I'm letting him down.

He knocks over the mostly full drink in front of me. It spills all over the table.

I push back, annoyed, looking at him like he's gone mad. "What the fu—"

"—You need to tighten the fuck up, Beej." My brother points at me.

Then he turns to the bartender, points to me and slides a finger over his throat. "Cut him off," he calls to the girl, then he walks away too.

I sit there, staring at nothing. Takes me a couple of minutes to catch that the bartender's just standing there, watching me.

I point to her, wag her over to me with my finger. She walks over slowly. There's no one around.

Bartender stands in front of me, staring down for a few seconds—and actually Bartender is insanely hot. She blinks a few times, then reaches down, takes my hand, pulls me up and leads me towards the bathroom.

As soon as we're in the corridor, Bartender has me pinned up against the wall; she wants this more than I do. Which is hard to articulate exactly because it's somewhere between needing it more than anything and not wanting it at all. Maybe she fucked up today too.

Bartender gets down to business pretty quick. Her busy hands unbuttoning my jeans and we're not even in the bathroom yet.

Her mouth is hungry for all of me, doesn't commit to one location. She undoes my shirt. The one I bought for Parks—don't think of Parks—kisses my chest. Same chest Parks spent the day against.—Fuck, she's my worst habit.

My hands are up her skirt, both of them slipped under the cheeks of her knickers.

Good arse. Squeezable.

She cocks her leg up around me—and I wonder whether we'll even make it to the stall?

Bartender's lips drag over me and my mind starts to wander to Parks the way it always does. That same memory, that boat, her on the lake, the lilac bikini—god, I love her in lilac—and then I think, fuck it—no.

I'm not going to think about her.

I'm going to think about Bartender, who's hot as shit, with her hands down my pants.

So I open my eyes, make myself look at the girl I'm about to shag and then—

I spot her.

End of the corridor.

Eyes glassy. Bottom lip quivering. Heart on her sleeve, mine in her pocket.

Holding her own hands in front of her, looking about five years old like she's watching her nightmare unfold in front of her.

Our eyes lock.

She turns—

I shove Bartender off me. "No! No, no, no, no, no—"

Parks runs. I run after her but she's fast and I lose her as she rounds a corner.

THIRTY-FIVE

Magnolia

I went back for a hair clip. I left it in the bathroom when I went in to check that my lips were still the shade of pink I need them to be to make my eyes the brightest. And I took my hair pin out to adjust it and then I forgot to put it back in, and I wouldn't normally go back for a hair pin but I did, because it's a £2000 white gold, diamond-encrusted hair pin by Suzanne Kalan and I'm trying to be more financially economical these days, so the economical thing to do would be to go back and at least look for the lost one before ordering a new one on Net-A-Porter.

So I ran back to the bathroom.

Tom offered to come, I said no, it was okay—I'd just be a minute.

It never gets easier, seeing BJ like that. I don't even know what I saw. They could have actually been having sex for all I know.

His hands were gripping her arse. Properly gripping it. Indented in her flesh of her bottom, were BJ's fingertips.

And her bottom lip—which was huge, by the way, was dragging up his chest like it was a fucking salt lick—and her hands were nowhere in sight.

And his head was back against the wall, his eyes were closed, his neck all exposed, muscles taut, and I remember when he used to lean back like that with us and I don't know what he was thinking about, but I know for sure it wasn't me. I stood there for I don't know how long. Could have been seconds, might have been minutes. 'Til he saw me, and then I ran.

I don't really like running. It's always felt quite pedestrian to me, but I'm faster than he is. I always have been. He says I waste it. I say it's not a skill I've any interest in or appreciation for. Until tonight, when I needed it.

I run back to my room, throw the door open, slam it shut, leaning against it. Squeeze my eyes tight shut, trying to get a handle on myself.

Tom looks up from the couch. "Are you crying?" he asks, standing. "Again?"

I wipe my face clean of tears and scramble for a way to stop feeling like I'm falling down a well.

I don't know what I'm doing.

I've given this very little thought.

None, actually.

Except that when Tom stands up, frowning with this concern on his face for me, the way he rises, the width of his shoulders, all of him feels safe, and I don't right now... feel safe anymore. And I'd really like to.

I walk over to him, acting far more confident and self-assured than I'm feeling. I slip my arms around his neck and pull his head down to me, and I've never done this before. I wonder whether I'm going to feel like a stranger when we kiss, like the girl who was kissing BJ, but I don't. When I kiss Tom I just feel like me.

A lost version of me. Maybe a concussed one. But still me.

The kiss starts slow, but I kiss him deeper and more and I feel him frown on my mouth, confused.

"What are you doing?" he says on my mouth, not really committed to pulling away entirely.

I pull back and look up at him. "On the day we decided to climb into the foxhole you said you were definitely trying to have sex with me—do you still want to have sex with me?"

He exhales all the air from his chest like I've asked him a trick question and his jaw goes a little lax.

"Yes."

"Okay then." I nod, leaning back in towards him.

He swallows once as he pulls back a fraction. "This—seems like a bad idea."

He says that but his hands don't move from my waist. If anything, maybe they hold me tighter.

"It's not," I tell him, eyes stubborn as I stare him down.

A frown whiskers over his face. "How much of this is about BJ?"

I pause, blink twice, swallow once. "Do you care?"

He thinks for a moment, his breathing louder than normal, almost huffy, his mouth pouting a tiny bit as he does—then he shakes his head.

"Nope." And then he kisses me like he's got my face in a headlock.

I'm moving backwards but my feet aren't on the ground anymore.

I unbutton his Cocoon oversized, logo-embroidered, crinkled, cotton-poplin shirt from Balenciaga. Six buttons. I stumble at the third—his chest feels like you're running your hand over a block of Cadbury's.

I take a breath. Measure myself. I've never done this with anyone else. Just BJ. Don't think about BJ. I need to change that.

BJ has probably at this point, done it with a hundred girls? Hundreds? I don't know. And here I am, saving myself still, for... him? Maybe? But for what? To change?

I think maybe, he changed already, and I think maybe, I don't like it.

When I see him with other girls I'm, well, I'm first of all confused as to why people like pornography so much because so far, my two close brushes with erotica have only made me want to gouge my eyes out. But also, when I see Beej with other girls it makes me quite sure that, actually, I don't really know him at all.

I'm wafting, in my mind. I'm mentally wafting. Dodging the full situation I've put myself in. It's a coping mechanism, probably. Probably I'm not ready to do this.

Probably this will be a mistake.

Probably need to still do this anyway.

Head in the game, Parks.

Tom lowers me onto the bed, hovers over me, head tilted, looking down, one hand holding him up, the other he uses to slide the strap of my Aya tie-detailed, tiered, shirred, floral-print, cotton-voile mini dress from Loveshackfancy from my shoulder.

His finger lags over my skin and I'm surprised how easy it is to keep BJ at bay in my mind every time Tom has his hands on me.

"You have very lovely eyes," I tell him.

He smiles at me, a bit amused. Slips the other strap off. He looks back at me, pushes some hair behind my ears. "You're not selfish," he tells me. "Or childish." I give him a small, grateful smile as I try not to cry all over again. "And I think you know what you want." He nods to himself. I swallow heavy as his hand slides up from my leg, slowly over my arse, landing on my waist,

holding me fast. He shakes his head. "Not a brat—"
Then he gives me a measured look. "Gotta say, a few
months in, you are a bit of a handful—"

I start laughing and instead of his face lighting up
how it usually does when I laugh, it goes serious. He
tugs my dress down and off my body, his hands trail me
as he goes, and then he climbs back up to my face.

His eyes go from eyes to my mouth to my eyes to my
mouth and then I pull him down on top of me because I
need to not be BJ's anymore and this will sever me from
him once and for all.

This acts almost as a bit of a kick start. He rolls me
over on top of him. I unbutton his jeans, and he kicks
them off. My hands are busy, so are his…

It's been so long since I've done this—when was the
last time I did this? Don't think about that. Don't think
about him. He rolls me again. Him on top, me on the
bottom. I like it better this way.

There's something so fundamentally comforting
about being this close to another person, maybe that's
why casual sex is such a big thing. His body on mine,
like a flack-jacket, protecting me from all the things I'd
otherwise be feeling in this moment, but can't because
his mouth is where my bra was a second ago, and it's
hard to focus on anything more than the task at hand
once the task has begun, don't you think?

His hands go up into my hair. His kisses are major,
deep earth, tectonic plates shifting, and we haven't even
gotten to the actual major parts.

And his parts are major.

It hurts, more than I remember. It's a good kind of
pain though, do you know what I mean? A deep muscle
pain. A pain you lean in to, not away from. Like a knot

in your shoulder where you lean into the hand kneading it out. And I remember this feeling with BJ—different though, because nobody knows my body like BJ does. Our bodies grew up together.

And I wonder if I'll ever feel like that with anyone else again. I wonder if BJ has? Or is it a once in a lifetime thing? How many loves do we get in a lifetime? I really don't know anymore—my heart's racing so fast now and the dam is building—and there are all sorts of love in this world and mine is killing me, I think. And even still, it's his face in my mind—even with Tom's perfect face and golden hair flopped over his eyes that are so blue, even the sapphires stare—even with Tom right here, my mind goes running back to BJ. The task at hand fails to keep my mind off him and I hate what that says about me and him and us, because maybe I'll never be free.

And do you know what, it's not even sexy stuff, it's him brushing his teeth in my bathroom—toothbrush hanging out of his mouth as he tries to peek in the shower wall at me. Him yelling at me every time I knock my water bottle over in the middle of the night. How he hugs Bushka from behind like they're a couple at the prom. His Vans at the foot of my bed.

And all this shit pulls a number on me, because my mind keeps drifting to BJ just like my heart is tethered there and I wonder if Tom's mind is drifting to Clara, and I wonder what the fuck we're doing—but it's too late to stop, I can't stop. And I don't even know that I want to anyway when I think of the way BJ's hands were gripping that other girl's arse because there used to be a time in our lives where he'd grip no one like that but me.

Tom presses into me more, pulls me in closer to him, I'm thinking about BJ lying on my side of the bed so

I'll fight him and he'll touch me and hold me and he'll have the same smirk he has every time he does it. I'm thinking about where his jeans sit on his body, how his Calvins always poke out no matter what belt I or his mother buy for him. Tom's very good at this, I think. I wish I could focus on what was happening to my body, but my mind won't let me. I'm thinking about BJ's mouth when he talks because the way his lips move is like some sort of ancient, wordless poetry. I'm thinking about his face in the sunlight, the gold flecks in his green eyes. I'm counting the tattoos Beej has on his body that no one really sees because they're fairly hidden but most of them are overtly about me.

A magnolia—chest.

My birth year—inner elbow crease, right arm.

His birth year—next to mine.

National Geographic—down his forearm.

My back begins to arch.

A bee—left hand.

Another bee—right shoulder.

The Uno Reverse Card—left calf.

A deer—left arm.

Tom presses my hand into the bed.

'Billie'—along a rib, left side.

A beach umbrella—left upper arm.

Coordinates from Dartmouth—inner elbow crease, left arm.

The date we first kissed—along his left thumb.

My breath is fast. Soon I'll lose it.

A lilac—left middle finger.

The date we first slept together—left forearm.

'In every lovely summers day'—right forearm.

'If someone loves a flower'—right forearm.

Tom pushes in deeper, and my breath turns jagged.

A plaster—upper left thigh.

His breath is hot on my neck as he brushes his lips over mine, and I wish I could see into his mind so I knew whether he was as fucked up as I am right now.

Forget-me-knot—right thumb.

The build of sex has always fascinated me, the climb up towards the end. And we're climbing, we're almost at the peak, I can feel it—see it in his face—and we're quite good at this, actually? All things considered, like how I'm not thinking about Tom England at all, which is insane because it's Tom England. Do you know what I mean?

East Winds—chest.

Tom's neck arches back the way BJ's did with that girl in the corridor.

Paddington Bear—right arm.

I can feel the breath in me being drained, sucked out as feet press down into the mattress, looking for anything to steady myself against.

The Maserati M—right foot.

And then the smallest sound escapes my mouth as my head falls back suddenly untense into the pillow. Tom falls on top of me. His chest is heaving, so is mine. I like the feeling of him sweaty on me.

And I'm so confused about what that means. How I just came, counting the tattoos of my ex-boyfriend but I don't want Tom England to move from on top of me? What does that mean?

What does that say about me?

I think it just says that I'm broken.

It didn't work, by the way. It didn't sever anything. If anything, it just tied me to another person.

BJ's twenty-second tattoo? The DeLorean from *Back to the Future.*

What have I done?

THIRTY-SIX

BJ

I don't know what I was expecting from a knock in my hotel door at 2 a.m.—but Magnolia Parks wasn't one of them.

Not after how she looked when she saw me. Not after how we spoke to each other earlier. But there she is, other side of the peephole. Holding her own arm and wearing a jumper she stole from me about forty seconds after I got it from Gucci. She's frowning, face a new sort of sad I don't think I've seen on her before.

I open the door and it's one look at her and I don't give a fuck about anything else, and I wonder if that'll always be us. Are we just those people who always find a way back to each other no matter what? Probably.

We're the wooden figurehead carved at the front of an old, sinking ship.

I step into the hall, close the door behind me.

"What happened?" I wrap her in me.

She pulls back and looks up at me and I don't know what gives it away—her eyes, the smell of him on her.

She doesn't have to say anything. I know.

I wince a bit. Out loud. She hears me, I know, because she presses herself harder into my chest when I do.

"Oh." Is all I say. Nod once. Hold her tighter.

Fuck, it's a solid burn.

Is this what I've been doing to her all these years? Is this how her chest feels? Because it feels like I've got carpet burn inside my chest. This weird slow sinking like my ribs are collapsing in on themselves and that maybe I'm actually finally losing her.

Maybe the ship's not still sinking, maybe it's sunk. Maybe we're on the seabed now. Maybe the ship's wood is starting to rot and all the anchors in the world can't save us anymore.

"Are you okay?" I ask her because I don't know what else to say. She just cries more. I hold her against me, my hands in her hair, and I pretend I don't notice that it's clearly just been pulled and messed up by someone else.

What are we doing? Other than hurting each other. I don't know what we're doing anymore. Because I love her in a final way. This unbeatable, can't trump it, will always win out, no matter what, fucked up kind of way—but I can smell him on her and I could actually. Probably will later.

"I'm sorry," she barely says, all muffled into my chest.

I tilt her chin up to look at me. "I'm sorry too."

She blinks a few times and her eyes remind me of raindrops on leaves on cold mornings.

"I hate you," she says, swallowing heavy.

"Yeah." I nod. "I kind of hate me too."

She pulls back to look up at me, I hold her face in both my hands—heavy, light eyes, that blushing mouth of hers with those cheeks that always go pink when I'm with her. The caramel skin, the hand I've held since I was fifteen, the curves of her body that fit into me like we're split from the same stone. How will I ever get past her?

I won't. Can't. Couldn't.

She holds my hand against her cheek, not letting go, not wanting to know what comes next for us once she does. I don't think either of us know anymore. We used to, I think.

Thought we did, anyway. It used to be all roads lead home to Tobermory—a quiet life in a coastal town up north because one night we had an unstoppable lust and a belligerent sense of fearlessness, and we'd have grown old there. Fell asleep on the couch holding each other, leave the curtains open and drown in the morning light of loving her every day and it's what we should have done but then that day happened. Probably should have done it anyway. Should have pulled her out and away to the life we both wanted even still, but I didn't. If I had, we wouldn't be here.

And then my hotel door opens, and Bartender fills the frame wearing my T-shirt and nothing else. Magnolia freezes in my arms and I close my eyes tight, like maybe if I squeeze them enough, Bartender will vanish, but she doesn't and I know what comes next.

Brace myself for it.

It's a shove this time. She pushes me crazy hard, but I know it's coming, my feet are planted—Parks moves more than I do, and her little body rebounds from the push into the corridor wall behind her where she stumbles a bit.

I go to catch her, but she smacks my hands away, looking up at me like an animal that's been kicked.

"Parks—" I reach for her again.

She jerks away from me. "No—"

"Magnolia—" I call for her, but she's already gone.

05:23

Parks

Hey

284

How's the weather, Parks.

Fucked.

THIRTY-SEVEN

Magnolia

I go to Paili's room after that and cry in her bed for a couple of hours. She cries with me. She's such a good friend. Patient. She's one of those people who are so good at caring about the things the people they love care about. She cried with me the night BJ cheated on me. She cried with me the night I started dating Reid. She's been here for all of it. She doesn't say much.

But what could she say anyway?

I should have gone to her after Tom, not BJ, but I barely could even help it.

Truly, it wasn't even really conscious, me going to BJ. I was lying awake, staring at the ceiling, my heart hammering, Tom peacefully asleep next to me—and I'll say it here because it's pertinent—that Tom England really is something akin to spectacular. Me thinking about BJ before, that's not a commentary on Tom at all. That is the residue of a habit I've had for half my life that I don't know how to break. I wish I thought of Tom. I should have thought of Tom. As he lay there next to me sleeping, I wondered whether I should wake him up to try again so I could only think of Tom this time, but instead I found myself walking to BJ and I guess that sort of says it all.

How stuck I am.

He's the moon, and I'm the tides.

When the girl walked out of his room, it was low tide. Pushed me out and away.

He stared at me, his eyes a familiar roundness. The way they go every time we lose each other, which is I don't know how many times at this point.

Too many.

Tom was asleep when I crept out to see BJ. He's a heavy sleeper, I've worked out this trip. I knock over my water bottle all the time and he never wakes up, even though it sounds like a Chinese gong every time I do. He was still asleep when I crept back into our bed a few hours later. He kept sleeping for hours.

I kept not sleeping.

In the morning I take a long shower and scrub my skin hard all over, try to wash off all the mistakes I'm making, but it doesn't work. I put on the comfiest clothes I have with me—the oversized Vetements, multi-button cardigan with the Loulou Studio ribbed. mélange cashmere shorts and crop top.

I order up some breakfast to the room for both of us and bring it out onto the balcony so I don't wake him, but I do. His eyes blink awake and he gives me a tired half smile—and something punches me in the stomach. Surprises me. Some kind of want?

He rolls out of bed, walks out to me. He's just in black Tom Ford boxer briefs and I have a brief and inexplicable desire to lick him but just for a second and then it's gone because how unrefined.

My legs are resting up on the chair across from me and Tom picks them up, sits down and then rests them on himself.

And it's a funny picture of familiarity, my legs stretched out over on top of him, mostly naked, him squinting at me in the Greek morning sun and another feeling in my stomach stirs, and I swallow as I worry that my cheeks might give away something I don't even fully understand myself yet.

He stares across at me for a few seconds, all stoic and statuesque.

"You went to see him after," he says eventually. Not a question, not an accusation. Just an observation.

My eyes fall from his, embarrassed. "Just for a minute."

He nods, his eyes not meeting mine anymore either. "Why?"

I purse my lips. I wasn't sure when this would come up but assumed it might have eventually, and I was quite sure that he'd not be thrilled about it either way. I take a breath, breathe it out through my nose. "I've never slept with anyone else, besides him."

Tom blinks a couple of times as his head pulls back in surprise.

A few more blinks, then… "Fuck. Magnolia!"

I give him a tight smile and swat my hand. "It's not a big deal."

He grabs my legs, yanks me and the chair I'm sitting on over to him so we're closer, my limbs now tossed all over him like a pile of pick-up sticks. I don't shift. I'm happy to be a pile of pick-up sticks on him. He stares at me. "It is."

It is. He's right. But we already did it and now it's done so I shrug.

"Yeah, well. I needed it not to be, so—"

Tom's hands have found their way to my ankles and he squeezes them.

"Why didn't you tell me?"

I hug my knees. "Because I knew you wouldn't do it then."

He gives me an unimpressed look that's scolding-adjacent, which, for some reason I find very sexy. Father issues, probably.

"That's being deceitful," he tells me.

"No," I correct him. "That's being withholding." I annunciate the last word.

He rolls his eyes, a little amused, then nods his chin at me. "So you went to see him?"

I nod a few times and I find myself unable to hold his eyes again. He knows I love BJ. He knows more about me and Beej than most people at this point so why am I so embarrassed about Tom knowing I went to see him? "Yeah," I nod. "Yeah, and he was with someone else."

Maybe that's why.

"Fuck." Tom's head falls back in exasperation, but his grip around my ankles tighten. "You two are—"

"—Fucked." I nod. "Yes, I know."

He stares over at me, trying to dissect what Beej and I—an impossible task, I can assure him here and now that he—like the countless number of people before him—will fail miserably. Because BJ and I are unquantifiable. It's the nuances of all the ways we love each other and have loved each other and keep on accidentally loving each other and it's the intricacies of our threads we've knotted together and it's the secrets we know about each other and it's that one broken heart we share.

"Why"—he asks eventually, squinting—"are you like this?"

And I'd love to tell him, I'd love to tell him so it makes sense, but I can't, so it won't.

Instead, I offer him a weak shrug. "I—we just, fell in love too young, I think… and we don't know how to be without each other now."

BJ and I—I think we're like a fine-chain gold necklace all tangled. Not impossible to undo but it feels like it is. You can sometimes manoeuvre the chain free of itself but not very often. Most of the time you have to undo it at the clasp or break it completely for the knots to come undone.

"You're like Sam and Closs." Tom nods to himself and he looks a bit sad. "Fuck," he adds as an afterthought, mostly under his breath.

"I'm sorry," I tell him, and I feel as though I could cry.

"No." He shakes his head, rubbing my ankle mindlessly. "I'm sorry—if I could unstick you I would."

My heart slumps in my chest and I sigh instead of formulating a sentence. There are things to say, many actually. But all of them are contradictory.

Yes, I love BJ. And no, I don't know how to make myself stop. But please don't leave me. I don't want you to leave me. I'd be afraid without you. You make me not lonely. And I'm worried that maybe Gus was right.

They're the things I'd say if I could, but they're stuck inside my throat.

He takes my coffee from my hands and has a big sip.

"So," Tom says, brows furrowed as he stares at me. "Where does this leave us?"

"Pertaining to foxholes you mean?" I clarify, as I reach over and wipe a rogue bit of cappuccino foam from his top lip. My hand hovers. His cheeks go pink.

Tom clears his throat. "Yeah—"

"I don't know," I say and shrug, mostly with my eyebrows. "Where do you want it to leave us?"

"Well, I still need a foxhole." He looks over at me. "You still need a foxhole. We're both still waiting out for our feelings to pass." He shrugs. "Might as well wait them out together."

I nod and feel a strange rush of endorphins. A little giddy that I can keep pretending to be Tom's. Giddier still that I don't have to face BJ without my own version of an AK-47.

Tom nods his head back towards the bed. "We probably shouldn't do that again though…"

"Oh." I nod. I don't think my face conceals my disappointment well at all. "No, no, I guess not—"

He squints at me playfully and his face fights off a smile. He's a bit pleased.

I put my nose in the air and peer over at him. "Wouldn't be the end of the world if we did though," I add as a caveat because something pangs inside of me at the thought of that being completely off the table.

His eyes soften and he nods once, leaning in. "Listen—we can do it again, any time you want. I just—I don't think you wanted to last night. I think you think you had to." He shakes his head. "You didn't have to."

"I know," I tell him, my nose in the air.

"You look so sad," he tells me with a bit of a confused and feeble laugh, then his face changes a tiny bit. "I don't want to make you sad."

"You didn't," I tell him.

"I know!" He blinks. "You did. But you made me an accessory."

I nod. "I'm sorry."

He squints at me, a bit playful. "This is a prime example of you being a handful."

THIRTY-EIGHT

BJ

Fucked. That's what she said. It's what I am. What we are, I guess.

Still, nothing could have fully prepped me for how it'd feel to watch Parks round the corner into the lobby with the only other man she's been with besides me. And here's the fucking kicker—they're different now. I can see it on them.

Sex is special to her. She wouldn't have done it if she didn't want to, even if she did it a bit to spite me; she's spited me a thousand times in a million ways and never once has she had sex with anyone but me, but Tom—

It's different with Tom. Even if she doesn't realise it yet.

"Oy." Henry grins at them because he doesn't know.

Magnolia smiles at him weakly, and he looks over at me, confused. Perry and Gus trade quizzical looks. Tom whispers something to Parks, brushes some hair behind her ears—he's too familiar with her now. Touches her like she's his—and then he goes to speak to reception. I look for her eyes, but she purposely won't meet mine. Pails rushes over to her, linking her arm with hers, kind of using herself to shield Parks from me.

I try not to look too hurt, but I am. I'm fucking dying inside. Christian looks from me to Parks, brows low. Reading the room.

I reckon he knows.

Tom walks back over towards Parks, clocks me, barely gives me a chin nod and then tosses his arm around her lazily. That hurts. The casualness of how he's touching her, and then she mindlessly reaches up and holds two of his fingers with her whole hand—and then they just stand there... like that... like a couple. Like an actual couple. With real feelings and real sex between them.

The quiet intimacy that passes between them right in front of me makes me feel like someone just scooped out my fucking soul with a soup ladle and I turn away because I can't look.

Henry notices, frowns. "You good?"

I nod quick because it's obvious I'm lying. "Be back in a sec," I tell him.

Jog to the bathroom. Do a line. Walk back out. Try to catch her eye but she won't cast me a line. That's all she'll give me. Nothing. And nothing from her is something because nothing between us is unnatural and something about that makes me feel a bit better.

Our car arrives; it's a stretch. Tom leads her to the car—the whole ride there she's quiet. I don't think she says a word once, not to anyone. Not even when people speak to her. Tom answers or Paili. And he doesn't let go of her hand—what are they? Superglued?

We get to the airstrip and my chest feels tight and my girl feels far away.

As they're unloading the car, I come and stand by her. "Can we talk?" I ask, quietly.

She tilts her head in my direction, but her eyes don't meet mine. "No." Then she walks away, back over to Tom. My face falters as I watch her with him again. She's not her comfortable self with him, she's not her usual self, she's not talking, or quippy, or funny or bright; she's none of those things around him today—she's hurt. She's her wounded self around him, and that might feel worse. Because the only other person I've ever known her to be that exposed with is me.

I watch them and feel like I'm watching my own life in a car wreck. We start boarding England's plane. I sit at the back same place I sat on the way over, leave the seat next to me wide open, hope she sits next to me again. It's not really like her to leave loose ends, doesn't do good for her brain. So, I sit there, waiting for her to get on the plane, waiting to catch her eye to nod her over to me—but when she boards, Tom's hands are on her waist.

He nods his head towards the cockpit. She nods and follows him and they close the door. I don't even get a look in.

Henry lets out a long whistle. Paili elbows him.

She was right. The weather is fucked.

10:12

Christian

Oy

What's up with you and Beej?

I don't know what you're talking about.

Liar

Did he say something?

Nope

He won't say shit about it either.

What happened?

Nothing

Tell me

We just had a big fight, is all.

...?

I saw him with a girl

?

I saw him saw him

Like.. 🥀

What?

Actually?

I think so. I don't know.

I ran away.

Where to?

To Tom

I was there

I know.

You could have come to me.

I know.

But I couldn't have.

You can always come to me.

You should know that.

I know.

Thank you xxxx

xx

THIRTY-NINE

Magnolia

Tom insists on dropping me home after the flight.

We land in Luton this time. A smidge less than an hour's drive at this time of day. I said he didn't have to, but he did anyway. Since our breakfast talk, he's become this funny, self-appointed guard dog. He didn't leave me alone once, wouldn't let go of my hand.

I don't know completely whether it was just because of what happened with BJ and how sad I was, or another reason—because regular foxholery aside, I felt a peculiar kind of relief to be holding Tom's hand anyway.

And when he told me to come and sit up with him in the cockpit, I knew it would hurt Beej so I did it, and I was right. I saw him sitting at the back of the plane, waiting for me to come sit next to him—I didn't.

Even though a bit of me wanted to. Because I think a bit of me will always want to. It sounds hypocritical, I know—that I'm this angry at him for sleeping with someone else when I did as well. I don't know why it feels heavy around my neck, a bit like it's choking me, and why I feel like he's betrayed me, but I've not betrayed him.

Or maybe I do feel like I betrayed him but maybe I had to?

The spare seat next to BJ was for me, that much was obvious from his eyes, even though I didn't meet them—I didn't need to, I could feel them on me, waiting for me, hoping for me.

And then I went into the cockpit with Tom.

And a part of me hoped that Beej felt what I feel whenever I see him with his hands on other girls, hoped that it consumed him while we flew—what was happening behind the closed door.

What happened was making out.

"Am I allowed in here?" I asked, as he closed the cockpit door behind us.

He gave me a look. "I'm the pilot."

"You didn't ask me in here last time."

"Saw Ballentine at the back of the plane with the spare seat next to him," he said. "You just strike me as the sort of girl who'd be powerless against a backseat with the love of her life."

"Excuse me." I blinked, indignant. "I'm powerless before nothing but Gucci."

He sniffed a laugh. "Go back out there then."

"No," I told him, my nose in the air. "I fancy my chances better in here but only because he's wearing grey and I love grey, and he knows that so he did that on purpose."

He looked down at himself in a plain white tee from Tom Ford. "How do you feel about white?"

My eyes fell down him and I was being flirty, I knew I was, but it's fun to flirt with Tom England. "It goes alright."

He smiled at me with pinched eyes and a mouth that said nothing while simultaneously saying many things.

I sat in the co-pilot chair. We flirted more. Tom showed me what to do, all the buttons to press, talked me through taking off as he did it, and then once we were in the air, he asked me if I wanted to fly it.

"Maybe?" I glanced over at him, nervously. He patted his lap. "Oh, I see." I rolled my eyes and he laughed.

He bit down on his bottom lip. "Come on," he said. I walked over to him gingerly, eyeing him, amused. He pulled me down on to him and positioned me for peak plane-flying position, wrapping his arms around me, holding my hands to the yolk of the plane. He rested his chin on my shoulder, guiding the plane through my hands—I wasn't doing anything, I knew I wasn't. But I also wasn't moving because I liked the feeling of Tom England against me.

It felt like I was lost at sea and he was this saviour piece of driftwood that I could cling to.

His breath on my neck caught on my skin and so I turned back, my eyes flicking from his down to his mouth and back up again.

He does this thing with his mouth, Tom England—and it's unbelievably sexy—it's this almost smile, no teeth—nearly a smirk but not smug at all. He does it when he wants something or he's being clever, and it was of my opinion in that moment, that he wasn't being overly clever, ergo he wanted something and the thing Tom England wanted was me.

He swallowed heavily.

Then I brushed my mouth against his. Quick and gentle, shyer than I wished I was.

I don't know why I did it. Not very like me, actually. I just wanted to.

He smiled, maybe surprised, definitely pleased, and then he leant in again, mouth hovered above mine, close enough that you could feel the touch before the touch, and my breathing went weak at the knees, and then our lips touched, slowly at first and then not at all, it was just rushy-rushy, time racing past us and through us.

He spun me around so I was facing him and then we were just kissing. We stayed kissing until we hit an air pocket and the plane dropped a few feet, and I nearly went flying into the ceiling, but he grabbed me, and he was laughing, and then he apologised to everyone over the loudspeaker, told them his co-pilot was a bit distracting and not overly-attentive in the aviation arena.

I didn't know whether he said that for me or for himself, but I hoped it hurt BJ either way.

We stopped kissing after that though, and he sat in his chair and I sat in mine, but every now and then, he'd look at me out of the corner of his eye and his nostrils would flare a bit as he tried not to smile, and then I'd start laughing, and then he'd start laughing and I think he's become one of my best friends.

There's a moving lorry out the front of my house when I get home. I look over at Tom, confused. We walk inside and we're only in for about 4.5 seconds when my sister flings herself into my arms. "Thank god," she cries. "It's been a madhouse."

"Oh?" I blink. "Why? What's happened?"

Bridget pulls away, hands pressed into her temples. She's wearing the maroon and custard, yellow, horizontal-stripe, logo cardigan from Miu Miu that I left hanging in her closet, hands on her hips—she looks from me to Tom.

"Everything." She shakes her head. "Everything!" I wave my hands impatiently, waiting for more information. BJ would have flicked me for doing that to Bridge. "Well, Mum's moving out," she starts, and I roll my eyes.

Wow. "Okay."

"They're getting a divorce."

Geez. I nod. "Okay."

"Mars is moving in."

I frown. "She already lives here."

Bridge gives me a look. "Into his room."

I scrunch up my face, make a "yuck" sound.

Tom glances at me and has a fairly solid lid on that smile of his but BJ would have covered my mouth to shut me up.

"I heard that," Marsaili says, walking out. "Magnolia—" She goes to kiss me and I dodge it. Not just to be petulant (though I am) but because we're not kissers. We weren't before she had an affair with my father. We aren't now that she has. "Lovely—" She clears her throat. "Still acting like a child, I see." She nods at him. "Hello, Tom."

He gives her a curt smile. "Marsaili."

My mother wanders out of a living room wielding a Carolingian sword from the 12th century.

"That's mine!" yells my father. "That's mine, put it back."

"I'm taking it," she tells him.

"You hated that sword—you said it was a waste of money!"

"Yes, but see, you love wasting money, darling, don't you?" My mother bats her eyes at him. "That third breast augmentation I had was just money down the drain, wasn't it? Money down the drain! Didn't even look at them once."

"Mum, don't say 'breast augmentation' in front of Tom England," Bridget tells her.

Tom tosses Bridge an amused look.

"Oh!" She looks over at us. "Tom! Magnolia, what a surprise."

"Is it though?" I frown.

"Hi." Tom smiles uncomfortably.

I wobble my head around, considering it. "I mean I do live here—"

"And I do not," she tells me with an indelicate nod.

I walk up a few stairs feeling like I'd rather like to be taller than the rest of the room, except I'm still not taller than Tom.

I stare at my mother for a few seconds. "Are you wearing a ballgown?"

She looks down at herself in the black Puff-sleeve, cotton-blend, Chantilly-lace gown from Dolce & Gabbana. "Yes."

"Why?"

"This is my moving ballgown."

"Practical." My sister nods appreciatively.

"Well, I was going to wear it at our recommitment ceremony." She eyes my father dangerously. "But that plan's in the toilet now."

"I never asked you to marry me again," he tells her, unceremoniously.

"Harley—" Marsaili smacks him in the arm.

I flick her a look. "Bit of a weird time for you to jump in—"

And I wish for a second that BJ was here. He's so good when things go pear-shaped like this. He's so good at diffusing my familial stupidity.

My mother folds her arms over her chest. "She's right, Harley, our vows might have gone to the wolves but there's no reason your manners need to."

I look only at my sister and give her a look. "I hate this."

She mirrors it. "Welcome home."

"Well—" I look between them all with a grimace. "I'm going to go upstairs—find a builder to soundproof my bedroom walls."

Marsaili rolls her eyes. "We've had sex here before."

I quickly stick my finger in my ears. "Lalalalalalala."

"Marsaili." My father gives her a look.

She looks annoyed. "She didn't hear us then—"

"And I shan't now," I yell.

"Do mine too, actually, will you?" Bridge tells me, and I give her a point and wink.

I turn to run up the stairs, Tom following me.

"Actually, darling"—my father makes a step towards me—"can I speak to you alone for a moment?"

I stand still and look back at him. Tom shifts in front of me. "No."

My father's jaw goes tight. He's annoyed but also a bit sad.

"No?" Mars says, incredulous. Tom shakes his head, indifferent. "Listen Tom," Marsaili sighs. "It's very, very sweet that you're so protective of Magnolia but she's perfectly fine to be left alone with her father, and frankly, this isn't any of your business, so—"

I shake my head. "Don't speak to him like that."

"Magnolia, with all due respect, Tom is new around here, and he's getting himself involved in our family affairs—"

"—You are not my family anymore." I shake my head as I point to her. "And he"—I point to him—"is my boyfriend."

Tom looks over at me and smiles with just the corner of his mouth, and it feels like maybe for a second, he's not just my fake boyfriend.

"Well," Marsaili sighs, "I'm sorry you feel that way, Magnolia. I've only ever treated you like my own daughter—"

"Oh!" I nod, thinking it through. "Is that why you've been fucking my father all this time?"

My father sighs with a groan under his breath. "Come on, love—"

"I don't know what you want from me." I look between them. "My approval? You won't get it."

"Darling." My father steps towards me. "I haven't been in love with your mother for a very long time."

"Fine," I nod. "That's fine—I don't have a problem with that. What I have a problem with is the spineless act of cheating. Which you do." I gesture towards him. "You cheat, I know you do. But with her?" I gesture to Mars. "Who was ours? Our one grown-up who loved us and cared for us and raised us—you had to ruin her?"

"Magnolia," Mars says, shaking her head. Her voice sounds a bit high and hopeful. "I'm not ruined, I'm just—"

"A hypocrite," I tell her.

FORTY

BJ

It was a few days before I went to her house—and they were fucking long days too. I don't do good with long days, don't do that good without Parks either. I have a penchant for filling the space she leaves with shit things, that's what Henry said to me last night when I took home a girl from Madrid.

Not that the girl was shit. She was nice, hot. Engaged—bit shit, I guess, not really my problem though. Didn't think about it again after a couple of lines.

Parks didn't text me though, and that's weird. Weird for us. We've always done this thing where if something's off between us, one of us caves, tries to restore the balance. I'll text her a bee. She'll send me an article from *Nat Geo*. Neither of us did that this time and I'm a bit scared to let myself think about what that might mean.

I stand outside her door and listen. Bridge is in there with her. "Stupid dress," Bridget declares. The sound of a page turns. "Stupid dress. Stupid dress." Page turns. "Stupid dress."

Magnolia hacks. "Your head's cut—" Makes me smile. She says that because my dad does. It's an Irish saying. "—That's Valentino at his best."

"It's still stupid. So is that one."

"I have that one." Parks sounds annoyed.

"So it's extra stupid then," Bridget says and I can imagine the look on her face.

I sniff a laugh as I listen to them. I miss them both, admittedly in very different ways, but I miss them, and I know their conversation could go on forever so I round the corner. I knock-knock at the door, stand in the frame. Parks glances up from the bed. Blinks a few times. Swallows. Her perfect face is a balanced mix of relief and nerves. Our eyes hold for a few seconds. She puts her hand over that little B necklace she's wearing that I got her. A good sign.

"Can I come in?" I ask.

Her face falters. "You've never asked before if you could come in…"

I shrug, shoving my hands in my pocket. "Never felt like I needed to."

Magnolia and I stare at each other and there's only been two times in our lives where there's been shit this big between us. When I cheated. And the other time when I fucked up pretty bad—climbed through her window at 11 p.m. on a school night to say sorry, invented the Tobermory plan, kissed her 'til the sun came up.

But I don't have balloons and I can't kiss her.

Parks does this weird hand gesture, telling me to come in. It's permissive and dismissive all at the same time. Bridget lets out a long, low whistle, takes a sip of her coffee, watching us closely.

"Okay," Magnolia says and rolls her eyes. "Can you sod off now?"

"Rude." Bridget huffs as she rolls of her bed. Walks by me, jumps on her tiptoes, kisses my cheek.

"Miss you, buggerface," she says, poking me in the stomach as she leaves.

Parks sits on the edge of her bed, hugging her knees to her chest. I stand in front of her, fold my arms over my chest. "Hey."

She sniffs a small laugh and shrugs her shoulders. "Hey."

"You didn't call."

She glares at me a bit. "Neither did you."

"You have a boyfriend."

"And your hands were very full…"

My eyes pinch a bit. She's exhausting. "You ran away from me," I tell her.

"I did." She nods, nose in the air.

"And then you had sex with him," I say.

She nods slowly once. "I did." Our eyes catch and the edges of her face go sad. Or soft? Shit. I hope it's sad. I want to fight with her, feel the closeness I feel when we do—when we say things we shouldn't and go too far and the other night when she shoved my face away it broke me and made me fly at the same time, because she can only hate me how she hates me because she loves me how she loves me.

"Are you okay?" I ask.

This small laugh come out of her like a choke. "I don't know."

She's not.

Her mind is so busy, I can see it—it looks like a Richard Scarry book.

"Are you sad?" I ask.

She wrings her hands. "I'm lots of things."

I want to reach out, touch her face. Pull her into me, hold her tight… I would have a week ago but now I'm not sure I can. She feels too far away for me to fix. I know why and I could boke if I thought on it too much.

"Are you into him?" I ask, my voice low. "Properly?"

She scoffs, tugs on her earring—ones I bought her last time I was in New York. Little diamond hoops. Don't know by whom. She'd know.

"I don't know what you mean," she says eventually.

I give her a look. "Yes, you do—" But she just stares at me, blinking. "Fuck." I press the fist of my hands into my eye socket.

She stands, grabbing my wrist, looking for my eyes— she finds them, doesn't say a thing. Just stares up at me, looking a little scared. I push some hair behind her ear because her hand on my wrist says I still can.

Shake at the girl of my dreams. "What the fuck is going on with us?"

"I don't know." She sighs. "Do you know?"

This annoys me and I pull away from her, scowling.

"How the fuck would I know what the hell is going on—you're the one holding all the cards."

She breathes a breath all the way out and glares up at me.

"Well, that's not true though, is it Beej? Because you're the one withholding information that had the potential to make things different to what they are—"

That hits different and I wonder whether it's true... If I told her, would she move past it? "Would it have changed things?"

She squares her shoulders defiantly. "I'd have thought so."

Fuck.

But I can't. So I dig in.

Shove my hands through my hair. "I gave you an answer."

Her face looks like I've hit her. She swallows and her eyes go glassy.

"And if that's your answer, then here's mine: We're done."

Someone could have hit me in the stomach with a pole.

Her mouth twitches and the glassiness of her eyes spills over a little. Fucks me up worse than it does her because she can't see her own face when she's crying but I can. Those fucking emerald eyes. I'd sell my liver on the black market to stop her from crying, sell everything I own, rip my heart out of my own chest—but I think I've already done that.

I shake my head at her, trying to level my breathing. "You don't mean that."

She carefully presses her tears into her own face and then looks up at me, face proud, eyes resentful.

"No. I don't." She clears her throat. "And I hate you for that."

16:42

Jonah

Oy

What's the go with you and Parks?

Any joy?

I don't know man. It's a fucking mess.

She's into him.

Actually?

Yeah I reckon

Shit

Yeah

It'll go right, man.

It's you and Parks. You always figure it out.

Yeah

You're alright though, yeah?

The boys said you were racking up a bit in Greece

Nah I'm fine.

Okay

Fine people don't often do drugs alone.

Just... for the record.

Right, yeah. Good point.

Oy, how's that crime syndicate you run going?

Good man. High stress but yeah, I mean. I'm not racking up alone in my hotel room, so...

FORTY-ONE

Magnolia

I come home after a long(ish) day at the office (lunch) and find Tom's car out front. He's not in my bedroom, not in the living room, not in the parlour, not in the other living room, not in the library, so I begin to wonder if maybe he's just parked here and gone for a walk around the park.

And then I hear Paili laugh from the kitchen.

I walk into the kitchen and Tom, Paili, and my sister all look up at me.

"What's going on here, then?" I look between them all brightly, flattening the skirt of my dark green Leona velvet mini dress from Khaites.

"Tom's teaching us to make a martini," Paili tells me.

"And how to order one," Bridget adds.

"Is he now?" I smile at him and he puts down a jar of olives, walks over to me and gives me a covert wink before kissing me.

"He is," he tells me as he pulls back. He looks so handsome. Bumblebee yellow, contrast-tipped, ribbed, cotton sweater and the tapered, pleated, linen and cotton-blend, drawstring trousers, both from Brunello Cucinelli. "How was your day today?"

He walks back towards my sister and best friend and eyes their handiwork. "It's either one or three olives, Bridge. Never two."

She nods obediently. I nod, watching him, my cheeks going pink. Why is he such a goodie?

"I had a work lunch with Kitty Spencer—"

"A work lunch?" Bridget blinks. "What's she doing in leisure for *Tatler*?"

"Well, it was a lunch during work hours so—"

My sister laughs.

"Paili"—Tom gestures to the refrigerator—"will you get the glasses out of the freezer for us?"

She obeys.

"Okay, now—" He glances at the ingredients in front of him. Gin, vermouth, olives. "Dirty?" He looks between Bridge and Pails.

"Filthy!" Bridget declares, delighted. Then shakes her head. "Just kidding, I've just always wanted to say that."

"Come over here." Tom nods me over towards them. "You should learn too."

"Everyone should know how to make a dirty martini," Paili tells me and I can tell she's just regurgitating what Tom said and I find it endearing. I perch up on the bench next to him.

"As much ice as you can in the glass, please Bridge," he tells her and she nods, piling in the ice cubes.

Paili passes him the spoon and he starts stirring. He's slotted right in and it strikes a chord in me I can't quite understand. A sigh of relief and a nervous tummy at once.

"Not shaken?" I ask, blinking away the most confusing parts of my mind.

He shakes his head.

"We want it smooth," Bridge tells me proudly and I can tell she likes him and that makes me like him more.

"Good girl," Tom says, and nods approvingly. "We're going to stir it for just shy of…" He trails and looks at Paili.

"One minute!" She grins.

"Very good." He nods.

He pours us each a martini, and Bridge plops in her little olive garnishes.

"Tada!" she sings as she gestures to it.

They cheer each other, but I look at Tom with pinched, suspicious eyes.

"You came here to teach my sister and my best friend how to make a martini?"

"No." He swipes his hand through his hair. "I came here to ask you on a date."

I take a sip, amused. "…We're already dating."

He shakes his head and takes me by the hand, pulling me off the bench and out of earshot of the girls.

"Foxhole business, I'm afraid," he tells me.

"Ah."

"Clossy's birthday."

I nod. "Okay."

"So you're free Wednesday?"

I nod again. "I will be."

His face looks strained for a second. "I think she's seeing someone."

I blink a few times. "Oh."

His face shifts from strained to frustrated. "Maybe. I don't know—"

I hold his arm and look for his eyes. "Are you okay?"

He gives me a tight smile. "Can you wear a dress that makes the whole world stare at you?"

"Do they not already?" I blink playfully.

He makes a "hah" sound as he kisses my cheek. "Thank you."

Paili

Babe, so you and Tom are like… a thing.

Pails, we've been dating for months.

Yeah but you were "dating"…

And now you're DATING

That's because we're TOGETHER.

🙂 you know what I mean.

I do not.

How's Beej.

I don't know.

Fine.

We left it in a weird spot the other day.

He'll come around. He always does with you. 🐦

For the record, you two are
also TOGETHER.

22:26

Christian

Hey x

Oy xx

Question..

Yep?

Is Beej fucking around a lot?

Hah

Beej is always fucking
around

How much though?

Come on

Don't make me answer that

Right.

That bad?

I didn't say a fucking thing.

FORTY-TWO

BJ

"Good of you to come up for air, lad," Jonah says, nodding his chin at me. His eyes are a bit dark. He's a bit off me, thinks I'm going too hard. That might be saying something in and of itself, I don't know? I mean—Jo's hardly a monk.

I actually think he's sort of into Taura Sax these days. Which is maybe a bit shit because I think Henry is also (reluctantly) into Taura? Probably why Jo's a bit tetchy?—I mean, definitely shagging her. And Henry knows it and doesn't seem to care, and Taurs, I think, is maybe intrigued by Henry not caring? I'm not sure. It's a mess. They think me and Parks are a mess, but they're making their own.

Admittedly it's been a rough week or so. Drank myself stupid, fucked 'til I was numb. Don't ask about the snow. I can admit it, I've been a bit off the handle since I saw Parks last, but this is just how I deal when things go to shit with us.

Usually within a fortnight she'd be texting me with a fake emergency like a flat tyre or she thinks someone's in her house trying to kill her and I'd come and I'd save her and we'd reset and be okay.

But she hasn't called. She hasn't even texted.

"You and Parks sorted yet?" Jo asks as I jump up on the counter, eating dry cereal from the box.

"Mope—" I chew through Frosted Shreddies.

"Seen her?"

"Nope."

"Called her?"

I scowl at him. "Get fucked."

"Texted?"

I throw some cereal at him and without skipping a beat, he pegs a remote at me and it hits me square in the chest with terrifying accuracy.

Fucking gang lords...

"What the fuck, man?" he groans.

I give him a look. "She likes Tom."

"Yeah, I wonder why, man? You're palming cereal into your mouth at 3 p.m. on a Tuesday, he's probably flying her to Barcelona as we speak—"

"I have a plane." I rub my tired eyes as I glare over at him. "You have a plane. So does she. It's not that special, we all have planes." He rolls his eyes. "And what's with how he calls her Parks? Don't you think that's weird?"

"That he calls her 'Parks'?" Jonah repeats, frowning. I nod. "Are you asking if I think it's weird that Tom calls Magnolia Parks 'Parks'?" he says again.

"Yes," I say, giving him an impatient look.

Jonah gives me a long look that makes me feel like a twat. "No, I do not think it's weird that Tom calls Magnolia by her last name."

"Yeah, but it's my name for her."

"Yes, but it's also her last name—"

I swat my hand at him because he's the idiot here who doesn't get it. Jo gives me a long look and I don't like it. He and Parks are the only ones who can make me feel like I'm made of glass.

"Beej, what are you doing?" He shakes his head. "What happened? You were nearly together and now she's shagging Tom."

"Once." I shake my head. Need that to be true. "It was a singular event. A sexual anomaly—" I wave my hand dismissively. He looks at me dubiously again. I sigh. "She wanted to know what happened. On the date."

"Oh." He nods, presses his mouth together. "Maybe you should tell her…"

I shake my head. "Can't."

"You could."

Shake my head again. "It's too late."

It is too late and I can't. I pore back over the night for the billionth time. Sadie Zabala in the little black dress, eye fucking me from the other side of the room. My hands went sweaty… went dizzy for a sec—everyone knew I was with Parks, had been for years by then, what was she doing? I went downstairs to my bathroom. Thought I might throw up. Maybe I was drunk? I wasn't. Not drunk enough for what happened next anyway.

She followed me to see if I was okay.

I wasn't.

And what would Parks knowing do anyway? Give her a visual to pair with her waking nightmare? There's nothing I can say that could make it better. I can't explain it away neatly how she needs me to.

I fucked up, I hurt her. I can't change it.

I need her to want me anyway. That's the only way.

"So, what?" Jo shrugs. "You're chucking in the towel?"

"With Parks?" I blink. He nods. "No." I shake my head. Never.

"What then? You already took her on a date and fucked that up."

I roll my eyes because I don't know what else to do. I did. He runs his tongue across his teeth as he thinks. "I reckon you should just kiss her."

I scoff. "What?"

He shrugs. "When was the last time you actually kissed?"

I scrunch my face back as I pretend to try to remember, like the last time we kissed isn't just singed into my memory, like I don't drag it out like my favourite sweater every time I have a minute in my brain to spare.

Shrug like it means nothing. "About two years ago."

He blinks twice. "What?"

I pull back, self-conscious. "What?"

"You haven't kissed in two years?"

I give him a look. "You were there—it was at the movies after I—"

"That was the last time you kissed?" he yells.

"Yes!"

"Hold on, wait—are you telling me that all these years you've been having 'sleepovers', you've actually literally just been having sleepovers?"

"What? Yes, Jo—" I shake my head. "I tell you everything, man—you'd know if we'd—"

"Nah, Beej, it's Parks." He shakes his head. "You never talk about her like you do with other girls, you hold that shit tight to your chest." He's right. He looks at me confused. "Are you sure you haven't shagged her once?"

"Jonah."

"Wow!" He shovels both hands through his hair. "I mean really, wow."

He's so taken by this revelation. I can see him rewriting the last few years in his mind—eyes ticking like a clock as he lines things up, undoing his assumptions—

"That was really your last kiss?"

I nod, mouth tight. "Pretty much."

There was one other time. Me and Parks don't talk about it.

"Bro—" He gives me a look. "Kiss her."

I give him a look, roll my eyes. "Come on."

Jo walks over to me, half-baffled, half-amused. "What, are you scared?"

I scoff. "No."

"Lad, I've seen you walk up to supermodels and kiss them."

I shake my head. "Different."

He gives me this exactly-my-point kind of look and he's a pain in my arse.

"Oy, Beej—man to man—" He whacks me in the chest. "Fucking kiss her."

FORTY-THREE

Magnolia

It's Clara's birthday and as promised, I wear a dress that will make the entire world stare at me.

Dolce & Gabbana's strapless, woven, raffia mini dress with the leopard print, tie-fastening sandals.

Tom at least picked me up this time. Suede bomber jacket from Brunello Cucinelli, a black and white striped T-shirt from Jil Sanders with the Fit 2 Slim-Fit, Rag & Bone jeans.

They've hired out Adam Handling's venue. The Sloane Street one.

"He's a friend," Tom tells me on the way there, then his eyes drag up and down my body, smirking. "That dress…"

I peek up at him, proud of myself as though I've done a great deal more than just look pretty.

"Are your parents going to be here?" I ask.

He shakes his head. "They're not feeling too good about Clossy seeing this boy—"

I nod. I feel sad for them—it would feel quick, I think. I feel sad for her too, because how long are we expected to sit in our grief? Longer than eight months seems to be the consensus of the England family.

"Are you?" I asked. "Feeling good, I mean."

His mouth goes tight. I think he thinks about brushing it off. "No."

"Are you sure she's seeing him?"

He glances at me, jaw pulled tight. "No."

I think I'm here in case. In case it's a worst-case scenario. Because I probably wouldn't bring Tom to BJ's birthday unless I was afraid BJ was going to throw a grenade at me.

I think I'm here to shield him in case.

When we arrive, Clara looks pleased to see me. I wish I felt the same way, but something about seeing her makes me feel a lot of feelings that have faces I don't recognise, and none of them have names.

"Wow"—she throws her arms around me—"I love that dress!"

"Yours too!" I smile at her. Jacquard, pleated, bustier dress from Dolce & Gabbana. Cream. A bit boring, but nice enough.

I hand her a present.

"What's this!" she marvels, like she's never been given a gift in her life.

I understand why Tom's in love with her, actually. Why both the England boys are. Were. BJ thinks I'm doe-eyed? Not compared to Clara England. Get a load of the richest girl Britain, whose eyes boggle when given a Net-A-Porter gift box. I wave my hand dismissively. "Just little Maria Tash diamond sleepers. The receipt's in the box—"

Clara looks up at Tom, smiling at him with a strained brightness. "She's a keeper."

He matches her smile. It's stiff and forced. "She is." He nods, and my heart feels sad seeing him like this. Everyone who doesn't know the truth would think the pain between them is because of her dead husband, but I know better. And I think the boy who's with her knows better too, so I squeeze Tom's hand because I should and also a bit because I want to. Clara grabs my hand and pulls me towards her may-or-may-not-be date.

"Sebastian, this is Magnolia—Magnolia, this is Sebastian."

I hold out my hand to the dreadfully sexy boy beside her: olive skin, brown eyes, tattoos up and down him, sulky mouth, razor-sharp jawline, messy hair. I don't recognise his clothes really, except for the Black XX chino, slim taper trousers from Levi's and black Vans, so I think he's probably not from money, not that that matters, I don't care. I'd kiss him myself all the same with a face like that. Just curious, I suppose. Nothing like Sam. Or Tom.

Speaking of, Tom's not even watching my exchange with the handsome boy, he's just watching Clara.

I hold my hand out to the boy. "Hi."

"The infamous Magnolia Parks." He grins down at me. American accent.

"Ah." I pull back, delighted. "You've heard of me."

"I have."

"All good things, I hope?" I smile.

He gives me a crooked smile with devilish eyes. "Not all good things," he says, then winks and saunters away. Clara apologies profusely but I don't know whether he was being insulting or flirtatious. She goes after him; Tom gives me an apologetic look and goes after her.

I sigh probably in a more overt way than I mean to and head to the bar to order a Lemon Drop Martini.

I drink it quite quickly so I order another.

"Babe—" Gus saddles up next to me, tugging on the skirt of my dress. "Love, love, love—"

I brush my hands over it—possibly get a splinter, nevertheless, I persevere—I grin up at him.

"At the fake-boyfriend's real love-interest's birthday bash—what a good fake-girlfriend you are."

I flick him in the chest as I tug on his red, Kiton single-breasted, cotton blazer. "Good to see you too—"

"Heard you're being quite the hell-raiser at home these days?" He smiles down at me.

I roll my eyes and laugh. "Only for the infidels."

And he chuckles—launches into a story about the artist he and my father are working with this week. I glance around for Tom and find him fairly quickly the way you might spot someone who you might have a crush on because they're your eye kink, but I think he's just that because he's my fake-boyfriend.

Tom catches my eye and gives me the nod that asks: you alright?

I give him a quick smile and nod, not wanting to be a bad foxhole buddy.

I laugh on cue for Gus's story that undoubtedly deserved more than the ears I didn't just give him and he notices. "Getting harder, isn't it?"

"Hmm?" I blink at him, confused. "No, no. Quite the opposite. Getting easier," I lie.

"Mmhmm." Gus looks at me suspiciously.

"It is." I nod emphatically. "I am easy breezy. Very casual, very—"

"You've naffed," he tells me.

I frown immediately. "How do you do that?"

He chuckles. "He told me that one."

"Oh." I roll my eyes but find myself laughing.

Tom party-jogs over. You know—it's not an actual jog, rather it's a hasty walk with intention. He puts his hand on my lower back. "You good?"

"Yeah! Fine! Yeah," I say, smiling a lot. "I'm fine." I keep nodding. "Yeah." Big smile to round it out.

("What the fuck?" mouths Gus.)

"Sure?" Tom frowns a bit.

"Mmhm. You're good—" I nod my chin back in Clara's direction. "Be free."

He squeezes my hand and smiles, and I wonder if I feel a sliver of sadness that he took me up on my offer, but also, no, I think. I'm not sad because what would I be sad for?

Gus raises his eyebrows up and down. "Unsolicited hand squeeze. How intimate."

I smack him in the arm, laughing. Then Gus looks past me and makes a delighted sound as he moves into hug someone.

It's a massive bro-hug, back-smacking, shoulders trying to increase in width in live time to overcompensate for the raw emotion they're displaying—and when they part I see that the other bro is Rush Evans.

The movie star. You know that hot boy in that teen movie? With the boy and the girl and the family drama, and he's a bad boy, and she's kind of annoying, but whatever anyway and they fall for one another? It was huge. Really put him on the map.

He's in the navy blue, logo-print bomber jacket from Off-White, blue, torn-knees Ksubi's and that fifties signature print, destroyed T-shirt from Saint Laurent that Beej has in black.

"Magnolia, babe." Gus pushes me towards him. "Do you know Rushy Evans? We all went to Hargrave together."

Rush shakes his head and takes my wrist in his hand gently. "Never met—know who you are though." He kisses my cheek.

I let out a tiny laugh that's more like a breath. "It's good to meet you."

He nods, smiles and he has eyes that get girls into trouble. "Likewise." Then he looks over at Gus. "You meet Clossy's new boy?" Gus nods, his face fairly neutral. Rush shakes his head. "Fucked up." Then he leans over the bar and orders a round of drinks.

("Rushy was Sam's best friend," Gus tells me while Rush is out of earshot. "Oh." I nod, feeling sadder for everyone.)

Rush hands me and Gus a shot; we clink, toss them down, and then he hands me another lemon drop martini and a negroni for Gus.

"Catch me up with you and Tommy," he tells me, leaning back against the bar.

Rush Evans really is rather charming. Impossibly handsome, quick and quippy, less Hollywood than I'd have imagined, but absolutely without question going to break your heart if you let him.

I tell him the official foxhole party line story about the bar and the kiss and always having a crush, etc. He nods along; Gus is displaying unhelpful facial expressions throughout, but Rush is mostly just looking at me.

"But I thought you were with what's-his-name." He clicks his fingers twice. "Fuck. The Instagram one girls throw their knickers at."

My mouth twitches and I swallow a bit heavy because I miss him.

Why hasn't he called me?

"BJ." I nod and then drink the rest of my drink.

Rush gives me an intrigued look.

("Bartender," he calls, then nods his head at me.)

"A lot going on there?" Rush asks and Gus leans in, eyebrows raised, waiting like the pain in my arse he is.

"Nothing at all," I declare in defiance and, I'm afraid, in truth.

"So anyway, Parks, riddle me this," Rush says, nodding his chin over at Tom, who's practically shadowing Clara, who herself is sitting with her hot maybe-boyfriend at a table by themselves. Tom's hovering inconspicuously close by, he's talking to someone, some girl who looks very pleased to have an audience with him, so pleased in fact that she's willing to look past the fact that Tom doesn't seem to give one genuine fuck about anything she has to say.

"If you're shacking up with Tom—"

"I'm not," I clarify. "I was born in W11. I don't shack—"

Gus laughs and Rush raises his eyebrows, amused.

"I said riddle me—"

I roll my eyes, wave him on as I finish my drink.

"—If you're with Tommy, why is it that he can't take his eyes off Closs, hm?"

I inhale sharply but catch myself—breathing it out slower.

Gus' eyebrows are up—waiting for my answer.

"Don't know." I shrug my shoulders dismissively. "Protective perhaps?"

Rush looks at Tom, then to Clara, then to me. "Protective?"

I nod, quite sure. Rush's eyes pinch.

I clear my throat. "I actually think his gaze is less sexually-charged and more perhaps"—I'm improvising—"you know, mother...ducky."

Gus suppresses a laugh. Rush doesn't, he just snorts.

"What the fuck kind of ducks are you hanging out with?"

"Absolute duck wits," I say, proud of my stupid joke.

He grins at me and then I start laughing, and he looks pleased with himself.

"Oh man." He shakes his head. "If you weren't fake-dating my best friend, I'd be all over you—"

"What?" I frown and blush all at once. "I—no! Pff!"

Rush Evans gives me a look.

"What? You don't think I know a PR relationship when I see one? Come on"—points to himself—"I'm fucking in one."

Gus gives me a smug look and I breathe out an exasperated breath right as there's a huge crash from the other side of the restaurant.

We all look over and it's Tom, with the hot maybe-boyfriend by the lapels, shoved against a wall.

Tom's a bit bigger than Sebastian, but the boyfriend looks like he knows how to fight.

Sebastian shoves him off of him—Gus and Rush run over.

Gus pulls Tom away, Rush shoves Sebastian again, yelling something, pointing. Clara's face is devastated.

I kind of just stand there, still at the bar. I'm slightly dizzy and I'm confused about my place in all this. I feel a protectiveness over Tom as I notice the blood that's dripping a bit from his busted lip.

I also feel sad for Clara, who looks caught—I think between her past and her future.

And then I feel sad for me, because same.

I hang back, waiting for it to diffuse. There's some yelling, mostly between Tom and Clara. I can't really hear what they're saying—and I get an overwhelming feeling that I shouldn't anyway.

Clara's eyes look bleary with tears.

The hot boy takes her hand and pulls her away.

It takes what feels like an age for Tom to glance around the room and remember I'm in it. His face falls, and he looks apologetic as he dashes over to me.

"I'm sorry." He shakes his head.

I grab a napkin and dab away from blood from his bottom lip. He winces but his eyes soften.

"I'm sorry," he says again, and I don't know why. I don't know what to say, so I just shake my head and shrug. I don't know what happened. I don't know what he's sorry for. I don't know why he's sorry to me.

"Let's go, shall we?" I offer him my hand.

He takes it in his, kissing the back of it absentmindedly, then nods at his boys as he leads me out.

("He kissed your hand!" Gus mouths dramatically, gesturing at his hand. "Shut up!" I mouth back.)

Tom is all scowls as we climb into his town car.

"My place, James," he tells his driver.

So I guess I'm not going home then? Tom's looking out the window, and I can feel it on him—his mind is a Peloton bike in gridlock traffic. Wheels are spinning, but he can't go anywhere.

"Can I do anything?" I ask eventually. Tom looks over at me and breathes out when he does, smiles a tiny smile.

"Not really." He does a grimace-smile. "No."

I nod and I'm sad for him, I have a brief and fleeting urge to kiss him because I wonder whether it'll make him feel better.

I don't do it because I'm a chicken.

"Hey." I poke him in the arm instead. "I think your friend knows about us."

He nods. "Yeah, Gus? You already said."

"No," I shake my head. "Rush."

"Rush? Really?" He pulls back, a bit surprised. "How do you know?"

I purse my lips before answering but decide to just be honest instead.

"Because he said if I wasn't fake-dating his best friend he'd have a crack—"

Tom's jaw immediately goes tight and his eyes pinch, but a small smile still surfaces before he chuckles.

"Of course he did, the smarmy shit—" He shakes his head, laughing. "Yeah, he'd love you. You're just his type..."

He looks a tiny bit annoyed by this and that actually makes me happy.

"Am I?" I try to keep my smile at bay, though I don't quite.

Tom rolls his eyes. "Great mouth. Leggy. Excitable. Ridiculous. Bit of an attitude."

My face falters a bit. "—Sorry, are you trying to be mean?"

"No." He frowns, shaking his head quickly. "—Sorry. No. You're just—" He looks at me thoughtfully, breathes out sort of loudly. "I should've seen it coming."

I stare at him for a few seconds. "Are you jealous?"

He pauses. Our eyes are locked.

"Yeah, actually. I am." He laughs. "I know that's particularly shit because I spent the entire night focused on another girl." He gives me a mildly remorseful look.

"Oh," I smirk. "So you were aware of it."

The look turns into full-blown remorse. "Sorry."

I shrug, pretend that my feelings aren't at least a tiny bit hurt. "It's why I'm here."

"I'm still sorry," he tells me and I nod and smile and look out the window.

He keeps watching me; I can feel his gaze on me, so I look back.

His face pulls as he mulls on his thoughts.

"You want me to tee it up with you and Rush?"

"What?" I blink, surprised.

"If you like him—" He shrugs and swallows. "I mean—you and me, we're just—you know. Whatever, right? So if you're attracted to—"

"He's very attractive," I concede. "In that obviously sexy, slick, Hollywood, playboy kind of way."

Tom lets out a small laugh.

"Yeah, obviously sexy is the worst kind of sexy." He gives me a look.

I press my lips together, amused. Tom looks out the window.

"Do you know who else is obviously sexy?" I say, wanting his attention again.

He looks back, raising his eyebrows. I poke him.

He sniffs a laugh and then his face goes back to serious. "Do you want me to?" he asks again.

"No, thank you."

He blinks. "No?" I shake my head. "Really?"

I roll my eyes with a demure sigh. "When would I possibly fit Rush Evans in between you and BJ?"

He laughs, but I think he looks relieved.

"Was tonight hard for you?"

"Yeah." He nods. "They're together."

"Tom—" I touch his arm. He looks down where I'm touching him and back up to my eyes. "I'm sorry."

He shakes his head and shrugs. "Not like she could have been with me anyway."

"But still."

He nods, looking back out the window.

"Are you bringing me back to your house on purpose?" I ask after a moment.

"Fuck—" He shakes his head once, looking sorry. "No. I wasn't thinking—James, can we—"

"—I'll come back to your house," I cut in. All the drinks I've had make me braver right now than I am in real life.

He looks over at me, eyes big, doesn't say anything.

"If you want me to," I add. He nods.

We pull up to those newish apartments on Victoria Street in Westminster. The ones designed by Stiff + Trevillion, do you know what I mean? Angular? Grey bricks?

We head upstairs and we're not touching.

He opens the door to his apartment and he's still quiet, but I think he's just sad. It's a three-bedroom penthouse—big enough for one, that's for sure.

His style is surprisingly minimal. A lot of neutrals. A bit of rattan. Splashes of marble.

"This is your place?" I blink.

"What?" He glances over at me. "You don't like it?"

"No, I—I do. I just thought—I don't know?" I shrug. "You're Tom England. I thought maybe there'd be your own McDonalds in a corner?"

"I'm not Richie Rich."

"A state of the art robot servant—"

"He's in the country house." Tom smirks.

I gesture to the apartment around us. "So, how many girls have you had here?"

"Do you mean over?" He looks confused.

"No, I mean sexually—" He laughs. "How many girls have you had sex with?" I clarify.

"Here?"

"Here," I nod. "Anywhere—?"

He considers this. "Here—Erin and one other girl. Somewhere else—three other girls, not including you."

"Six!" I blink, in disbelief. "You've only had sex with six people?"

He frowns defensively. "You've only had sex with two."

"No," I say, shaking my head. "I mean, I can't believe it—you're Tom England. And you look like Thor—" He laughs. "How is it possible you've only been with six women?"

He takes a big breath, breathes it out, and pours me some sort of brown hard spirit I don't like but I sip it anyway, because I want the warm feeling it gives me when it hits my empty stomach.

"I had girlfriend at school, slept with her. Met Erin in university, we were together eight or so years." He shrugs. "And then I fell in love with my brother's wife." My mouth twitches away a smile. "Tried to sleep with a few people to get over it—didn't work." He shrugs. "And then… you."

"And then me." I give him a tiny smile.

"Why?" He nods his chin at me. "How many girls has BJ slept with?"

I swallow. "He won't tell me."

Tom's face falters a bit.

"But I think we're safely in the vicinity of the hundreds."

His face pulls back, blinking. "Multiple?"

I shrug like it's nothing, even though I could be drowning in all the women I've lost him too. "By my count"—I give him a quick look—"I try not to count."

"Fuck." He sighs. "I'm sorry, Parks."

I walk back over, stand toe to toe with him. It's closer than I need to be, but I feel like I want to be. "Are you actually okay?" I look up at him.

He brushes some hair behind my ear. "Yeah."

I purse my lips, thinking barely for a second before I say it. "Would you like to have sex?" How many Lemon Drop Martinis is too many?

"Oh." He blinks a few times, surprised. "Uh—maybe?"

"Maybe?" I frown.

I haven't had too too many, because my face isn't tingly at all, just my chest is warm, and my mind is floaty, and my heart is numbed enough to maybe not think about how much I miss BJ for a half an hour. He tilts his head at me, and his hand is already a bit in my hair.

"You had a bit to drink?"

"A tiny bit!" I nod, and he laughs. "I'm not drunk though."

"Really?" he asks, suspicious.

"Merry, if anything."

"How merry?" He laughs.

"Quite." I lift up his shirt and take a peek at his stomach. "More so by the second."

"I see." He nods, thoughtfully. "Are you angry at BJ?"

"No more than usual."

He smiles. "Has he had sex with anyone regrettable this week that you're trying to process by sleeping with me?"

"Oh," I nod emphatically, "I'm quite certain he has, but I possess no definitive knowledge of such events."

He snorts a laugh, licks his bottom lip. "Are you going to sneak out of my bed in the dead of night to scurry off to an ex-boyfriend?"

I roll my eyes. "I shall try to restrain myself."

His eyes pinch as he gives me a long look. "Is this a good idea?"

I shake my head and shrug all at once. "I don't know. It could be a terrible idea—"

He grimaces in thought. "Probably fun though..."

I nod. "Probably..."

FORTY-FOUR

BJ

Kiss her, is what Jonah said.

I don't know why it was such an insane suggestion to me—it's not like I don't want to do it all the time, it's not like our relationship up until now hasn't been dotted with an infinity of almost-kisses—it's the permission, maybe?

Someone telling me to do it, validating my feeling that I should have actually just done it all along.

I chew on it for a few days.

Pretend like I'm mulling it over but actually, I'm just finding my balls because I think I know it'll probably be the most important kiss of my life.

I know where she is on a Friday.

Likes to round her week out with a little shop on New Bond Street; of course, "little" is relative to her. Anywhere from a new handbag or two to buying out a whole store. Depends on her week, depends on me probably—how shit I was, how happy we were…

I walk into Gucci—it's the first store I try and she's there because she's predictable—I stand by the counter, watching her file through the racks. Do my best to keep my face in check, not look like a massive knob who's too in love for his own good. Hard not to smile when she's wearing my black bomber though. From here, got it a few weeks ago. She picked it. Red and blue on the shoulders—I wondered where it got to... It found a higher purpose sitting on the shoulders of the best girl I know.

She's standing in the mirror, staring at herself in these indigo blue denim flare jeans and cropped T-shirt with cherries on it that I immediately want to take off of her because she looks so good in it.

"You'll never wear the jeans," I tell her and she spins around, eyes wide, cheeks pink as soon as she sees me. I walk towards her and she tugs at her clothes almost feverishly which is stupid because she looks so hot it's insane. "Get this though," I tell her as I slip my thumb under the hem of her top, rubbing it between my fingers.

I don't need to stand as close to her as I'm standing, but sort of I do.

She takes a conscious step away from me—forces herself to do it. She blinks a lot, looks flushed. I try not to smile about it. She pushes her hair over her own shoulders, trying to control what she can. "So you don't like the jeans?" she asks, squinting at herself in the mirror.

"No, I like them," I say and nod. "You just won't wear them."

She snaps her head in my direction. "Will too."

"Won't."

"I will! You don't know me," she tells me, nose in the air, and even before the sentence is out of her mouth completely she looks like she might laugh at it.

She doesn't. She's too proud.

"I know you, Parks," I tell her as I walk over towards her, my eyes softer than they are for anyone else ever.

I stand behind her.

Our eyes catch through the mirror and she swallows, nervous.

She's flustered. Her chest is rising and falling quickly.

"You here for your weekly Gooch?" I nod at her through the mirror and she turns around quickly with a scowl. I'm already laughing.

"I have asked you repeatedly not to call it that—" She eyes me. "So has Alessandro Michele for that matter." She gives me a stern look.

"Sorry." I shove my hands in my pocket. "Where's your boyfriend?"

She moves to a different rack, picks out half a dozen pieces and hands them to the shop assistant wordlessly, waiting for them to leave before she speaks.

"He flew out yesterday for a few days." She tilts her head at the jacket I'm wearing. Squints. "Oversized-checked, cotton-flannel bomber jacket?"

Jut my chin at her. "Who by?"

"Balenciaga," she says, without looking at me. "And your jeans are from TAKAHIROMIYASHITA TheSoloist."

I sniff a laugh, shaking my head at her a bit.

She looks up at me and her eyes pinch a bit. "I've heard you've been a busy boy."

My face falters, surprised. "Have you?"

She watches me closely. "Lots of girls…"

I frown. "Who told you that?"

She shrugs all coy and shit and then whips shut the heavy, velvet curtain in the changing room. Probably sprains her little arm she does it with such force. She emerges a minute or so later in a short, little blue and gold dress. Not my favourite thing she's ever worn but I'd still take her in a heartbeat.

I swallow, fold my arms over my chest. "Have you been busy?"

Her eyebrows curve up. "Not as busy as you."

My brow drops a bit. "Busy at all?"

Her eyes go a bit round, cheeks go pink. She swallows, nervous.

"Yes."

I stare at her for a couple seconds not blinking and then I yell "Fuck!" Loud. It startles her.

"Sorry—" I look over at the shop assistant. Shaking my head. "Sorry," then look back at Parks, whose eyes are round and alarmed. "Sorry—but fuck."

Her bottom lip looks like it could go any second. It's not full-blown trembling, but the tremble is there.

"Sorry," she says in a tiny voice.

I shove my hands through my hair as I shake my head. "Fuck—no—it's your... I mean, I—"

"Yeah." She frowns, defensively. "You—"

"—You're killing me, Parks." I cut her off.

"Am I?" she asks, eyes heavy.

"A bit." I nod.

"Just a bit?" She tosses me a quarter smile. "That's not so bad then, is it—"

I sniff a laugh. "I'd like it better if you weren't killing me at all, to be honest—"

Our eyes lock. She's the deer and I'm the wolf and there's a massive truck headed right for us in the middle of a dark night.

She swallows. "Me too, actually." Then she pulls the curtain shut again.

I breathe out big, lean against the wall outside, knock twice.

"Oy."

"What?" Even though I can't see her face, I know it's huffy.

"Can I come in?"

"What?" She sounds nervous.

"I want to come in," I tell her.

"Why?" She sounds urgent.

I toss my head around, thinking for a decent excuse.

"I want to see how you look in those clothes," I lie.

"Well—no!" she sputters.

"Why?" I ask with a shrug, even though she can't see it. "I've seen you without clothes on before."

"I thought you wanted to see me in the clothes."

"Oh," I snort a laugh. "Well, I was lying before."

"You don't want to see me in the clothes?" She pouts.

"I want to see you... not... in clothes."

"Well," she huffs, "you can't."

"Nothing I haven't seen before..."

"Well, that was different!"

"How?" I roll my eyes. "Besides, you can't have a real conversation with someone through a curtain—"

"We're having a real conversation right now!"

Pause. This is it. Make or break. Proceed with caution. But definitely proceed.

"Oy, Parks. Do you really not want me to come in there, or are you pretending that you don't want me to come in because you like to play hard to get because it makes you feel in control of me, or us and whatever the fuck we are but actually, you'd be fucking stoked if I jumped in there and felt you up against the wall?"

There's a pause. A long pause.

Fuck.

And then, from the other side of the curtain... a small crestfallen voice.

"The second one."

I slip inside the change room, and there's a space between us. I stare at her, shyer than I want to be for a couple of seconds. Her eyes look like big windows on a stormy day; she's scared. It's all over her. Me too.

My breathing's gone to shit; I can see my own chest moving... Stomach feels like there's an animal burrowing into it.

She's blinking a lot, sucking on her bottom lip which is a thing she does both when she's afraid but also when she loves me extra.

My eyes fall down her body—and she stands there, waiting for me.

I've probably never been this fucking nervous about anything in my life. I shake my head at myself. "Fuck it."

And then I rush her. One hand in her hair, and with the other I lift her up onto my waist—bang her backwards into the wall. She laughs as she looks down at me, her gaze flicking between my eyes and my mouth.

I give her a crooked smile, and I can't fully believe that I have her pressed up against a Gucci change room.

She gives me an exasperated look. "Come on, then..."

"Alright, alright." I roll my eyes. "I will when I want to."

"You don't want to now?" She blinks. "Are you serious? Are you completely insa—"

"Parks," I interrupt.

"Mmm?" She frowns.

"Shut up," I tell her and then it feels serious.

I move my hand down to her face, pull her in close to me and our mouths brush.

Then I kiss her, slowly at first... slowly like how you drink a top shelf whiskey—feel it in your mouth, let it roll around for a couple of seconds before you go back for more. Bask in the flavour of my old, always love. Slowly, slowly, and then more. I kiss her deeper and her breath gets caught in her chest, and I remember how much I used to love it when that would happen, so I do it more.

We're like a broken faucet where the water's drip-drip-dripping out and then full force—but we've always been like this. It's one choked breath and a heavy swallow from her and I'm pulling the dress off her body. She scrambles for my shirt, undoing the buttons with unfocused fingers.

I drop her from my waist, and she tugs my shirt from my body. We're good at this. Years of practice, I guess. And even though we haven't practiced in years, we haven't seemed to have lost any ground—just time. I wrap my arms around her, bang her backwards into the wall again as she fumbles the button of my jeans. Undoes the zip and just as she's about to reach for me…

And then—a knock.

My head drops a bit defeated on top of Parks, but I hold her tighter still because I'm not done with her yet.

"Um," Magnolia clears her throat. "Yes?"

"Hi, um." The shop assistant coughs nervously. "I think—uh—whatever you're doing in there is, I think, maybe against company policy?"

I'm about a second away from keeling over with laughter and Parks can tell, smacking her hand over my mouth to shut me up.

"Um, I'm not doing anything," Magnolia says, airily.

"I know there's a boy in there," the girl says, getting a bit more confident.

"No," Parks sings, unconvincingly. "There's not—"

"I saw him go in there," the shop girl says.

And I accidentally snort.

Parks scowls at me, shaking her head. "That was me! Are you saying I look like a man?"

"I can hear him!" she says, sounding nervous.

I lean into Parks, kiss her big time, feel her tense, little, uptight body relax as I do—how much control I have over her has always been something I love and I'm scared of at once. Suppose that's how I feel about her in general though.

One sec, I mouth to Parks and then I walk over to the curtain, poke my head out.

"Hello," I grin at the shop girl—give her what Parks calls "the magic smile." Girls do weird shit when I flash them the magic smile. One time a girl fainted.

"Hi," she says, shyly, instantly blushing.

"Just clarify for me," I say, pushing my hand through my hair. "What exactly is the company policy? Is it one person per change room? Or is it no sex in the changing room? Because there's a lot of wriggle room in between those two, if you know what I mean... Like, can I feel her up in the changing room? Can we go to third in the changing room? What are we working with here?"

I don't even need to look at Parks to know she's blushing—she is—but so is the shop girl, who eventually manages to wring out of herself an apologetic smile.

"It's a one person per change room policy, I'm afraid."

"Fuck." I frown. "Just my luck," I look back at Parks, nod my head. "I'll wait out here."

She touches her mouth, nodding, thinking, blinking.

I sit out there, waiting for her, grinning from ear to fucking ear. I don't know what it means. Don't know what any of it means.

All I know is that kissing her felt like a shower after a particularly brutal rugby game.

Mum would drive me home, I'd be so wrecked, so mudded up, sore and shit—and every week the shower would blow my mind.

Like I hadn't showered in years is how it felt.

Sometimes Parks would join me. That'd blow my mind extra.

But kissing her just now, I could feel the mud coming off.

She emerges ten minutes later with her yes pile. I take them from her, take them to the front.

"You don't have to get them," she calls after me.

I throw her a look. I pop them down on the counter. "How's your day going?" I ask the shop girl.

She smirks, looking from me to Parks. "Probably not as good as yours."

And I go, "Hah. Well." I cock an eyebrow playfully at her. "Don't worry, day's still young. One of your ex-boyfriends might dander on in and give you a snog in a change room."

She blushes and laughs. I take the bags and Parks follows me out.

She stands on the street, looking up at me—eyes big and round, chewing on her bottom lip like I wish I was.

"I'm sorry we were interrupted," she tells me.

I nod with a small laugh. "Me too."

I load her bags into her town car.

She gestures at them. "Thank you."

I swat my hand at her, and she stands close to me. I don't even mean to do it when I slip my arms around her waist. Just happens, like holding her is the most natural thing in the world.

"Do you want to come home with me now?" she asks in a small voice.

"I do, actually." I nod. "Yeah. Very much—but you have—"

"A Tom." She nods.

I give her a strained smile. "I don't even know what that means."

She lets out a tired laugh, but she looks a bit sad and confused behind it. "Neither do I."

I take her face in both my hands and press my mouth against hers. Kiss her twice. "You figure it out and let me know," I tell her.

And then I walk away.

21:42

Beej

> Hi

Hey

You good?

> Yes, are you?

I am.

Weather okay over there, Parks?

> Very good.

And the bees?

Oh, they're grand.

Yeah?

Yes. I actually think they'll never go extinct. I've no idea what Attenborough is prattling on about...

Never hey?

FORTY-FIVE

Magnolia

I saunter in, eyeballing both my father and Marsaili as I indelicately throw myself into a chair next to my sister for theatrics. Marsaili rolls her eyes.

"Why are you dressed like that?" My sister frowns at me in my Metallic Monogram tweed skater dress with signature V belt by Louis Vuitton.

"What?" I glance down at myself. "Nicely? You should try it sometime."

She gives me a smarmy look. "You laid this out for me."

I swear under my breath because she's right—I did. And she looks completely fantastic in the Rainbow, cashmere, striped-knit shorts from The Elder Statesman with the navy, lace-up jumper from the Michael Kors Collection. I see she picked her own shoes though. Some sort of sad, brandless espadrille. Espadrilles! In London! In the Autumn. My god.

"A dinner with all my girls," my father says as I reluctantly sit down at the table.

This is a dinner I've been coerced into: Bridget, my father and the step monster—at our house, obviously. Apparently they're not willing to risk me yelling at them in public, those little snowflakes. Catered, obviously—because Marsaili doesn't lift a finger around the house anymore, that lazybones.

I wonder if that's why she'd grown so lax about serving my breakfast properly over the years?

The coercion came about because my father said he wouldn't pay my credit card bill this month unless I attended, and I clarified whether attendance was the only prerequisite and he said yes, so firstly, he's an idiot and secondly, obviously I had that drawn up by my legal team and now that bitch is iron clad.

"Thank you for joining us, Magnolia." My father smiles.

"Sure, yeah," I say. "Yesterday I bought an electric hydrofoil surfboard."

"Okay." My father nods at the same time my sister frowns and says, "Why?"

"It was about £10,000," I say, sipping my water.

"Of course it was," he says and sighs.

"You don't even surf," Marsaili tells me.

"But I could."

"Where?" Bridget scoffs. "You going to zip around the Thames?"

I ignore her.

"How's it going with Tom?" my father asks.

"Yes, fine," I say, as I shovel the honey-garlic butter roasted carrots around my plate. "He's been away the last five days. Home tomorrow."

"Anything interesting happen while he was gone?" my sister asks a bit pointedly.

I glare at her. "No."

"Nothing at all?"

I give her a weird look. "No."

I take a sip of my wine.

"You didn't nearly have sex with someone in the Gucci change rooms?"

I choke on my wine.

"Who told you that?" I stare at her.

("Who did you nearly have sex with in a Gucci change room?" Marsaili asks.)

"BJ and I get lunch," my sister says with a shrug.

"When?" I blink.

("BJ?" Marsaili whines. "In a changing room?" And my father holds his head: "I think I'm getting a migraine.")

"Wednesdays, usually," my sister says and forks a piece of chicken.

I pull my head back in surprise. "Usually?"

She makes a "mmhm" sound with her mouth full.

"What do you talk about at these lunches?" I ask, frowning.

"You." She nods at me. "Them." She nods at my father and Mars. "Him—him and you. You and Tom. Jonah and that Taura girl—"

("Jonah's with Taura Sax?" Marsaili asks, eyes wide. She knows that's who BJ cheated on me with.)

I glare over at Mars. "Don't be such a gossip, Marsaili."

Marsaili gives me a tired and exasperated look and my father pours himself an extra big glass of wine.

"Why didn't you tell me?" Bridget asks, maybe hurt.

I shrug, demurely. "It's complicated."

"It's BJ," she clarifies.

Marsaili looks between us, very, very unthrilled.

Me, however? I'm delighted that BJ's ruining this family dinner without even being here.

"How close to sex were you?" Marsaili huffs.

"Not very." I roll my eyes.

("Hands on the equipment," my sister says under her breath but loud enough for everyone to hear.)

"Oh, fuck me," my father says and does two wide blinks.

No one says anything so I glance over at our resident infidel.

"Marsaili." I look at her with tall eyebrows. I nod my head in my father's direction, "I believe he's talking to you."

And at that—Marsaili snorts, which turns into a laugh, which makes me nearly laugh but I get a handle on it before it gets away from me.

Marsaili looks at me for a few seconds. "Will you help me with something in the kitchen?"

"Absolutely not." I shake my head.

Bridget kicks me under the table.

"Oh, fine." I roll my eyes, dragging my feet as I follow her.

Marsaili folds her arms over her chest and peers up at me. "Are you really going to hold my affair with your father over my head while you're cheating on Tom?"

I glare over at her, at her presumptions. "Tom and I have an arrangement."

"Oh, you and Tom have an arrangement?" She blinks, unimpressed. "How terribly modern of you. Enlighten me, what is this arrangement?"

"Sure, yeah—the condensed version is, he's in love with someone he can't have, and I'm in love with someone I was told would hurt me if I stayed with him so I didn't and I should have and now, everything's a fucking mess."

"Because you've slept with Tom too," she says. Says, doesn't ask.

"Well, who told you that?" I throw my hands into the air, as I lean back against the bench.

She sighs. "I ventured a guess."

"Oh."

"You've never slept with anyone else," she tells me.

"I know."

She gives me a look. "Not even Christian."

"I know."

"Didn't much like it when you were dating him—"

"I know." I roll my eyes.

"Gang lord and all."

"Just a little baby one." I shrug.

And Mars laughs and then she gives me a parental look.

"Are you being safe?"

I scoff. "Are you?"

She laughs again.

"I've missed you," she tells me.

"Yes, I'm sure." I nod. "I'm an absolute treat."

She rolls her eyes exaggeratively. "I can see in my absence your ego's gone completely unchecked."

"Not entirely, no." I shake my head. "Life's beaten me down some… I broke a nail last week. The barista used the wrong milk in my coffee thrice in the last fortnight. My sister is apparently having regular lunches with my ex-boyfriend. I had a sesame seed between my teeth when I bumped into William at Harrods—"

"Which William?"

"…Arthur Phillip Louis."

She snorts a laugh. "Oh, well—that's your very worst nightmare."

"I saw BJ having sex with someone else."

"BJ slept with someone else?"

I frown. "He's always sleeping with someone else."

She rubs her temples, she goes to say something— she doesn't. She fiddles with her bracelet.

"What did you mean when you said he almost died?"

I stare at her for a few seconds, wondering how I can get around this without telling her—or if even that's the right thing to do.

I sigh.

"He overdosed once." She gasps quietly. "Right after Reid and I started...dating." If that's what you'd even call it.

"Magnolia"—she shakes her head—"I had no idea."

"No one knows," I tell her.

She nods solemnly. "Is he still on drugs?"

I shake my head vehemently. "He promised me he'd never again."

She nods, relieved.

"So, now what?" she asks.

And I pull up empty with a shrug.

"I have no idea."

00:51

Vanna Ripley

Hey

Hey

Miss you

I'm in town for a few days...

Are you? For work?

And pleasure.

Hah

Come over...

Can't

What?

I can't.

You can't?

Sorry x

FORTY-SIX

Magnolia

"Oy," Tom says, standing in my bedroom doorway. He gives me a small smile and wanders in.

"Hi." I stand up to hug him and bury my face in his Textured, loopback, cotton and camel hair-blend sweatshirt from SSAM.

I've been thinking about Tom coming back since really the moment he left for this work trip.

A bit because I miss him when he's gone now and also a bit because I know I have to tell him about BJ, and it makes me feel a little queasy.

Tom hands me a La Mer gift bag full to the brim and I marvel up at him.

"Peeked in your bathroom before I left," he says.

I empty the contents out on my bed. "How was your trip?" I ask the jar of Creme de la Mer.

"Good." He nods. "Bit longer than I like, but I always like New York."

"I quite like New York too," I tell him. "Were I not in London, that's where I'd be."

"Magnolia Parks—not in London?" He smiles playfully at me. "Wouldn't be London."

He sits down on my bed, leans back against the headboard.

We don't do sleepovers like BJ and I do.

Did? Do? Will do again?

BJ and I haven't been doing sleepovers much ourselves anyway—but if we were, he'd never sit on my bed with outside shoes on.

BJ would never. BJ would do a lot of other things though.

Tom picks up my Paddington Bear that I've had all my life and tugs at his ear.

It makes me feel funny because the only other person who I'd ever let hold him is Beej and Tom's holding him now and maybe that means something.

"I had fun with you the other night," he tells me but his eyes are on the bear.

I chew my bottom lip. I'm nervous. What am I nervous for?

"Me too." I take my Paddington from him and set him on my bedside table. I look down at Tom, fight the urge I have to push my hand through his dark blonde hair. "Are you feeling better about Clara?"

He rubs his stubble absentmindedly as he nods.

"Kind of," he says, eyes and mind somewhere else. Then he looks up at me. "We could never happen—I know that. I didn't mean to—you know? It just..." he trails.

"Right." I nod.

"It's hard." He shrugs. "Me aside, for Sam—I'm wrecked but—" He shrugs again.

Shrugs it off, almost? Like he doesn't want the fullness of thought that's bashing into him right now.

I sit down on the bed, tucking my feet under me.

He gives me a tired smile that I know is the smile he does when he's in his head about his brother. "What'd you do while I was gone?"

357

I lick my bottom lip and take a breath. "Um—right," I sigh. And I see it on Tom—he steels himself. "Beej and I kissed," I tell him.

"Oh, whoa." His head pulls back and he blinks six times in quick succession. "Wow. Okay."

He nods to himself, and then looks up at me, face all strained. "I'm happy for you."

My face falters. "Are you?"

I almost don't want him to be.

Tom sniffs a laugh. "No, not really."

He lets out a single laugh again, and I match it. I feel myself frowning a lot. And my chest feels heavy. And I hate the eyes Tom's giving me without meaning to. A bit sad, a bit lost, a bit alone.

He breathes out. "So this is probably the end of the line for us?"

I purse my mouth and barely shrug. "I guess?"

He nods a few times then scowls. "Fuck."

"What?" I chew on the inside of my bottom lip.

"I don't know—" Tom shakes his head, shoves a hand through his hair. "So we're really calling time on this?"

I blow out a breath, my hands on both my cheeks. "I don't know?"

He blinks again, surprised. "You don't know?"

I don't say anything—I just frown.

He swings his legs off my bed and stands, scratching the back of his neck.

"Are you with BJ?"

I stand up, but I don't feel too tall. "I don't know."

"Do you want to be?"

My frown deepens. "I think so, but—"

"But what?" he asks quickly, all of him on edge.

I give him a look and he raises his eyebrows at it.

"You're going to make me say it?" I blink at him.

He nods, obstinate. "Yeah, I think you should—"

"Why?" I frown. "This was your fucking idea."

"My idea?" He gestures at himself, eyes wide.

"It was literally your actual idea," I yell. "In the bar. After the club. In the corner. It was y—"

And then he grabs my face and kisses me, so I stop talking, I think. It would have knocked me over were he not already holding me—

"You still haven't said it," Tom says, his mouth still against mine.

I kiss him once more and then pull back.

He plants my feet back on the ground, but I didn't realise I'd left it.

"I like you," I tell him with a small nod, whose decisiveness feels like an assault to BJ.

He smiles down at me. "I like you too."

I cover my face with my hands. "Goddamn it."

He peels my hands off of me, and ducks down so we're eye to eye.

"This is me tossing my hat in the ring," he tells me. "Just so you know."

Then he pecks me on the lips again and walks out the door.

FORTY-SEVEN

BJ

Jonah's launching a new club of his tonight and all the crew is piling in.

I head over to Parks' to pick her up because I'd usually do that anyway, but I'd definitely do it now that I've felt her up in Gucci.

Been a bit in my head about how she hasn't called me yet, confessing her undying love for me, but I guess these things take time. She still wants me, I knew that from the kiss, from the hands, from the lean in.

I walk into her room. "Parks?" I call out because she's not in there.

"In here," she replies from the bathroom.

She looks over at me from the mirror, and her eyes light up. I walk behind her, slip my arms around her waist, press my nose into the back of her head. She lets me for a second before she spins around to face me.

"Like my dress?"

Short. One shoulder. Spotty.

Nod as measured as I can, pretend I don't love her in spots like I don't just love her in everything.

"Saw it in Saint Laurent the other day," I nod. "Was going to grab it for you."

She tugs on the collar of my shirt. "Amiri, camp-collar, printed silk-twill shirt," she tells me.

"It has birds on it," I tell her stupidly and she smiles. She slips her arms around my neck and I actually a bit can't believe it, that I'm standing here, in her bathroom, holding her like this—and I'm awake, and she's sober and it's all coming up roses. I lean in to kiss her—it's slow and measured, and it's still blowing my mind that my mouth is on hers when she says, "Can we talk about something?"

I frown on her mouth before pulling away, but not letting go.

Never letting go.

I look at her face, all frowns and eyebrows like an angry cartoon bunny. She doesn't need to say it. I know it before she can even put words around the sentence.

"...You like him."

And then the worst thing imaginable happens. She says nothing. Part of me, I think, was expecting some push back. Denial, refusal, anger... being incensed. But none of that's here and that's probably worse than her liking him.

I shove both my hands through my hair, breathe out one, long breath.

"Fuck."

She reaches out, holds my waist. "I'm sorry—"

I put my hand on top of hers without even thinking. I shake my head.

"No, I—it's Tom England," I shrug. "I get it. You've always had a thing for him—"

"Not a real thing," she clarifies unhelpfully.

"Look, if he wasn't poaching you from me, I'd probably try to shag him too," I say, forcing myself to laugh because I don't know what else to do. "So you're picking him?" I say that like it's not the end of the world.

And then—her face falters. "No."

"Then what?" I shake my head a bit, waiting for an answer and she pulls away from me, distressed and sad.

"I don't know!"

I glare over at her. "Well, don't ask me to pick—"

"I'm not," she says like I've wounded her. "I wouldn't."

Her head hangs. She's sad. Fuck. I hate it when she's sad. She could have lopped off my entire arm and if she looked a bit sad about it, I'd offer her my other one if it'd cheer her up.

"What do you want from me, Parks?"

She shrugs all hopeless and beat. "A time machine?"

"...That I can give you," I say, louder and clearer.

She reaches for my hand, takes it in hers. Plays with my fingers, traces them with her own.

It's an act of recalibration for us—touch always has been.

Even in the Dark Ages where we'd fucked around and each other over, even then we'd find ways to touch, find our ways back to the centre of us.

I don't know what the centre of us is, by the way.

Sounds romantic as shit, I know. But it's more than that. Also worse than that.

The problem with me and Parks is, I think we love each other more than ourselves.

Again, that sounds romantic but it's not—

Because if she loved herself more than she loves me, she'd have fucked off years ago. I don't deserve all the chances she half-tries to give me.

And if I loved myself more than I love her, I would have cut the ties between us as soon as she started to strangle me with them. If I loved me more I would have let me drift away, into the dark, out of her light but I didn't, and I couldn't and I won't because when it comes to her, I have zero instinct for self-preservation. I'll die in her arms or at her doorstep trying to get back into them, I don't give a fuck.

I kiss her hand. "Parks, where am I losing you?"

She holds her hand against my face and sighs.

"With you—I don't know. I keep trying to walk through the wardrobe, wait for the feeling that I can't trust you to fall off me like a coat but it doesn't. It's just always on me—" She shakes her head. "I'm wearing it all the time."

Fuck.

I sigh. "And you trust him."

She nods.

I shrug in a way that feels like I'm conceding. I'm not. But the truth is—

"He's trustworthy," I tell her.

"Are you?" She blinks, eyes too hopeful.

"We belong together—"

She shakes her head. "That's not what I asked."

"And I'm always going to be here—"

Her eyes go wet. "That's still not what I asked."

I hang my head, breathe out. She turns away from me, facing the mirror and the shields go up.

She tucks her hair behind her ears, touches her perfect face that needs no touching.

I turn her back around, look all over her face for a door number two…anything else but the door she thinks she needs me to walk through so we can be together. I know what she thinks she needs to feel like she can trust me again, and she's wrong.

"Kiss me," I tell her.

She frowns a little, but I can tell already her resolve is paper thin. "What?"

"Kiss me," I shrug. "You'll feel better."

A hint of a smile appears on her mouth. "Will I just?"

I nod. "You will."

"Come on," I say and poke her in the ribs. "It's what we used to do if we were fighting and about to go out—"

She shakes her head. "No, it's not. We stared at each other."

"Staring, kissing—" I wobble my head side to side. "Stare at me and see if it doesn't end in a kiss anyway."

She stands on her tip-toes and presses her lips into my cheek. I turn my head so our mouths meet and she smiles. I kiss down her cheek, down her neck, I pick her up off the ground and she wriggles and jerks around in my arms as I bury my face in there because she's ticklish—

Everything that happened just before is a snooze alarm on your phone.

It'll go off again soon, but we've got some time.

"One more thing," I say, muffled by her neck.

She slumps in my arms. "What?"

"I think Taura's going to be there tonight."

She pushes back from me and I accidentally drop her to the ground.

She shoves me backwards.

"Are you shitting me?"

My head rolls back, already exhausted. "Parks—it wasn't her—"

"Then who was I—"

"Magnolia," I say through clenched teeth. "Can we not?"

She glares over at me, and I shake my head at her.

"Give me a week," I beg. "Just give me one week or—fuck, I don't know—a month even, of just getting to lie in the fucking sun of kissing you any time I want again before we start pulling at all our threads."

She swallows once, her little shoulders pouting in the way they move.

"Okay."

"Okay?" I blink. "Really?"

"Yes." She crosses her arms over her chest. "But I like Tom more."

I smile at her because she's a shit and I take her hand in mine because she's also everything.

"Are you still going to come?"

She considers this. "Do you promise it wasn't her?"

I nod.

And then she takes my hand places it over her heart.

"Swear it," she tells me. "On me. Swear it on my heart, that you're holding—that you didn't cheat on me with Taura Sax."

I nod again and look her square in the eyes. "I swear."

"Okay." She nods.

"Okay?"

"But you have slept with her," she clarifies, I don't know why.

"Yes."

She frowns. "That's not my favourite thing."

"No," I chuckle. "No, I don't imagine it would be…" I pull her towards the door. "Come on, we'll be late."

We are late… later still because I asked Simon to drive us the long way round so I could kiss her extra in the back seat. We sneak in through the back door because Parks wants to avoid the vultures out front. I toss my arm around her, leading her back to where Jonah will be in the roped off section and I have this sort of euphoric high about being like this with her in public.

Spot my best friend, nod at him. "This is sick, man. Well done—"

He ignores me.

"Parks!" Jo cheers. "Your lipstick looks great—on BJ." He can barely get that delivery out with a straight face.

Magnolia rolls her eyes and goes around hugging all of our friends, and especially not hugging Taura, whom I toss a consolatory smile to.

Taura's sitting with a friend of Jonah's, but I'm pretty sure she came with Jo—there's no Henry here. Weird, maybe? Don't want to ask about it because I reckon this whole thing could get messy fast, so I order a round of shots for us all to take the edge off.

A few celebrities, Christian's coming later with the Haites. Maybe Hen's coming then?

The vibe of the club is pretty cool. Somewhere between the Playboy Mansion and the 90s Viper Room.

I know clubs aren't Jonah's real job, but he has a knack for them anyway.

Parks sticks pretty close to me the whole night, tossing daggers at Taurs with her eyes, holding my hand like I might wander off and get lost if she lets me go— which I think is how she feels.

I get that though. That's how I feel about her too. We wander off, we circle back, find each other. I wonder how much Tom will change that?

I'm in a conversation with Jo, who's trying to convince me about how he's not into Taura in a legitimate way by telling me all the girls he's slept with in the last month, but I'm rolling my eyes at him, nodding my head at Parks, trying to tell him without telling him that it means fuck all because I've loved her since I was seven and I've been with hundreds of girls.

And then I hear Perry, as I watch him nod his chin at Taura, whisper to Parks, "What's she doing here?"

I don't turn my head to watch the exchange, stay still, use my peripheral vision.

Parks shrugs, a bit hopeless. "He promised it wasn't her—"

Paili presses her lips together. "Do you think maybe he's lying, though?"

And then I turn around. "What the fuck was that now, Paili?"

"Uh," she stutters.

"What did you say?" I lean in towards her, scowling. "Say it again—what did you say?"

She swallows, nervous. "Nothing—"

I shake my head. "I've never lied to her."

"Okay." She nods.

"Fuck you." I point at Pails, angry.

"Beej," Parks says, touches my arm. "It's okay, she's just being—"

"Fuck her?" Perry sniffs, talking over Parks, which already makes me angrier. "Fuck you. It's not like Sax is innocent here—"

I shake my head at him. "What's your measuring stick for that, Lorcs?"

"Your dick, mate—"

Taura shifts uncomfortably. She and Magnolia eye each other in a way I hate. I pull back, surprised at him. Impressed almost. Annoying timing though.

"Quiet," Paili whispers to Perry.

"No—he can't talk to you like that," Perry tells her, not talking his eyes off me.

"Can't I?" I blink, squaring my shoulders. "You going to do something about it, big man?"

"Beej—" Magnolia pulls my arm. "Stop."

And Taurs is watching on, paying attention too closely.

Fuck. If Parks looks at her right now it'll all go to shite anyway, but she won't look at her. Can't. She's locked on me.

Hands on my cheeks, sweeping the hair from my face. Trying to calm me down—succeeding at it too—because her eyes have got a shock factor. If I look at them properly any time it's like someone pushing me into a river. I go under real quick, gotta kick my way back up to the surface, body chokes up, I'm just treading water.

"It's okay," she tells me again, rubbing my cheek with her thumb. "She didn't mean anything by it."

I shake my head and stare down at Paili with my jaw set.

"I went straight to her." I point to myself. "I might be a fuck-up, but I'm not a fucking liar—"

Jonah sits there, watching it all, looks uncomfortable, looks uneasy.

"Oy, let's bounce." He nods towards the door.

"Nah—I'm good." I shake my head, sitting back down. "I'm good—"

Jonah gives me a look, points his chin at the door.

"I'm calling it," he says, gesturing to me, Parks, Taura and himself. "Us four are heading somewhere else. You two"—he points to Paili and Perry—"can piss off."

Perry glares at him. "Really, Jo?"

"Yeah, really." Jo gives him a sharp look. "You're a shit-stirrer, Lorcs—"

Perry shrugs. "Shit-stirrer, truth-teller—they're the same things to liars."

My eyes shift from Perry to Paili and I scowl at them both. Parks kisses them on their cheeks and we head out.

I'm holding her hand absentmindedly, not thinking straight, just thinking about what happened, angry as shit, when we walk out the front and a billion flashes go off and then the yelling starts.

"Magnolia! Where's Tom!"

"Are you and BJ back together?"

"BJ, are you and Magnolia dating again?"

"Are you and Tom over?"

About thirty variants of these questions assault us at once and Magnolia just freezes.

It catches her completely off-guard, and I'm still holding her hand, and they're getting too many photos that will make her life too complicated, and I'm about to hit the photographer next to me who's physically leaning over my body to get a photo of Parks' face right now, which, if I was to caption it, it'd be: my deer's in headlights.

And then Taura breaks free from Jonah's linked arm, grabs Magnolia's face and snogs her. Jonah looks at me with wide, baffled eyes as the flashing lights flash faster and the voices yell more but differently now. Not about us, about them.

"Magnolia! Who's this!"

"Is this your girlfriend!"

"Does Tom know you're a lesbian!"

Parks is frozen still, doesn't pull away, doesn't recoil—lets the kiss happen and just blinks at Taura as she finally pulls away. "Magnolia's with me now," Taura declares obnoxiously and the cameras love her. She nods over at me. "She's had enough of his shit—"

I snort a laugh. "We're not hiding our love anymore," she declares triumphantly, and then grabs Magnolia's hand, pulling her into Jonah's Escalade.

Jonah and I exchange amused and confused looks and follow them into the car.

Inside Jo's tinted, bullet-proof Cadillac the two girls stare at each other—it's dead silent for a long few seconds and then Magnolia blinks a few times before she cracks up.

"You are so weird." She shakes her head at Taura.

Jonah and I look at each other; I swallow a smile.

"And that is Magnolia for 'thank you,'" Jonah tells her.

"It was a panic move," Taura says and shrugs.

Parks sighs, leans her head against the window.

Taura keeps watching her. "They're aggressive with you, aren't they?"

"Invasive," she tells the window, then looks over at Taura, perking up a bit. "That should keep them at bay for a few days though."

Magnolia gives her a small smile and looks away.

Taura looks over at me and excitedly mouths, "Oh my god."

I sniff a laugh and throw my arm around Parks.

02:02

Perry

Sorry bro.

Yeah, me too.

I love you, Beej. Didn't mean to be such an arse.

Those girls...

They'll getcha.

Yep.

19:45

Beej & Tom

You're both Texting me at the same time.

Tom

Oh, good.

Beej

Hey Tom.

Tom

Hey Beej.

Very civil. Love to see it.

So listen. As you both know tomorrow is the Grand Prix ball and you have both asked me to go with you so I'm not going to go with either of you.

Beej

Stupid.

Beej

We'll both take you.

Tom

We will?

Beej

Unless you don't want to, England?

Fine by me. I'll take her myself.

You want us to go... together?

Beej

Yes.

The three of us?

Beej

A throuple, if you will.

Tom

I won't.

Hahaha

Beej

You in, Parks?

I suppose.

Beej

England?

Tom

See you tomorrow x

Beej

Sleep well, cutie @Tom

Alright, bye then?

FORTY-EIGHT

Magnolia

"There was a shooting at a night club—did you hear?" Bridget tells me.

I look up at her, surprised.

"No?"

"Yeah," she says and nods. "At Clean Slate."

"Oh my god." I frown. "Was anyone hurt?"

"A couple of people were shot." She nods. "No deaths."

I frown and shake my head.

"London these days," I sigh.

I'm getting ready for the ball. I've had my hair and make-up done—by George Northwood and Ruby Hammer respectively, and I'm in the red and white ruffled, tiered, metallic tulle gown by Rodarte and I'm practically dying over myself. I look like a fairy god-princess. Bridget's helping me get dressed because I'm practically just a gorgeous marshmallow at this point—I've begged her to come, but she keeps refusing me.

"I hate these things," Bridget says.

"But you love me!"

She shakes her head. "Not that much."

"I come," Bushka declares from the doorway.

Bridget and I exchange looks before I say rather indelicately, "Er—no."

Bushka frowns. "You never bring me to the places—"

"Yes," I nod emphatically. "Quite intentionally. You're terribly uncouth and quite a racist—"

"White people think they better than everyone, but they not so good."

I twist my mouth and my sister clears her throat. "Bushka, you are white."

"I Russian."

Bridget and I exchange a look.

"Anyway." I flick my eyes.

"You bring me," she demands.

"No." I shake my head, straightening out my dress. "The last event we took you to, you tried to goad Princess Anne into a fight."

"I could take."

Bridget nods her head at our grandmother. "She is a Soviet defector."

I pinch my eyes at both of them.

"All I do for you…" Bushka shakes her head ruefully.

"You don't do anything for me." I look at her like she's crazy. "Bit of a relational deadweight, actually—"

"I give you money when I die—"

"Yeah but you're still alive."

"Nice," Bridge says. I roll my eyes. Bushka swats her hand at me. "Oh," my sister growls. "Just take her."

I make a sound in the back of my throat. "Fine."

Bushka cheers and she riffles through my closet, pulling out a very short, skin-tight Herve Leger dress. "I vwear?"

"Absolutely not."

She ignores me, carrying the dress out of my room. "Party vwith two boyfriend and grandma—"

I look at Bridget for help.

"Well," she says, "I'm obviously coming now."

Tom's the first to arrive—no surprise there.

BJ is merry of heart, the best kiss of your life and is probably actively making an Instagram story with a puppy or something, but Tom is a grown-up man, with a wristwatch and a sense of self and time.

Tom is also wearing black Brunello Cucinelli trousers, the Shelton slim-fit, shawl-collar, velvet tuxedo jacket and the white, pintuck-detail tuxedo shirt both from Tom Ford.

It's hardly fashion forward but Tom has these ridiculous eyes that add the wow factor to everything about him.

Opens the door for me? Wow.

Drinks from my water bottle? Wow.

Ties his shoe? Wow.

Breathes? Wow.

"Hello," Tom says when he sees my dress, taking me in. "You look incredible."

He walks towards me, brushes his lips against mine and my cheeks go pink.

"Am I the luckiest man or what?" he asks me, smiling.

"Well," I grimace, "BJ's on the way—so I'm going to go with 'or what'."

Tom sniffs a laugh.

"It'll be fun," he tells me with a mostly certain nod. "It'll be good. Tonight will be good—"

"Yeah, keep saying it." I give him a look. "That'll make it true."

He laughs as the front door opens again and in walks the other one.

Beej jogs up the stairs towards us, and Tom doesn't let go of me.

"Hey bro!" BJ says, walking over to Tom and smacking him on the arse playfully. "That jacket! Looking spiff."

Tom lets out a bewildered laugh. "You too, man."

Then Beej gives him a look. "Sorry, but would you mind taking your hands off the girl of my dreams for a second?" Tom obliges him, steps away.

"Hello Parks." BJ smiles at me, kissing me on the cheek like he owns the place.

"Hi," I say shyly.

"You look like you're crown princess of the candy canes."

"Is that a compliment?" I frown.

"Course it is—you think I'm dumb enough to insult you while I'm trying to make you choose me?"

I consider this. "Yes."

He flicks me a look.

Beej looks from me to Tom.

"So what's the vibe here, guys? Are we both kissing you? Neither of us are kissing you?"

"I think you should kiss each other," Bridget declares from the top of the stairs.

"Don't need to tell me twice," says BJ. He jovially skips towards Tom, who shoves him away with a chuckle.

Bridge is wearing the completely-to-die-for-gorgeous, pale, egg-shell blue, lemon-print sleeveless gown.

"Sorry," I blink up at her. "Did you just casually have that Oscar de la Renta lying around?"

She glances down at herself and shrugs, all indifferent.

BJ looks back at Bridge. "Wait a minute, are you actually leaving the house to come to a society event?"

"Yes," she says, nose in the air.

"Why?" BJ frowns. "Did you lose a bet?"

Bridge scowls at him.

"You look beautiful, Bridget," Tom tells her.

Bridget smiles at him, genuine and pleased.

And then she says, "Not as beautiful as—"

And right on cue Bushka appears at the top of the stairs, thankfully not in my Herve Leger. "I come."

"Shut up!" Beej looks from Buskha to me, eyes wide. He can't believe it. Neither can I. I sigh. Beej squints at me. "Are you drunk?"

I give him a look. "I'm going to be."

"You're coming!" Beej yells jovially. He jogs up the stairs to help her down them. "My favourite of the Parks women!"

("She's actually not a Parks," I growl under my breath. "But yeah, okay.")

"You're my favourite Parks woman," Tom tells me.

"Well, that's because you don't know me very well," my sister tells Tom as she links arms with him, leading him out the door.

Beej walks Bushka out and down the steps.

And I stand there watching my grandma with one of my boyfriends and my sister with the other.

I yell after them dimly, "I'll just lock up then, shall I?"

FORTY-NINE

BJ

Parks isn't into it. The whole dating us both thing. Could tell the whole ride over. She looked nervous. Nervous about what the papers would say about her, because they're not always nice.

She's either their darling or their slut and there's no telling which she'll be on which day.

On a good day she could walk in straddling one of us and kissing the other and they'd call her progressive but when they want to, they'll fault her on everything, shred her to pieces, write things about her that makes her cry in my arms like she's been bullied in the school yard.

I walked in arm in arm with Bushka, half for Parks' sake, half because the old girl's a good time—she's always got a flask on her, she had a crack at David Beckham, she's out-drunk Jonah twice, made a Nazi joke to the German ambassador at the last gala they brought her to. The woman's an absolute loose cannon.

Plus, I can see Magnolia's heart going mush as she watches me with her grandma, which isn't why I'm doing it, but it's sort of the cherry on top.

Once we're inside, Parks darts away from us at the speed of light. She says it's because she spotted Kate Middleton—

"Really put all my eggs in the wrong basket, bonding with Meghan Markle, didn't I?" She shakes her head.

"Now I've got to go and butter up the Duchess of Cambridge—"

"I'm friends with Wills," Tom calls after her.

She stops, turns, rolls her eyes. "Of course you are."

"I'm the love of your life," I remind her. Our eyes catch—does her best not to smile at me for that one.

"—Can't believe they left the monarchy. What a terrible day for everybody. Me in particular," Magnolia mutters under her breath, walking away. "And Lilibet, probably."

An afterthought.

I look over at Tom, who's watching the girl I love like he might love her too.

"Well, fuck," I sigh.

He looks at me and laughs. "Yeah."

I nod my chin at Parks. "She's struggling—"

He looks over at her again, looking for whatever it is that I can see. It's got to be shit for him... to want to see it but not being able to spot it because I don't think you can see it with your eyes.

I can see it in how the butterflies flap in the halo over her head, in the way the light reflects off her thoughts, the way that willow tree shudders—

"Yeah?" Tom says, not looking away from her.

I nod. "She's avoiding us."

"I mean"—he gives me a look—"it's pretty weird."

I look over at him and sniff a laugh. "Is it?" Tom looks at me strangely. I shake my head "Yeah, I guess it's weird." I shrug. "Feels kind of normal to me."

"That's pretty fucked up," he tells me.

His mouth pulls like he's sorry for me, but I don't fucking want him to be sorry for me. I've had her for all my life, she's mine, I fucked it up and now I have her like she'll let me. I don't need his pity. I don't even need his understanding. Just need her.

I watch her, the girl of my dreams, love of my life, alpha, omega, beginning and end, 'til death do us part and even then I'm still hanging on—and all I say is, "Yeah."

"She's put you through the ringer," Tom tells me.

I consider this, frown a bit as I do. "I dunno—I can never tell if we're dancing in a burning room or taking turns dragging the other unconscious up a mountain."

Tom sniffs a laugh, looks at me like I'm crazy. "Both pretty shit to be honest, man—"

"Yeah," I concede as I stare over at her. "One ends with a pretty good view though—"

Tom watches me closer than I want him to. He's got an intense stare. I think it's worse because his eyes are so blue. Sounds dreamy, but I don't know—aggressively blue, you could say?

He's just watching me, nearly frowning but not at me.

"You two are something else." He shakes his head. "It's weird."

We are, I know. All I do is give him a nod and a shrug.

He's watching her, eye pinched. "You think she does it to everyone?"

"Does what?"

He shrugs. "Makes them feel like they're—I don't know? The sun."

I feel bad for him. He's still new to her. New to watching other men around her and Parks not even knowing she's the focus of everyone in the room.

This little ray of sunshine even when she's acting like a solid git.

"It's nearly intimidating the bond you have." He looks back at me.

I sniff. "Just nearly?"

"Yeah," he says. "I can't have the whole story, and I refuse to be intimidated by something I don't fully understand." I nod a couple of times. Fair enough. "Your chemistry though—" He gives me a look and I wonder why he's here still.

Forget the metaphors about the jumper cables and the sparks, we're all of them and none of them—Parks and me. It's in the fucking stars.

"It's a lot," Tom says and nods.

"Not intimidating enough to keep you away though." I give him a look.

"Yeah." He pauses. "It's that gunpowder fire thing from Shakespeare. Your chemistry is what makes you— no doubt, man. It's unparalleled." Pause. "It's maybe what'll kill you though."

And I fucking hate this shit because that wasn't a threat. He's not being an arrogant son of a bitch; he's just thinking out loud. Sitting there shooting the shit all sage and shit and I fucking hate him, because sometimes I worry maybe he's right.

"Hey." Tom elbows me. "We were fucking around with you before—"

I purse my mouth. Nod.

"I'd wondered with the dropping her off to me with the Harley shit—"

Tom shakes his head. "No, I already liked her by then—but she didn't need me." Shrugs. "She needed you."

"What the fuck?" I frown. "You're so annoying." Likes her and drops her to me anyway because I'm what she needs? "How are you this fucking chill, man?"

Tom sniffs a laugh. "I'm not." He glances at me for a sec, then looks away. "I watched you hurt her in that club, thought I could help her level the playing field. But now I think I'm a bit in love with her—"

I nod, getting it. "She has that effect on people"

"I know," he says, solemn. "I'm sorry."

I clock him. "For what?"

"Because I like you, man." He smacks me on the back. "But if I have a shot here, I'm taking it."

I give him a look. "Same, bro."

Tom nods—glances at me, a bit nervous. "She doesn't know."

I sink my Negroni. "Know what?"

"That I love her."

"Ah." I nod.

Lock my mouth up, put the key in his lapel pocket.

He smacks me on the back.

"Good man." And then he slides me over my drink, raising his.

"May the best man win."

I snort and shake my head.

"Nah, bro—fuck the pilot. I'm pulling for the obviously worst man—he's real fucked up but a heart of gold."

Tom laughs and so do I.

Stings though, I think because we both know it's true.

17:41

Tom

> Are you sure you don't want to come to Julian's birthday?

I'm sure.

It'll be fun...

Nah, I'm too old for clubs and shit.

Actually, I think you and Jules are the same age.

'Jules' now is it.

We're old friends.

Hah. Okay.

Also, you and I met in a club like 5 months ago, so—

Actually, we met at The Queen's Cup when you were 7. I was 16. You've been a real hanger on.

Come?

No, I'm good.

Have fun x

FIFTY

Magnolia

It's Julian Haites' 30th tonight. Me and the boys are going. BJ thinks he's bringing me as his date. He doesn't realise Julian sent me an invitation himself.

I spot Daisy Haites before I spot her brother. She's perched on Christian's lap. I wave at them both. Christian doesn't really do anything; his face pulls funny and I don't understand—Daisy raises one hand and offers me an unenthusiastic quasi-wave.

I do my best not to over-analyse this lukewarm reception and look for validation in other ways, like slipping my hand into BJ's. He lifts it to his mouth, kissing it without thinking.

"Ballentine," Julian jeers, a drink in each hand as he walks over. He downs one quickly and offers the other to me before he picks BJ up, jostling him around affectionately.

"Happy birthday!" Jonah grabs him by the shoulders, and Jules claps his face.

Julian would probably be Jonah's other best friend, which might make the scene extra tense when his eyes catch mine the way they do over Jonah's shoulder.

He stands tall in his logo-appliqué, wool-blend varsity jacket from Amiri and smirks down at me. "Magnolia."

"Jules," I nod up, matching his face.

And the tone of familiarity between us strikes a bizarre chord in the boys. BJ looks over at me, frowning with concern.

Jonah and BJ have always been very clear with me about Julian:

Avoid him at all costs. Unless someone is trying to kill me, and then I'm to run straight to him.

I did once. Run to him. No one was trying to kill me, but I was dying. A few weeks after BJ and I had broken up. You know after the adrenaline stops and the numbing agent hasn't kicked in and you're not medicated and your heart's just dying of thirst, completely on fire and suffocating at once—and I don't know why I thought to do it—I hadn't left the house in two weeks—but I made Paili come out with me.

"I don't think this is a good idea," she said about 90,000 times on our way in. "You just need to grieve…"

I shook my head. "I'm done grieving him."

Paili gave me a look. I wasn't. How could I be? Even a layman could have told you:

I'd never stop grieving that boy.

At his birthday, Julian and I standing next to each other, too familiar for Beej to be comfortable with, he does this laugh that's meant to sound airy, and it would to everyone in the room but me and Jonah… to our fine-tuned ears, it's strained.

"Didn't realise you two knew each other?" BJ glances back and forth between us.

Julian lets out a "hah", and shrugs his burly shoulders, all indifferent. "Everyone knows this one."

"Right—" BJ's eyes pinch looking from him to me. "How?"

Julian sticks his tongue into the cheek of his mouth and peeks over at me, cheeky. Eyebrows high, waiting for me to handle this.

We went to a club. McQueen, I think it was, and in a horrible twist of events (for me), a boy from our old school—Ed Bancroft—whom Paili always had a crush on but nothing every really happened with, was there. And he was very interested in Paili.

And I don't know what happened, or why it was happening—it was oddly out of character for her, like she had something to prove, even though she had nothing to prove. She's never been a real hook-up-in-a-club kind of girl, neither have I—but that night, she was just going for it.

Next to me. On a couch. And she'd been such a good friend the last few weeks, hadn't left my side. Lain in my bed with me, cried with me, sometimes for me.

She was so present, so heartbroken for me—I could hardly be cross that on a night I'd dragged her out to a place she thought neither of us should be in that she finally decided to enjoy herself.

So, I was sitting there dressed to the nines and vaguely suicidal as Ed Bancroft practically dry humped her on the spot. I sighed, threw back a few drinks in quick succession to make my mind quieten down and to dampen my blaring discomfort, when a guy ducked into my line of sight.

Messy brown hair, big blue eyes, five o'clock shadow. Drop dead gorgeous.

He smirked at me. "I know you."

I offered him a small smile and singular nod. "You do."

"Do you know me?" he asked, eyebrows up.

I gave him an amused look. "Everyone knows you—"

"Well, I really only care if you know me," Julian Haites said and grinned. "Do you remember me from school?"

And from his *Vanity Fair* spread, his *VICE* interviews, his *GQ* shoots, he really was (is) the world's most famous, handsome "arms dealer."

"I mean, I was eleven—" I gave him a tiny smile. "But you were quite fast on that field,"

He smiled appreciatively. "But not as fast as—"

"Don't!" I interrupted, shaking my head. "Don't say his name."

Firstly, I can't quite believe that BJ doesn't seem to know about any of this? If BJ doesn't know it means Jonah doesn't know, and if Jonah doesn't know it's because Julian strategically never told him. I wonder why? BJ's staring at me, waiting for me to tell him how his friend knows me but in all honesty I'm quite sure he actually doesn't want to know how Julian knows me and in which specific ways.

Two and a bit years ago, Julian's eyebrows shot up in that nightclub with intrigue. "Wow, okay—they around?"

I shook my head.

He was unbearably hot. Is still, actually.

Jawline, razor sharp. Eyes, like the dark parts of glaciers. Six feet, three inches. Tattoos up and down his body. Also, the head of the most notorious family in London. I don't know what exactly it is that they do but I do know it's not legal.

"They not around for a reason?" he asked. I nodded. "You need a drink then," he told me, pulling me up off the couch, taking my hand and leading me over to the bar. The crowd parted for him like the Red Sea, no one wanting to be in his way, but he didn't even seem to notice. I knew people's eyes were on me—not how they are these days, back then it was less. The real public fascination with Beej and I began when we stopped being something that made sense to them.

There were rumours at this point that BJ and I were on the rocks but nothing definitive, and were I with anyone but Julian, I think people might have taken photos, might have leaked them out to the press, but I remember I had a distinct feeling that no one was going to tell anyone about this. You don't mess with the Haites family.

My hand in his made me feel a surge of relief and also somewhat free.

"Do you like whiskey?" he asked me.

"No," I pursed my lips, leaning across the bar.

"Give me two of the Johnnie Walker Baccarats," he told the bartender. "Put it on my tab."

He slid me over a shot glass. "You might like this one. It's £500 apiece." He smiled.

We clinked glasses and threw them back.

He looked down at me, eyebrows raised expectantly. "Like it?"

"Nope." I smiled apologetically.

"Fuck!" he cried, his head fell back, laughing. "Lie to me?"

"Loved it," I said with a grimace.

He gave me a despondent look.

We took a bottle of vodka to a table in the corner of the room, and we laughed a lot, and we drank even more and I wasn't thinking about BJ or what he did to us barely at all, and all I was doing was staring at Julian Haites' mouth. His lips were so pink. Bottom heavy and almost like he's angry even when he's happy.

He pushed some hair behind my ear.

"Can I take you home?" he asked me, tilting his head so we were eye to eye. His eyes were steady, and I liked them.

I nodded quickly, not giving myself a chance to think about it and say no.

He took my hand again, leading me out the back door and to a town car that was waiting for him. Black, tinted windows—bullet-proof, just like the Hemmes cars—he opened the car door for me, and I climbed in, him after me.

We sat perfectly still next to each other for a few seconds, staring straight ahead, then he turned towards me and I climbed onto his lap, kissing him quickly with lips on fire, pulling his shirt off over his head.

He chuckled, holding my face in his hand and—can I just say—he is a phenomenal kisser. Phenomenal enough that it didn't immediately kill me that I was kissing someone other than BJ—that feeling would come later, like I was cheating on him, like I was breaking us— that'd come eventually too but Julian was so good and so smooth and so handsome that it delayed the inevitable.

I never thought I'd say that about anyone besides BJ in my whole life, but I can guarantee you, Julian Haites is the boss of every room he's in. He lay down across the back seat, pulling me down with him. He's good with his hands, I'll tell you that much. I didn't even notice when the car stopped moving.

We slipped inside his house. Huge and excessive. Everything white or black marble, with gold trimming on everything. He guided me up the stairs, silently, still shirtless, to a room. I followed him in and he closed the door behind me, then walked over to a desk and emptied his pockets, then looked back at me, quizzically. I leant against the door, pursing my lips together, holding my clutch in front of me like some sort of chastity belt.

He laughed to himself, then sat on his bed, scratching his head.

"So." He smiled.

"So." I nodded. I wasn't awkward before. I don't know why I was suddenly. Maybe the lights?

He tilted his head, looking at me softly. "You good?"

"Me?"

"Yeah," he answered, leaning back a bit.

"I'm fine." I nodded, emphatically. "I'm totally fine."

"Okay." He nodded, then paused. "Girls don't say 'fine' when they're fine, usually—"

"Well, I am," I told him, my nose in the air. "Fine."

"Okay." He nodded again, squinting. "Great..."

"It is great." I nodded again. "I am great, and you're great. And we're going to have great sex. And it'll be great."

"Okay." He smiled and rubbed his hand across his mouth.

"And I can't wait," I told him, blinking a lot, sounding really enthused and not thinking about BJ at all. "— Didn't mean for that to rhyme."

I swallowed nervously.

He smiled a tiny bit, then pressed his lips together, watching me closely.

"Okay!" I said, clapping my hands together and taking a deep breath as I walked over to him. "Let's do this. Can you just help me with this zip?" I sat down on the bed next to him, offering him my back.

He reached for it, then his hand hesitated.

"I have a sister, you know?" he said, looking for my eyes.

"Weird time to bring her up—"

"Shut up." He rolled his eyes. "I just know girls."

"—I'm sure you do," I butted in.

He rolled his eyes. "You know what I mean."

"I don't."

He scratched his neck, smiling wryly. "You're beautiful, Parks. Really, really beautiful," he added with a hint of a frown. I looked at him with dark eyes, sensing a "but" on its way. "You sure you want to do this?"

"Yep," I over-accentuated with a nod.

He leaned in, cupping my face with his hands, and kissed me softly and then I burst into tears.

He laughed and pulled away, shaking his head. "Magnolia." He pulled me up into his lap, held me into his chest, and then he just let me cry. That's probably not on-brand behaviour for a gang lord, maybe that's why he never told Jonah. Ours is hardly a story regaling his sexual prowess: I just cried on him for about two hours. Big, shoulder heaving, snotty sobs. His bodyguard made me pancakes, and then I cried more. He played with my hair. I spent the night in his bed, and I told him everything that happened, and he offered to kill BJ and I was afraid he meant it. We talked all night until I fell asleep on him, and then that was it. He drove me home the next morning, gave me his number, and said if I ever needed anything...

"Would you believe me if I said we're in a book club together?" I offer BJ.

He shakes his perfect head.

"Julian loves... historical women's fiction and also, is quite partial to a biography."

Julian starts laughing, unhelpfully.

BJ squints. "Mmhm."

"I offered to help her out with something." Julian catches my eye. "She never took me up on the offer." He elbows BJ playfully. "She's still slumming it."

"Behave," I say and give him a stern look. Julian grins back. All the while BJ looks terribly uncomfortable at the air between us.

"But for real, Parks—if you're ever looking for a good time, with an actual bad boy, not one of these silly *Vogue* bad boys—call me."

I roll my eyes at him and try to curb my enthusiasm over all the attention being paid to me in the moment. "Perhaps just let's get me through this present love triangle I'm in and once I sort that out, you'll be next in line?"

"Yep, fair." Julian nods and then smacks BJ on the arm, winks at him playfully.

BJ watches him walk away, incredulous.

"Are you kidding me?" He blinks.

I try not to laugh at the face he's wearing and pull him aside, holding his hands. "We kissed once."

"Once?"

"We nearly had sex once," I concede.

"When?"

"Um"—I grimace—"immediately after you and I broke up."

He pulls his head back. "What?"

"Like, a fortnight after or something—"

"Parks! He's a dangerous guy—"

"Right," I say and give him a look. "You know we're at his birthday party? Like, right now."

"We're here with Jonah, and you're my guest."

"Actually"—I pull a face—"he invited me himself."

BJ sighs. "Of course he did."

He rubs his face with both his hands.

"You nearly had sex with him?"

"Well—you have sex to completion frequently with people who aren't me," I remind him. "All the time."

He tries his best not to laugh at that, but he sniffs anyway.

He gives me a long look. "Why was it just almost?"

"Uh." I purse my mouth. "Because when he kissed me on his bed, I burst into tears. Over you—" He squashes away a smile. "And I cried in his arms, his head of security then made me pancakes and then Julian drove me home."

BJ nods, pleased with the answer, and pulls me in towards him, wrapping his arms around me.

"And who's going to make you pancakes tomorrow morning?"

"I don't know?" I smile brightly. "Shall I see if his security guy's available?"

The night goes on from there, everything seems good and fine and normal—Christian's drinking a bit though—but BJ and I are wonderful.

He doesn't let go of me, hovers like a shadow in the noontime sun. I don't know if it's because of what he just learnt about me and Julian or it's just because he can, but I don't care either way.

We feel good.

The kisses on my neck when I'm not looking, the hands around my waist at all and any given moment, and everything feels kind of how I always thought it would before we fucked it all up—us together, our hands in each other's, him talking to Jo, me talking to Henry—and without looking at me, no words, he tosses his arm around my shoulder, pulls me in towards him, kisses my ear, keeps talking to Jo, and it's so minor in the scheme of affection, such an absolute non-event, but it makes my heart feel like it's carrying around a diamond in its pocket and that nothing, no time or heartache or infidelities have passed between us, and maybe this is how we'll always be—stuck together, drifting back to each other if we somehow pull apart. I hope that's what we'll be like. I hope we'll always find our way back.

And then there's yelling. Loud and aggressive.

Jonah cranes his neck looking over—then jumps to his feet because it's Christian.

He nods his head over towards his brother and the boys and I follow.

"—the fuck do you mean, why do I care? We're together," Christian says to Daisy, staring at her wide-eyed.

She's with a boy. I've never seen him before.

"Are we? Don't bullshit me" She glares over at him, angrily. "I've never been under any illusion of what I am to you—I'm the girl you're fucking while you're thinking of your best friend's girlfriend."

And then we all go tense. Not just me and the boys, but the entire room. My eyes are wide. BJ's whole body goes stiff.

"I—" Christian stutters, jaw agape and my heart pangs because I hate to see him like this.

He looks hurt and sad, maybe a bit betrayed? I don't know if Daisy's talking about me, but probably she's talking about me?

And what the absolute fuck is she doing saying that out loud in front of everyone?

"Oh." Daisy Haites blinks, all big and innocent. "Did you think I didn't know? You're confusing me for someone who has a little bit of self-respect, because I know what I am to you and I still stayed, hoping that one day you'd want me more than you wanted her. But you never wanted me. You never liked me—"

And Christian's watching her how I've never seen him watch anyone else before: eyes round, shaking his head a little bit. He looks scared.

"And we might be a fucking mess—" She gestures back to Romeo Brambilla. "But you know what? One thing I know for certain is when I take Rome home tonight, he's not going to be thinking about Magnolia fucking Parks."

All our jaws hit the floor, and Daisy's out of there like a light. Legs it, hand in hand with the boy who isn't Christian.

And Christian's frozen still, eyes on the ground. He doesn't meet my eyes; he won't dare look at Beej or his brother.

He shakes his head and walks through the crowd, pushing past them.

And then Jonah charges after him, so BJ goes after Jonah, so I go after Beej, and I have this peculiar floaty feeling that perhaps I have loved too many boys and maybe I've made too many boys love me.

There are all sorts of loves in this world, I know that now. I don't know it completely—it's not a full moon of knowing just yet, maybe at best I'm at the waxing crescent of understanding what I can about love. They say it conquers all, but does it? Can it even? All is so vast.

I've lost BJ hundreds of times to hundreds of different women and he's nearly lost me twice now to two men I loved more than I meant to. Do I love Tom? I suppose I do if he's on my mind right now. What does that mean?

What could it mean? Because it's not the same as it is with BJ, which is the only love that matters to me, I think. And even then, me and Beej, we keep losing each other, and it doesn't seem to matter that we love each other how we do, which is with a fullness—kind of like those animals that will eat themselves to death if they're left to their own devices. I'll love him 'til I die, love him 'til it consumes me whole and kills me dead—so maybe love doesn't conquer all but just some. Because all is vast and love is so varied, like light in a prism; if you move it around a room, depending on how it catches, it changes. It means different things and there are so many different things love can be to people.

I know that some love is beautiful, and some is freeing, some unravels you, some love poisons you, some blinds you, some betters you, and some loves break you in invisible ways that no one else knows about until you have to stand up and the weight of your love crushes your bones. And as I watch him scream "fuck" again and again in a back alley while he punches a wall, I wonder if maybe I accidentally made Christian love me like that?

"Tell me Daisy Haites has lost her fucking mind." Jonah shakes his head at his brother.

Christian spins on his heel to face him, eyes ragged.

Jo shakes his head at Christian, placing a threatening finger on his chest and I get a nervous feeling. I hate it when they gang up on him. It's only ever about me.

"What the fuck is she talking about?" BJ asks, brows low. Christian says nothing, but his eyes catch mine finally—just for a second before Jonah gives him a push. "Don't look at Parks—look at me."

And then something surprising happens: Christian shoves Jonah off of him. Harder and more aggressively

397

than I've ever seen him be with his brother. "Don't fuck with me tonight."

"Boys," Henry says, standing next to Christian and I'm glad he's there. Henry levels the playing field a bit.

Jonah's not backing down—he's got Christian backed up against the wall, the collar of his shirt in his hand.

"Jonah." I shake my head at him, yanking his arm. "Let go of him—what are you doing?"

"—What are you doing?" Jonah barks back.

BJ looks from me to Christian and then cries to the sky. "Are you fucking kidding?" He looks down at me with wild eyes, wide and sore. "Is two of us not enough?"

I reach for him, my heart breaking in my eyes. "Beej—"

"Did you know?" BJ asks me with eyes as tattered as his heart.

My face falters. "Of course I didn't know."

And I wonder whether I'm lying to him—

Is that lying to him?

I didn't know with any absolute certainty.

I didn't want to know. Didn't want to have to change how I am with Christian, didn't want to not be able to rest my head on his shoulder at a movie if I wanted to, didn't want to have to lose the one boy I knew I had in my corner, the one who'd tell me the truth about BJ, no matter what.

Did I know he loved me? No.

Did I know for certain that he didn't love me? Somehow, also no.

BJ hooks his arm around my neck, pulling me away from them, pressing his mouth into my cheek.

He doesn't do it because he's okay, he does it because he's not. He's trying to level himself. Breathing me in like an essential oil.

"I'll take you home," BJ tells me and I nod.

I look back at Jonah. "Don't hurt him, okay?"

All Jonah does is grunt.

My eyes lock with Christian's and I wish I could make sure that they won't hurt him. I want to tell him I'm sorry and I hope he's okay and he can call me later if he needs to, but I don't think any of those things are okay things anymore.

So instead, I tell him I'm sorry with my eyes, but he doesn't speak the language of my eyes, just BJ does, so Christian thinks I say nothing at all.

BJ doesn't stay the night. He doesn't speak to me in the car ride home—but he doesn't let go of my hand either. He walks me up the front steps, kisses my head and turns to leave.

"BJ—" I call after him.

He presses his hands into his eyes.

"I can't right now, Magnolia." He shakes his head. "I need to think."

09:56

Beej

How's the weather, Beej?

I don't know.

You're cross.

I don't know what I am.

I'm sorry.

For what?

I don't know.

Everything?

I'll call you tomorrow, okay

Okay

I'm sorry.

🐝

X

FIFTY-ONE

BJ

I'm reeling afterwards. Mind's on fire, an ache in my chest that feels like a hole. Everything's slipping. He still into her? What else don't I know? Is she lying to me?

She never lies to me, not about actual shit.

Might tell me she hates me or she's done with me, but that's as close as she'll get to a lie. But now I'm thinking—why the fuck is he thinking about Parks while he's with Daisy if he and Parks didn't actually fuck? Right?

So she's lying.

I dropped her home and headed straight back to mine. Did a line. Waited ten minutes. Did another.

Helps me focus and I needed to focus.

Pored over the cracks in our timeline, wonder if she filled them with Christian.

These are the days that follow. I don't call her. Don't text. Reply when she texts me though, but only because if I don't she'll go into full-blown panic mode, and I can't right now—can't figure out what the fuck any of this means or how I feel about it if I'm having to make her be okay too.

Cancel all my shoots for the week. I go to the café by our house, order in at night, do lines in between. Before I felt bad when I did the lines, like I was fucking Parks over but now I reckon she's probably the one fucking over me, so rack 'em up.

That's all I do for four days. Read a bit. Try to watch TV but can't because pretty much everything I've got left to watch I promised I'd watch with Magnolia and so I start *Narcos* again.

Halfway through season two, Christian appears in my doorway. I frown over at him. He disappeared after that night. None of us have seen him since.

"Where'd you fuck off to?"

He shrugs, walks in, stands on the other side of the room with his hands in his pockets. "Just needed a minute."

I don't say anything. Don't know what I'm supposed to say.

He breathes out, tired and impatient, watching me carefully.

"I'm in love with her, Beej—"

My jaw goes tight. Heart falls down five flights of stairs. He's in love with her?

I sniff out this laugh that's suspended in disbelief.

"What?" he asks, nervous.

I shake my head. "You're just not the first person to tell me that lately."

"That's fucked up," he tells me. I nod. He shakes his head, happy for the connection point, I think. "She's fucked in the head," he tells me.

"Oy," I growl reflexively, even though I don't think I disagree. Even if I don't, no one can talk shit on her except me; it makes me angrier that he feels like he can.

"She is, man...she needs everyone to love her," Christian says. "You, me, Tom, Jules—it's fucking shit. And she—"

"Stop." I frown. "What are you doing? This isn't about her." A lie. It's always about her. "It's about you being my best friend and loving her—"

"I didn't mean to—"

I let out an incredulous laugh. "You fucking dated her. Behind my back."

"Beej—" He bangs his head back against the wall behind him "It was an accident. We were hanging out— we've been friends forever—longer than you—"

I give him a warning look. Fuck him.

"I was just with her, the same as I'd been with her a billion times before. And then one day we kissed." He shrugs. Shrugs like it's nothing. Like it's not the biggest fucking betrayal in the history of time.

"Oh," I say and nod, over-emphatically. "You kissed."

"It was rainy, in a phone box—"

I shake my head quick. "I'm not asking for a fucking play by play—"

"Then what are you asking?" His voice getting louder.

"Why her?" My tone meets his.

"Because she's Magnolia fucking Parks."

I look away, shaking my head a bit. How much shit is she going to get away with in this lifetime under that hat?

"And she was sad. And I wanted to make it better." He shrugs like he can't help it. Maybe he can't. I can't. "But she was sad because of you. Because for her, it's always you—"

"That's not true anymore."

"Yes it fucking is, man—how can't you see that? Everything she does is because of you, or about you, or trying to fuck you up because you fucked her up first—"

I cover my face with my hands, feeling weird and exposed. Peek through my fingers at my old friend. "Why didn't you tell me?"

"Because she's yours." He glares over at me a bit. "And even when she isn't, she is." He glances up at me. "And I don't want her. I just—I don't know how to get past her."

I grind my jaw, feel my own eyes soften a bit. Fuck.

"Yeah." I breathe out my nose. "Know the feeling."

Christian rubs his jaw, watching me carefully for a few seconds.

"Beej, I've gotta talk to her."

I bang my fist on my bed absentmindedly.

"What are you going to say?"

He gives me a long look, doesn't have to tell me what he's going to say, I already know. He's going to tell her. I feel sick for a second. Wonder if he'll go to her, tell her he loves her. And I wonder for a second whether he's more worthy of her than me? In some ways maybe he is.

In every way imaginable, Tom's more worthy than us both.

He shrugs, a bit helpless. "I have to."

I give him a wary look. "I trust you."

He nods once, then he leaves.

FIFTY-TWO

Magnolia

"—And he hasn't really spoken to me since."

My sister grimaces as she leans back in her seat. We're having brunch at Neptunes.

"He never doesn't talk to you." She tells me like I don't already know, like it's not my every waking thought.

I told Tom what happened. He wasn't so upset, he said he saw it coming. Actually, he said Gus saw it coming and gave him a head's up.

Tom's been around a bit, a numbing agent in the wound of an absent Ballentine.

He's even stayed over a few times.

I'm not sure that'd placate BJ, but it's placated me.

I think I'm starting to see why BJ has sex all the time now.

It does make me feel better, it's a brief kind of betterness, very little permanence to the whole thing but there's this euphoric few seconds where you can't really focus on anything at all other than the good thing you're feeling, and it's so good and for twenty seconds I can't think about how far away BJ feels or how fucked everything is these days, or who I'll pick, because I know I'll have to pick one of them soon, or how I'm worried about hurting Tom when I don't pick him, because I don't know how to pick anyone over BJ, or how Christian's relationship's seemingly gone to shit because of me without me even lifting a finger—all of it is all I think about when my mind isn't forced to think about something else, and thusly—Tom and I have been having sex quite a lot.

He's gone away for work for two days though, leaving me in the lurch with all my thoughts and the boy I love ignoring me.

"It's actually wild, isn't it," Bridget considers. "Your capacity for male-driven drama."

I give her a look.

"What?" She shrugs. "It is—you've got a lot of boys in the air."

"I've got two boys in the air." I pet my dark green, asymmetric, pleated, wrap skirt from Marni.

"Christian might beg to differ."

I take a long sip of champagne, glaring over at her a bit. And she's doing this thing she does—it's shit and I hate it. She's watching me, thinking, processing, reading. She leans back in her chair, squinting a bit at me—usually she's doing this to me and Beej, trying to solve the unsolvable.

But me, she can read like a book. Crack me open, get straight to the core.

"I don't know if it's because of BJ or Dad," she says. "Both probably." She considers. "You might be addicted to male attention."

"Fuck off." I blink, horrified. "I am not."

"It's not your fault." She shrugs. "Look at your face. Your face is the first part of the problem—"

I frown, touching it absentmindedly. "What's wrong my face?"

"Nothing," she says and laughs, pulling a piece of lint off of her script-logo, crew-neck jumper from Saint

Ivory NYC. "Hence the origin of the problem."

"I don't much feel like being psychoanalysed, Bridge."

"Too bad." She leans in. "Dad never paid much attention to us, not enough. Not the amount little girls need from their father, anyway. But BJ—" She gives me a knowing look. "He was your saving grace. He... looks at you and sees the sun. So, you were covered. You didn't need a dad, you had a BJ. For years, you were fine. For years, boys probably paid attention to you and you just didn't even know, because all you saw is BJ. And then he cheated on you—"

"I'm aware."

"—And that undercut all the attention he'd paid you 'til then."

My brows drop a little.

"Sullied it. Made it untrustworthy and invaluable. So now I think, maybe you just collect the attention of men—"

"Fuck you—"

"—Keep it in your back pocket for a rainy day."

"You're being ridiculous." I shake my head.

"Am I?" She arches her brow.

And I worry that maybe she's not. I fold my arms over my chest.

"This thing with Christian is hitting Beej harder than I thought—"

"Well, yeah." She shrugs. "He's his best friend."

"It's not like I was shagging Jonah!" I say, mostly to make myself feel better.

"Right," she says. "Just his other best friend who's as close to him as his brother. Much better."

I sigh, deflated.

"We weren't shagging."

She looks at me, dubious. "You and Christian really never slept together?"

"No." My nose in the air.

"It's okay if you did." She gives me a look.

"Well, we didn't."

She gives me a look. "Why the fuck not?"

I shrug like there's no reason, like it's a mystery to me too, but it's not. I know why. And there's so much more to it than I can say.

"Beej thinks you did," she tells me, and I have a pang of jealousy that my sister knows the innermost thoughts of the boy I love.

"I know. He doesn't believe me."

"That's because BJ doesn't know how to not have sex with people."

I nod, glib. "Excellent."

"Do you think you guys will ever work it out?" she asks, tilting her head as she watches me.

And honestly, the question hits me like a slap.

The idea that there's a chance we might not has never been a reality on my horizon.

But all of that feels too personal to say out loud, even to my sister. I don't want her to know I always assumed we'd just wind back up together and I also don't want her to know that until this waking moment, I hadn't realised that maybe we might not.

FIFTY-THREE

Magnolia

I'm in my room by myself when I get the feeling I'm being watched—it lasts only for a second before I look over and see him, hovering in the doorway. 4 X 4 Biggie Hoodie in jet black from Ksubi, the hood pulled up, hands shoved deep in the pockets of his drawstring, drop-crotch trousers from Rick Owens DRKSHDW. It's been nearly a week since Julian's party. I haven't seen him or heard from him. I rush over to him, pull him into my room and yank the hood off his head.

"Did they hurt you?" I blink up at Christian.

His eyes flicker down my knitted, candy pink, hooded, pompom-embellished mini dress from Gucci before shakes his head. I sigh relieved and he pushes past me, walking into my room.

"You did but—"

"What?" I blink.

"Honestly Parks, fuck you." His tone is aggressive. "Like, really, fuck you. I mean it."

"Christian—"

"You're a bitch, Parks."

I'm baffled. I can't believe he's saying that to me.

"I'm in love with you," he tells me, frowning.

He slips his hand around my waist.

"What?"

And then he kisses me.

It happens too quickly for me to stop it—he grabs my face, and he kisses me, and I don't stop him because it's oddly familiar and the familiarity of it is the first thing I register, not that I shouldn't be doing it.

By the time I register that the kiss should stop, it's already stopped.

"And I hate you," he tells me, and he's angry.

I swallow and try not to look gutted. "Why?"

"Because you let me be," he yells, exasperated. "There's a reason you turn to me over the other boys—"

"Yeah, because we—"

"Don't." He shakes his head. "You know why."

I don't mean to, but my bottom lip starts to go. I don't really like it when anyone's angry at me but Christian feels particularly bad.

I give him a tiny shrug. "The other two, they're too loyal to Beej. They'll lie to me for him. And I know you'd—"

"Do anything for you," he says. "Yeah, I would. But fuck you for letting me—" His anger peeks through again. "Do you need the whole fucking world to be in love with you?"

My eyes go teary. "Christian—"

He rushes towards me, takes my wrists in his hands, pushing some hair behind my ears.

And it's bad, all of this is bad.

I know it's bad.

Bad that he feels like he can be like this with me, bad that he can touch me without a second thought, bad that I'm not stopping him.

He looks for my eyes. "I'm done with this now, okay?"

"Christian—"

"And I need you to let me be, Parks." He shakes his head, eyes stern. "Let me be over you."

I nod, tearier than I should be. Nervous that I'm losing him.

"Are you not going to be my friend anymore?"

"I'll always be your friend." He gives me a look. "But I haven't been your friend for a long time."

I drop my eyes from his, feeling embarrassed. I don't know how active a role I played in him loving me still. It's not like we hang out by ourselves—Henry's almost always there. Usually. Sometimes we text, occasionally we talk on the phone. Our eyes catch when we remember things we probably shouldn't anymore, but he can't have thought it meant anything. I don't know—maybe sometimes I did treat Christian like a safety net for when Beej lets me fall, which he does. Often.

"From now on"—he searches for my eyes—"if you wouldn't ask Jonah to do it, don't ask me."

I nod, solemnly. "I'm so sorry—I don't know what's wrong with me, I—"

"I let you." He shrugs. "We could have had this conversation three years ago but we didn't because I didn't want to. Loving you was a good reason not to love anyone else."

"Do you love her?" I ask, and I'm not jealous as I do.

He nods, sitting down on my bed. "Yeah."

I give him a small smile. "Lucky girl."

"Oy." He points at me, squinting almost playfully. "None of that shit—we're strictly business now, you and me."

"I'd say that to Jonah." I frown, defensive.

"Nah, how could you? It's completely irrelevant." He shrugs. "His heart's dead in the water."

I watch him for a few seconds. "I love you," I tell him. "Do you know that?"

He stares straight ahead, nodding two, three, four times.

"Yep." He looks over at me. "Not how I love you, unfortunately."

"I did once," I remind him, I don't know why.

He nods again, thinking about it. "Not how you love him though."

He puts his hand on my knee, squeezes it once.

There's a finality to it. Like we're closing the chapter, finally, on what we used to be.

How many loves, I wonder again?

Some loves, like ours was, are like wrecking balls in glass houses. And wrecking balls have no business being in glass houses like I had no business loving Christian how I did once upon a time, except that sometimes, some loves keep your head above the water when you're drowning. Some loves might fog up a phone booth on a rainy London afternoon and make you feel less alone than you did before your lips touched.

He's leaving what we had behind, like he should. Like I should have let him so long ago. But I'll miss him on my rainy days.

He stands and walks towards the door, pausing as he looks back.

"Don't fuck it up, Parks. I'll be fucking pissed if you do."

11:16

Tom

Heard from him?

No

You doing okay?

Do you want me to have heard from him?

Hah

No, not really.

I do want you to be okay though.

Cute.

I miss you.

I miss you too.

Dinner tonight?

Yes please.

Be ready for 8. I'll grab you.

Don't bring BJ...

😳

Sorry.

FIFTY-FOUR

BJ

She's sitting there, perched up on one of the walls, her legs tucked under her. Wearing some red checked skirt and top set thing, I don't know—she looks like my dream girl, whatever it is. Everything she wears I want to take off her body. Sounds like a sex thing, maybe it is a bit but also, I just want to see all of her. I don't want anything, not even clothes, between us. And fuck—we have so much between us these days.

I go and sit next to her wordlessly. Funny because I honestly didn't come here to meet her. Maybe I was hoping I'd bump into her? I don't know—it's not just her spot, it's mine too. It's where we'd go when we were teenagers if we needed to think.

St Dunstan in the East.

I can't go there without thinking of her, but I suppose what else would I be thinking about anyway?

She looks over at me, waiting. My move, I guess.

It's always my move. I shake my head.

"Do you have any idea what it's like to be in love with someone and have to watch everyone else be in love with them too?"

She gives me a long look with dark edges. "I have an idea."

I sigh. "Then why the fuck aren't we together, Parks?"

She doesn't say anything, she just stares straight ahead as she shifts her legs, kicking them out in front of her, dangling them down. It's not fair. I love her legs. I wonder if she does it on purpose, to distract me. I wouldn't put it past her these days.

If you told me she was a master manipulator or, I don't know—a witch?—I'd probably nearly be relieved. Relieved to have a reason to be stuck on her how I am more than just because I love her in a way I can't undo.

The way we're sitting—shoulder to shoulder—one of my arms sitting on the concrete behind her, her leaning back into me without even knowing she's doing it.

This is what we're like.

This is what we're always like.

I look over at her, breathe her in. Same smell as always. If she ever leaves me for good I'll take baths in Gypsy Water to get to sleep at night.

"Christian said he was going to come and talk to you—" She nods. "He did?" I look at her, waiting for more, but she doesn't say anything. "What'd he say?" I ask. She shrugs. I frown at her. "What do you mean—" I imitate her shrug.

She shrugs again. "I don't want to say."

"You don't want to say?" I blink a few times, and then it flares up in me like a hot flush. "What the fuck, Magnolia—what'd he say?"

And then she gets a look in her eye. I recognise it. It's the same look she'd get in her eyes whenever Mars would give her shit for bringing me home, because no one can give me shit but her.

Those were always my favourite nights because she'd grab my hand, pull me to her room, slam the door and throw me against it, pretending we were hooking up just to get a rise out of Mars, but it always meant she'd touch my body all over, more than she needed to, and she'd let me hold her against me under the guise of a ruse, but the ruse was the guise.

Whenever Mars gave her shit, the look in her eye was always a massive "fuck you and watch me come out swinging," and she's got that look now here, swinging those legs, kicking down my inhibitions more and more by the second.

She sizes me up.

"I'll tell you what he said if you tell me why you did it—"

Fuck me.

I sigh.

"I told you why I did it."

"And I told you, I don't believe you," she shoots back, quick as light. "I don't believe you."

I shrug, trying to look indifferent, because I can't deal with this right now. "That's not my fault."

She shakes her head, shaking off the hurt my indifference there caused her—I can see it swim across her face, pool in those lake eyes that I'd swim in forever if she'd let me, and I don't know why the fuck she won't let me?

"Fine," she says defiantly. "Then tell me who."

I shake my head. "I'm not telling you that—"

"Why?"

I give her a look, wide-eyed and begging. "Because it'll make it worse."

She shakes her head like she knows. "It couldn't be worse than not knowing."

"Yes, it could," I say. "It's the specificity of a face. It's nearly fucking impossible to see past—I see you and Tom in my mind all the time. I used to think of you and me to fall asleep, and now I just see you with him." I shake my head, trying to clear the image from my brain. Her face falters at the way I sound. Her heart's knees buckling at the sight of me. It's quick—like a flash—the sympathy for me before it's back to stubborn and digging in.

"I didn't cheat on you."

Which is technically true—technically—but too fucking on the nose to bring it up today.

"Are you shitting me, Parks?" I look at her with wild eyes. "Why the fuck are we talking about this? Again. We're not talking about how I fucked up, we're talking about your colossal fuck up. With my best friend. Who's in love with you now."

She frowns. I don't know at what.

How angry I am? Being put in her place? That he loves her?

"You had to know—" I look over at her, cautious. Search her face, make it feel impossible to bullshit me on this because I need to know. "Did you know?"

She stares at me for a couple of seconds and then her eyes go extra heavy. She nods. She looks guilty. "What the fuck, Parks." I push up off the wall, start pacing.

She jumps up after me. Because if I move, she moves.

"I mean, I had a feeling—" She sounds a bit panicked. "I didn't ask—"

I give her a look. "Yeah, you didn't need to."

She reaches for me. "He's just my friend."

And maybe for the first time in the history of time, I pull away from her and give her a ragged look. "Yeah, but you're not just his friend, are you?"

"Beej—that's not my fault! I didn't feed into it." I give her a look. "I didn't!" She shakes her head wildly.

"When you can't get on to me and you're in trouble—who do you call?"

"Tom," she says quickly.

"No." I shake my head. "Before Tom. The last two years. Who do you call?"

Magnolia's eyes drop from mine and she looks away.

I point at her. "Henry's been your best friend since you were four—it's fucked up, Parks"—I shake my head—"that you'd call Christian before him." I'm vindicated.

Shake my head more. "You don't treat him the same as Henry and Jo—" Magnolia replies, "Because he's not the same as them. We have a history."

"Yeah, well, whose fault is that?" I spit.

She looks at me, eyes so wide that when she blinks the lids barely touch. "Yours!"

"Mine?" I repeat. Loud enough that people are looking—maybe a phone or two flashes—I don't know. "I made you fuck my best friend?"

Now she's yelling. Proper yelling. "We never slept together."

"Never?" I repeat back louder.

"Never," she repeats.

I glare over at her. "What's all that shit about orgasms then, hm?"

She gives me a look—baffled.

"Beej—you are substantially more sexually active than I am—I feel like you should know the answer."

I shovel my hands through my hair, try my best not to laugh at what she said because I don't want her to get the upper ground. I get to stand up here so infrequently, I'm not getting down just yet.

"And how was it my fault?"

She gives me a look, head tilted, jaw tight, eyes dark.

"Are you shitting me?" I yell. "I made you do it? Because you broke up with me—"

"You had sex with someone else!"

"One time. One time, Parks! And I came to you and I told you straight away. It was a mistake, I fucked up. But it was just one time."

"And how many times now?"

I groan and glare over at her. We're stuck on a loop.

"I mean it," she asks, nose in the air. "How many times now?"

I shake my head. "Don't."

"Tell me." She grabs my arm to wrangle herself into my view.

I jerk out of her hold. "No, Parks—"

And I'm fucking over it. I can't keep having this talk. I can't keep telling her the reason I did it is because I wanted to. It's fucking me up and it's fucking her up, and she wants answers from me that I will never, ever give her.

I take a step away from her. "You know at some point in all this, you're going to have to look your own shit in the eye, Parks. Yeah, I was the first one who fucked up first, but you've fucked up constantly ever since."

She pulls her head back, like I've hit her.

"You dated my best friend—you went home with Julian Haites, apparently," I say. She rolls her eyes. "You got scared because your nanny told you some bullshit about me that you know is bullshit, but then you started dating these fucking random dudes to make yourself feel better and me feel like shit, but all that was you, not me." I shake my head at her. "I didn't make you do shit. You were the one who started dating Tom—"

"You were getting a fucking lap dance from a stranger in the middle of Raffles!" I'm trying to read her face, trying to figure out how far away she is from crying. "Do you know how embarrassing that is?"

I nod, conceding.

"Yeah, I'm a fuck up, Parks. I know I am—I can stand here and tell you all the ways that I've put us in the ground, but it wasn't all me." I give her a look. "I didn't make you run to Christian. I didn't make you run to Tom. I didn't make you run to any of your fucking playthings that you dangle in front of me to make me jealous—"

"Yes you did, of course you did—you with your shag count of girls so high you'd put Mick Jagger to shame—"

"Yeah, Parks—okay. I get it. I fuck around a lot. It's because I'm in love with an idiot who doesn't want to be with me—"

She looks angry, shakes her head. "That's not true, you know that's not true—"

"Okay, fine." I nod, jaw tight, eyes glassy. "Maybe she thinks she wants to be with me, fuck it—maybe she even actually does, but she cannot, for the fucking life of her, reconcile that I did a bad thing once, and I hurt her, and I can't change it—"

She's blinking a lot. Trying her best not to cry.

"More than once," she says, voice quiet.

"Yeah, well." I shrug. "She's hurt me more than once too." Our eyes lock, she's glaring up at me, I'm staring down the barrel of a rifle that's about to snipe us out of love. "And until you can admit that we're fucked up because of you too, we're never going to work."

Her face goes a bit blank and I wonder if she's hearing me—like, actually hearing me.

Then her eyes go dark.

"Then we're never going to work."

FIFTY-FIVE

BJ

I decide to throw a party—full Park Lane blow out. No Parks, no Paili, no Perry. Jo tried to talk me out of it—told him not to come.

It's been a week since Dunstan, haven't heard from Parks once.

Seen pictures of her pop up from around town with Tom. Holding hands, her looking up at him how she used to look up at me.

So, I guess she picked him, then?

Hence the party.

Every hot girl who has DM-ed me the last few months, every girl I've shagged that's still in my phone, every girl Parks felt nervous about in high school, I message them all. Invite every single one of them.

Definitely invite Alexis Blau, who's been tuning me since the 9th grade but has popped up again heavily in the last few months, trying to hook up constantly. Palmed her off 'til now. Parks saw her name pop up once while she had my phone. In response, she put on *The Notebook* and Ubered in McDonalds just for herself. Didn't speak to me 'til the next morning.

Alexis Blau is a sore spot.

Don't know why—I've never touched her.

I'm going to later though.

Christian walks through the door, glances around—looking for Hen, probably. Henry's off talking to some girl in a corner, chewing her ear off about a book she no doubt gives zero shits about, she's just happy to have his attention and his hand on her upper thigh.

And he's just happy to be doing something that's making Taura look how Taura looks right now.

"You came here with Jo—" I tell her.

"I know." She keeps watching Henry with these round, sore eyes.

"You're sleeping with Jo."

She gives me a look. "I know."

"Fuck, I hate girls." I shake my head at her.

Her eyes pinch. "Actually, I believe you're in this mess because the reverse of that is true."

I shake my head. "I'm not in a mess—"

Christian wanders over.

"Speaking of messes," Taura says and grins, "how's our biggest one of the lot?"

Christian tosses her a dirty look. Our horns lock, me and him. And then I pass him a beer. He sits down next to me, doesn't say anything. Stares straight ahead for a good minute or two. Glances at me once. "You okay?"

I shrug once. "Yeah, why wouldn't I be?"

"You and Jo only throw these parties if one of you is fucked in the head."

"Your brother's always fucked in the head."

Christian laughs. I pull out a bag. Taura walks away, looking annoyed. I glance at Christian; he nods but he's watching me closely.

"How many you done tonight?"

I shrug. I'm not being evasive. I actually don't know. A lot.

"Who gives a fuck, man—I love a girl who doesn't want me. You love a girl who doesn't want you. Actually, you love two girls who don't want you—"

He gives me a dry look. "Thanks, man—"

"How fucking wild is it that one of them is the same girl?"

Christian gives me a look. "Are we okay?"

"Yeah, bro." I pat him on the back. "If anyone's going to get being caught up in her—" I blow some air out of my mouth. Shake my head.

I do a line. Pass him the rolled up £20.

He takes it, snorts it, toss it on the table and leans back. "So this is what we're doing tonight."

"And that." I nod my chin at Alexis Blau.

His eyebrows go up. "Alexis Blau?"

I nod, take a big drink. Too big a drink for Christian's liking, I guess, because he takes it from my hand.

"We're not doing that tonight."

I roll my eyes at him. "You overdose one time…"

He gives me a look, picks up my drink and walks away with it.

I stand up, walk past Alexis Blau, nod my head at the stairs.

She excuses herself from the conversation she's in, slips her hand in mine and we're not even halfway down the stairs when my hand is up her dress.

Christian probably did the right thing by me—taking my drink—because the world's starting to look a bit blurry.

Just how I want it to be if it's a world where I don't have Parks. Dulled down enough where the curves of the body I'm touching could be Magnolia's. And I'm fucking kidding myself—because I'd know her body with my eyes closed. This body isn't her. She doesn't grind on me like this. Parks makes me work for it, how she makes me work for everything—this girl's doing it all for me.

And I don't care anymore. I lean back against my headboard. Find a weird comfort in behaving exactly how Magnolia expects me to... Feel justified in it for the first time in years. Stare at the ceiling, breathe out as Alexis Blau climbs down my body.

I guess I'm higher than I realised because it takes me maybe a full five minutes to clock that there's another girl in my bed too—don't know where she came from.

And here I thought Alexis Blau just had magic hands. This one's another from school. Something Talbot.

Parks' year too. She'd fucking hate this. This is the version of me she despises.

I close my eyes. Breathe her out of my mind. Switch into gear. Reach over to my bedside table, rack up a few more lines—tell myself I'm not losing her, I already lost her.

Now it's time to lose myself.

FIFTY-SIX

Magnolia

It's Perry's birthday, and I don't really want to go but Paili says I have to.

She says Perry will be too upset if I miss it, and that if anyone should miss it, it's BJ, but we both know BJ won't miss it, so I guess I'm just seeing him later then.

We haven't spoken since Dunstan in the East.

That felt more final than I meant it to. That we're never going to work? Of course we're going to work, even if I'm a round peg and he's a square hole—I don't care, I'll shave down the edges of myself to keep him.

I'd do anything for him.

I can't remember the last time we didn't speak for this long. This has been more than a fortnight that's felt like a year, just a constant state of fretting. Like he kicked my world off-kilter, an undeniable imbalance in the universe of myself, and imbalances are peculiar because they manifest in ways you don't expect.

My heart's got a limp—it's had a limp for a while now—but it's found a crutch in Tom. Not just a crutch, but a goddamn hospital wing. If he were a surgeon, I'd be in trusty hands. But he's not and I still am anyway.

I wish I had the words to wrap around Tom, a pedestal tall enough, a spotlight bright enough to show you actually how perfect a man he is—

And I don't know what we are anymore, if you're trying to keep track. I've stopped trying to define it, he doesn't ask. We're definitely not friends, but somehow he's also probably my best friend these days. Sleeping together—and there are feelings there. Open wide window, birds on branches, raindrops on roses feelings—but we both know he loves someone else whom he can't have, and I love someone else I probably shouldn't.

We're honest. I tell him everything—what's the point in lying?

Together—that's what we are—I suppose if I were to label it, and I shouldn't because it's too confusing to try. All I know is that he's a safe harbour. If BJ is the storm that's sinking me, Tom is the place where my heart's ship is getting patched up.

Tom took me shopping in Harrods this afternoon and asked, "Am I coming with you tonight?"

I think I'd mentioned it in passing a few days ago.

"Oh." I stick my head out of the change room. I'm trying on the wool, cable-knit mini dress from Weekend by Max Mara, which admittedly is much more casual than my usual style, but Tom and I don't much leave the bed these days, and tulle is quite annoying to wear in bed.

"I didn't really think that you'd want to." I blink up at him.

He leans back against the wall.

"Sounds like foxhole duties—"

I step out of the change room and walk over to him, looking up. "Are we still in the foxhole?"

He frowns a tiny bit while he thinks, pushing some hair behind my ears. "I'm going to let you use my body for as long as you want it." He shrugs. "Foxhole, shield, jungle gym—I don't care."

I frown a little. "You should care maybe, a little—"

"I care—" He scrunches his nose up. He shakes his head. "Care about you more though, and your face does this thing when it's hurt, like you're a deer caught in a bear trap—and I have to help you." He says that like it's an unchangeable fact. "And I can see you trying to untangle yourself from this fucking idiot you've been tangled up with for half your life and one day you'll be free, and when you are, I reckon I'm first in line."

I hook my arm around his neck and kiss him on my tip toes. "You are."

"Does he know I'm coming?" Gus asks on the car ride there.

"No," I say and shake my head. "You're his birthday present."

Gus gives me a look. "You can't afford me, babe."

"I'm very rich." I frown at him. "Tom's richer. Let's go Dutch, Tommy."

Gus laughs, and Tom sniffs at me, amused.

I feel a wave of gratitude that Tom is looking as handsome as he does (light grey, brushed wool and cashmere-blend sweater by Incotex, black slim-fit, stretch denim jeans by Dolce & Gabanna, and the full-grain leather Chelsea boots by Common Projects), mindlessly fiddling with the hem of my skirt.

It's the embellished, pleated, houndstooth wool and mohair-blend mini skirt—super cute. BJ bought it for me that day. The coat I'm wearing too. The faux shearling-trimmed wool coat, both by Gucci.

I've got embellished, ribbed-knit camisole by Versace under it (so much embellishment, literally and meta-phorically) and the Kronobotte 85, leather knee boots by Christian Louboutin—I look like BJ's dream girl and I did it on purpose.

I know he'll know he bought me most of these clothes, and I hope he thinks about Tom taking them off my body later.

We arrive at Dolce Kensington about forty minutes later than we mean to, and I brace myself for an earful from Perry when we walk in but he and Paili beeline over to us, both clapping and grinning and sort of forming a wall.

"Oh my god!" Perry claps my face in his hands. "You're here! I love you!"

I wonder if Tom sees something being about two feet taller than I am, because his eyes snag on something and he sort of moves his body, joining the wall.

"This is your present." I shove into Perry's arms. "Happy birthday!"

And Gus, that old sport, grabs Perry's face and gives him a snog.

Perry's cheeks go red and I toss a Saint Laurent gift bag into his arms.

"Bar!" Paili sort of yells. "Let's drink—"

I look at her strangely. "We don't have table service?"

She swats her hand. "Of course we do, but bars are fun. Shots are more fun at bars—don't you think?"

She looks at Tom for help.

Tom nods. "She is correct."

And they all start sheep-dogging me towards the bar and away from whatever I assume BJ is doing that they don't want me to see. Another lap dance? Taura Sax? I don't know.

We do some shots with a vulgar name and I've barely swallowed it when Perry's clapping his hands saying,

"Again, again!" And Tom's ordering them, and I've had enough. I push past them to see what the fuck is going on.

It's BJ and Alexis Blau. On the couch.

I've never liked Alexis Blau. I overheard her in the school loo once telling people that if I didn't have a famous father, BJ would be with her but that's bullshit because I'm way prettier than her too.

She's always had a thing for him. She messages him all the time.

He's never told me that—he wouldn't because he knows I'd get jealous—but he didn't need to tell me anyway, because I guessed the passcode on his phone. (It's 7989—the years we were born, backwards. It took me two months of trials to crack it.)

I try not to look at it. It's mostly things I don't want to see, mostly me putting knives in my own heart. Anyway, to his credit with Alexis, he really never gave her the time of day. Not even when he didn't know I could see. He's giving her more than the time of day now though. Heavy petting. Making out. His hands pretty high up her skirt. Not all fingers accounted for.

I turn back to my friends, trying to look brave—all of their faces contorted into some sort of grimace.

"I'm fine," I laugh. Not a one of them buys it. I smile more. "Guys, I think I once literally saw him having sex with someone else—some gross girl's tongue in his ear." I shrug.

Paili's hands are on her cheeks, because her hands are always cold and she's trying to calm her flushed cheeks now. "I don't care," I tell them all—I look up at Tom for some back-up, but his face looks strained.

I sigh, roll my eyes, take his hand and pull him back over to the party.

429

"Oy, oy," Christian calls to us, lifting his eyebrows in an unenthusiastic, wordless hello. Henry smiles, standing up to hug me. His eyes look nervous too. Do they think I'm some kind of time bomb? He holds me longer and tighter than he should and something in it makes me nervous.

"You good?" he asks as he pulls back, looking at me. He doesn't wait for an answer as he shakes Tom's hand. "Should we go to the bar?" Henry points to it.

"No." I frown, impatient. "I don't want to go to the bar—what's going on?"

"Nothing." He does this breezy laugh that feels forced.

I watch BJ for a couple of seconds. I can't tell whether he's seen me yet, and I don't know whether it's better or worse if he has. The way they're hooking up is this weird sort of desperate but not in a sexy way.

It sort of feels like the kissing version of when the American football players run off the field and pour the cooler of Gatorade over their heads.

He looks kind of sweaty. Flushed, or something. I get a wave of nausea. I hope they move it to the bathroom soon—this is embarrassing for all of us.

"Why is he so drunk?" I ask Henry, frowning.

It's like 9 p.m.

"Maybe because you're here with Tom fucking England, mate," Jonah says loudly as he glares over at me.

And at that, BJ pulls away from Alexis, looking over at me. His face doesn't show any emotion. He just blinks at me. How drunk is he?

Tom's standing behind me, holds both my arms with his hands, steadying me.

"I just got here," I tell Jonah and gesture at Beej. "That's not my fault."

"Whatever, man-eater." Jonah swats his hand, annoyed.

BJ snorts a drunken laugh.

"What did you say to me?" I blink at my old friend.

Jonah stands. "You heard me."

"Oy," Christian says and stands, frowning.

Jonah puts his hand flat on his little brother's chest. "Are you fucking joking me?"

"Are you?" Christian steps between me and Jo. "If Beej wasn't so fucked up, he wouldn't let anyone speak to her like that."

And with that, BJ pushes Alexis off his lap. It's mindless. Pushes her off him like she's a heavy duvet and it's the first thing in the morning. She's not even completely off of him when he stands; she sort of tumbles off him onto the couch, staring after him in disbelief—and me too, honestly. I've never seen him treat someone like that—like they're not a person, just a thing he's playing with.

He walks over and stands toe to toe with me, staring down.

Something about him is unrecognisable but familiar? There's a far-ness in his eyes I can't immediately place. Less than a school ruler between us as he stares down at me.

Jaw set, brows low, eyes dark. Tom doesn't let go of me, but BJ doesn't even acknowledge him. He sees no one but me.

He scrunches his nose. Sniffs big.

I stare at him for a few long seconds, my eyes flicking between his. And then I recognise it.

My face goes still.

"Are you high?" I ask quietly.

He stares at me for a split second, then sniffs a laugh. "No."

I lean into him closer, but it's dark—I can't see. "Are you?" I ask louder.

"No," he answers quicker.

My heart's beating fast. "BJ—"

"I'm not," he says too loudly and does this strange shrug with his whole body. "Don't be fucking weird, Parks."

He wipes his nose with the back of his hand unconsciously.

I look at the people around him—the boys are all standing now, hovering and something about that strikes me as weird—and if I was a body language expert I would have seen it all: Christian's eyes avoiding mine, Jonah's clenched fists, Henry with his hand pressed into his mouth. But I'm not a body language expert. I see none of that, but I feel it anyway—in my bones, that something's amiss.

I wait a few seconds, staring back at the love of my life who's barely blinking but when he does, those blinks drag slowly over his bleary eyes.

And what happens next happens so quickly, I don't even do it with a conscious thought—I'm standing toe to toe with him one second and the next, I'm shoving him backwards into the light, grabbing a fistful of hair and jerking his head to the ceiling.

"Are you fucking high?" I demand, angling his eyes so I can see his pupils.

"Get the fuck off me!" He pulls my hands off him gruffly, tossing my arm away from him because he is absolutely high as a fucking kite. And me—I'm in some sort of aggrieved shock, and suddenly I'm lobbing my hands at him, smacking him and hitting him and he—high—shoves me away from him. I fall backwards and Jonah catches me, staring over at his best friend him wide-eyed, Beej stares at me terrified and I stare at him in disbelief—and then Tom comes in swinging.

It felt like the whole club had stopped to watch us by now.

I think there was music playing, but I swear to god you could hear a pin drop anyway.

It's a solid crack and BJ does nothing to stop it—you could hear the bone-crunch-bone sound of hand meeting jaw.

Tom winds up to hit him again and then a bouncer grabs his wrist, another grabs BJ and they're pushing them towards the door—and Jonah's still holding on to me, but I shrug him off—the fucking traitor.

"Parks!" Jonah calls after me.

"Stay away from me," I yell, smacking him away as I rush outside after them.

FIFTY-SEVEN

BJ

I don't even know what to do—I'm choked up. I could cry, I could throw up, I could kill myself—I'm glad he hit me. Needed it. Deserved it and he should have.

It's what I would have done if I weren't so fucked up but as it stands, I am. Fucked up, ready to fuck it all up, throw it all to the wind. Ready to lose her finally to someone who's actually worth her time.

We're on the street now—bad place for me and Parks to be because there's always cameras somewhere, but I don't give a shit anymore.

I just want him to hit me again. Take the sting off what I just did for another second. And then out she tumbles after us, Jo hot on her heels—he's trying to grab her away, I think.

I actually think he's probably trying to keep her away from me.

Because I pushed her. Holy fuck—I pushed her.

Her, who I love more than everything, who I've spent my whole life wanting, who I've hurt more than anyone.

The boys run out. Gus appears behind Tom. Magnolia's still fighting with Jo, who's practically wrestling her to keep her from me, and then Henry shoves Jo away from her.

There's a look between them, Jonah and Henry, that fucked up as I am—I know has nothing to do with Magnolia. Easier to pretend that it does though.

"Get the fuck off her," Henry snatches Parks from our best friend.

The wheels are falling off. Or I'm tearing them off? I can't tell.

She sort of lets herself fall into my brother's arms—glad she does, she's safe in them—and I'm watching Henry hold her how I wish I was, how I wonder if I'll get to ever again, and then I'm smacked in the face again.

The crowd that's gathered around us gasps.

I lick my lip, taste blood. Look back up at England. He shakes his head. I want him to fuck me up and curse me out but there's nothing left he could say to me now that I don't already think about myself.

"I hate you," Magnolia tells me from the safety of my brother's arms.

"You know what, Parks—fucking same," I spit. "I hate you back."

She breaks out of Henry's grip and rushes over to me, eyes all glass. "What's the matter with you? What are you doing?"

I place my hand on her chest and put some distance between us. "Stay away from me," I tell her. It sounds like it's because that's what I want but it's really because now I'm afraid of myself.

Her chin is shaking when she asks in a tiny voice, "Why are you using again?"

"Because you're killing me, Parks," I yell. "You're fucking killing me."

I wipe my eyes. Don't know when they got wet.

She shakes her head, frowning. "Are you really trying to blame me for this?" She takes a broken breath, looking at me like I'm an insect. "What the fuck are you doing?"

"Losing you," I tell her.

She reaches for me. "No, you're not—"

I push her hands away from me. "Stop it—"

She blinks, confused. "—Well, maybe now you are."

"Good," I yell with a definitiveness I hate.

She blinks. "Good?"

If I had special goggles to see invisible things—which I don't need with her, I can see her invisible things anyway—that was what I'd call a fatal blow.

I don't know why it was, what about it was that delivered such a punch in the middle of her, but I see all these cracks appearing, rippling out from the centre of her.

I wipe my face again. Hands come back wet. "I—fuck! What do you want from me, Parks?"

She looks confused. "Nothing!"

"You want nothing from me?" I pull my head back. "Then why the fuck am I here? What have I been doing these last three years?"

"That's not what I mean." She shakes her head. "I don't care, Beej. I don't care that you don't do anything with your life. I don't care that you get too drunk on the weekends. I can even get past that you're a raging slut—"

"I'm a slut?" I cut in, shaking my head and laughing meanly. "You're a fucking joke, Parks—"

I stare at her, giving that sentence enough distance to reach her before I hit her with the next one.

"You love me. Everyone knows you love me." I gesture around us. "I know you love me. Your boyfriend knows you love me. Even you know you love me. Except you're fucking him," I yell, and I sound savage. "So who's the real slut?"

Tom shakes his head, pulling her behind him. "That's enough," he tells me.

Good lad, a part of me thinks. Grateful for him for being to her what I can't be.

She peeks past him. "You promised me—"

She's crying now. Really crying. She hasn't cried like this since that night I came to her smelling like someone else.

"Yeah, well"—I shrug like I'm indifferent about it—"I promised you a lot of things."

She stares at me, nodding barely. "Yes, you have." Her eyes blink, begging for me to fix this before she has to say what she should have said to me all along.

I say nothing, do nothing. Watch her slip away. Watch me push her away.

She nods with a finality that scares the shit out of me. "I'm done waiting for you to be who I thought you were."

"You're done?" I repeat, taking a sharp breath.

"Yes," she barely says.

I shake my head at her. "Don't say shit you don't mean—"

"Listen to me, okay?" She shakes hers back at me. "I'm done with you. We're done."

I press my mouth together, clap my hand over it and wipe away some snot I didn't realise was there.

I nod.

"Finally," I sniff.

And she starts crying, shoulders bobbing like a buoy in rough seas, and she's never cried like that in front of anyone but me before and she's crying here on Harrington Road for all the world to see, and even though I'm about as fucked up as I've been in years, high as a fucking satellite—I start to wonder how many people in your lifetime do you get to love how I love her? Can't be that many. How many loves do you get? Tell me it's two.

Fuck.

Please, tell me it's two.

Jo pulls me backwards and away from her and I think the ties that bind us, I think I hear them snap. It's not two.

Jo drags me away.

"Come on man, that's enough—" and I fight him because it isn't.

It won't ever be. There's no such thing as enough when it comes to her. No enough and I'll never be done.

FIFTY-EIGHT

Magnolia

I don't know how I got home after that. I don't remember. I remember BJ saying "finally" and I remember Tom putting his arm around me and pulling me away, and I remember the smell of him—patchouli, bergamot, lavender, oak moss—I think I was breathing him in, crying into his chest.

I had one of those sleeps where your head hits your pillow and then you're gone. It was the crying, I think. I haven't cried how I cried tonight in years. And the sleep acted for me almost like a momentary eraser.

Because then I woke up and it was morning.

Past morning, actually.

Tom's lying next to me, watching me. His face looks quite sad, quite serious.

"Hey." He gives a smile that's really a frown.

"Hi."

He brushes some hair from my face. "How are you feeling?"

The question feels foreign, and for a second I wonder what happened—what did I miss—why would I be feeling bad? I force my mind back—past the big sleep, past the car ride home, through the crying—why was I crying so much? This happens in a matter of seconds. Why was I crying? BJ.

The answer's always BJ.

What does that say about us?

There is no us.

I grab Tom's hand, turning it over in mine to inspect it. He got in two solid punches—a couple of grazed knuckles and it's a bit swollen.

I sigh. "Sorry—"

He shakes his head.

"I'll get you some ice—"

"No, I'm fine—"

I ignore him and kiss him quickly before scurrying downstairs. I'm in a T-shirt of Tom's. It smells like him. I lift the neck of the shirt to my nose and I breathe him in, and I feel a tiny bit calmer.

I walk into the kitchen downstairs and my whole, entire family looks up at me. They're all assembled there—all of them—standing around the marble counter.

Even my mother, who I'll remind you no longer lives here.

"Are you okay?" My sister rushes towards me.

"What?" I frown.

"The papers, the socials, the internet—it's everywhere—"

I feel myself frown a bit. Marsali approaches me gingerly. "They're saying you had a physical altercation…"

I say nothing, instead moving past my sister to get the ice.

"Well?" Bridget blinks. "Is it true?"

I say nothing again, instead finding a tea towel and dumping a bunch of ice into it.

"Did he hurt you?" my father asked.

Not in any way you can see with your eyes. "I'm fine," I tell him.

"What ice for then?" Bushka asks with pinched eyes.

I consider the question. "BJ is less fine."

Marsali's eyes widen. "BJ's upstairs?"

I shake my head. "Tom's upstairs—"

"You just said BJ's upstairs—"

"No, I said 'BJ is less fine.' Because he was hit by Tom, who's upstairs, with a bruised hand—so if you'll excuse me—" I glance at my mum in Cult Gaia's brown, Serita cut-out, cotton-blend maxi dress. "Interesting choice for an almost-winter's morning…"

She looks down at herself. "You don't like it?"

I look her up and down again. "No, actually I love it."

"Thank you, but wait—" My mother's shoulders slump as she frowns at me. "So you're fine?

"Yes."

"The papers said you're over—"

I nod. "We are."

My mother looks confused. "But you're fine…"

I nod curtly.

"Well, what did I schlep all the way over here for in the early hours of the morning for then?"

Bridge checks her watch. "It's noon."

"And don't you just live across the park?" I wonder out loud.

"Some parents might consider her fineness a positive—" Marsali whispers.

My mother rolls her eyes at all of us.

"I'm glad you're fine, darling—honestly I am. You and BJ will work it out, you always do."

I give them a tight smile. "Not this time."

I turn on my heels and jog back up the stairs to Tom. Bridge scurries after me.

"Not this time?" She blinks. "What do you mean not this time?"

"I mean we're over now." I keep on up the stairs.

"Bullshit."

I ignore her and keep walking. "I'm serious."

"No, you aren't," she calls after me.

I pause and look back at her. She loves him, always has. He's been around in some capacity all her life. She grew up with him too. Vacation with the Ballentines, sleepover at Allie's. She took him cheating on me as hard as I did—harder, in some ways. Took her longer to welcome him back. I think it would frighten her, for BJ and I to be really over—he's so important to her. And she'd choose me, I know she would. But she wouldn't want to have to.

"He's using again," I tell her.

She gasps quietly. She stares at the carpet for a few seconds. "Are you sure?"

I nod. "He pushed me."

Her head drops as she walks up the stairs towards me and unsolicited, throws her arms around me, squeezing me tightly. "I'm so sorry—"

"Stop it," I tell her, not moving.

"You need this," she tells me.

"I don't—"

"I'm upping your dopamine and serotonin levels."

"Please stop."

She grunts and lets me go, shaking her head. "Why are you acting like you're fine?"

I meet her eyes, look at them for a couple of seconds. "I'm not fine."

I go back to my room, climb onto my bed and crawl towards Tom. He pulls me onto his lap and wraps his arms around me. I hold the ice against his hand and lean back into him. He rests his chin on my shoulder.

"Parks—" I look back at him. "We could be real," he says. "This could be real."

I think about this. "What are we now?"

He sniffs a laugh and presses his mouth against the corner of mine.

"—Fucked if I know."

"Not real though?" I clarify.

He kisses my shoulder absentmindedly. "I don't know," he says, his mouth muffled by my shoulder. "What am I to you?"

I lean back into him, pursing my mouth at the question. "The oxygen mask"—I glance back at him—"that falls down from the ceiling of the planes."

He hugs me tighter.

"That's good enough for me."

10:12

Henry

Oy

Hey

I love you

I love you too

Always will.

I know.

Pain in the arse.

I'm sorry, by the way. That all that happened.

Yeah, me too.

You're still my best friend forever though, Hennypen.

More than Paili?

More than anyone.

Are you okay?

I don't know.

What can I do?

Don't let him overdose.

Promise.

FIFTY-NINE

BJ

What happens in Amsterdam stays in Amsterdam. That's always been the motto. I don't really give a fuck anymore if that sticks. All cats are out of the bag, I don't have shit to lose.

Amsterdam is where me and the boys always seem to go when shit goes sideways. And I cannot express this enough: all the shit is sideways.

Me and Christian have sworn off loving girls ever again. Henry and Jonah may or may not be in love with the same girl.

It's a mess.

And we can't talk about it. Can't talk to Christian about losing Parks. Henry is shitty at me because he's default on her team. And Jonah's Jonah, he's not telling me shit right now—he's just watching, making sure I don't unravel completely.

Talking is obsolete for us all at the minute. There's a lag between what happens and how long it takes for us to process.

I can never really tell how I feel about something 'til I get a bit fucked up over it.

How many drinks, how many lines, how many girls does it take for me not to feel it in my chest anymore?

So off to the Netherlands we go for a lads trip.

Usually when we do these trips I come back wracked with regret, worried a picture will leak, someone will talk, that it'll get back to Parks and she'll see me for what I am—which is, regrettably—substantially less of a man than she thought I was, but not this trip.

I'm a fuck up and she knows it. I'm the fuck up she's done with, so I hope to god that whatever it is I do tonight it's enough to be plastered all over the internet and she sees in the morning when she wakes up and she feels like shit.

Because I feel like shit.

I hook up with the hotel concierge within an hour of being here.

Been drinking since we got on the plane. I'm shit-faced by the early afternoon and we end up in one of those underground 24/7 clubs this city is famous for. Stay there 'til sunup the next morning—fuelled by cocaine alone because all the boys are mother hens now apparently and keep sniping the drinks out of my hands.

Had sex that night too. Or at least I think it was night? Hard to tell. You lose time there. Which is the point, I guess. Trying to bleed time 'til she takes me back.

Which, by the way, Henry says she won't. Says that a few times

I'd explain more if I could, but I can't. Can't remember the first four days.

Telling.

How fucked am I over this?

11/10.

Christian's as bad as I am. Worse maybe. I've lost Magnolia before… The Daisy shit's hitting him pretty hard.

Loved her more than he knew.

On the plane ride back to England, Christian looks up from his phone. "Round two in a fortnight?"

Henry squints over tiredly. "When's a fortnight?"

Christian shrugs. "First week of December?"

I look up, purse my mouth.

Jonah nods. "Yeah, I'm in."

Henry toddles his head side to side. "I've got some uni shit, but I'll try to make it work—where are you thinking? Prague?"

"Yeah." He shrugs. "Or Funchal?"

"Can't," I tell them, looking at my phone because I don't feel like meeting eyes.

"Why?" Christian asks.

I shrug. "Got something on."

"What?" Henry asks.

I look up at him. "Something."

"Yeah, but what?" he asks again. I give him a long look and then stare out the window. "Do you know?" Henry asks Jo.

Jonah shakes his head, shrugs.

"For work?" Henry presses, the nosey shite.

"Yep," I lie. "For work."

SIXTY

Magnolia

Tom take us to the Grand Resort in Bag Ragaz—it's just an hour outside of Zurich and we haven't run a piece on them in a while at *Tatler* so I don't even need to pretend to have the flu so I can go away.

There's a peacefulness here and it makes me feel further away from London than I am.

Us being, by the way, Tom and I and Paili and Perry. Insisted upon it, actually. He said he didn't know them that well and that he feels he should know them better.

On the flight over Perry sat with him up in the cockpit and Paili and I drank wine at the back of the plane.

"He must be softening the blow at least a little bit," she told me, and I nodded. "Are you sleeping together?"

I nodded again.

She smiled a little. "Look at you! Having sex—god, you might actually be moving on..."

I glanced over at her, and even in retrospect I can't tell whether what she said made me feel relief or sadness. Maybe both.

"What's he like?"

"Compared to BJ?" I clarified. She shifted uncomfortably and shrugged, but they're the only people I've been with, so I assume that's what she meant. "Well, I've not had sex with BJ for years—not since—well, you know—" Her eyes went sad and her mouth pulled, sorry for me. "—but from memory, it's quite different. I learnt about sex by having it with BJ. We always talked a lot and laughed a lot and—" I trailed. "He knows my body better than anyone—"

It grew up in his arms, after all.

She gave me another sad smile. "And Tom?"

"And Tom?" I smiled. "It kind of always feels like a day-dream."

My cheeks flushed a little. "I don't know—whenever we do it there's at least one occasion every time where I open my eyes and I think, 'Gee! Look at us! Doing this! How'd this happen?'"

She laughed. "Does he live up to the reputation we gave him after seeing him in that boat?"

I blushed more. "He does."

The hotel is beautiful, by the way. Of course it is. Everything about Tom is beautiful. From his choices to his eyes to his hair to his voice to his shoulders to his smile to his hands.

I don't know why he brought me here, if it's for any other reason than to get me away and give me space, but in the space he gives me all I wonder about is what my life would be like if I can do what I'm trying to do.

How would my life be if I actually cut BJ out? Because the life I think I could have with Tom would be good a one... and it's not a money thing—money I have. It's the calmness of him, the way he moves in a room, the way he holds my knee when I'm sitting next to him, his watchful eyes, how I can just barely fold my whole hand around only two of his fingers. The thoughtfulness of him.

And he isn't mine completely, I know that. I know he loves someone else but so do I, and maybe that's okay because maybe you do get more than one love in a life-time. Maybe BJ is the great love of my life not because he's great but because he's been defining, and maybe Tom will be the redeeming love of my life, and maybe that's better?

It's fun being away with Perry, Pails and Tom. It's a very drama-free combination.

Paili and Tom get along swimmingly. Perry tends to get a bit jealous when Paili likes anyone more than him, but the England charm once again overtakes.

I love being away with Perry because he's always down to try weird things with me.

Tom guffawed at my suggestion of a singing bowl massage but Perry was automatically enthused and required no bribery whatsoever.

"You heard from any of them?" Perry asks me, while we're waiting in the sauna. I shake my head. "You haven't even spoken to Henry?"

I shrug. "I always speak to Henry—but never about his brother."

Perry grimaces. "They went pretty hard in Amsterdam."

"I'm sure they did." I keep my face very straight. He watches me for a few seconds. "What happened before that you haven't told us?"

I look over at him.

"You didn't care that that girl's tongue was in his ear, you cared that he was doing drugs—what happened?"

I stare at him for a few seconds. I consider lying, consider throwing him off the scent of the truth he's picked up, but I decide against it. "He overdosed." I don't want to cover for him anymore. I don't know much about him anymore at all, I suppose.

Perry blinks a few times. "When?"

I purse my lips, pretending the date isn't etched in my mind, pretending I don't see his clammy forehead and bleary eyes and raw nose and love bites all over his body at least once a week when I have bad dreams about it still. "Two years ago. A bit more."

"Fuck."

"Yeah."

He thinks to himself. "The kiss," he says. "At the cinema in Leicester Square—Paili and I always wondered about that." I glance over at him, and my eyes soften at the memory—the feeling in my chest and an indomitable need to kiss him at all costs.

"And like, why the fuck were we at the cinema anyway? We go to premieres, not afternoon matinees." Perry scrunches his face up. I laugh. "Are you really done with him?" he asks, after a few seconds.

Probably not, but I mean what I say genuinely: "I hope so."

SIXTY-ONE

BJ

I come here expecting I'll see her. It's one of her mum's things, The NSPCC Gala. Raising money for the children. Don't know what children and I'm a prick for it, but I didn't come here for the children, I came here for the girl.

I'm so sure she'll be here that by the time I arrive at One Marylebone I'm already three lines deep, all steeled to watch her walk in, hand in hand with fucking England, in a dress that makes me want to top myself and feel her up at the same time.

I watch the door feverishly.

"Sweetheart," my mum pats my arm, "give her a minute, she'll be here."

She fixes my hair and I unfix it with a bleak look.

"Mum—"

"What? It's messy—"

"I styled it." I frown.

"Yes," she nods. "Messily, darling. It looks like you just rolled out of bed."

I lift my eyebrows at her. "That's the idea."

"Stupid idea," she mutters under her breath, then glances over at me. "Is Magnolia coming here with that Tom England?"

"Probably," I say and nod. "They're dating."

"He's probably never cheated on her," Mum says, rueful.

"No, probably not," I give her an exasperated look and throw back my drink in one go.

"Ooh, eggrolls!" she sings and scurries after the waiter.

I sigh, a bit relieved she's gone and then I check the door again and then Magnolia's dad walks in with Marsaili on his arm.

Everyone sort of stares at them for a few seconds, the volume of the room dropping right off—and then it's as if everyone there realised there was silence at the same moment, and the room sings back to life.

My heart's in my throat waiting for her. I don't care that she'll be with England, I'll just be happy to see her. Her eyes that'll glare over at me angrily—her pouty mouth. Maybe I'll start a fight with her, so she'll say something to me?

I miss her voice.

How she sucks in her bottom lip when I do something she doesn't like; I wonder who's here that I can kiss in front of her to make her angry?

And then a Parks walks in.

Bridget, not Magnolia. Our eyes catch and I feel my face falter. She gives me a sad smile and walks towards me gingerly. Looks a bit like Cinderella, actually.

"Two social events in one calendar year?" I gawk, kissing her cheek. "Pick this one out yourself?"

She flicks me a look. "She thinks I'm her life-sized doll."

I nod a couple of times. "She avoiding me?"

Her mouth pulls tight. "She's in Switzerland."

"Avoiding me."

"Can you blame her?" she asks, brows up.

I pull out my phone, check the date. December 1st. "When's she home?"

"Um," she says, plucking a champagne off the tray of a passing waiter, "tomorrow, I think."

I don't mean to, but I sigh, a bit relieved.

Bridget watches me for a few seconds. "Who are you here with?"

"Came with Mum." I give her a cheesy grin.

She nods, coolly. "Does your mum know you're high?"

I squint over at her, a bit annoyed. "She doesn't."

Bridge raises her eyebrows for a few seconds, then shakes her head. "Are you trying to drive her away?"

"What?"

"This." She gestures to nothing. "It seems like self-sabotaging behaviour."

I grind my jaw, not in the mood for an unsolicited Bridget Parks diagnosis. "It's not," I tell her.

She ignores me. "It's just—you did the one thing that you knew she'd never forgive you for."

I shake my head, annoyed. "Why is there something that even exists that she won't forgive me over? If she loves me." I shrug and I mean it. "Shouldn't it be enough? Love conquers all and that shit?"

She sits down at a table, not ours—chin in her hand.

I sit next to her. Happy to be with her. Makes Parks feel less far away.

"She's watched you now with what"—she shrugs aimlessly—"how many girls?" Answers it for herself. "Too many, actually. It's manky—get tested—"

"I do." I smile at her smugly. "Regularly."

"Wouldn't brag about that myself, but okay—"

I roll my eyes.

"She knows you cheated on her. She knows what you've been like since you broke up—you hurt each other, it's your thing, I get it. It's what you do to feel close to each other, but still, it's fucked up and it's dumb and you're stupid for doing it but it's not uncommon for two co-dependent idiots—" I frown, even though an equally appropriate response would be to laugh. "The only thing she'd find categorically unforgivable is you dying."

I roll my eyes. "I'm not d—"

"Don't interrupt me," she interrupts me. "You weren't there. You didn't see her after."

"She hit me." I give her sister an incredulous look. "In front of my parents and my doctor—in a hospital bed."

"Good." Bridget nods, merrily. "She should have. You overdosed. You nearly died. You did it to yourself—"

I sigh. "Not on purpose—"

I promise, not on purpose. I'd not do that to her.

Bridget looks at me thoughtfully. "It was worse than when you cheated on her—"

And I don't buy it for a second. Not for a second. After we broke up I read the articles the *Daily Mail* and *The Sun* ran about her. Shit like, "Close sources say sorry-looking Parks is on her way to rehab after worried parents obsess over weight-loss," and other ones about her having diabetes, one about her picking up a parasite, but really she was just sad.

So Bridge's lying.

It couldn't be worse than that.

"She wouldn't shower. She sat in a ball in her bed for nearly a week. She didn't eat. She didn't drink—"

"She eats like a bird anyway," I say and shrug, like none of what she's saying is killing me.

"She blacked out," Bridget nods. "We had to take her to the hospital for dehydration."

My heart sinks. Parks never told me that.

Fuck.

Bridget shakes her head at me. "You can't make someone love you how she loves you and then be as reckless as you are. It's not fair—"

I scowl at her. "And she can't make me love her how I love her and then keep me at arm's length because I fucked up once three years ago—"

Bridget scoffs. "You've fucked up more than once—let's get that straight first. So has she," she adds when I open my mouth to complain. "I'm not saying she's blameless—she's not. She's more gormless than you are some days."

I smile at her, a bit validated.

"But the root of what she's doing here is self-preservation," Bridget keeps going. "She thinks if you die, she'll die." She gives a small shrug, happy with her conclusions.

"Bridget." I give her an uneven smile because she's being stupid.

"And obviously that's ridiculous," she says loudly over me. Bit big for her boots for a twenty-one-year-old, if I'm being honest. "And untrue. But can you imagine—if you did die, what that'd be like for her? Because she has. That's all she's imagined since it happened." Takes a sip of her drink. "Plays it on a loop in her mind."

"She doesn't." I frown.

"She does. She told me." She drums her fingers on the table. "And then here you are—doing the thing that caused it." I open my mouth to say something. "Are you trying to hurt her?"

"No," I say and glare.

"Are you trying to see how robust your love is?"

"No."

But it's more robust than you know, Little Parks.

She gives me a long, curious look.

"Then what the fuck are you doing?"

SIXTY-TWO

Magnolia

I make it home for London just in time for the 3rd. Not that it matters. It doesn't matter anymore—well, it does, but I'm with Tom now, I think. In a proper way.

Or at least I'm going to be.

That's what I decided as I drove away from him earlier.

"Where are you going anyway?" he asked.

"Devon," I shrug. "For work."

He looks confused. "Why Devon?"

I think on my feet. "Research for a 'in our own back-yard' kind of piece."

"Oh." He nods, then brushes his mouth over mine. "I'd come with you if I didn't have to fly out—"

I shake my head. "Don't be silly. It's just Devon."

I hug him tight.

He's who I should be with. I'm sure of it. That's what I think the whole way there, and it doesn't matter now anyway because when I told BJ that we were done, he said finally, like he'd been waiting for me to do it. How long had he been waiting for me to cut him loose?

I probably should have done it all those years ago, but I'll worry forever that I'll never love another person the way I love him.

Fated: that's what I thought we were. That no matter what happened—how far we went, how much we hurt each other, that we'd always sort of find our way back to each other.

Now that I'm twenty-three and we're here and all we've done since losing each other is lose each other in different ways over and over, being together again sort feels like a childish daydream. A bedtime story I clung to that eased the growing pains of having to leave him behind.

Leaving him behind was never going to happen passively, I could have told you that from the start. Leaving him would always involve pain, an act of violence, like ripping my heart from my own chest, leaving it on a bench somewhere, hoping for the best until I could make it to a hospital and be patched up, but I don't think you can live too long with your heart outside of your chest.

I pull up to our family home up here in Dartmouth.

It's a big old manor house on twenty-nine hectares of land. Indoor pool, outdoor pool, a lake, path to the beach, some horses and sheep.

I used to love it up here. Not so much anymore.

I look around for the groundskeeper. Mr. Gibbs. He's worked for my family for years—my whole life, actually. He's a good man. Quiet.

A widower, I believe.

I often wonder if he's lonely up here.

He and his two Saint Bernards that live with him on the property.

I pull together the Embellished, suede-trimmed, ribbed, camel hair cardigan that I'm wearing, hug myself because no one else is and I walk around back to the garden and follow the path that isn't there down to the lake where the tree lives.

I always loved this willow tree, even before. There's something poetic about it, even before there were poems to write. It weeps into the water, leaves swinging low like a chariot, bending like it's broken, but none of that makes the tree less beautiful.

And now… I still love this willow tree—even before I spot BJ Ballentine standing underneath it.

I stare at him for a few seconds.

Black, cashmere hoodie from the Fear of God x Ermenegildo Zegna collaboration, Paccbet tartan trousers, trashed black Vans.

His hair is messy, his eyes are heavy. His mouth hangs open a bit as he stares over at me.

I blink that I miss him and the turned down edges of his mouth tell me he misses me too and I have a feeling running right through like being tucked tightly into your bed at night, like a safe certainty that I will major in the minor details of him forever. I will never unlearn the shape of his mouth.

"You're here," I say softly.

"Course I'm here." He looks a bit annoyed. "I promised."

"You've broken promises before."

He looks over at me. "Not this one."

I walk over and stand next to him, further away than I want to be.

There's a noticeable distance between us—when is there not these days? Minutes go by without us saying anything with our mouths.

At the altar of the tree, I make a thousand soundless prayers and offerings, beg whoever's listening to align our stars and let him be who I thought he was. If he can't be that, I pray, may I be free of him and not have it kill me. But he is worth dying over and that's the part that gets me, I guess.

He's watching me with the eyes of someone who's known me for too long, reading things on my face he doesn't have permission to.

"You okay?" He looks down at me.

I nod, even though it's a bit of a lie. "Are you?"

He shrugs. "This day always kind of fucks me up."

I nod again. "Yeah."

He stares at the tree, smiling a little. "I think about that night all the time."

My cheeks go pink. "Do you?"

He presses his index finger into his nose, amused. "Yep. Don't you?"

I try not to is the honest-to-god answer.

"Who was it that walked in on us?" I squint up at him.

"Thatcher," BJ laughs. "Hendry."

He shoves his hands through his hair.

"Yes." I grin up at him. "You were very cross."

"Well," he says, wiping away his smile with his hand, "you were practically naked."

I frown as my cheeks flame. "So were you."

"Yeah but I don't give a shit if someone sees my arse—"

Our eyes lock. I swallow, then shake my head trying to keep my composure.

"You just never could make the lock on that door work."

"It's a fucking dud lock, Parks." He laughs once and a million memories are swimming on the surface of his face. "I'll never not be happy that door didn't lock though—"

If there was a fire in my mind and I could only save three things, one of them would be that night—the feather down quilt we muddied up at the foot of the tree and seventeen-year-old BJ's impatient eyes and wandering hands.

"Do you remember afterwards how a family of ducks walked out from the pond shrubbery?" I ask and he starts laughing.

"You were so upset. Like the ducks knew what we were doing."

"They did!" I shake my head. "I bet those ducklings have been in therapy for years after what they watched you do to me."

He gives me a playful look. "I don't recall you having a problem with it at the time…"

I stare over at him, lifting my chin. "I don't have a problem with it now."

His mouth twitches and his eyes fall from mine, he drops his head into his hands, shaking it.

"Parks, how the fuck am I ever going to get over you with all this shit between us?"

I purse my mouth. "Trauma bonds, you mean?" And he sniffs a laugh, annoyed at my sister all the way from here.

"I'm quite glad for them, actually," I tell him.

He looks down at me tenderly. "I've had the best life being fucked up by you."

We look at each other with eyes that are saying more than our mouths ever could.

The air between us begins to thicken—like how a tropical island feels before a storm breaks. Heavy and charged. Tangible.

And maybe this tree is a wormhole through space and time or maybe the coat finally falls off, or maybe I just love him in an undoable way.

His eyes flicker over my face, landing on my mouth, and then it's happening before I know it's happening. Like waves crashing into a cliff face, that's how we kiss.

I don't know whether I'm the water or he's the rock, but his hands are everywhere, all over me, up my white, cotton midi dress from Bottega Veneta and I'm moving backwards—I pull off his shirt, run my hand over my old stomping grounds—and then I'm pressed up against the tree—his mouth is on my neck—his breath has jagged edges that snag on my skin—and I'm up on his waist—our eyes lock. They're always greener than you'd think they are—almost the colour of the leaves of the tree we're about to do this under once again.

He stares at me, blinking, his face all serious.

"I love you," he tells me, his voice low and throaty.

I swallow, nervous. "I love you too," I whisper. And then he pushes into me. A tiny gasp gets caught in my throat and I rest my forehead on his. I hold his face in my hands, kissing his stupid mouth that I love, I push my hands though his hair 'til they're tangled in it.

And the world falls to black. It's just me and him in all the universe. The stars have exploded, the sun's burnt out. And it's rushy, and I love him and it's urgent. I love him, and it's like someone's put a fire under us or maybe in our bones and we need to put it out, but maybe we don't want to—and I love him.

I'll burn the coat, I don't care.

His mouth on my skin is like snow falling onto water. And it's unforgivable of me, really—that I dragged other hearts into this. But I did, and I'm sorry and my mind is swimming as he holds me against him and maybe I'm tired or maybe it's just that I'm here in his arms again as my eyes fill with tears and the whole world trembles in time with our bodies, all the flowers in this world and any others that might exist bloom all at once and the leaves of that tree we love rustles a whisper that I'm home.

SIXTY-THREE

BJ

We stay up here for the night—neither of us have anything.

No clothes, no toiletries. Nothing. Just each other, which is probably how it's meant to be.

That was the plan before it all went to shit. That quiet life we planned: breezy, open windows in our little house next to the ocean in a town on the other side of the country and we don't miss London at all because London, not us, is the problem.

It's my goal now, to get us there. It's what I'll spend my life doing here on out. Untangle her and me from our fucked-up lives in London and whisk us away to a place where we're better versions of ourselves and we'll be the best versions of us because we are when we're together.

We don't leave the bedroom—that room with the lock on the door I can't use for shit—we don't leave it. Talk for hours, kiss for hours, we laugh. She cries a bit; I cry a bit. I feel her up a bit—rest my chin in the dip of her bellybutton and stare up at the only girl I've ever loved—try not to cry again because I'm holding her how I've thought about holding her since the last time I did.

It's the best day of my life.

We order in a pizza, eat it in the bed. Shower together. Do stuff in the shower together. Back to the bed.

She falls asleep on my chest, and I breathe, relieved for the first time since I lost her.

She wakes up the next morning and for the first time probably ever, I'm awake before her—never happens.

She always wakes up first, but I guess I really wore her out yesterday, because she sleeps past lunch, so I don't move a muscle until her eyes flutter awake.

She looks at me for a few seconds, blinks, glances around the room, and then back at me.

"Not a dream." She smiles.

I kiss her. "Not a dream."

She wriggles in towards me, goes forehead to forehead.

"Parks?" I look at her.

"Mm?"

"This is it—isn't it?" And I fucking hate myself a little because I sound more nervous saying that than I want to.

"Like, we're in. No more fucking around. Yeah?"

She nods.

"I'll be done with all the girls and all the other shit—and you—no more Tom."

"No more Tom," she repeats, nodding.

She could nearly sound sad about it. Won't think into it too much because I know they got close. "And you'll let go of what I did?" I ask, searching for her face. She nods again. "For good?" She nods. "Can't bring it up in fights for years to come." She rolls her eyes. "Even if you never get the answers you want from me?" I gauge her eyes. "Cause those answers don't exist."

She considers this.

"Okay." She nods once.

I nod back. "Okay."

SIXTY-FOUR

Magnolia

We leave Dartmouth the next day, stay on the phone talking to each other, laughing as we drive beside one another—we pull off on the M3 just before we hit Lightwater.

We kiss again, have sex again in back of his car—because we've got lost time to make up for—and then when we get closer to London, the dread hits me.

It could barrel me over, the juxtaposition of how I'm feeling... such a peculiar mix.

I'm so happy, so in love, so relieved to be finally with Beej, properly, out loud, confessedly in love with him.

But there's an encroaching shadow in the corner of my mind about having to tell Tom. About having to let him go. Because he's important to me now, and I adore him.

It's different than with BJ and we can't pretend that it's the same—it's not. Tom wouldn't even think it is.

If BJ's water to me, Tom is wine. I don't need him to survive, but I love him anyway; he tastes good, makes me feel better, makes me feel braver.

He's nice to have around, and actually, in all unmetaphorical seriousness, I have no idea how I would have stayed afloat this year without Tom.

It's strange, don't you think, the way we attach to people.

The way our best intentions are cast aside, and the seed gets deeper into the soil of us than we planned and their place in our lives grow roots. I don't think we're supposed to love people lightly. I don't think we're supposed to love them a little bit and move on. Tom grew roots. It's not his fault. I let him.

And I have a horrible, nervous feeling that maybe my sister was right about me, and if she was—what kind of person does that make me?

I ask for Tom to meet me in the park by my house.

He's waiting for me on the bench.

The navy, Horsey lounge pants from Loro Piana with the brown, wool polo shirt and the matching suede sneakers from Fear of God for Ermenegildo Zegna.

Handsome as ever. The eyes Billie Eilish wrote the song about, I'm sure of it.

I walk towards him, swallowing nervously as I do. And I suspect he knows as soon as he sees me. It's probably written all over me—BJ usually is.

Tom England looks up at me—this strange, closed mouth, sad-eyed smile.

He breathes out, his eyes drop from mine. "You're back together."

I sit down next to him, my hands heavy in my own lap. I nod, my mouth pulls into a reluctant smile. He shakes his head and gives me a small shrug; his eyes look a bit remorseful. "We kind of saw this coming—"

"I suppose." I nod. "I didn't see you becoming my best friend, though," I tell my hands because I can't face him.

He looks over at me, picks up my hand and holds it in his. "No, I didn't see that coming either."

He puts his arm around me, sighing as he looks out over the park. "So, are you already back together or just deciding you'll be?" I glance over at him and my cheeks are pink. "Ah," he says and chuckles—albeit a bit flatly. "You had sex."

I twitch my mouth from side to side.

And then he asks me as though he genuinely cares, "How was that?"

I look up at him. "Do you really want to know?"

"No." He smiles a little. "I don't."

I lean into him. "Thank you," I tell him without looking at him. "For what you did for me."

"What did I do for you?" He tugs on my blue, pavilion pleated, cotton shirt dress from Aje.

"Lots of things," I say. "But mostly that you loved me."

His mouth goes tight and he looks a bit embarrassed. "He tell you that?" I shake my head. "How'd you know then?"

"Because I know you now, quite well."

"Oh." He gives me a look. "I suppose you do."

I watch him closely. "Are you okay?"

"I'll be fine." He nods, not meeting my eyes.

"You'll need a new foxhole."

He lets out a dry laugh. "I think I'm done with fox-holes for a while."

I sniff a laugh. "Me too."

He nods, mouth pursed and then drops his arm from around me, turning to me. His face goes serious, eye-brows dropping in a sort of serious low. "I've got to say something—and it might sound self-serving, but I'm not trying to be."

I shake my head at him. "You never are—"

"He's going to hurt you again," he tells me without flinching.

My heart climbs a little up my throat.

I shake my head. "No—"

"Yes." He nods.

"Tom—"

"Magnolia." He shakes his head. "I'm not telling you to change your mind. I couldn't, anyway. You two are"—he pauses, looking for the word—"bound."

He says that like it's a hopeless thing.

But he's right. We are.

"I can't undo that—I'm not trying." He shrugs. "I'm just telling you, so someone has—he's going to hurt you again, and I don't know that I'll be here when he does."

SIXTY-FIVE

BJ

I walk into my parents' home in Belgravia, unannounced. It's after dinner, but there's always dinner here. Mum's a chronic over-caterer who's in denial that Henry and I don't live here anymore. Sometimes we do. Each have our own places now, but sometimes it's nice to come home.

I walk into the kitchen and my mum looks up from the sink, her face lighting up.

"Sweetheart, you're here!" She pulls off a rubber glove. "Darling!" she calls out to my dad. "BJ's here!"

There's a vague rumble of response from my dad and my mum wraps her arms around me.

"Hungry?"

I nod. "Starved."

I perch up on the marble counter that's covered in cleaning shit—I don't know why—we've always had a cleaner but Mum just runs around pre-cleaning before the cleaner gets here. Bit redundant, Dad hates it but he loves Mum, and she'll never fire Nel. Will pay an annual salary to sit and have tea and biscuits 3 days a week with her though.

She fixes me a plate with too much food. Two different kinds of meat (chicken and steak), four kinds of carbohydrates and some broccoli, all slathered in her gravy and it's way too much food and I eat all of it in under five minutes.

She's sitting there, chin in hand, watching me pleasantly.

"And to what do we owe the pleasure this evening?"

I sniff a laugh. "Can't a lad just come and visit his mum for no reason?"

"A lad can, but alas, my lads do not." She gives me a look. "Henry's upstairs." She nods in the direction. "What's going on with him and Jo?"

I give her a look. "How do you know something's going on with Jonah?"

Her eyes pinch. "Because nothing ever goes on between him and Christian and if it was between him and you, I'd know about it."

Annoyingly observant, she is.

I squint over at her. "Into the same girl."

"Ah," she says. "Is she a goodie?"

I nod. "Yeah, she's sick—"

She pours me some wine. Pours herself a bigger glass.

"And you, my darling?" She tilts her head. "What have you come here to tell me?"

I take a drink, say nothing just to annoy her.

She frowns. "Good news or bad news?"

I take another drink, smirking.

"BJ!" she scolds me.

And I stand and carry my plate back to the kitchen, rinsing it off in the sink. She scurries after me, yelling my full name—she plucks the plate from my hands, rewashing it herself before putting it in the dishwasher.

She turns, hands on her hips.

"Baxter James Ballentine—"

I spread my arms out wide and lay my torso down on the marble island in the middle of her kitchen, grinning up at her.

"What?" She frowns.

"Parks and I had sex."

A small scream escapes her mouth as she claps her hands over it. Would I ever tell my mum I had sex with anyone else? Nope. Never. Never in a billion years, but that outburst is the reaction it deserved, and I wanted it, so I told her.

She rushes towards me, shaking my shoulders.

"Oh my god!" Shakes me again. "Hamish! Oh my god—"

Dad rushes in.

"What's going on?"

"BJ and Magnolia are back together," she practically squeals.

I give Dad a wide-eyed, amused look and his face cracks a smile. "Really?"

I nod.

He squints at me suspiciously. "Does she know you think you're back together?"

"They had sex!" Mum yells.

And Dad and I both give her a weird look.

And then her face turns to a scowl. "—For the first time ever, I assume. Because until this moment you were a virgin."

I shake my head once. "—Wasn't."

"And she's the only girl you've ever been with."

"—She's not," my dad tells her.

She scowls at him, then looks at me. "And will be with…"

I smile at her. Here's hoping, Lil.

"You were safe, yes?" She nods to herself.

"Mum." I roll my eyes.

Henry walks into the room. "Mum, they've been having sex since they were—" I throw a dishtowel at him. He laughs.

473

"—twenty-three and twenty-four respectively," she tells Henry with the utmost conviction.

"Lil"—Dad shakes his head—"you walked in on them at the chalet."

"Did not." She shakes her head vehemently.

Did, definitely did. Could have died—most embarrassing day of my life. Parks was seventeen, I was nineteen. Mum was… mortified… apparently to the point of total denial.

"Oy," Henry says, nodding his chin at me. "How was that work thing, Beej?"

I smirk. "Good."

My brother chuckles. "I bet it was—"

My dad walks over, looks at me for a few seconds, then hugs me.

"I'm glad for you."

There's a champagne pop—Mum's grinning in the corner.

I glance between my dad and my brother. "This feels embarrassing."

"It's not," she sings.

"Sorry," my dad says. "Is that my 2002 Dom—?"

Mum shrugs. "It's the occasion for it—"

Dad considers. "Is it?"

Henry starts laughing.

Dad begrudgingly gets out some glasses and Henry comes over to me, smacking me fondly in the face.

"This legit?" I nod. "Bro," Henry says and hugs me. "Fuck me, that was a long drive—"

"Henry." Our mother shakes her head. "That language isn't going to win you the girl you like—"

Henry gives me an exasperated look and hits me in the stomach.

I flinch in a tiny bit of pain but mostly I'm laughing.

"She forced it out of me." I shrug, helpless.

Henry points to me. "He and Parks did it on Dad's company plane on the way to Monte Carlo when he was sixteen."

Mum's jaw drops. I grimace.

"Highly premeditated—" My traitor-brother continues. "They planned it for days."

"Henry!" I yell.

I glance at Dad, nervous. Like I could get in shit for something I did nearly nine years ago.

Dad starts laughing.

"Twice." Henry shrugs, drinking his champagne, walking out of the room.

SIXTY-SIX

Magnolia

I swan downstairs the next morning and into the kitchen. My sister's leaning over the counter eating a bowl of cereal and Marsaili is leaning against the sink drinking a tea in a black and white, silk blend skirt from Ecru that sits above her knee and it feels horribly inappropriate, because I don't want to see a forty-five-year-old's knee.

"Morning," Bridget smiles, dressed in head-to-toe Gucci—the sky blue, tech-jersey tracksuit. Must stay calm. Don't react. Don't frighten the wild thing who's finally well-dressed away from the nice clothes... I blink a few times, probably look like I'm having sort of brain malfunction as I recalibrate my reaction to a hearty nil.

"You look nice," I tell her and she looks down at herself, doesn't even vaguely acknowledge the compliment.

"Where'd you disappear off to this week?"

I shrug demurely.

"Your phone was off." My sister squints at me.

"Oh, yes." I sigh. "I stayed overnight somewhere unexpectedly."

"Oh." She nods, getting it. "So you were with BJ."

I frown.

"Where'd you go?" Bridge asks, shovelling Coco Pops into her mouth.

"Dartmouth," I tell her, my nose in the air.

She pulls back confused. "Dartmouth?"

"To the house?" Marsaili clarifies. "Why?"

I open my mouth to say something and find myself not quite sure what to say.

I wave my hand through the air dismissively. "Long story."

They both do different variants of nodding and seem dramatically disinterested in me and I feel cross about it. They go back to talking about something on Graham Norton last night, and he's a good friend, I'm terribly fond of him but I'm wearing the logo-jacquard stretch-knit and leather knee boots from Fendi which are cute as fuck, and I'm looking impossibly bright-eyed because I'm sleeping so well because I'm sleeping with my boyfriend, which is the spectacular news they don't even know about yet and I can't get a fucking look in.

I clear my throat to get their attention. They glance back over at me, not looking dreadfully thrilled.

"Do either of you want to ask me anything?" I give them a dazzling smile.

"No," Marsaili says, indifferent. "Not really…"

"Nothing?" I frown. She shakes her head. I frown again. "Nothing at all?" Bridget gives me a weird look. "Nothing about… my… time away?" I ask, lifting my neck and scratching it in a tragically unergonomic way, exposing a—

"Is that a hickey!" My sister lunges towards me, knocking over her cereal and grabbing my neck, inspecting it. "Is it?" she yells again, looking at my face.

I do a tiny nod.

Her eyes go wide. "From BJ?"

I nod again.

And then she squeals and turns wide-eyed to Marsaili. "A hickey from BJ!"

Marsaili rolls her eyes a little, hardly thrilled but barely angry. "And what about Tom?" Marsaili asks from the sink, sipping her tea in a very controlled manner.

I sigh a little bit. "I ended it with him yesterday."

Bridget frowns a little. "How was he?"

"Okay." I press my lips together. "Quite gracious about it all, really—"

Mars nods. "He's a good man."

Bridge gives her a stern look, then grabs my hand. "So is BJ."

Marsaili nods diplomatically. "I didn't say he wasn't."

"Are you happy for me?" I ask Marsaili, smiling.

"That you got a hickey from your ex-boyfriend?" She gives me a little smirk and rolls her eyes. "Thrilled."

Bridget scowls at her and pulls me into the dining room and sits us down at the table.

"So how did it happen?" She leans in. "When did it happen? Where? How many times—"

"Um. How—" I consider the question. I hate lying to her. "Fluke?" It's hardly true, but what else could I say? "Same time, same place?" I offer as a companion answer. She nods, accepting it. "When?" I tug on my ear, mindlessly. "The day before yesterday. Where—?" I press my hand into my mouth, cheeks going pink. "Under the willow tree? By pond."

Her eyes go wide.

"What if Mr. Gibbs saw you!" she asks, horrified.

And I can't help but laugh. I give her a tiny shrug. Besides, Mr. Gibbs has seen so much more than that. I take a big breath, then breathe it out.

"And how many times..." I grimace, then shrug hopelessly.

She smacks my arm. "Minx!"

I roll my eyes.

Then she thinks to herself for a moment.

"What about the questions he won't answer?"

"It was nearly three years ago now—"

"Yeah, but," she sighs, "it was a big deal. He's not given you any closure."

And she's right. He hasn't. He seems like he never will. And I think a bit of me might wonder why forever, but will I let that wondering rob me of being with him anyway?

I don't know what answer I'm looking for anymore. And maybe he's right?

How much could knowing who he slept with change now anyway?

It's done. It happened already and just once.

And maybe I am too stupid and fucked up in love to think straight, but it seems silly to me, suddenly, to throw away what BJ and I have because he had sex with a random girl at a party once when he was drunk.

I shrug at my sister.

"What closure could he give me more than loving me how he does?"

"Magnolia," she says, sitting back, surprised. "How very enlightened of you."

I give her a smug smile.

"You know, you're going to have to choose to forgive him some days," she tells me.

"It's not always a feeling, forgiveness."

"I know," I tell her, though I didn't.

Fuck.

Oh well.

"And this is official?" I nod matter-of-factly. "So when's the world finding out?"

"Later, I'm sure." I smile. "We're going to stay at the Mandarin tonight—"

"Cute."

"And we're meeting everyone at The Rosebery before-hand for some cocktails." I give her a little smile. "They don't know yet, just Henry."

"Can I come?"

I blink at her, surprised. "You want to come out with me and my friends?" She nods. "Voluntarily?"

She nods again.

My jaw drops into a delighted smile. "Of course!" I frown. "Are you dying?"

"Uh—" She frowns. "Not presently, no."

I stand up, walking to the door.

"Okay, I'm going to get ready—"

"Do you think he's going to propose tonight?" my sister calls, excited.

I let out a laugh. "I really don't."

"But when he does propose," Bridget says, thinking aloud, "you'll get married at the Mandarin Oriental, won't you?"

I give her a look like I haven't thought about this myself a million times before. "Maybe?"

"Who will be your maid of honour—me or Paili?"

I give her a look. "We just started dating."

"Yeah," she says, "but he's the one."

SIXTY-SEVEN

BJ

She walks into the Rosebery wearing a coat and one of the dresses from Gucci that I bought her. Full Box Set tonight plus Bridge. It's me and the boys at the table—Pails isn't here yet, and I haven't said anything. I stand as Parks skips over towards the table—don't know why—gives us away before we have a chance to tell them ourselves. She throws her arms around my neck and jumps to kiss my mouth. Like a fucking Disney kiss. Feet off the ground, her hands in my hair, one hell of an entrance. Few flashes from cameras, a murmur through the crowd, but that's what she wanted. If it wasn't, she wouldn't be kissing me like this in here.

She pulls away from my mouth and smiles at me as I put her back down on the ground. She turns to the lads, and gestures to me. "Have you met my boyfriend?"

Bridge cheers. Jo lets out a triumphant crow. Henry wraps his arms around Parks and they say words to each other that I can't hear, but her cheeks are pink, and he pokes her nose.

Christian stands up and we stare at each other for a few seconds and I briefly feel like shit—and then he hugs me.

Parks kisses Perry (with his slack jaw and wide eyes) on the cheek as she passes him, perching on my lap, and the world is as it should be.

Forgot what it's like to be like this with her, and what strikes me the most about it is it feels like a weight off my back—getting to be with her like this, like not touching her, not holding her, not being with her, has had my whole body holding its breath 'til now and now everything's good.

No more touching around touching, just touching. Touching for touching's sake. Touching her because I can—because she's mine, because we figured it the fuck out—finally.

She does a button up on my shirt.

"Who are you trying to seduce with all these buttons undone?" She gives me a playful frown.

"You," I say into her ear and she swallows heavy, her little body goes all rigid, her grip on my arm tightens and—fuck!—I wish no one else was here so we could go upstairs right now—why the fuck did we bring other people here?

Because it's worth celebrating, she said. That's why.

And that we've put all our friends through so much shit the last three years, we owe them several drinks at least.

And then Paili walks in.

Clocks me quickly how she often does—glances at Parks on the rebound.

Parks on my lap, my hands tossed around her waist. Her eyes go wide and then her jaw drops into a surprised smile.

She points between us. "Are you—"

I nod, smiling at her coolly. And everything is fine. Magnolia jumps up off my lap and bounces over to her best friend, making excited girl sounds, throws her arms around her neck,

Paili puts her hands on Magnolia's cheeks, holding her face and smiling at her.

"I'm so happy for you," she tells her and she means it.

Parks puts her hands on top of her best friend's affectionately, and turns her face a little, kisses the palm of her hand. "You smell nice—" Parks says, smiling at Paili absentmindedly as she turns away.

"Oh, thanks." Pails puts her bag down on the seat. "I haven't worn it in a while, it's from—"

Magnolia freezes.

"Orange blossom," Parks says, voice far away.

And the room falls into slow motion.

Magnolia takes Paili's wrist, lifts it to her nose to smell it.

Breathes it in. "Musk."

She breathes in again. Magnolia looks up at Paili, not blinking. "Tuberose."

"Magnolia—" Paili starts.

Parks drops her wrist, takes a step away from her.

"Magnolia, listen—"

"It was you?" Parks says in a tiny voice and I'm already on my feet.

Shit. Paili and my eyes catch. She's panicked.

"Parks." I grab Magnolia by the arm, pulling her back towards me.

She moves when I move her, looks up at me, eyes like a hummingbird with no place to land.

She stares up at me, mouth open, frozen in an old grief that has a weight that hasn't even hit her yet.

"Was it her?" she asks in almost a whisper.

"Parks." I shake my head.

"Was it?"

"Magnolia," I whisper.

She jerks her arm out of my grip. "Did you fuck my best friend?" she yells and the room halts to a silence.

The talking stops, the volume sucks away. Cutlery clangs on plates. Everyone stares.

"Yes," Paili says from behind us.

I always want to think I was drunk; I was a bit but not enough—not how I should have been to take the edge off of what we did. I felt dizzy and weird, walked downstairs and she followed me. I guess she saw I looked off.

We'd been friends for years by then too, obviously—wherever Parks goes, Paili goes. We were always close.

She followed me into my room.

"Are you okay?" she asked.

I ignored her, walked into my bathroom. Water. I needed water. Ran the tap, splashed some on my face. Gripped the sides of the sink hard.

I turned and looked at her, she frowned when she saw me.

"You're not," she told me. "What's wrong?"

I smelt her. "New perfume?"

She nodded, pleased I noticed. "Yeah, I just got it last week, it's Frédéric Malle, Carn—"

And then I grabbed her face and kissed her.

Don't know why? Never thought about kissing her before, just did it. I wasn't dead surprised when she kissed me back. I always thought she had a bit of a thing for me, most girls do—but she was so loyal to Parks, she'd never—

So that… kissing there in my bathroom. Weird.

I pulled back, looked at her.

We had this moment of like, what the fuck are we doing?

484

I was breathing fast, panting almost. I don't think she was breathing at all. Her gaze went hungry girl. Seen her look at Jo like this before, but not me and then she just threw herself on me.

And you want to know the god honest truth? I wasn't thinking of Parks. All I was thinking about was that was what I wanted. It was what I wanted. I was choosing it. That was what I wanted to be doing and I was doing it, and I had a girl in my hands that I wanted there, and we were touching and kissing and that was what I wanted.

I was sitting on the side of the bath; Pails was sitting on my lap—she was a better kisser than I would have thought—good with her hands.

I remember I fell backwards. Tumbled back into the bathtub.

She fell on top of me. We laughed.

She looked down at me, a half-smile, half-frown on her face, and reckon it's important to say because it's true, we could have stopped. Throughout. In every sexual encounter there are multiple organic check points—breathing breaks, taking clothes off, kissing breaks, shifting positions—we could have stopped several times.

We didn't.

Then I pulled her down on top of me and we had sex in my bathtub. And it was—I feel sick to say it—good. Great, even.

I know that's not what anyone wants to hear at this point. You want it to have fucking sucked, been the worst experience I've ever had. You want me to have felt nothing, hated it, not come, been thinking of Parks the whole time—none of that's true.

I wanted it.

And the only times I thought of Magnolia was when my brain was like, you should be thinking about Magnolia.

But after…

Holy fuck.

It was like a spell wore off.

She jumped off me, holding her clothes against her body. "What did we do?" she asked—white as a ghost.

"Fuck." I hung my head in my hands. "Fuck!"

"What do we do?" she asked, urgently.

I shook my head. "We have to tell her—"

"What?" She pulled back. "No!"

"We have to!" I shook my head. "I have to—I can't keep this from her—"

"You have to!" Paili yelled.

"I can't!" I yelled back. "I'm telling her—"

And then Paili started to hyperventilate. I mean—couldn't breathe—gasping for air. I rushed over to her, held onto her arm. "Look at me—breathe—you've gotta breathe—"

And I was standing there coaxing her breathing and she still wasn't dressed, just in her underwear. My shirt was off, and then the door opened.

"What's going on in—" Jonah started, then froze in his tracks. "Shit."

Jo looked over at me, clamped his hand over his mouth. My eyes dropped to the ground. Embarrassed and guilty. Jonah looked at Paili who was having a panic attack, and he walked over to her in two strides. Grabbed a cup of water on my sink. Threw it in her face.

She froze. Looked up at him, wide-eyed. Petrified.

"You two are fucking?" Jonah asked through gritted teeth.

"I-It just happened," she said, eyes teary.

I was sitting on the toilet lid. Hands shaking.

"What the fuck, Beej?" he yelled.

"I have to tell her." I looked up at them both. "We have to tell her," I told Paili. "It's the right thing to do—"

"No!" She shook her head. "She'll never forgive us."

"I can't lie to her—"

"But you can cheat on her?" Jonah spat.

I ignored him.

"Paili." I shook my head at her. "It was a mistake, she might… maybe she won't—"

Paili started crying.

"Listen, listen," Jonah said, tossing me my shirt. "Put that on. We can figure this out."

He took Paili's dress out of her hands, pulled it over her body. Dressed her like she was a rag doll. She watched Jonah with scared, grateful eyes.

"Did you use protection?" he asked, looking between us.

Hadn't even thought of protection—I was only sleeping with Parks and she'd been on the pill she since she was sixteen. I shook my head.

Paili barely shook hers. Started crying more.

Fuck.

Jonah clapped his hands to get her to focus, then held her by the shoulders.

"I've got emergency contraception in my bathroom," he told her. "You'll be fine. It's fine—we'll go take it now." He started leading her away. "And you—take a shower—"

I shook my head.

"I'm going to tell her—"

Paili started crying again.

Jonah put his head in his hands. "Paili, shut the fuck up—I'm trying to think." Her mouth snapped shut the way you'd expect it to when a gang lord tells you to be quiet.

"She's going to end it, Beej," he warned me.

I shook my head at him. "I can't pretend I didn't do it, I won't lie to her—"

Paili's shoulders were convulsing, she was crying so much—

"Fine, but just don't tell her who—"

"She should know," I yelled.

"She shouldn't have to know," Jonah barked back. "You shouldn't have fucking done it—but now you have and here we are. Paili's about to have a fucking meltdown. It's her story as much as yours now. You want to tell Parks you cheated, fine." He looked at Paili. "And you want to lie to your best friend, fine." He pointed at me. "You were at the party, you got drunk." He grabbed an open beer that was in my room, splashed it on my clothes. "You fucked up." I nodded at him. "And you," he said, looking at Paili, "you and me hooked up tonight, if anyone asks, okay?"

She nodded obediently, eyes red.

"Okay." Jonah nodded.

You know what happened after that.

I went to Parks. Told her. Left out the most significant detail. Lost her anyway. Lost her then how I'm losing her now in a Gucci dress at The Rosebery.

"Parks—" I reach for her again.

"My best friend?" she whispers.

We're all frozen—fucking suspended in time in my worst fucking nightmare—

Christian can't believe it. Perry's eyes are on the floor—confirmation for me, finally, that he knew all along. Henry's going to fucking kill me, I can see it—Jo's just watching Parks. He looks a bit afraid, actually.

"Did you know?" Magnolia asks Jonah in a quiet voice.

Jo nods.

She turns to Perry. "And you?" she asks, throaty.

He nods too.

These bonus revelations crush her extra, I don't know why.

"Magnolia." I reach for her but she's walking backwards away from me, afraid. Like she doesn't know me. Like I'm a danger to her.

"Don't touch me." She shoves my hands off her and I fall back a bit, crashing into a waiter with a tray of food.

"Parks, please," I call for her, but she's already running.

SIXTY-EIGHT

Magnolia

I slip out in the commotion of Beej falling on the waiter and I run out of The Rosebery like it's on fire. The room parts for me like a sea, all the people in the room moving aside, like my devastation is a disease they could catch.

I'm grateful for it. Grateful they aid my escape because I can't see straight, can't think straight, there's a black hole in the centre of me and I'm giving in to it.

My best friend?

My best friend and my best friend.

It's worse. He's right. It is worse. Knowing her face. Was it planned? Had they liked each other a long time? Did she see him naked? Did they use protection? Oh my god, I hope they used protection.

It nearly wallops me to my knees, the idea of him being inside of her with nothing, not even a flimsy piece of plastic between them—I think I'm going to be sick— what parts of her body did he hold?

Did he think of me? Why her? And why him? Where did he kiss her? Where did her hair fall on his body? Did he hold her hand how he holds mine when we have sex? Did he look at her? Eyes open, watch her? Did he come? What was he thinking of when he did? How stupid am I that I didn't see it? Was there something to see? How does this happen?

I'm so dizzy, I could fall. And then BJ grabs me.

I don't know where he comes from, it feels sudden, even though it's not—it felt like I was alone in a dark sea, adrift and suddenly there are hands on me.

He's holding me by the arm and my waist and he's shaking his head like mad. "Parks, listen to me—"

I shake my head, but I don't fight him off because I don't want to. It's too hard. Counterintuitive. I love being touched by him; I want to be touched by him. And held by him and kissed by him and had by him and I haven't been for nearly three years and I've had him for three days and now I'm losing him again and my skin feels like there's acid on it with the betrayal—it took me so long to stave off the wildfire for him in my belly and now it's back and it can't be.

But I'll douse it out however I need to, because I'll never have him again. This is the end.

"Parks, please—"

"She's my best friend!"

"Magnolia—listen. It's already happened—you said you'd forgiven me, it's still the same thing."

"No."

"It is! I haven't done it again, it's still the same—"

"No, it's not the same thing because you fucked my best friend," I over-annunciate. "You had me think all these years that it was some random girl, a perfect stranger, an accident, something that just happened—but you did it with my best friend."

"Parks—"

"And we're together all the time! We're with her all the time! Do you watch her when we go on holidays—think about how you've been there—"

He looks horrified. "Parks, no. It's—"

I look at him like he's the stranger he feels like to me now. "How could you do that to me?"

He grabs me, pulls me in towards him, holds me tight against him and I tell myself to remember this.

Remember how this feels. Being in here, in his arms. Remember how it feels to be folded up inside his chest, how it feels to have his arms pressed against my back, where my legs fit between his, how he ducked his chin a little so I can live under there, remember all of it because this is the last time.

I breathe him in once more.

And then I rip him off me. Do it quick, like a plaster.

I'm shaking all over, my hands are trembling, my legs are jelly—

"You'll never touch me again," I barely say out loud but he hears it.

I pull the chain around my neck where his crest ring has lived for the better (and worst) part of a decade— snap it off my body, throwing it to the ground.

He looks up at me in a quiet disbelief. He shakes his head, moving back towards me and then he's pushed backwards again. Not by me but by his brother.

"No," Henry growls. BJ shakes his head, annoyed and put off, tries to push past his brother. Henry shoves him again. "You stay the fuck away from her." Henry points at him, teeth gritted.

Beej lunges towards me but Jonah grabs him from behind, holds him against him like a seatbelt and Beej goes limp.

He stands there, watching me in his brother's arms. He breathes out and his head swings low in a mixture of sadness and guilt. He shakes his head a tiny bit, trying to steady himself, chest heaving.

I want to touch his face, kiss the corner of his mouth, breathe with him until he's normal again but we'll never be normal again.

Henry looks down at me. He looks pale. "Magnolia, what do you need? What do you want me to do? I'll do anything—"

"I need to go," I choke out.

He nods and pulls me down the front steps.

"A cab," he tells one of the bellman. "Now. Get her a cab."

One pulls up in front of me and the bellman opens the door.

Henry pushes me in.

"I'm so sorry, Parks," he tells me and his eyes are teary too.

I nod. I think. I think I nod? Maybe I don't.

I can't feel my body anymore, really.

Henry closes the door and I get one last look at his brother on the steps, watching me leave him.

He's crying now, choked sobs in Jonah's arms.

Our eyes catch, he blows some air out of his mouth, drops his eyes from mine.

Can you die from a broken heart, do you know?

And if I did and they cut me wide open, would I bleed loving him? When they lift my heart out of my chest cavity to weigh it, does it weigh the same as his top lip? Is his name carved into my third rib to the left? Bone of my bones, flesh of my flesh. He's killing me. Loving him is killing me too, and I'm afraid because how many loves really, do you get in a lifetime? How many chances do you give it before you let it go?

I'm letting it go.

"Where to?" asks the cabby.

I look out the window to the city that's filled to its brim with daydream kisses and perfect poor decisions all made with a man I think I used to know.

"To Heathrow."

Acknowledgements

Though you have well and truly passed the timeframe which was allotted to you for you to read my book, I'll still say thank you to you first.

You have not just believed in me and supported me, but paved the way for me. Paid the way for me. Afforded me so much time and space to be, long before we could afford to. No one has believed in me how you have believed in me, and all my favourite things about being a human I can tie to being yours. I love you, Benjamin William Hastings.

Emmy. We were in the stars all along. It took us a decade to work together but we did it and I'm grateful for the decade any and either way. And I'm always, always grateful for you, my blue moon. It's the cover of my dreams. I've believed in your art since the second I saw it, and I will keep believing in it because actually it's a bit divine. Thanks for being so business oriented.[1]

David Hedlund, without whom this book I think would never have happened. You have helped me more than I can say. You've clarified for me, helped me find my way back when I'd lose it, stuck with me when I cut your favourite character (R.I.P. AVS) and have read too many versions of this book to track. Thank you.

---

1. No, but actually really that has proven helpful so thanks.

A rapid fire of completely necessary thank yous: Jesus, for every good thing. Luke and Jayboy—for finally giving me space to be on a board even if it's fake and just on our group chat. You got the book, you made it come to life, you're two of my favourite people, complete geniuses. Mum and Lis— for all the times you selflessly helped me with my kids so I could visit this world I made. Bronte & Rach, for being the only ones who believe in that post-milly jet life. Grandma, for everything. Grandad, for everything else. Viv and Bill, for letting me have weeks of space and silence in my favourite house in the world. Maddi, for being the most enthused and excitable person. AJ for being the fastest reader in the west. Jarryd & Mystique, a lot of this story was formed at the desk you'd let me work from to escape my beautiful[2] baby when we were neighbours. Amber, we couldn't have done this ridiculous season without you. Tori, for answering my billion questions. My editor—for seeing through the haze of commas and persevering through my DE trauma. I was very deflated when we found each other; thank you for your kindness and patience with me. I will check in to Comma Rehab now. Laura, my typesetter and my two final proofers, Nikki and Felicity. Sarah,[3] Karalee[4] and Aodhan.[5]

Jackson Van Merlin, you actually made me believe in me in a way I don't even think you know about—don't know where you are these days, your weird tendency to fall off the planet—hopefully you're alive. And well. I do hope you're well.

---

2. occasionally impossible and insane
3. Because it'll never fly if I don't mention her.
4. Because I can't mention my other two best friends and not mention you.
5. Because otherwise I'll never hear the end of it.

Alana Fragar, you gave me the book[6] that made me want to be a writer.

Joel Houston, you told me I was a good writer when I was eighteen and because you're a good writer, I believed you.

To my year 11 English teacher who was so exasperated with me for interpreting that WWII essay question as a creative writing exercise, sorry.[7]

To my beloved Helen from the best book shop in the world[8]—you fed my mind for years and years and even though we're far away now, I think of you often and only with tenderness.

And actually probably most of all—Juniper Ruth Magnolia Hastings. You were the most difficult 6-month-old imaginable and you stretched me more than I knew I could be stretched, and in that stretching I began to write a version of what would become this book. So thank you. And please don't do that again. Bellamy[9]... you didn't do that much, I'll thank you next book.

---

6. *Extremely Loud & Incredibly Close* by Jonathan Safran For, so thank you Jonathan also.
7. You were pretty rude about it though.
8. Which, by the way, is Blues Point Book Store, and it doesn't have an Instagram or a Twitter because Helen would never, but it really is divine and you should go there.
9. Sorry. Love you though.

About the Author

Jessa Hastings is an over-thinking puzzle enthusiast who likes *Friends* more than you but doesn't likely have the social graces nor stamina to prove that point to you. She feels breakfast foods are superior to all other foods except maybe a Sunday roast. She lives with her husband and their two children in Marina del Rey, CA and has loved stories and words all her life. *Magnolia Parks* is her debut novel.

CPSIA information can be obtained
at www.ICGtesting.com
Printed in the USA
BVHW040959101022
649064BV00006B/156

9 781737 281108